Jude Fisher is a pseudonym for Jane Johnson, publishing director of HarperCollins' SF imprint, Voyager. She holds two literature degrees, specialising in Anglo Saxon and Old Icelandic texts, and is also a qualified lecturer. For the last seventeen years, Jane has been the publisher of the works of J.R.R. Tolkien. She is the author of the official Visual Companions to Peter Jackson's movie trilogy of THE LORD OF THE RINGS, and with M. John Harrison has had four novels published under the pseudonym of Gabriel King.

Sorcery Rising

Book One of Fool's Gold

Jude Fisher

EARTHLIGHT

SIMON & SCHUSTER

London • New York • Sydney • Tokyo • Singapore • Toronto • Dublin

A VIACOM COMPANY

First published in Great Britain by Earthlight, 2002
An imprint of Simon & Schuster UK Ltd
A Viacom Company

1 3 5 7 9 10 8 6 4 2

Simon & Schuster UK Ltd
Africa House
64–78 Kingsway
London WC2B 6AH

www.earthlight.co.uk

Simon & Schuster Australia
Sydney

A CIP catalogue record for this book is available from the British Library

Hardback ISBN 0-7432-2091-9
Trade paperback ISBN 0-7432-2092-7

Typeset by Palimpsest Book Production Limited,
Polmont, Stirlingshire
Printed and bound in Great Britain by
The Bath Press, Bath

My thanks to Joy, Jim, Dick, Emma, Mike and Jo for their encouragement on this long road; to Henry Teece, JRR Tolkien and the saga-makers, who started me dreaming; to Viggo and Iceland for ravens, words and warriors; to sea cliffs, gritstone and granite domes; and to John, Danny and Russ, for the care they take.

Prologue

The day the Master showed him the world was the day Virelai became a man, which was a dangerous thing indeed, and not at all what the mage had intended.

When the great ice door swung open before him, Virelai experienced a moment of pure terror. He felt the chill air inside reach out for him, as if the pitch-dark heart of the tower-room contained a sucking vacuum that might swallow him up forever. Rahe's grim intonation as he ushered him inside – 'Welcome, Virelai, to my world' – had hardly been encouraging, either, for the mage had been acting very strangely of late.

Virelai had caught him on numerous occasions setting small fires – in the grounds, in the kitchens, and once in his own study; fires which gave off noxious fumes and left behind in their ashes scraps of charred hide and stinking hair; roots and tubers, claws and teeth and little bits of bone. Which had been alarming, to say the least; since the only other occupants of Sanctuary, to Virelai's sure knowledge, were himself and the Master's familiar, a black cat he called Bëte. And things had been disappearing, too: scrolls and parchments, tomes of magic, journals and notebooks gone from the library; collections of plants and vials taken from the herbarium, torn down in such a hurry that dried leaves and flowers were left scattered on the ground, smashed underfoot along with shards of pottery and dried smears of something that looked suspiciously like blood. And in the *curiositar*, the chamber in which Rahe kept his most prized objects – row upon row of specimens (fine crystals, cut and uncut; rocks of every size and shape and hue; ores and metals and gems, all labelled with their names and magical properties; artfully-worked figurines and jewellery, knives and swords, spearheads and arrows, as well as many items mysteriously unnamed and defying any attempt he could make to categorise them) all elegantly arrayed under the thinnest sheets of translucent ice (no doubt to prevent his clumsy apprentice from laying his grubby hands upon them) – where there had been the most exquisite order, now there was a chaos of destruction. Nothing, it seemed, had been left intact. The artefacts were broken and twisted; the stones and metals fused together into a horrible, misshapen lump with what must have taken an immense blast of spellcraft. Even the great wired skeleton of a beast that Rahe called the Draco of Farem had been torn asunder and strewn around the chamber as if in a giant's fit of rage.

Virelai could only deduce that the Master had caused this terrifying destruction, but to what purpose, he could not imagine. And if the Master had at last gone completely mad, then how long could it be before he began to vent his murderous spleen upon his companions?

So now, as he stood at the dark threshold, panting after the long climb up the narrow, winding stairs, feeling the cold air leaching his body-heat away and the hot breath of the mage on the back of his neck, Virelai thought seriously about taking to his heels. But just as he felt the first tremor of his intent to flee run through his thin frame, the Master clicked his fingers and a pale-blue fire limned the chamber, revealing the oddest sight Virelai had seen in all his twenty-nine years in this odd place.

In the centre of the chamber lay a huge oval bowl of light; and inside it lay what he could only describe as a world.

Clouds floated over expanses of blue and green and brown – oceans and islands, lakes and continents. Sunshine – from no source that could be determined from this vantage point – lined the clouds with burnished gold and rose and cast moving shadows over land and sea alike. Virelai gasped. He took a step closer.

'Touch nothing, boy!' Rahe placed a restraining hand on Virelai's shoulder.

For once, Virelai did not bridle at the term, so entranced was he by the sight before him. 'What magic is this, Master?'

The mage made no reply. Instead he reached beyond his apprentice and pulled on a cord. There was an abrupt change in the light in the chamber and when Virelai stared up, he saw that a great contraption of levers and pulleys and crystals had been constructed around the open top of the ice tower. Where the sun struck the crystals, prismatic beams shot down at a myriad of angles into the bowl, and as the angles changed, so did the view. And where before there had been oceans and swathes of land seen from the greatest distance, now Virelai found himself staring down into a more intimate landscape – rooftops of wood and turf, cows and sheep dotted over steep pastures, people like insects scurrying about their tasks. A gull slid past in a flash of white and involuntarily Virelai shied away.

'The island-kingdom of Eyra,' the Master declared. He pulled another lever and the ground swarmed up towards Virelai with dizzying speed. Children ran laughing across a shingle beach, pursuing a small brown dog; women hung washing out on long lines across an enclosure. Boats bobbed in a sheltered harbour.

'And this is the southern continent, wherein lies the empire of Istria and the great wastes—'

Now there was a city of towering stone and hundreds of people in bright clothing milling about its streets; then the light became harsh and bright and a broad sandy vista stretched across the bowl, its braided pattern of dunes undisturbed except for a single line of dark figures trekking across the sands. Another twitch of the levers and Virelai was stunned to be confronted by an old woman with a white topknot of hair adorned with shells and feathers and a dozen or more silver chains around her thin brown neck. She stared right at him and opened her mouth to say something he could not hear, and then he was whirled away, up into the clouds and over a range of magnificent snow-capped mountains.

'It's beautiful,' he whispered, awed. 'But I don't understand.'

'Virelai – Virr-eh-*lay*! Think, boy, think. It's Elda.'

The mage pulled back the focus so that the view became once more a sketch for a world, all abstract shapes and blurred colour.

Elda.

Virelai thought suddenly of the maps he had pored over in the study – ancient, curled things all brown with age on which had been scrawled ideograms of mountains, crude triangles repeated over and again, little wiggly lines to denote the ocean's waves, abstract patches of brown amid the blue to represent land; and the word 'Elda' emblazoned in a rayed sun at the top or the centre or off to one side; and something clicked in his head. How stupid never to have understood that those flat marks represented anything more than themselves. To think that Sanctuary was all there was.

'Can I go there?' He gazed back at the mage, his face rapt.

The Master laughed, not kindly. 'Oh no, I think not. You wouldn't last a minute. Look—'

The crystals realigned themselves and there followed another vertiginous descent. At a market, a woman wrung a chicken's neck and reached for the next bird while the first lay flapping disjointedly. In a dark chamber a man lay upon a flaming rack and another applied vile instruments to his flesh. Somewhere else – it was impossible to tell the location, the images changed so swiftly – men fought each other on a blood-soaked field. Virelai watched in horror as a man's arm was sheared off. Another pull of the levers and now he saw two men hold down a slight figure in a full black robe while a third rent the fabric to reveal pale flesh and a fourth man pushed the writhing figure's legs apart and inserted himself with a grunt. Under a pitiless sun, chained men hacked stone and metal from a gaping hillside, watched over by mounted guards with whips and goads.

Virelai stared and stared. He saw: a mountain village over-run by soldiers, women and children pierced by spears; a man hanged from a tree; people and animals with their throats cut and shrouded women catching the spurting blood in great dishes; he saw a group of folk adorned like the old woman with shells and feathers and silver chains being stoned to death by an angry mob; he saw naked women burned on pyres and men pinned to masts of wood in the baking heat; then the view changed and he was on a ship far out at sea, watching as a speared whale was hauled in close to the waiting boats and men made the water run red as they hacked it to death.

'No more!' he cried and tried to move away.

'Why do you think I came here, boy?'

Another twitch of the levers and there was a tiny island, serene and white against dark-grey seas ringed about with drifting ice and veiled by swirling mists.

'To get away from all that. Sanctuary, I named this place, and sanctuary it is. You should thank me for bringing you here and saving you from all that greed and horror.' He sighed. 'It all decays and falls away, boy: life, love, magic. There's nothing worth saving in the end. May as well break it all up, let nature take its course.'

Rahe gave the levers a vicious twist, and images of the stronghold tumbled around the bowl: Virelai watched as a view of the kitchens was replaced by one of the ornamental lake with its ice swans and statuary, which in turn was displaced by a vista of the inner courtyard, then by a maze of corridors. A moment later there was a sudden blaze of gold amid the cheerless greys of the ice walls and he caught a glimpse of a naked woman, her long pale back all rosy in the candlelight, a swathe of silver-blonde hair veiling the curve of her buttocks as she slept – on the Master's bed.

Rahe swore, pulled a cord and abruptly plunged the chamber into darkness once more.

Virelai, about to question the mage as to the identity of this miracle, was distracted by the sense of something unfamiliar stirring in his breeches. He reached down to investigate and was horrified to find that a previously innocent part of his anatomy had become hard and misshapen. Alarmed, he pushed it away between his legs, but the image of the woman returned again and again, so that no matter what he did the offending item sprang back up, throbbing and insistent.

It plagued him all day as he went about his tasks; that naked flesh, his unruly member. But what plagued him worst of all was the realisation that there was a world out there – other people, other places, endless possibilities – and that Rahe had kept it from him, as if he owned no more life or will than any other of the mage's exhibits. He felt like apparatus in one of the Master's experiments, stuffed full with volatile substances, ready to explode at any minute.

As soon as he was able, he made his way back to the secret tower-room, counting every step: third turn out of the east corridor, fifty-nine paces, then the hidden door; followed by the one hundred and sixty-eight winding ice stairs. He had memorised the route with grim determination, even though on the way there and back he had felt the Master try to maze his mind. It took him some time to understand the workings of the levers, but soon, in a fever of excitement, he found himself able to conjure all manner of images of Elda, and he fed upon them until he was dizzy and intoxicated. At last he turned his attention back to the matter of the woman he had glimpsed in the Master's chamber, but no matter how delicately he manipulated the pulleys, he could find no sign of her.

He was just about to abandon his attempt when he came upon a view of Rahe himself standing in the middle of the hearth of the great hall with his robes on fire. Poisonously-coloured smokes billowed up from floor to ceiling. It was an arresting sight. Virelai held the lever still and watched. On the rug before the fireplace sat Bëte, her head cocked, her green eyes wide, studying the old man intently as, with a great shout (though no sound reached Virelai), the mage flung wide his arms. The smoke, which had been escaping lazily along the beams to collect in the hollows of the roof, was sucked suddenly backwards into the Master's mouth, leaving only a few tendrils of purple and green to wisp gently from the old man's nostrils.

Virelai frowned.

An instant later, the cat was in the Master's arms and nose to nose with him. The mage opened his mouth and, a distorted mirror-image, Bëte did likewise. As if triggered by this action, smoke began to pour from man to animal until at last the cat's eyes flared once with fiery light. Then she leapt down from his arms, made herself comfortable once more on the hearthrug and began to groom her posterior with overstated care.

Rahe stepped out of the fireplace, leaving behind him embers as cold and black as ancient lava, made, with a rudimentary gesture and a scatter of words, an incantation Virelai thought might be one of the eight Parameters of Being, and brought a huge oak crashing into the centre of the room. Its boughs creaked and swayed dangerously in the enclosed space. Bits of the ice roof crumbled and fell, but the

Master took no notice of any impending disaster; rather, his face creased with concentration, he called the tree towards him as he had called the smoke and flame, and the tree obeyed, flowing like an ocean of leaf and bark across the chamber. Great braids of green and brown made a maelstrom around him, a maelstrom with the mage's mouth at its vortex. Down it went, leaf and branch, bark and root, till there was no trace of it in the room.

Bëte, who during this latest display, even with her fur blown this way and that by the force of the spell, had not moved an inch, now considered the old man expectantly. He squeezed his eyes shut and coughed. With a muted plop, an acorn fell at the cat's feet. She nosed at it curiously, then at the Master's hand as he retrieved it.

He pressed the acorn to the cat's face; but she made bars of her fangs. The Master pressed harder. A second or two more of resistance; then the sharp teeth sprang apart and Bëte had the acorn in her mouth, one of the mage's hands clamped over her muzzle, and the other rubbing at her throat. Her eyes bulged, as if in panic; then she swallowed.

Rahe smiled distractedly and said something soothing to the cat. Then he bent and picked a speck of dirt – or else something indistinguishable – from the floor. After inspecting it minutely, he muttered over it, turned twice upon his heel and cast it aloft. The chamber seemed to ripple before Virelai's eyes, then, where the oak had previously been there abruptly appeared a great winged creature, twelve feet tall and covered from spiny head to clawed foot in luminous scales.

Even in the relative safety of the tower-room, Virelai gasped in terror. Unbelievably, it seemed that the beast had heard him, for it turned its head ponderously and regarded him with eyes as multifaceted and unreadable as any bluebottle's. It opened its monstrous jaws.

Then it seemed that the mage addressed it, for the appalling creature swung its head away. Released from that terrible scrutiny, Virelai pulled back the focus of the crystals in time to see the beast begin to dwindle, then to spin and rush towards its creator. A moment later the Master stood untouched and alone. Protruding slightly from his mouth was a small white object, which he gingerly withdrew and held out to his familiar. Upon his palm lay a single leathery white egg. Bëte showed considerably more interest in this than she had in the acorn. Her nose twitched, then she carefully set her teeth around it and, leaping light-footedly down from the table, carried the egg back to the rug, where she ate it slowly with the side of her mouth.

Something the Master had said in the tower-room came back to Virelai then. He had been so distracted by the visions of Elda that it had not registered at the time, but now it all came into clear focus. *There's nothing worth saving in the end. May as well break it all up, let nature take its course.* Rahe was reversing his spellcraft, destroying all his magic.

A red mist boiled in Virelai's head . . .

The Master straightened up, passed his hand across his exhausted face and began to pace the chamber. Avoiding his feet nimbly, the cat sprang up onto a table upon which a large crucible held a pile of ashes and what looked like a pair of charred brass hinges.

Virelai stared at the hinges. His head itched. He knew them; he *knew* them . . . His hand made a minute adjustment to the lever and the vista skewed around the chamber. Where was the great leatherbound volume in which the Master recorded each of his procedures and findings, adding to the wisdom of his predecessors? Where was the Grand Register of Making and Unmaking?

The terrible suspicion hardened into certainty.

Virelai abandoned the tower-room and, taking the stairs three at a time, hurled himself down into the familiar corridors of the stronghold. *Such a waste; such a stupid, senseless waste!* Anger surged and flowed inside him. *The old fool! The old monster!* A fount of lava bubbled under his pale skin; yet over the years he had learned to control his temper. No trace of his fury showed in eyes as cold and pale as a squid's. Twenty-nine years: twenty-nine years of unreasonable demands, of useless tutoring, fetching and carrying and general humiliation; twenty-nine years of being beaten on a whim and called 'boy'. And now Rahe was eradicating all those paths to magic that Virelai had been so patiently following, eradicating them and storing them out of his reach in the blasted cat, and just as he was beginning to gain some understanding of the processes, some mastery of magic's complex structures. It was too much to bear.

By the time he reached the chamber, both the Master and his familiar were gone. Virelai crossed to the long table and stared down into the crucible. It did indeed appear to contain the last remnants of the Book of Making and Unmaking. He fished out the two hinges and weighed them in his hands. They felt lumpen, bereft of magic, useless without the great tome it had been their purpose to enclose. He put them down again, his heart as heavy as the cold metal.

On the floor beneath the table a couple of torn and crumpled pieces of parchment lay abandoned. He picked them up. The first had lost its top third and started midway through a sentence. He scanned it rapidly, recognised it as the charm for making a charging horse dwindle to stallion's seed, and cast it down again. The second piece was almost entire and he could remember the missing words; and while he could think of no immediate use for a spell to remove rockfalls from choked caverns he pocketed it anyway. The third scrap of the Book contained a rather fiendish recipe of the Master's own devising, that and a grim description of its effects. Virelai read it through once without much interest, then stopped.

His head came up. His eyes narrowed. He read it again. A sweat broke out on his brow and his heart began to thud.

Clutching the parchment in his hand as if it were his pass-key from hell, he scurried to the kitchens.

Sanctuary had been carved so deeply out of the ice and into the rocky bones beneath that its walls were like the stone of unvisited caverns: dark and ungiving, ready to chill you to the marrow. Even the torches burning in the sconces lining the dim passageways in the heart of the stronghold seemed to make little impression on their surfaces. They barely flickered as Virelai passed them at speed later that the evening, carrying the Master's meal on a tray. It would be the last time he did so. The chill he felt as he walked the corridors that encircled the mage's chambers was not just a physical temperature, for the Master's magic bore its own cold with it.

Where the ice gave way to rock strata, minerals glittered in the flickering candlelight: feldspar and pyrites; cristobalite and tourmaline; greywacke and hornblende and pegmatite. To Virelai, taught to respond to natural harmonics, each one bore a different resonance to its fellows, each a different voice. He liked to think of the voices as the souls of the earth: bound in its crystals, trapped there for millennia: and perhaps they were. Virelai had seen the Master speak to the walls; even before he had thought him mad.

Towards the heart of the labyrinth, the walls gleamed gold and silver. Virelai had learned from his reading that although many of the minerals had little worth in the lands beyond – the world he now knew as Elda – others were considered as 'treasure'; though it had to be said that if this were the case, the peoples of Elda must confer most arbitrary value to the different rocks, for some of the so-called worthless ones (which were extensive in the tunnels) were remarkably close in appearance to those that men fought over in the old stories.

Fourth passage: dead end; take the first door past the hanging icicle; go down three steps; press the wall behind the tapestry.

Once in the vicinity of the Master's suite of rooms, Virelai became furtive. He lifted the metal dome that covered Rahe's meal and sniffed it again, although he was careful not to take the vapours too deep into his lungs for fear that even in steam they might do their damage. But despite the virulent ingredients he had added to the stew from the old parchment's recipe, he could sense none of them, through any of his senses, natural or attuned. He smiled.

When he reached it, the door to the Master's chamber was slightly ajar and he could hear voices within. His heart hammered.

Balancing the tray carefully, Virelai applied his eye to the door-crack.

What he saw almost made him drop the dishes. The blood rushed to his head, his chest; his loins. His jaw sprang open like an unlatched gate. He stared and stared, taking in detail after detail of the scene. Then he grinned wolfishly. *To the opportunist shall be granted opportunity, and he who takes Destiny by the throat shall be rewarded threefold*: was that not what the books said? Virelai counted his blessings. Threefold indeed.

He knocked smartly upon the door.

'Your supper, lord.'

There was a hush, followed by a soft scuffle, the rustle of heavy fabrics. Then: 'Leave the tray outside, Virelai,' came the Master's voice, a trifle querulous. 'I am somewhat engaged just now.'

'Indeed, lord: may you have pleasure of it.'

Bëte the cat emerged from the Master's chamber and watched Virelai retreat down the long corridor. She hovered for a moment beside the tray, sniffed at the covered dish and recoiled with a sneeze.

The only witnesses the next morning to Virelai's departure were the terns that frequented the bay beneath Sanctuary,

and a single storm petrel, the light of the brassy winter sun
lending its wings an oily iridescence. The petrel flew on,
uninterested in the drama that was being played out below:
it had many miles of berg-strewn ocean to cross on its long
journey. The terns, though, were curious as to the nature of
the large wooden chest the cloaked figure was manhandling
into a single-masted sloop that looked perilously close to
overturning. They dipped and wheeled in expectation of a
tidbit or two. Bëte the cat, swaddled unceremoniously in a
blanket laced with leather ties, lay motionless save for the
flick of her eyes as she watched the flash of their plumage,
their bright black eyes, their pretty red beaks: so close but so
infuriatingly inaccessible.

Virelai, having eventually succeeded in his battle to stow his
oversized cargo, boarded the little vessel himself, untied and
shoved off from the natural breakwater, and rowed inexpertly
out into the ocean, followed by the birds, distracted from their
search for food, in a stream of white. Once out of the shelter
of the icewall, the chop of the waves made the boat roll
alarmingly. The cat, splashed with freezing seawater, mewed
piteously. Virelai missed his stroke; cursed, shipped his oars
and after a certain amount of fiddling around, managed to
put up the sail. For some moments the sail hung as slack as
a turkey's wattle. Then, a little breeze bellied the fabric and
began to drive the sloop slowly, inexorably, back to shore,
until the prow, its painted eye staring blindly ahead, bumped
the ice of its home, and the seabirds shrieked their derision.
Virelai put his head in his hands. He was a fool, a fool, a fool:
he could not even sail a tiny boat. *Idiot*, his inner voice chided
him. *Use the magic!* A wind spell: it was a simple thing, but
even so his memory had deserted him. Digging in his bag
he pulled out a small notebook and riffled through its pages.
Then he unbound the cat's head from the swaddling, and
made a short incantation. Bëte fixed him with an unforgiving
eye, then made a choking cough. The sail went slack, then

swelled on its opposite side. The terns, caught unawares by the sudden change in wind direction, banked to correct their coverts. The sloop sailed smoothly out into the ocean.

Virelai shaded his vision against the rising sun and watched as it delineated the deceptive curves and rises of the place he had regarded all his life as his home. To the untutored eye, it might have been no more than the usual vast jumble of ice you would expect to find in such an arctic region: great blocks and floes that had been piled one atop the other by a thousand ocean storms, ice that had been carved into bizarre and unlikely shapes by wicked seawinds; all bleak and wild and uninhabitable by any except the seabirds and narwhal. But to the mage's apprentice Sanctuary revealed itself in all its sorcerous glory. Where a shady cornice met a cliff of ice, Virelai, narrowing his eyes, saw how the curving wall of the great hall met the stern face of the eastern tower; where higgledy-piggledy blocks lay as if scattered by the hand of a god, he noted how elegant stairways twined up from the statuettes and balustrades of a formal garden that to another might offer nothing but the unrelieved whiteness of an untouched snowfield. Spires and pillars, columns and masonry, all perfectly proportioned and crafted; cold white surfaces now limned in dawn-golds and pinks by the romantic sun.

The Master had brought his exacting eye to bear on every detail of his ice-realm. Nothing here was natural: nothing occurred by chance. Virelai wondered if he had viewed it from this very point, perhaps even from this very boat, when he had conceived Sanctuary's form.

How it or he had come to be here, and for what purpose, Virelai had no idea: but he meant to find out. Turning away from the island of ice, he set a course south, to where the world began.

PART ONE

One

Sacrilege

Katla Aransen stared out across the prow of the *Fulmar's Gift* as it ploughed through the grey waves, the foam from the ship's passage spraying back into her face and wetting her long red hair, but Katla did not care. It was her first long voyage and they had been at sea these past two weeks, but she was nineteen years old and hungry for the world: she could not bear to miss a moment of it.

Behind her, she could hear the great greased-wool sail cracking and roaring in the stiff wind, the wind that carried away her father's voice as he shouted orders to the crew. Many of them, she knew, would be hunkered down amidships amongst the cargo and sea-chests, trying to stay warm around the tub-fire. A sudden hissing signalled the start of preparations for the evening meal: they stored their meat in leather buckets full of seawater till it tasted more of brine than anything else, and cooking it by putting it directly onto the embers was the only way to make it palatable.

A warm hand on her shoulder. She spun around, to find her twin brother, Fent, beside her. His long red fringe was plastered to his face; the rest he had bound up with thongs to stop it whipping into his eyes.

'Listen to this, small sister,' he said teasingly, bracing himself against the gunwale with a knee, 'and tell me what you think.' He pulled from his tunic a length of twine that had been knotted at intervals in the complicated Eyran fashion that

served both as memory aid and language. Moving his fingers
nimbly up and down the knots he began to declaim:

> 'From Northern Sea to Golden Sea
> Smoothly swam the swan-necked ship
> On the backs of Sur's white horses
> On the line of the lord's Moon-path
> Easily from the Eyran Isles
> Came Rockfallers to the Moonfell Plain.'

He wrapped the twine around his hand and into a loop
and folded it carefully back into his tunic before looking to
his twin for approval.

'You repeated "moon",' Katla said with a grin, and watched
Fent's brows knot in consternation. 'And I'm not sure about
"Rockfallers", either.'

'I couldn't fit "the Rockfall clan" in,' Fent said crossly. 'It
wouldn't scan.'

'I'd stick to swordplay, if I were you, brother. Leave the
songmaking to Erno.' Their cousin, Erno Hamson, for all his
skill at weapons, was at heart a quiet and serious young man,
and he was currently conveniently out of earshot.

'As if you'd know a well-made verse from your ar— Ow!
What?' Her fingers were suddenly tight about his biceps,
digging into his skin even through the sturdy leather of
his jerkin.

'Land: I can feel it.'

Fent stared at her, his pale eyes mocking. 'You can
feel land?'

Katla nodded. 'There's rock ahead. My fingers are tingling.'

Fent laughed. 'I swear you are a troll's get, sister. What is it
with you and rock? If you're not climbing it, you're divining
it from the depths of the whale's path! We're miles north of
Istria yet: Father reckoned on landfall at first light.'

But Katla was shrouding her eyes with her hand, gazing

intently at where a dark smear lay between sea and sky on the horizon. 'There—'

'A cloud.'

'I'm sure it's not . . .'

There were clouds aplenty, piled up above the horizon in great lumps and towers, strewn about the upper reaches of the sky, which was darkening already and streaked with red, the sun having lost its daily battle with encroaching night: a blood-sky, as Erno would term it.

A shrill cry broke into their reverie. Above them, suddenly, a white bird veered past the ship, banking sharply. Fent watched it go, his mouth a round 'o' of surprise. 'A gull,' he said, like a simple child. 'That was a shore gull.'

Katla squeezed his arm. 'See?'

And now the outline on the horizon was becoming clearer by the minute; not a cloud-bank, after all, but solid land – a long, dark plateau, bordered to the west by higher land misting away into the distance.

'The Moonfell Plain.'

She could hear the delight in her father's voice without even having to see his face; even so, she turned around at once, eyes alight with excitement, seeking his attention. 'Land, Father: I saw it first.'

'And sensed it before that,' Fent muttered, clearly put out.

Aran Aranson grinned, revealing sharp white teeth amid weather-darkened skin and a close black beard barely touched by grey.

Ahead of them, the dark shape began to resolve itself further so that tiny dots of colour against the stark black gradually revealed themselves to be brightly-hued pavilions, the more vivid pinpricks of light between them as campfires. As they sailed into the sound they could see a whole host of other vessels bobbing quietly at anchor off the shore. 'Istria: can't you smell it? That's the smell of a foreign land, Katla; that's the smell of the Southern Empire.'

All Katla could smell was salt and sea and the sweat of bodies that had lived for a half-month in close quarters without fresh water to spare for washing, but she wouldn't say so.

'A foreign land . . .' she whispered, awed.

'Aye, and a load of bastard Istrians,' Fent said under his breath.

> *'To the south, sweet and fair*
> *They lie, slumbering and fat*
> *Ripe meat for the wolf.'*

He didn't need a knotted string for that one. Yet how his father could be so blithe at the sight of the old enemy's land, he could not understand. He turned to make further comment, but Aran was already calling for the rowers as he ran back along the deck, nimbly skirting the boxes of cargo, the cook-fire, the startled crew. With a dark look at Katla, Fent followed his father and took up his oar-place with the others.

Katla watched as the great striped sail was taken down and furled as they came into the shallower waters. All over the ship, men leapt to their tasks. She saw her father take his customary position at the steerboard to guide them in through the reefs and the long, grey breakers and turned her face back to the new land.

The Moonfell Plain.

A place from legend.

It had taken hours, it seemed, to make camp. By the time they had unshipped the two skiffs and put in to shore, the Navigator's Star was shining brightly in the sky. Lying on the strangely still ground, tired to the bone, Katla had been unable to sleep for the sheer novelty of it all. She'd heard about the

Allfair for as long as she could remember – all the lads' tales of horse-fights and boulder-throwing and swordplay; the gossip, the trading stories, the marriage-makings, the lists of extravagant-sounding names and internecine political allegiances. And she'd seen with her own eyes the intricate silver jewellery her father brought back for her mother when trading had gone well for him: and the monstrous, shaggy yeka-hides that covered their beds at home in the winter months – but this was her first Allfair and she could not wait for it to begin.

Wrapped in a sealskin with the pelt turned to the inside for warmth, she peered over the snoring bodies towards the distant campfires of the fairground and gazed again in awe at the great rock that rose steeply from the plain, illuminated by the flickering light. *That was what she had felt, all those miles out at sea*, she knew it now, twisting around to stare at its massive presence. It must be, she realised with a little thrill of excitement, Sur's Castle: hallowed ground. It was here – according to her folk, the Eyrans, the people of the north – where their god Sur had first taken his rest (having fallen from the Moon onto the surface of Elda) and surveyed his new domain. And having contemplated the whole great vista and found it sadly wanting, he had waded into the sea, thinking that by following the track of the moonbeams on the waves he might somehow find his way back home. *The Moon-path*, Katla thought, remembering Fent's verse. *Poor Sur, lost and lonely in an empty land*. The god had marched right across the northern ocean, skimming stones on his way to take his mind off the numbing cold (and of such great size were the stones that he cast about him that they formed the islands and skerries of Eyra) until at last he had disappeared into the fogs at the edge of the world of Elda. There, resigned to the fact that he would never find his way back home, he had raised a great stronghold beneath the waves, deep down on the ocean bed. This, the Eyrans called 'the Great Howe', or sometimes 'the Great Hall'. Lost sailors shared the long table there with Sur, it was said: and once one member of your clan had drowned and gone to the Howe, it was well known others would soon follow.

Katla had heard that the Istrians had a different tale to tell. They had no love of the sea, and did not believe even in the existence of Sur, an appalling heresy of itself. Instead, they prayed to some fire-deity, a creature – a woman – rumoured to have come walking naked out of a volcano in the Golden Mountains, unscathed by the lava, leading a great cat on a silver chain. Falla the Merciful – that's what they called her: a misnomer if ever there was one, since in her name the southerners burned unbelievers and wrongdoers by the thousand, sacrifices to appease her and hold at bay the molten heart of the world.

Sur's Castle. Her fingers began to itch. She'd go and look at it first thing the next morning: there would surely be a route by which she could climb to the top. Fighting and jewellery and monster-skins – *and* a new rock to climb: truly the Allfair was a wondrous event, to encompass such diversity.

She lay there, smiling at this thought, until she became drowsy. When at last she closed her eyes, she dreamed that she could feel the pull of the great rock deep inside her, as if it was somehow a part of the Navigator's Star and she nothing but a lodestone, drawn to it through a dark sea.

At first light the next morning, Katla kicked off the sealskin and crept away from the camp like a fox from the coop. In this area of the shoreline, no one else stirred. Up the shore she went, as fast as she could, the loose black ashy ground loud beneath her feet. In the shadow of Sur's Castle, she stared up. The great rock reared over her, enveloping her in its chill shadow, seeming higher, suddenly, from here – and steeper, too – than her first assessment of it from the beach. Dark clouds had gathered above it, promising rain:

she'd have to be quick. Her stomach fluttered and her heart gave a little thump: a familiar reaction before she attempted a climb, but a useful one, she'd found: anxiety tended to sharpen her concentration. Above her stretched a vertical chock-filled fissure – the most obvious line of ascent as far as she could see. It looked wide enough in places to jam a knee for balance, narrowing down to a crack that should accommodate a fist above the halfway mark. On either side of the line, little rugosities could clearly be seen where the crystals in them caught the early light: *useful footholds*, Katla thought. She reached up and found her first handhold: a jagged flake just inside the crack. It felt cold and a little damp beneath her fingers: sharp, too, but solid. As she took hold of it, a line of energy ran through her hand and jolted up her arm. For Katla, this had become a familiar sensation: this magical connection with rock and stone and the minerals they bore. She waited until the burst of energy had charged through her chest and up into her head, waited for the disorientating buzz to die away, and then gave herself to the rock. Letting the hold take her weight, she swung a foot up into the crack.

The move off the ground was always the hardest. Once established in the fissure, she readjusted her balance and went easily upward, hand over hand, methodical and careful, occasionally stepping outside the crack for better stability when the angle became too steep. The texture of the stuff reminded her of the sea-eaten cliffs back home: all pitted and sharp-edged from the corrosive appetite of the waves, and as painful on the skin as barnacles. She could feel it biting into the soles of her feet even through the leather. Sur knew what her hands would look like by the top, even though she'd been placing them with more consideration than usual. It was not that she was a vain girl – far from it: but there would be awkward questions to answer if she came back covered with cuts and scrapes.

The sheer pleasure of the climb soon erased any sense of

worry: past the halfway mark it started to rain; but the angle of the rock eased so that she was able to stand in balance and look around, taking in the brightly-coloured tents of the other Fair-goers, their wax-treated surfaces repelling the drops of water that pattered down upon them. She had never before seen such vibrant shades: in the islands the only eye-catching dye you could produce was a rather putrid yellow that appeared to have been obtained by soaking your clothes in pig's urine but actually derived from an innocuous-looking lichen, scraped painstakingly and in vast quantity from the granite cliffs that formed the bones of her homeland. (Though it had to be said that even then, you did actually need a bit of urine to fix the colour so that it didn't bleed down your leg in the first storm. It didn't smell for too long. Only a week or so.)

It was among these granite cliffs where Katla had first learned the magic that lay in the veins of the rock. It was there she had started to clamber around in such a casual fashion, barely conscious of the yawning gulf beneath her feet, the sucking maw of the ocean; the bone-shattering consequences of a fall. There, she'd collected gulls' eggs in late spring; samphire in the summer. She'd fished from precipitous ledges and pulled line after line of iridescent mackerel out of secret zawns. And sometimes she'd just scaled the cliffs for the sheer pleasure of being somewhere no other person had set foot.

Two more moves and she had her hands on the flat summit: using a sharp incut for her right foot to gain more height, she pushed down hard till her arms could take her whole weight, skipped her feet up the remaining stretch of rock; and suddenly she was on top of Sur's Castle, on top of the world.

Sitting there, with her feet dangling over the edge, with the Moonfell Plain stretching away below, a glorious sense of well-being descended upon Katla.

So she was surprised and not a little dismayed when someone started shouting, apparently at her.

'Oi, you there!' The second shout was in the Old Tongue. She looked around.

At the far western edge of the rock, a couple of elderly gentlemen were climbing, haltingly and with great puffs of effort, a line of carefully-chiselled steps. Someone had thoughtfully arranged a pair of taut hemp handrails on either side of the stairs, and the grey-hairs were hanging onto these even as they bellowed at her. They both wore long dark-red robes with elaborately-worked brocade facings; even from her perch seventy yards away, Katla could see the silver thread glinting in the weak light. Rich men, then, she thought. Not Eyrans; at least like none she'd ever seen. The northerners could never afford clothes like that – they'd be worth a ship's cargo apiece – and even if they could, they'd never climb a rock in them . . .

'Get down from there at once!'

The first of the old men had reached the top step and, lifting his voluminous skirts, was picking up speed.

She cupped her hand to her ear and shrugged: the universal gesture for 'can't hear a word you're saying'.

Infuriated, the grey-hair waved his stick.

'The Council and the Allfair Guard—'

'Of which we are on the ruling committee—'

'Indeed, brother. Of which we are on the ruling committe, have declared Falla's Rock as sacred ground!'

Falla's rock?

The second had almost caught up with his fellow. He was shaking his fist at her. 'You'll pay for not showing the due observances, young man!'

Young man? Katla's mouth fell open in amazement. Young man? He must be blind. She stood up, and with aggressive haste unbound her hair. She always tied it into a tail when she climbed: otherwise it could be a damned nuisance.

Unconfined, it fell around her shoulders in tumbling waves. At the same moment, as if to emphasise the point, the sun came out, so that the slanting rain became a shower of silver and Katla's hair a fiery beacon.

The second old man cannoned into the first.

'Oh, Great Goddess, Lady of Fire, it's— a woman!'

They looked extremely unhappy.

Katla, deciding not to find out exactly what it was that pained them so badly about the situation, made her excuses and left, reversing with considerable alacrity and no little skill the crack-line she'd just ascended.

There was a saying that the old women had in the north (they had a saying for everything in Eyra: it was that sort of place): *the heedful outlive the heroes*. Like her brothers she'd always thought it cautious nonsense; but it was possible in this particular case that they had a point.

Saro Vingo emerged, blinking, from his family pavilion into the light of a day still making its mind up whether to rain or shine. His head hurt as if someone had trampled on it in the night. For some reason his father had decided that Saro's first visit to the Allfair should be marked by a major araque-binge, and his uncle and cousins and older brother, Tanto, had all conspired to line up glass after glass of the vile smoky stuff for him and watched him down each one in a single swallow until every flask was dry. They had matched him glass for glass; but they had had a lot more practice. He had left them all sleeping it off, tumbled on the floor amid the dogs and the vomit; collapsed upon silk-strewn couches, snoring their heads off in the pile of rich tapestries and shawls they'd brought as a gift for the northern King at this, his first Allfair. Though why the people of the Empire should bother to flatter a barbarian, he could not imagine. Falla knew what he'd make of the gorgeous Istrian fabrics, now reeking of araque and bile. Still, the Eyrans were known to be very

unsophisticated people: he'd probably think it had something
to do with the dye-process.

Saro was curious to set eyes upon the women of the north.
All the lads whose first Fair this was were equally fascinated;
it had been their major topic of conversation on the journey
here from the southern valleys. King Ravn Asharson was
coming to the Allfair, it was said, to choose himself a bride;
so the Eyran nobles would surely be bringing their daughters
and sisters in the hopes of making a royal match. As far as
Saro was concerned, it was the focal point of the Fair: not for
him the dull complications of deal-making and point-scoring
with a load of fat old merchants who knew exactly what game
they were playing with one another and made him feel a
complete fool for not being a party to their subtly coded
rules and haggling. The women of Eyra were rumoured to
be amongst the most beautiful women on Elda, and *that* was
interesting. Although he would be the first to admit that he
had no real idea of what a woman looked like; let alone
how to assess her beauty. At home, the women were hidden
away for most of the time: since the time he'd turned fifteen
and had been initiated into the sexual world, he had barely
even seen his mother.

He thought of her now; how, swathed from head to foot in
a fabulously-coloured sabatka, she would flutter silently from
room to room, with only her hands and mouth showing, like
some wonderful, exotic butterfly.

A moment later, and he was remembering the encounter
that had brought him to manhood: how his father had paid
for him to enter that darkened room in the backstreets of
Altea; the smell of the woman inside it – musky and rank;
the feeling of her cool hands and hot lips upon him; his
uncontrollable climax, and the shame that followed.

Yet it was rumoured that not only did the men of the
northern isles allow their women to wander freely, but also
that they showed off not just their hands and mouths, but their

entire faces, and occasionally even their limbs and chests. The thought of such sacrilege made Saro's heart palpate. And not just his heart.

His fair cheeks were still flushed from these unclean thoughts when he heard a shout. Turning around he saw in the near distance how two of the Istrian elders who sat upon Istria's ruling council of city states – Greving Dystra and his brother, Hesto – were laboriously climbing the stairs to the summit of Falla's Rock. They seemed to be waving their arms around and calling out. Intrigued, Saro made his way between the pavilions grouped below the rock, and, shading his eyes, stared up. Atop the rock sat what appeared to be a young man dressed in a homely brown tunic and long boots, who even now had scrambled to his feet, clearly embarrassed at being caught in this serious act of trespass. Greving was shaking his fist at the intruder and Hesto was just clearing the last stair, when the young man turned to confront them and with an impatient – indeed, rather extravagant – flick of the wrist pulled loose the cord that held back his hair. The light struck suddenly off a face revealed to be too finely structured for any boy's, framed by a flamboyant fall of blazing red, and Saro found that he could not get his breath. Even at this distance he felt the shock of seeing a girl – with bare legs and arms; and not just any girl, but a barbarian creature in defiance of all observance and decency, on top of the sacred Rock – like a physical blow. Quite unexpectedly, his knees became unreliable, and he sat down hard upon the ashy ground.

When he looked up again, she was nowhere to be seen.

If Katla had hoped to sneak back amongst the Rockfall clan unnoticed, she was soon to be disappointed. Cresting the ridge of the shore, she stared down across the dark and gritty sand to where the faerings and their snoring crew had lain like beached whales only an hour before; only to find everyone up and about and as busy as ants, under the watchful eye of her father.

'Sur's nuts,' she cursed softly. 'Now I'm in trouble.'

The *Fulmar's Gift* lay anchored a hundred yards offshore, bobbing in the pale light of the newly risen sun. At this distance she looked graceful and sublime, her clinkered hull as elegant as any swan's breast. But close up, Katla knew, she was a more impressive sight by far, the fine oak of her strakes marked by years of voyaging in rough northern waters; her gunwales gouged and split by rocks and collision and the violent grip of enemies' axe-heads; the soaring neck of her ornamented prow culminating in the fearsome shape of a she-troll's head, mouth agape and every tooth sharply delineated with loving, superstitious skill. But of course they'd taken down the provocative figurehead before entering the neutral territory of the Moonfell waters and laid it in sailcloth alongside the lowered mast. It would hardly do, Aran had said, to remind their old foe of worse times when you were preparing to fleece them blind.

A dozen or more of the crew swarmed over her, manhandling great wooden chests and barrels from their stowage places and lowering them one at a time into one of the narrow faerings, which shuddered and rocked under the weight of the heavy cargo.

The second of the ship's boats was even now beaching in the shallows. Four men in the bows leapt out in a flurry of surf, stark white against the black of the land, and hauled the little boat up the gentle rise as if it were as light as a mermaid. Katla could make out her elder brother, Halli, and her twin, Fent; the second pair comprising Tor Leeson and their cousin, Erno Hamson.

'That's all I need,' she groaned. 'An audience.'

Chin up, she strode resolutely down the volcanic dune to face the inevitable chastisement, the ashy sand crunching unhelpfully underfoot. Before she had got within even ten feet of him, her father turned around and regarded her grimly, his gnarled, weather-beaten hands on his hips.

'Where have you been?'

Aran Aranson was a big man, even by Eyran standards. His wife, Bera, often joked that before they were married, whenever her mother had spotted him riding up to their farm to pay court on his sturdy little pony (his feet so close to the ground despite its zealous efforts that it seemed that the pair of them might at any moment trip each other up and fall in an undignified heap) she would say, 'Here comes Aran Aranson, that great ogre of yours again, Bera. If you have children – hear what I say – they'll turn out trolls and you'll be split in two like a piece of firewood!' And then she'd cackle fit to bursting and fuss over him till the poor lad turned red, knowing that somehow he was the butt of her teasing yet again. She still had a robust sense of humour, Gramma Rolfsen: and her laughter could often be heard on a smoky night pealing out from the steading at Rockfall; but her son-by-law had never quite learned the trick of such humour, and as he stared at his errant daughter, he showed not even the trace of a smile.

Katla, having spent years learning to charm her father over her minor misdemeanours, took in the single-browed line of his frown and the flint in his eye and quailed. Her lips blue with the telltale signs of a fruit pie swiped from an unattended table, she wracked her brain for a suitable falsehood.

'I just went for a walk – to watch the sun come up over Sur's Castle,' she said, careful on this occasion not to present him with an outright lie, for the expedition had almost started so.

'We're not in Eyra now,' he said grimly, stating the obvious. 'You can't just wander around on your own at the Allfair. It isn't safe.'

So it wasn't anger, after all, but worry! He was *worried* about her. Relief swept over her: she laughed.

'Who's there to be afraid of? I'm not afraid of anyone, especially not *men*.' She grinned, teasing out the emphasis on the last word. 'You know perfectly well I can defend myself – didn't I win the wrestling last summer?'

It was true. Slim and swift and lithely evasive, there had been no one who could pin her down. Wrestling Katla was like trying to wrestle an eel.

She bared a biceps and flexed it as if to prove her point. Hammering metal and manning the bellows at the smithy had had its effect: a hard, round ball of muscle popped impressively into view. 'Who's going to tangle with that?'

But her father was not to be deflected. Moving far more quickly than you'd imagine likely for a man of his size, Aran lunged forward like a wolf going for a rabbit and seized her arm so hard that she winced. When he let go, the marks of his fingers were clearly visible in the smooth tan of her flesh. The smile faded from Katla's face and an angry flush rose up her neck. An uncomfortable silence fell between father and daughter. Katla, afraid of her own temper, stared hard at the ground between her feet and started sullenly to trace a knotwork pattern in the black ash with her toe. As the silence lengthened, she found her unpredictable mind considering how she might incorporate this pattern into the hilt of the next seax she worked.

'They're odd about women, the Empire men,' Aran said at last. 'You can't trust them – they have bizarre customs and it can make them behave dangerously. A few country grappling tricks won't see you through; and, besides: you're here on my sufferance. There was no need for me to bring you to an Allfair: it's a waste of a fare, for me. Two stone of sardonyx I'm down because of you, with Fosti Goatbeard desperate to come this year. Could have bought your mother a nice shawl and some good jewellery with the proceeds. So having deprived your mother of her Fair-gift, and old Fosti of his place on the ship, you can repay my generosity by doing nothing, and I mean nothing, without my permission. Is that clear? And you stay always in my sight.'

Katla opened her mouth to protest, then thought better of it. She'd wait until he was in a lighter mood, and then work her wiles on him, she thought with sudden savage resolve. Even in the islands, where women laboured as hard as men and were considered their equal in most things, Katla had found that her wiles provided her with a delightfully unfair advantage over her brothers.

'Yes, Father,' she said with apparent docility, and looking up through her lashes was gratified to see his expression soften.

'Well, mind you do,' he finished lamely.

Daughters. Why were they so much more difficult than sons?

At that moment one of his male offspring came crunching up the strand to join them. His brother and cousins were not far behind. Tall lads, and well-put-together, the Aransons and their cousins made a striking group. Halli took after his father: big and dark, with a nose that in age was likely to become as hooked as a hawk's. Fent, like his sister, had Bera's flaming hair, fine bones and skin – and their vanity, too, for he shaved like a southerner; but hard work had made whipcord of his muscles and packed his light frame with enough energy for three. As if to provide the greatest possible contrast, or to demonstrate the various appearances to be found in the Eyran Isles, Erno Hamson and Tor Leeson were so blond that their hair and beards shone like silver. Erno, whose mother had recently died, had plaited a complex memory-knot, complete with shells and strips of cloth, into his left braid. After two weeks at sea, the scraps of fabric were salty and faded, but the knots were as tight as ever. At night when he had sat his watch at the tiller, Katla had heard him quietly reciting the word-pattern he had made for his mother when first weaving the braid, his fingers retracing the loops and bindings to fix the pattern in his head—

'This cloth the blue of your eyes
This shell your openhandedness
This the knot for wisdom given but never compelled
This knot for when you nursed me from fever . . .'

—and she had been surprised how one who by day could be so distant and diffident could in the night hours become so tender; and for this she almost liked him.

'So, the wanderer returns!' Fent beamed. 'Thought you'd escape your chores, did you?'

'Shirk your family duties?' Tor made a face at her.

'Leave it all for the boys with the muscle?' said Halli, whose sharp eyes had not missed the flexed-biceps exchange between his father and sister.

Erno said nothing: he was always tongue-tied in Katla's presence.

Aran looked impatient. 'Did you bring the tents and the stalls in with this load?'

The lads nodded.

'Right then – Fent and Erno, and you, Katla, come with me to get the booths set up. Halli and Tor, you keep the crew working to unship the cargo. I'll be back in an hour and we'll get the sardonyx weighed in and registered.'

Fent grinned at his sister, his incisors as sharp as any fox's. 'You can carry the ropes,' he said. 'Since you're only a girl.'

He dodged her swinging fist with ease and jogged down the beach to the piles of equipment. There, light ash frames rested amongst rolls of trussed skins, waxed wool-cloth and coils of rope. Two huge iron cauldrons, together with their stands and pothooks, lay amid a welter of bowls and dishes, knives and hand-axes, where someone had thrown them down on the sand in a hurry to fetch the next load.

Fent swept an armful of the clutter into one of the cauldrons until a strange assortment of blades and bowls stuck out of the top. 'There you are,' he said to Katla. 'If you think you're hard enough.'

An iron cauldron this size was fantastically heavy – let alone one filled to the brim with kitchen implements. Katla knew this to be so: one had fallen once from a rusted-through hook and had almost crippled her: she'd danced aside quickly enough to avoid a crushed foot, but even a glancing blow had caused her to lose a toenail to it, and she'd had to bind her foot in cloth for a week, since she couldn't get her boot over the swelling. With a grim look at her brother she hefted the thing two-handed and managed to stagger half a dozen paces with the cauldron skimming the surface of the sand, before staggering to a halt. Every fibre of her arms protested at the weight: they felt as if they'd stretched a knuckle-length already.

The boys burst out laughing. Even her father was grinning. She watched them, narrow-eyed, then picked it up again with one hand, her other arm waving wildly for balance, this time straightening the carrying arm and her back to keep the tension running through the bones rather than the muscles, a trick she'd learned from climbing overhanging rock. The cauldron lifted reluctantly and bumped painfully against her leg. Katla bit her lip and soldiered on. When, after some minutes of sweaty effort, she reached the crest of the beach, she set the cauldron down and looked back. Taking her obstinacy for granted, the men were no longer watching her: instead, they had gathered up the rest of the equipment and were trudging in her footsteps. When they caught up with her, Aran took the cauldron away and exchanged it for a tent-roll.

'You have nothing to prove to me, daughter,' he said gently and his eyes were as green as the sea. 'I know your heart to be as great as any man's.'

So saying, and as easily as if it had been a wooden bucket, he picked up the cauldron, and strode quickly past her.

Aran and his family worked quickly and efficiently together, with barely a word of instruction passing between them, and less than an hour later they had erected a pair of tents, which would provide their living-space for the duration of the Allfair. And while the Eyran tents might not be as plush or as colourful as the rich Istrian pavilions Katla had seen at the foot of Sur's Castle, they were both weatherproof and spacious, almost twenty feet long, fourteen broad and over ten feet high at the centre – large enough to house family, crew, cargo and wares.

A cold onshore breeze seemed to have sprung out of nowhere while they were working, making the tanned leather of the roof bell and flap. Katla, her hair having long since escaped its braid, ran to tension the wind-ropes, and found herself confronted by an Empire man in a rich blue cloak. With his dark complexion and cleanshaven chin, it was clear at once that he was not an island man. He wore a thin silver circlet in his black hair, which complemented the dusting of grey above his ears, and his skin was so smooth as to look like polished wood. He was taller than she was, but only just; yet he stared down the length of his thin nose at her as though she were something unpleasant he was about to tread in.

She stared back at him enquiringly, not sure, for once in her life, what to say.

Aran stepped silently to his daughter's side. 'Is there something I can help you with?' he asked.

The foreign lord's eyes swept insolently over Katla's bare arms and wild hair, resting for a moment longer than propriety required on the hint of cleavage visible at the top of her sweat-streaked tunic, then turned to Aran. 'I believe you sell fine knives,' he stated smoothly. His voice was silky and light, and he spoke the Old Tongue with barely a trace of Istrian.

Aran nodded. 'But we're not open for business until after noon.'

'I would like to be your first customer, to ensure I have the pick of your wares.'

'Then you'll need to be here when we open up,' Aran said shortly. Katla could tell from his tone that something about the foreign lord irked him.

The Istrian raised an elegant eyebrow. 'I see.' He paused. He took a pouch from his belt, weighed it thoughtfully in his palm. 'Might I not persuade you to open your stand now, for a sum to be mutually agreed?'

Aran laughed. 'No. We won't be ready till noon,' he repeated.

The foreigner's eyes flashed. He adjusted his cloak to one side so that his house insignia was for a second apparent, then let it fall back.

'It is imperative that I have the pick of your wares. Only the best will do.'

'I'm flattered that our reputation has reached the far countries,' Aran said with care. 'We could, perhaps, open just before noon for your convenience and Katla here will take you through her finest blades. They are pattern-welded to the highest—'

'This . . . woman?' The Istrian seemed appalled. 'You let a woman show your daggers for you?'

Aran looked wary. 'Of course. They are Katla's own work, the finest in all of Eyra, even though it might not be seemly to boast of my daughter's skills—'

The lord took a step backwards as if Aran had fouled the air between them. He made a complicated sign with his left hand and said something in his native language that was quite unintelligible to Eyran ears. At last he said: 'I cannot buy a weapon touched by a woman, it would be quite unthinkable. Good day.'

He turned on his heel. Then, as if he had had second thoughts, he turned back again and addressed Katla direct. 'There is a rumour circulating that a young Eyran woman was caught on top of Falla's Rock at dawn this morning,' he said, and his voice was cold and dangerous. 'I hope, for your sake, and the sake of your family, whom I am sure are most fond of you, that that person was not you.'

Katla stared at him. 'Why, no,' she said at once and looked him right in the eye. They hadn't caught her, after all: so it was no lie.

'Because,' he went on, 'for a woman to trespass on Falla's Rock is a capital offence. The Rock is sacred terrain: sacred to the Goddess. For any other female to set foot there is the deepest desecration.'

Fent stepped forward then, his face furious. 'The Rock is Sur's own ground—' he started, but his father interrupted, his face grim: 'It could not have been my daughter for, as you can see, we have been labouring together for many hours, and she has not in all that time left my sight.'

The Istrian lord looked somewhat appeased. 'My apologies.' He made as if to leave, but Aran said quickly, 'Might I ask why you suspected the transgressor might have been my daughter?'

'Why, her hair of course. The two lords who came upon her described her most carefully. Long red hair, they said, long hair in a braid that she took down and flaunted at them.'

Aran laughed. 'It is our custom in the north, as well you know, my lord, for both the men and the women to wear their hair long; and many – like my son, Fent here – have hair both long and red. I fear the gentlemen who came upon the trespasser may not have been in the first flush of youth or have possessed the keenest eyes.'

The Istrian thought for a moment. He inclined his head. 'That is indeed possible, sir: the Dystras are quite elderly men. Maybe they were mistaken. I hope so for your daughter's sake; for the tale is becoming quite widespread and the officers are searching for the trespasser: she may encounter certain . . . difficulties around the Fair if others leap to the same conclusion.'

Aran held his gaze with complete composure, then the Istrian lord nodded. 'May you have a fortunate Fair,' he said formally, and walked away. His fine blue cloak rode the breeze behind him as if by elegant design.

The Eyrans watched him go. When he was well out of earshot, Aran grabbed Katla by the shoulder. 'You little witch! I promised your mother I would not let you out of my sight, and already you're in the deepest of trouble.' He looked her up and down, taking in her short tunic, her bare legs and unkempt mane. Then without a word he caught her in an armlock and grabbed the ornamented knife Katla wore always at her waist belt. 'Hold her hair up for me, Fent,' he said in a tone that brooked no refusal.

Erno, standing behind them, gasped. Katla, realising what her father was about to do, struggled. But her father was more than a match for her in comparison to the untrained lads against whom she had wrestled and won at the summer games. Tightening the hold with one arm, he sawed at the handfuls of flaming hair that Fent, with a pained expression, held up taut for the knife. The tempered blade, one of the best Katla had ever made and of which she was inordinately proud, proved its worth by shearing through her tangled locks as if through finest silk. Great swathes of hair floated to the ground to glow like the fire that had once created the black ash upon which it fell.

'Gather it up,' Aran said to Erno, who hesitated, then dropped to his knees and started to stuff it into his shirt.

Seconds later, Aran let his daughter go. She stood there for a moment like a cornered bear, the fury emanating from her in waves. Then she turned and ran as if all the devils in the world were after her.

Fent stared at the piece of hair he was still grasping – warm in his hands, like a little living creature of flame – then dropped it slowly to the ground. He looked up at his father.

Aran grimaced. 'It's for her own good. If they find her they'll want to burn her.'

He stuck the dagger into his own belt and rubbed his hands conclusively on his leather jerkin. Fine strands of red gold drifted away on the breeze. Aran watched them spiral away with an unreadable expression on his face, then, with a barked order to the lads, started down to the strand to see to the sardonyx.

Erno exchanged glances with Fent, his face white and strained. Fent stared back, his fair features in sharp contrast to his father's. 'You heard what he said.' And when Erno hesitated, 'It won't come to that. If they try to take Katla all of Eyra will be up in arms.' He kicked dust over the lock of hair, then stowed the mallet and remaining pegs swiftly inside the tent. 'Come on.'

They ran to catch up with the receding figure of the clan leader.

Two

The Footloose

Saro Vingo and his older brother Tanto had just finished grooming the second group of Vingo family bloodstock – a dozen of the finest Istrian colts: all dainty narrow heads, sheeny coats, long-limbed skittishness and sharp yellow teeth – and thanks to the latter, specifically a one-year-old beauty called Night's Harbinger, a tricksy beast with a dubious temperament, Tanto was sitting on the ground, nursing a bitten forearm.

'Bastard creature!' He rubbed the skin ferociously. Distinct toothmarks showed up purple-red against the brown, testament to where Tanto had lost his temper with Night's Harbinger – a fine-boned bay with a single white star on its forehead – and gripped him too hard when trying to brush out his forelock. Saro knew better than to force his will upon the animals thus: consequently they never bit him. It was a curious fact, though, that animals did not much like his brother. Tanto was always getting kicked or bitten by something. It was noticeable, too, how at home cats would slink silently past him, low on their hocks, close to the walls; while in the long, warm Istrian evenings, when the last rays of sun spilled through the tall windows to make honey-coloured pools of light on the polished floors, the greyhounds would watch him out of the corners of their anxious black eyes whenever he moved from his chair, which was rare enough, so long as there was a pitcher of bier or a flask of araque at hand.

'It'll be a killer, that one,' Tanto muttered darkly. 'I told Father the last time it bit me that we'd be better off serving it to the dogs than shipping it all the way to the Allfair on the bastard barge.' He picked up a piece of black stone, walked it adroitly between his fingers for a few seconds, then threw it with sudden vicious force at the offending animal. Accurate as ever, Tanto's shot hit the horse on the tender spot between haunch and flank, and the creature shied up and sped off to the other side of the enclosure, white panic encircling its eyes. 'Worthless runt!'

Saro frowned, but said nothing. Night's Harbinger was the best of their bunch, a rangy runner with a fine turn of speed, likely on a good day to win any race they set him to. Besides which, he'd long since learned never to get in the way of his brother's frequent tempests of rage; even commenting on them had earned him cuts and bruises as a child. Instead, he gathered up the grooming kit, replacing each brush and flask of oil carefully into the pockets in the soft cloth roll in which he kept them, and said: 'So, which contest do you think you have the best chance at?'

A climate change came over Tanto. It was as if all the black clouds had blown away and a sun shone down upon the world. A handsome, athletic lad, and well aware of it, nothing pleased him more than to have someone showing interest in him, even if it was only his measly little brother. He shook his head and the light played dutifully upon each black curl; upon the taut plane of his cheek and the hollow of his smooth throat, and came to rest finally upon his prized choker of sardonyx, its alternating bands of finest red chalcedony and lucent quartz a perfect foil to the dark warmth of his skin. His expression relaxed into a wide, delighted smile.

'Why, all of them, brother! I've been training, you know.'

It was true: he had. While Saro and the younger boys had their knuckles rapped by their humourless tutor in the dull, cool silence of the learning house, outside in the sunshine

Tanto was ploughing a furrow in the lake with his effortless backstroke; or casting a carefully-weighted spear across the homefield into distant straw targets under the discerning eye of their Uncle Fabel; punching mercilessly some poor slaveboy who'd been wrapped in padded leather and given some rudimentary fist-training; or out with their father, Favio Vingo, in the hills, triumphantly shooting rabbits full of quills from his short-bow. Seeing in his eldest son the Allfair champion he had never quite been, Favio lavished upon Tanto the finest of weapons – sabres of Forent steel and pattern-welded daggers from the north; bows crafted from aged oak and arrows fletched with the feathers of geese bred specifically for the purpose at Lake Jetra, way down on the Tilsen Plain. Tanto had the pick of everything – from the first cut of the roast, to the most exclusive of his father's courtesans: it was only fair, he said, when you considered the riches and the glory his prowess would bring to the family name.

Saro smiled back at his brother (a smile that did not quite touch his eyes), feeling for his sibling the usual resentment simmering quietly away beneath his quiet exterior, and let the neverending flow of boasts pass like hot air above his head. Saro himself had always failed miserably in the contests at which Tanto excelled. He didn't appear to have the necessary physical strength or coordination to compete with his brother, or anyone else, for that matter; his fear of water made him sink, stiff-muscled, to the lake floor; spears left his hand on unpredictable trajectories which had the slaves running wildly out of the way; the delicate southern swords – too light, surely, to be effective as a weapon? – slipped awkwardly from his fingers; and as for fist-fighting . . . Maybe it was just that he lacked the will to win. Probably it had more to do with the fact that with Tanto around, there was hardly any point in competing: why try and fail, only to be beaten and chastised? It seemed easier to accept his limitations and live with his father's inevitable disappointment. 'Saro: you will never amount to anything,' Favio Vingo said constantly, and Saro had now come to accept that as an ineluctable truth.

Besides, Saro thought to himself, seeing how his brother's chest was swelling from his inability to draw breath while talking so about himself, if you had to be like Tanto in order to succeed, who wanted to be a champion?

'. . . so it's the swordplay in which I should really excel, with that new damascened blade of mine, even though Fortran's father gave him a gilded guard for his sabre, and Haro's been taking lessons all summer from that swordmaster from Gila,' Tanto finished in a rush.

'Clearly brother, who could possibly match you?'

Tanto grinned in agreement, then uncoiled himself and strolled across the enclosure to supervise the slaves who were completing the stockade. Tall and muscular, he walked with an easy grace Saro knew he'd never possess, though as children kind aunts, the glint of their eyes bright through the veils of their sabatkas, their hands all aflutter with affection, had often remarked upon how alike the two boys looked: 'like fircones from the same branch!' Which had not pleased Tanto, and even though they shared a superficial similarity, Saro found himself feeling a fraud, guilty at the aunts' obvious error of judgement.

Now, Tanto was firing off loud commands at the work-crew without the slightest hesitation or doubt as to his right to do so. At once, the slaves redoubled their efforts, careful not to meet his eye. The colts, meanwhile, trotted to the other side of the pen, blowing through their noses and looking expectantly at Saro. With a quick glance to make sure that Tanto's attention was safely engaged elsewhere, Saro slipped his hand into the bag inside his tunic and drew out some of the horse-nuts he'd smuggled over with him. Neither Tanto nor their father approved of 'spoiling' the animals thus. 'They're here to make us money,' Favio had said. 'A great deal of money. They're not pets.' Fine-bred horses were considerable assets in Istria, for status, for spectacle, for racing and as a sweetener to attract the best officers for the standing armies that each province prided itself upon, and the trading of stock such as these was one of the Vingo family's major income sources. Only family members were allowed to tend the animals, for Favio, a superstitious man when it came to money, was convinced that the touch of an outsider's hand upon his bloodstock would somehow taint or subvert the purity of their Falla-dedicated breeding-lines. And so it was that both lads had travelled to the Moonfell Plain the long way, this year, along with several of their compatriots: for the livestock barges were too slow and cumbersome to deal with the fast waters of the Alta River, or the open sea, and instead had to make their meandering way up the wide, placid Golden River. Tanto, of course, had complained bitterly at not being allowed passage on the Vingo ship, *The Maid of Calastrina*, with the rest of the clan, but in this alone his father had not indulged him. 'My boy,' he had said, 'your marriage payment and future success may rest on the price we get for the bloodstock this year. Remember that: care for the animals with all diligence, and ride the river with a hopeful heart, for if all goes to plan, by Allfair next year you will be lord of your own domain, owner of a noble wife and a fair castle.'

Tanto had stopped complaining after that; but he'd avoided the horses as soon as they were out of sight of the family estate and had cheerfully left all the work to Saro, spending his time instead peering at charts and maps of the river's course, and delivering orders to the crew. Cognizant of Tanto's famous temper, the men deferred to him silently, though Saro caught them exchanging amused glances: for everyone knew a child could steer a barge up the Golden River.

As soon as they scented the horse-nuts, the colts were crowding around Saro, pushing at him with their velvety muzzles, until he had to drop the treats down inside his tunic and fend them off. Night's Harbinger, however, had hung back from the rest and regarded him warily. Slowly, Saro moved between the other horses till he was within arm's reach of the bay. He held out his hand to him, empty, palm up. The bay rolled his eyes. When he stretched out to rub Night's Harbinger on the cheek, he threw up his head, but did not back away. Carefully, Saro reached into his shirt and drew out a handful of the horse-nuts. When he scented them, the bay became strangely compliant. A few seconds later, Saro felt questing lips graze his hand, and then the horse-nuts were gone, as if by magic, and the next thing he knew, the bay was pressing his head against his chest, nosing deep into his tunic, until he had to push him away. As he did so, his shirt pulled loose from his belt, and horse-nuts scattered everywhere.

They made a sound like a miniature rockfall.

Tanto's head whipped around, and took in with a face like thunder the sight of six of the Vingo family's finest bloodstock yearlings scoffing worshipfully at his little brother's feet.

Aran Aranson's daughter ran until a sharp stitch under her ribs slowed her down. Rage had carried her a mile or more from the family booths, to the edge of the fairground and beyond. No one had taken much notice of a girl running urgently through their midst, since there were so many other people scurrying in all directions on errands and assignments; like the Aransons, setting up their stands, raising tents and pavilions, building temporary stockades for the livestock, tethering horses and dogs.

From the top of a rocky knoll, Katla looked back at the activity of the fair and pummelled her abdomen with a hard knuckle, trying to shift the stabbing pain. Stupid! She'd been so angry she'd forgotten to breathe properly. At home she ran for miles, tireless and steady, her long legs loping like a hound's across moorland and meadow, up hill and down dale. She never got stitches, not like this. Damn her father for his bullying ways! She was a grown woman now, and surely due some respect: how dare he manhandle her as if she were a wayward ewe at shearing-time! And damn Fent and Erno, too, for standing by like the useless wretches they were, not even bothering to lift a hand to stop him. It didn't surprise her that Fent wouldn't stand up to their father, for Aran's rages were elemental in their force; but she was disappointed in Erno, who might at least have remonstrated with him. She'd thought, from his shyness around her, that he might care a little for her: but clearly he was as cowardly and ineffectual as the rest of them. She ran a distracted hand over her head, feeling for the first time its strange new configuration, the remains of her hair uneven and spiky. Her head felt oddly light. It was – she noted with some surprise – quite a pleasant sensation.

Well, at least washing it wouldn't be the tedious chore it usually was, with the long tail hanging plastered like a wet cat down her back for hours on end. As short as it was now, it would dry in minutes. She laughed as another thought struck her: for clearly her father had no intention of parading her around before King Ravn, as a marriage prospect! When Breta, Jenna and Tian had heard she'd be coming to the Allfair, it had been all they'd talk about – King Ravn Asharson: so handsome, so dashing, and by all accounts as wild as a stallion in heat for a mate – and they'd giggled and blushed and gone on at tedious length fantasising about what dresses they'd wear to be presented, how they'd curtsey and gaze up at him; how they'd prime their fathers to put their case to the lords. Remarkably, Jenna had managed to persuade her father to let her come with him to the Fair this year as well, though Katla doubted she'd ever be able to talk him into entering her into the marriage contest. The Fairwater clan, though wealthy and with an old heritage, were a shipbuilding family, and Katla suspected they already had their eye on one of her brothers for Jenna. Halli, probably, as the older of the two, rather than Fent. Katla anyway suspected her dour older brother had something of a soft spot for the coy and flirtatious Jenna. And Jenna, with her liking for dark men would most likely choose Halli, if she were given her say; though not until she'd had her foolish infatuation with Ravn Asharson conclusively quashed. They would all be going to the Gathering: that much Katla knew, for any Eyran family who paid tithes to the King or provided him with ships, crews or fighters was welcome to attend any court event. The northerners were not much for ceremony, Sur be praised.

Though quite what she would do with her tousled crop for the royal reception, she didn't know, and it was only a couple of days away. She'd been planning to braid it up in the latest style, shown to her by Jenna when she'd come back from Halbo last month with a gorgeous new dress in the best southern silk – glossy as a holly leaf and edged with frothings of Galian silver lace. Katla had no gorgeous new dress at all. She had prided herself on her own hair being more lustrous and vibrant than Jenna's, and that what she lacked in finery she'd make up for with her crowning glory, as her mother so proudly termed it. Not much of a crowning glory now, she thought ruefully. Bera would be furious when she got home, would no doubt start castigating Aran for ruining his daughter's marriage chances, and not only to the King! Which, as far as Katla was concerned, was no bad thing in itself: she didn't think any husband would be so generous as to allow her travel to the Allfair with him as her father, for all his complaints, had done; let alone run wild around the islands, climbing cliffs and riding wild ponies. No, she'd be the one saddled and harnessed, with a brace of children before she could blink, and then more and more and more until she'd mothered an entire clan. The Eyrans regarded large families as a sign of Sur's blessing: a hard enough achievement, since they lost so many to feuding and the wicked seas.

The girls she knew talked about nothing other than wed- dings, it seemed: which lads were the nicest looking; which had the best prospects; what their settlements would be and what they'd wear for the handfasting; how many children they would have; what they'd call them all. To Katla such discussions were no more than a catalogue of constraints, and that the girls should conspire in their own confinement seemed perverse, to say the least. It was hard to maintain friends when you shared none of their dreams. Recently, she'd found herself drifting away from them, to pursue more and more solitary interests, and she hadn't really missed their idle tattle at all.

Oddly enough, she'd come to count her brothers and their cronies as closer allies than her own sex, finding with them a fine sense of companionship in the sharing of active tasks around the homestead; or adventures on the island. One day she'd taken Halli with her to climb the headland at Wolf's Ness, certain she'd seen a rock-sprite in a cave near the overhang. Using combined tactics and a rope made out of sealskin, with Katla wobbling badly on her tall brother's shoulders at the crux, she'd managed to grasp the ledge and haul herself over, only to be confronted by a furious gull which had rushed at her, wings spread wide, its squawks of outrage splitting the air and its mad little chick, with its huge eyes and ridiculous fluff, pecking bravely at her hands. So much for the rock-sprite. Halli had laughed so much he'd fallen off the ledge: but luckily the rope had caught over the lip of the overhang and, with Katla as a counterweight, the two of them had swung out over the sea, giggling at their recklessness till they were weak.

And that had been only last year. Not very dignified behaviour for a young woman of marriageable age.

She smoothed her hands down her tunic, saw where the salt-stains from the oars had left round, almost fungal patches; where sweat and food and animals had all left their marks. Even aside from its sorry state, she probably wouldn't be able to wear this tunic much longer, for propriety's sake: it was getting a bit short in the leg now, and surprisingly tight around the chest. Perhaps she'd sell enough knives to afford some new clothes at the fair. She'd seen leather brought back from the Allfair that was as supple as the finest cloth and could be sewn with an ordinary needle, instead of the vast, unwieldy bodkin used for tacking Eyran horseskins together. With such leather could be fashioned a luxurious jerkin. Not that Katla had any intention of sewing it herself: rather, she'd persuade her mother to sew it for her: sewing was not something at which Katla excelled: left to herself, she'd produce great long stitches half a knuckle long in order to get the garment finished, and when challenged would reply crossly: *It'll do the job.* Of course, she'd have to admit that there was more than one item of clothing she'd made for herself that had sprung apart at the seams, often in embarrassing circumstances; but it made her no more patient. Maybe, she thought, returning to her buying fantasy, I'll get a good shirt or two; and an embroidered waistcoat and some suede leggings, as well. And a pair of pointed shoes. And some fine, long boots to ride in . . .

She laughed: she'd have to sell the entire stand to afford such a collection!

Knowing that she should swallow her pride and return at once to the family booth and join the workers, but still smarting from her treatment, Katla stayed on the knoll and watched the clouds burn away from a sky revealed at last to be as blue as a robin's egg. The distant hills emerged from their grim shadows to expose slopes clothed in purple and russet, where most likely at this time of year bilberry and heather vied for space with brackens and grasses, like the hills at home. The thought came to her unbidden, that climbing the Rock had perhaps been a reckless act, since she had thought nothing of the circumstances, and that maybe she deserved her punishment: but she pushed it away, feeling instead a sudden, burning urge to keep on running, away

from the fairground, out into these strange hills, to take one
of the long, meandering black paths at random and run to the
summit, there to look out over the vast southern continent
on which she now stood.

So she did.

'Who was that man?' Fent asked, his face sharp with curiosity.
The Istrian lord had been everything he had expected from
a member of the old enemy's nobility: arrogant, dismissive,
outright rude, and fanatical to boot.

At the water's edge, Aran Aranson shaded his eyes and
watched as his two ship's boats crested the surf towards him,
packed to the rims with crew and cargo. Some moments
passed and the question hung, answerless, on the breeze.

At last, Fent was forced to repeat his enquiry.

Aran turned to regard him, taking in the volatile light in his
younger lad's eyes, his balled fists and chancy temper. 'He's a
man you should avoid,' he said mildly.

This merely served to irritate Fent further. 'Why should I
want to avoid him? I'd say I was more than a match for a soft
southern man like that, lord or no lord.' And when his father's
face went blank and unresponsive: 'In Sur's name, who *is* he?'
Fent persisted, goaded by the memory of the foreigner's haughty
demeanour, his contempt of Katla, his strange fervour.

Aran clenched his jaw. 'His name is Rui Finco, Lord
of Forent, and he's a dangerous man to cross. You leave
customers like that to me. We're here to trade and I'll
tolerate no trouble.'

'I don't like him,' Fent said stubbornly, but the fighting
light had gone out of his eye.

'Liking has little place in business.'

And with that, Aran strode out into the breakers to haul
the next of the laden faerings ashore.

The vegetation of the foothills turned out to be nothing that

Katla had encountered in Eyra: consisting largely of oddly-coloured sedges and lichens, and tufted grasses sprouting through all these like clusters of feathers. The gradient was steep, too; but the stitch didn't return and she made it to the top in less than a half-hour, breathing harder than she'd like but delighted to have explored further than any of her brothers into this new land. Near the summit she turned to look down on the fairground. From here, Sur's Castle seemed no more than a tiny crag, the people like insects bustling around, the ships as still and small as roosting birds on the glistening sea. But when she got to the crest of the hills, instead of being rewarded by a sunlit panorama stretching away to the exotic land of Istria, she saw nothing but mountain after mountain after mountain, ranges lining up one behind another like an army defending its territory; and then she remembered that the anchored boats off the shore of the Moonfell Plain had not been Eyran alone, but also those oddly elegant Istrian craft with the eyes carved at bow and stern so that the vessel could see in all directions. So most of the Istrians also came to the annual gathering by sea, not overland.

In which case, who were all those people a thousand feet below? Down there, the valley lay like a jewelled sash, impossibly green amid vast expanses of rockfall and scree, a narrow tract that wound its way like an emerald snake in and out of the mountains' feet. And on that path, as far as the eye could see, came cart after cart, wagon after wagon, and hundreds of great, black slow-moving beasts toiling ahead in a long, long line, tiny figures perched, as bright as ladybirds upon their backs.

Katla felt her mouth open in a great gasp of wonderment. Nomads: the wandering peoples of Elda, doing what they were most famous for: travelling the world. It was the most amazing sight she'd ever seen. She watched them making their way towards a col further up the range, which meant— They were coming to the Allfair! All at once she was laughing, her head tilted up to the sky, the sun warm upon her skin. Truly, Sur took with one hand and gave with the other: if she hadn't climbed his rock, her father would have had no cause to cut her hair; and if she hadn't lost her hair, she'd never have run off in a rage and ended up here, rewarded by this secret glimpse of another world.

As they said in the north: 'The likely may happen: also the unlikely.' And it was true.

It was the arrival of Fabel Vingo that saved Saro from the beating he might otherwise have won from his brother.

'Handsome beasts this year, eh Tanto?'

'Indeed, Uncle. As you can see,' he held out his injured arm for inspection, 'Saro and I have paid dearly to make them look their best!'

Fabel roared his approval. 'Ah well, it'll be the high-spirited ones that always fetch the best price; and it ain't the case only with horses − eh, lad?'

Tanto's huge, open-hearted laugh joined with his uncle's bellow. Saro looked on, smiling weakly. It would never do not to accede to the joke, though he had no idea what it was that had set them off so.

Uncle Fabel took his eldest nephew by the elbow and together they walked around the enclosure, Fabel indicating each horse's finest points, Tanto nodding discerningly, as if riveted by every word. Saro sighed. He kicked at the ground. Truly life could be mightily unfair. Surely any idiot could see that Tanto had no interest in the animals at all, that as far as he was concerned they were just walking bags of cantari, ready to be exchanged into nice fat dowry payments. It was ironic, Saro thought, tracing a pattern with his foot, that his brother had not the wit to make the rest of the metaphorical leap: for if the horses were there to be traded for money; how different was Tanto's own position? Endowed with sufficient funds, and enhanced by his status at the Allfair's contests, wouldn't he then also be auctioned to the highest bidder, married off into the family of the man who could offer the Vingo family the best deal, as far as social and political advancement were concerned?

For a moment, Saro was the recipient of a delightful vision: his brother, naked in the selling-ring, hair and muscles polished with linseed oil, eyes rolling in fear; paraded around on a lunge-rein with the rest of the marriageable lads. The dealer with his silver baton pointing out Tanto's fine pectorals, the proud carriage of his head, the curve of his neck, the neat turn of his calves and fetlock; flicking him lightly across the buttocks with the whip to show off his well-disciplined gait, his graceful trot; then running the baton down his flanks and lifting into view Tanto's private parts so that the audience might remark (disparagingly) upon the virility and length of his—

'Saro!'

Saro's head shot up so fast he cricked his neck. Favio Vingo had joined his brother and Tanto and was even now bearing down upon his second son. Thank Falla his people were not mind-readers, Saro thought wildly. If they were, it would not be Tanto on the receiving end of a whip.

'Hello, Father.'

Favio Vingo was a short man, though compactly muscled. He hid the shame of his encroaching baldness today under a fabulously-patterned silk head-wrap, fastened with a vast emerald on a pin. 'I have something to show you, Saro. Come with me.' His father beamed: clearly, Saro thought uncharitably, the effects of the araque must still be with him, that he should be so magnanimous towards one he so despised.

Garnering his most obliging and agreeable expression, Saro took his father's proffered arm and fell into step with him.

'What is it, Father, that you wish to show me?'

'Words would not do justice to the experience: you must see it for yourself and form your own responses. I remember witnessing a similar scene on my first visit to the Allfair—' he paused. 'By Falla! Over twenty-five years ago, now: can you believe it? *Twenty-five years*. Twenty-five visits to the Moonfell Plain, by the Lady! And still the memory of that first time as clear as if it were yesterday: such excitement, eh Fabel?'

Fabel Vingo looked over his shoulder at them. 'Ah yes. I remember my first time at the Fair – would have been a few years after you, though, brother.' He winked and then turned back to continue his conversation with Tanto. As if unconsciously, he ran a hand through his own thick cap of hair.

Favio grimaced. 'It wasn't just his *first time* at the Allfair, either,' he said in a voice too loud to be destined for Saro's ears alone, but there came no response from his brother.

They made their way past the rest of the livestock stalls and the temporary booths for the herdsmen and servants, and soon found themselves out on unoccupied ground. The sun, coming to its fullest point now, beat down on the volcanic ash so that in the miasma of heat thus produced, it seemed that the eastern mountains rose off the plain in great, rippling waves, like a tide. The sky overhead, early clouds now burned away to nothing, was the deep, unflawed blue of a Jetra bowl.

Favio shaded his eyes. Saro, following his example, stared out into the heat-haze. Tanto and Fabel, bored already, started to discuss the intricate silver inlay-work that could be commissioned from some northern craftsman they'd heard of who specialised in ornamental daggers and pattern-welded swords. Lovely work, apparently: though far from cheap.

'Oh!'

The gasp escaped Saro before he could draw it back. Out of the middle of the haze as from the heart of legend, or the gorgeously deceptive Fata Morganas reported by explorers in search of fabled Sanctuary, shimmering like a mirage and most eerily magnified by the waves of heat, a nomad caravan pulsed gradually into view – a weaving, many-legged millipede of a creature displacing clouds of dust as it travelled unerringly towards the fairground.

'Wanderers!'

'Aye, lad,' Fabel said cheerfully. 'The Lost People; the Footloose: here they come, ready to fleece the lot of us yet again!'

Three

Charms

Jenna Finnsen gazed into the polished metal mirror Halli Aranson had just brought to their booth as 'a gift for a maid on her first visit to the Allfair'. She'd heard him announcing himself at the doorflap and had promptly disappeared behind the partition, leaving him shuffling his feet awkwardly in front of her father. *What a clod*, she thought. Just a great big farmboy with no courtly manners at all, even if he was desperately in love with her. She giggled, then watched with alarm as her large grey eyes disappeared into fat little folds of skin and lines etched themselves around her nose and mouth. 'Oh no,' she thought desperately. 'Not at all alluring. You mustn't smile like that when you meet Ravn. Solemn and intense, that's the way to win his heart.'

She composed herself rapidly and returned to her favourite reverie.

Holding the mirror about a foot above her head, she gazed up under her fair lashes and addressed his invisible presence, mouthing softly: *Yes, sire, my name is Jenna Finnsen, daughter of Finn Larson of the Fairwater clan, who supplies your royal household with the finest seagoing vessels.*

To this the King always replied, *Had you not told me your name, I would have guessed it from the graceful curve of your neck, as noble as a swan's, and surely your father's inspiration for the prows of his lovely ships.*

And at this, Jenna would look modestly down, thus drawing

the King's eye to her rounded bosom, nestling like a pair of goose-eggs amid all the fine Galian lace, and he, overcome by her extraordinary beauty, would take her by the chin, and after murmuring even more wonderfully poetic compliments would address the assembled crowd (which would, of course, include all the so-called friends who told her such a thing could never happen, as well as all the young men from the local skerries, especially Tor Leeson who had once, when they were thirteen, told her she looked like his mother's milch cow) and announce that he had chosen his bride – the exquisite Lady Jenna – and that they could all now leave, as quickly as possible, so that he could be alone with his love. Then he would sweep her up (she could imagine the hard-packed muscle of his arms, the ease with which he would crush her to his chest, the thump of his excited heart) and—

Lowering the mirror until it was level with her face, she closed her eyes and kissed it passionately. The cold tin misted like a blush.

'You like your mirror, then?'

Guiltily, Jenna clutched it to her and whirled around to face the speaker.

'I— I thought you'd gone.'

Halli grimaced. 'I went outside with your father for a few moments to discuss some business.'

Jenna's eyes narrowed suspiciously. She hoped it was not the business she thought it might be, for she chafed at becoming part of some inter-clan land transaction – the codex to a bargain struck between men. 'What business?' she asked rudely, going on the attack before he could pursue the matter with the mirror.

'I am thinking to commission a ship from him.'

'My father's ships are the best in the world – they're not for just anyone!'

Halli blinked. 'Our money is as good as the next man's,'

he said mildly. When she did not deign to answer, he went
on: 'King Ravn is calling for men with their own ships to
pioneer a passage through the Ravenway with the Far West,
and I thought to volunteer my services, and,' he looked into
her face intently, 'to make a sufficient sum that I may buy a
parcel of land and take me a wife . . .'

'And you have someone in mind for this . . . honour?'

Halli met her gaze steadily. 'I might.'

'Pigs might fly.'

Halli had sparred too much with his impertinent little sister to allow such churlishness to throw him. 'You
know, at the midsummer fair at Sundey a couple of years
back,' he said, 'I seem to remember there was a man who
claimed to be able to make you see pigs fly – aye, and
sheep, too.'

Jenna scoffed. 'That'd just be some potion he'd be selling
– made with spotted toadstool for the truly gullible.'

'More than likely.' He let a pause develop. 'But when
I had my two coppers' worth it was a maid that I saw
flying: set her heart on the moon, she had, and was leaping up and down with all her might, and making quite
a show of herself into the bargain; but no matter how
high she flew, she just couldn't make that lofty old moon
notice her.'

She stared at him in disbelief.

'Wasted right away, she did, for want of what she could
never have,' he finished softly.

Comprehension dawned slowly. A hot and heavy red
flushed up her neck, across her cheeks and into the very
tips of her earlobes. Her hand tightened on the mirror.

'Well, I was going to ask if you'd like to come with me to
see the nomad peoples arrive, with their spotted toadstools
and magic potions for the gullible and all; but as I can see
such flightiness does not appeal to you, I'll bid you farewell,
for now, Jenna, till the Gathering, and perhaps we'll speak

again after that, eh?' He dipped his head and ducked smartly out of the tent.

There were a few moments of silence, followed by a gale of amusement from outside the booth. Jenna recognised her father's laughter, and that of her brother, Matt, and her cousins, Thord and Gar. Furious, she flung the mirror to the ground and stamped on it till its pretty surface was dulled and dented.

'Ever ride a yeka, Joz?'

'No.'

'What about you, Knobber?'

'No.'

''Ave you, Mam?'

'Oh, go away, Dogo.'

'I did, you know: I rode a yeka, when I was working for the Duke of Cera, commanding that troop that made the first crossing over the Skarn Pass. Did it stink? Man, it stunk.'

'Oh, do shut up.'

Undeterred, Dogo turned to the companion on his left, a huge, lowering mountain of a man dressed from head to foot in stained leather and mail.

'Doc, did you ever ride on one of them things?'

The big man regarded him solemnly. 'Bugger off, Dogo.'

'Right then, Doc. Sorry, Doc.'

For some seconds, silence resumed. The five mercenaries leaned on the stockade they had been hired to guard – one task among many at this Allfair, and an easy one, though as a result it wasn't paying too well – and watched the Footloose roll in to the fairgrounds with their great shaggy yeka and their rumbling carts, their wagons and litters and outriders in eccentric and colourful garments.

'Ever had yer palm read, Joz?'

'No.'

'Did you, Knobber?'

'No.'

'Mam?'

She gave him a hard stare.

'What about you, Doc? 'Ave you ever bin to one of them nomad fortune tellers and 'ad yer palm done, 'ave yer?'

'Let's have a look at your hand, Dogo.'

'Righto. What can you see?'

'A bloody short lifeline if you don't stop your yakking.'

'Oh.'

A long string of goats trotted past with red tassels in their ears, herded by a pair of piebald dogs and a lad doing handsprings. A six-wheeled cart rumbled behind upon which several sunburned women and two furiously moustachioed men all in tangerine silk headwear and row upon row of ivory beads and not a great deal else reclined amongst a pile of cushions and blew fragrant smoke from a huge spouted pot. A chorus of whistling and catcalling marked the wagon's progress.

'Ever had a Footloose woman, Doc?'

'Dogbreath—'

'Yes, Doc?'

There was a thump and a yelp.

Aran Aranson watched the great caravan come in and felt his heart lift as if he had just heard the opening notes to a favourite song.

Seeing the Footloose always had this effect on him – it made him believe in the existence of infinite possibility. There was something otherworldly about the nomads and what they brought here with them – something magical, provocative; something chancy. It brought into sharp perspective the mundanity of trade and gossip and court politics; it lifted the Allfair to another plane of being. It might just be the waft of their cooking spices they passed – complex and unfamiliar – or of their perfumes

– elusive, subtle, teetering on the edge of recognition; or the incomprehensible babble of a foreign language; or just the knowledge that these were folk who had travelled the length and breadth of Elda and as a result had seen and known more than he would ever see or know. If he were to admit it to himself, Aran Aranson envied the nomad peoples. He envied their rootlessness, their lack of responsibilities, their undemanding sense of community. But most of all, he envied those ever-changing horizons, the thought that each day might bring new discoveries about the world and your life in it.

He watched a nomad woman stride past in her voluminous silver-threaded robes of yeka wool; a man with his face tattooed from crown to chin; young lads laughing and running with a crew of mangy dogs. Little black goats and exotically feathered chickens. Whole tribes of children – all brown and gold skin and hair and flashing white teeth. A mule swayed past, burdened with saddlebags bulging with candles in every imaginable hue and shape, accompanied by a sharp-faced man carrying a dozen yard-high paper lanterns. However he had managed to keep them intact in the high winds of the Skarn Mountains, Aran could not imagine. He stared and stared and after a while became aware that something about his face felt stiff and odd. It took him a moment or two to realise that all this time he had been grinning from ear to ear.

'You look to be enjoying yourself, Da.'

He spun around. It was Katla, with butchered hair and a filthy tunic.

'What will your mother say when she sees you?' He looked her up and down in dismay. 'It was all I could think to do.'

Katla ran her fingers through the sweat-streaked crop. 'I quite like it, actually. It doesn't get in my eyes when I'm running.' She grabbed his arm. 'Aren't they fine, the nomads, I mean? I saw them arrive from the top of that hill back there – they came down over a mountain pass!'

'Aye.' Aran scanned the passing procession. 'They're remarkable people, the Footloose. True explorers. Nothing can stand in their way once they've decided on their route, not mountains, nor forests, nor deserts.'

Katla watched as his eyes went misty with longing. He was a frustrated nomad himself, she thought then, remembering the tales he had told of his ancestors' travel into the wild parts of the world as they sat around a winter fire, and seeing his yearning burn so clearly, she felt as close to him as she had ever done in her life. 'Imagine – crossing a desert, on the back of a yeka, with the sun on your face and the hot wind at your back,' she said. 'Or climbing up into the mountains where the snows never melt and you can see across all the continents of Elda.'

But her father was not to be drawn. He hunched his shoulders as if he felt the burdens of his life pressing down on him. 'You're a lass,' he said unnecessarily. 'You're not for exploring.'

Distracted by the unfairness of this, his daughter bridled. 'Why not? There are many women among the nomads: riding yeka, driving carts and wagons; and up there—' she indicated the stockades '—I saw a woman in leather armour who looked as tough as any man. Why cannot I choose such a life? I can run faster than a man; and climb and swim and break a horse; aye, and fight, too.'

'The nomads are different to us, Katla. They live by different rules. And as for sell-swords: they live by no rule at all.'

Katla's eyes flashed. 'That sounds like freedom, to me.'

Aran turned to face his daughter. 'Eyran women run farms and houses and raise families. What greater power is there than to make a haven for others, to cultivate the land and bring new life into the world?'

'Power?' Katla sneered. 'Eyran women get traded by their menfolk to the most convenient partner and put a good face on it; they bear child after child, only to lose them to the cold, or the fever, or to evil spirits – and if they grow to men they'll only lose them to blood-feuds or the oceans! Women drudge from dawn to dusk and then till midnight, and have never a moment to themselves. That's not the sort of power I ever wish to claim.'

'Brave words, little sister!'

Fent threw an arm around her shoulders. 'Perhaps you'd rather marry an Istrian lord, like the fellow who just caused our da to cut all your hair off?'

'Fent!' Aran's voice was sharp, but his younger son took no notice.

'Darling sister, I can just imagine you with your head all veiled and your body all trussed up in fine silks (pink? – purple? no, that would only clash with your hair, or what's left of it; scarlet, then; or green) and allowed only the company of other women by day and your husband by night. If King Ravn's going to choose himself an Istrian wife to take back to the Isles with him, I think the least we can do in exchange is to trade our Katla to one of their lords. She'd talk him to death! That, or wrestle him into submission. Just think, she could be Eyra's greatest weapon! No Istrian is going to get a chance to wage war against us with Katla as his wife: not unless he gags her and shuts her in a cellar!'

'Fent, be silent!' This time, Aran's voice held a dangerous note. 'I'll have no talk of war. There has been peace now for over twenty years, and I for one thank Sur for it.'

'Peace!' Fent said contemptuously. 'Our true homeland of a thousand years and more lies within spitting distance of these mountains, and the sons of the sons of the sons of the bastards who took it from us walk this fairground with not a quiver of fear in their hearts; rather they treat us as barbarian fools – they ridicule our customs, insult our sister and demand we open our stalls early so they may buy our weapons – but, no, we must not speak of war!'

Aran passed a hand across his face as if composing himself and when he spoke again it was in a lowered voice. 'When you have lost your father in front of your own eyes to an Empire mercenary, and taken a sword-thrust through the side trying to save him; when you have seen ships aflame and all the men in them screaming as the fire ate them; or seen a man so mad with hunger he would try to eat his own arm; or women kill their children rather than give them up to captivity, to rape and slavery – you will not be so keen to speak of war.'

Fent looked away. 'I know all that, Father: but everything you say just makes the truth more evident, and here we are at the Allfair, doing *business* with our old enemy.' There was contempt in that last phrase, but Aran decided to let it pass.

Katla, however, would not. 'Fent! You cannot speak to our father so.'

Fent stared at her in surprise. Then he smiled. 'Now *that*, I would say, is the pot calling the kettle black!' He turned to Aran. 'Father, I apologise. I will speak no more of enmity; but if I cannot kill the Istrians, then I will skin them in trade, and you will be proud of me. Besides, if Halli and I are to have the longship we have set our hearts upon, we will need to have a *very* successful Fair.'

Aran raised an eyebrow. 'Oh?'

Katla became very still.

'Halli and I have talked and talked about this. It's time we struck out on our own. I'd like to ask your permission, Father, to take our share of the profits—'

'If we make any—'

'If we make any – and commission a ship from Finn Larson – a big ship: one hundred and twenty oars, no less: it'll need to be a very substantial vessel if it's to weather the big seas of the Ravensway—'

'You're going to the Far West?' Katla was transfixed.

Aran's eyes gleamed with sudden interest.

'To join the King's call-up for the new expedition fleet.'

'Can I come?'

'Katla.' Aran's reprimand was gentle but firm. 'You, of all people, are not sailing off into the sunset. I have other plans for you.'

'What?' she said with alarm. 'What do you mean?'

'You'll find out soon enough,' Aran said, dropping her a wink. He turned to his younger son. 'I am not altogether sure that your and Halli's share of what we make on the sardonyx will buy you any sort of boat, let alone one of Finn's.'

Fent looked put out. 'But Halli said—'

Aran grinned wolfishly. 'But I'll make you a bargain, son. If your share won't buy you your longship, I'll throw in mine and your mother's, and Katla's, too.'

'Father!' Katla was scandalised. 'You can't do that, not without consulting us, at least. And what about our debts? There's the new pighouse, and we owe Uncle Margan already for the shieling . . . And—'

'Katla: the money you make from the weapons stall is all your own to keep, since it is your hard work's earning; but the outlay on the tradegoods was mine, and thus the risk in the trading is all mine, so I shall make the decision as to how any profit from it shall be spent. Fent and Halli's plan is a bold one, and I admire ambition in my sons: I know their mother would, too, and while there may be trinkets she hankers for from the Fair, I am sure she will see the sense in postponing her pleasure till it comes back a thousandfold from the Far West! Besides, daughter, I had not thought you would be wanting to have your bride-price in hand so soon!'

'I— no.' She tossed her head, was made aware again of the loss of her hair by the unexpected lightness of the movement. 'I want no husband at all!'

'Never say that, child.'

'I'll buy mother the silks and grains she wants out of my own pocket,' Katla said fiercely. She turned to Fent. 'But if you'd said I could come, you could have had my share from the sardonyx, and all I make from the swords, and welcome to it.'

Fent punched her lightly on the arm. 'Keep your pocket-money, small sister. Anyway, you'll need all you can get to bribe a man to marry you with your hair shorn like an urchin's!'

And then he dodged.

Aran watched the pair of them duck and dive their way through the growing throng until they had disappeared from view. Gradually, his eyes lost their focus.

'The Ravenway,' he breathed, staring into nothing. 'Ah, the Far West!'

'So, Halli: how did Jenna like her mirror?'

'Rather better than she likes me,' Halli replied ruefully. 'I caught her whispering love-talk to it as if it were the King.'

Erno laughed. 'She's a silly girl, Halli. I don't know what you see in her.'

Tor Leeson grinned. 'When did you become an expert in such matters, Erno Hamson? A girl has only to look at you and you go bright red and run away.'

Erno flushed now, and hung his head.

'Besides,' Tor carried on with a mischievous glint in his eye, 'if you are so vehement as to Jenna's failings, it must surely mean you have your heart set on another . . .'

'I do not!'

Halli, ever the peacemaker, intervened. 'She'll grow out of her fantasies once the King's picked his bride and she has a man of her own. And she comes from a good family.'

'You wouldn't have your eye on one of her father's longships, would you, Halli?' Tor asked shrewdly.

Halli held his look steadily. 'It would not be the sole reason for my interest.'

Tor laughed. 'It's not a bad one, though. I swear I could

almost tup plump little Jenna myself to get my hands on one of those beauties!'

'You're each as bad as the other!' Erno declared furiously. He stood up awkwardly, his arms wrapped around his chest as though to keep something in place, and regarded his cousins with burning eyes. 'I'm going for a walk.'

He clambered over the piled blocks of sardonyx, each piece weighed, registered and certified that long afternoon by the Fairmaster and his assistants, and pushed his way out through the doorflap.

Tor watched him go with a strange light in his eye. 'He's got it bad for Katla,' he said.

'Hmm.' Halli shrugged. 'She won't have him, you know.'

'Of course not,' Tor laughed easily. 'She'll have me.'

Erno walked unsteadily past the Eyran booths, his heart hammering in his ears. 'Idiot!' he said to himself repeatedly. 'Idiot!' If Halli suspected he loved his sister, he'd be sure to tell Katla, and that Erno could not bear. Katla Aransen was not, he had to admit to himself, a kind girl: no, she'd laugh at him, tell her friends and then go on ignoring him as she always had; except that from then on it would be worse, for he would know for certain she had no interest in him.

He passed Falko and Gordi Livson, who nodded and smiled and went back to building up the walls of their enclosure; then the Edelsons and their sister, Marin, a thin girl of seventeen with eyes as dark and wary as a seal's.

'Hello, Erno.'

He bobbed his head, but could think of nothing to say. Tor was right: he was a dolt with girls.

Despite this, Marin fell into step with him. 'Where are you going?'

'Oh, just walking, you know.'

'Can I come with you?'

'Surely.'

Jude Fisher

They walked together in an uncomfortable silence until they reached the stockades. A crowd had gathered there to lean up against the fences and watch the travellers arrive, but this was Erno's third Allfair and the advent of the exotic nomads cast less of a spell over him this time than it did over others. Marin, of course, was entranced.

'I've heard they have the gift of magic, the Footloose,' she breathed excitedly.

Erno stared out into the dust and noise. 'They certainly give the appearance of it,' he said. 'But how much of that is tricks and sham, I wouldn't care to reckon.'

Marin looked disappointed. 'I've been saving my coins,' she said, opening the leather pouch that hung at her neck and tilting it towards him. Inside, Erno could see the glint of coins. 'There's a potion I've heard about that I want to buy.'

'What is it?' Erno asked, his curiosity overcoming his embarrassment.

Marin blushed. 'I can't tell *you* that.' She ran her hands nervously down her overdress.

'Why not?'

In reply she gave him a steady look. 'You're a man. It's a woman's thing.'

Now it was Erno's turn to go red. No one had ever called him a man before.

They leaned up against the stockade and watched the last of the nomad caravan roll past. Once it had, the crowd started to disperse and Erno thought, with a sudden electric jolt, that he saw Katla Aransen running towards him through its thickest part, but when he looked again, he realised it was Fent, his long red hair swinging free and his sharp teeth gleaming, and then he was gone. Beyond the stockades, the black dust began to settle again.

'Let's go and have a look at the Footloose encampment,' Marin suggested.

'I'm not sure your father—' Erno started, but she was already dragging him by the arm.

'Come on!'

The quarter designated by the Fairmaster for the nomads' use was at the far eastern end of the fairground, where there was no fresh running water. In the tall cliffs that overhung this part of the campsite, seabirds shrieked all day and all night: great colonies of gulls and razorbills and guillemots and oystercatchers, clinging precariously to the narrow ledges, before launching off over the sea in search of more food for their incessantly ravenous young. The gulls, of course, made a nuisance of themselves all over the fairground – mobbing the foodstalls, dive-bombing the livestock, rummaging through the midden heaps and trash; it was said that Allfair gulls would even steal the food from out of your hand if you did not keep an eye on them. The nomads, however, seemed entirely untroubled by them, even collecting the guano from the rocks and the feathers that drifted down from the nests; for what purpose, Erno had no idea.

He was just telling Marin this, and she seemed interested in a way most girls would not be, though whether she was just being polite, he could not tell, when he felt something hit him on the back, and at once a tall woman in a striped turban and bronze earrings called out something in an incomprehensible language, while her two companions – a man with two silver rings through his eyebrow and another through his lip, and a boy with half his face painted black – began to laugh and point at them.

'What?' asked Marin, staring around. 'What are they laughing at? Why are they looking at us?'

Erno frowned. 'I don't know.'

The woman chattered again and pointed repeatedly at Erno. Then she pushed the boy, who rose good-naturedly and came over to them.

'*Ma-na, eech-an-jee-nay?*' he said, his head cocked to one side like a little monkey's.

'What?'

The boy smiled. He had enormous black eyes and very white teeth. 'Eyr-ran?'

'Yes.'

'My mother say, "You are receiver of great good fortune."' He grinned.

Erno's frown deepened.

The boy dodged behind him and ran a finger across the back of his tunic. Holding it up for inspection, he said again, 'Good fortune, see!'

Marin began to laugh.

It was a gull's dropping. The offending bird circled still overhead, calling raucously. The child grabbed Erno by the arm and pulled him towards the wagon where the woman in the turban and her friend were getting to their feet. The woman came forward, her hand extended. Bronze bangles ran the length of her forearm from wrist to elbow. They must, thought Erno, weigh a ton, but if they did, she did not move as though she noticed it.

In the Old Tongue she said, 'Welcome, young man. It seems you have been blessed!'

'Blessed?' Erno shook his head. 'This was my second best tunic, so I'm not so sure about that.'

The woman turned to Marin. 'Your – sister?'

'No,' Marin said, smiling.

'Sweetheart, then,' the woman winked.

Erno shook his head vigorously. 'No, no, just friends. We came here to find a potion-seller for Marin.'

The woman regarded Marin enquiringly. 'Fezack Starsinger?'

Marin nodded. 'Yes – that was the name!'

The woman turned and said something to her companion. He clicked his tongue against his teeth and whistled, then disappeared into the wagon. A moment later he returned with an old woman propped on his arm. She was completely bald except for a crown of brightly-coloured feathers and a single top-knot of white hair. A necklace of twenty or thirty thin silver chains lay around her meagre brown throat.

'I am Fezack,' she said in a birdlike voice. '*Rajeesh.*' Placing the palms of her hands together, she bobbed her head just like a bird plucking a worm from the ground.

'G-good day, lady,' Marin stammered, amazed.

'Go on, then,' urged Erno. 'Ask her for the potion.'

Marin stared at him wide-eyed. 'I can't, not with you here.'

Suddenly the old woman was at her elbow. 'Come with me, child, come in the wagon and tell me what it is you wish me to mix for you.'

Erno gave her a little push. 'Go on,' he grinned. 'Have an adventure.'

Marin looked uncertain. 'Don't leave without me.'

'I won't.'

He watched as Marin and Fezack Starsinger disappeared into the wagon together. The other woman smiled at him. 'No danger: no worry.' She held up her hand. In it she clutched a spotted cloth. 'I clean your back.' When she grinned, Erno could see that she had little jewels inset into her teeth and a tiny silver ring through the tip of her tongue. She turned him around and rubbed the bird shit off his tunic as roughly as his mother might have done, had she still been alive.

'Arms out.'

Erno did as he was told.

'*Eee-kor-ni!* What this?'

He looked down to find the turbaned woman kneeling at his feet with her hands full of golden-red hair. His heart thumped: Katla's, fallen from beneath his tunic where he had been holding it in. She held it up beside his own, her grin widening.

'Not yours?'

'No.'

Erno felt the heat in his face, his neck, his ears. He felt sick. He glanced guiltily at the wagon. What if Marin were to come out now and witness this odd scene?

He retrieved the hair from the ground and from the turbaned woman and stuffed it back down inside his shirt.

'No, not mine.'

'A girl's hair?'

'Yes.'

'A sweetheart's, then?'

'She is not my sweetheart.'

'Ah, but you wish she was.'

Mortified, Erno nodded once.

'Fezack can help with that. She take hair and weave a magical amulet: you wear it next your heart: girl will love you.'

Erno laughed. 'If only it were that simple.'

'It can be. Give me the hair.' She held out the spotted cloth, streaked now with white guano.

'I have no money.'

'You had the luck of the gull: for that we give you free charm.'

What could he say without being rude? Erno reached into his shirt then placed Katla's cut tresses carefully into the kerchief. The woman folded the corners in and placed it in her ample bosom. 'I give it to mother secretly,' she said. 'You come back tomorrow.'

The curtain over the wagon's door flicked open and Marin came out, clutching a dark glass bottle with an ornate silver stopper to her chest.

'Rub it in at dawn and dusk,' the old woman warbled. 'Dawn and dusk, mind you.'

'Thank you,' Marin said nervously. She bobbed a curtsey and skipped down the steps. She ran towards Erno, scanning his face anxiously to see whether he had understood the import of the old woman's instruction, but he was staring at the turbaned woman and his face was as red as sunset. 'Thank you again,' she called to the old woman.

The man with the pierced face whistled at her and made what might have been a lewd gesture. Marin grabbed Erno's arm and together they walked quickly from the nomad campsite through the fading light.

'Father!'

The figure who greeted him stood in the half-dark at the back of the pavilion, swathed in shimmering grey. Even when she stepped into the torchlight, all that was visible of her were her hands, clenched tightly at her sides, and her mouth – pale, unpainted, and currently set in a hard, thin line. Standing thus, tall and slender and absolutely motionless, she looked, Lord Tycho Issian thought, like a pillar of granite facing the relentless waves of the Northern Sea. The sabatka she wore – the traditional dress of the respectable Istrian woman – had once belonged to her mother. Demure in the extreme, it covered from sight every part of her from her slippered feet to her veiled head; even so, he knew that beneath its cool drapery she would have the same alluringly sleek curves as the lovely Alizon had possessed when he had first encountered her: sweet eighteen, on the slave blocks at Gibeon. It had been her mouth that had done it for him: revealed by a single gash in the severe black sabatka that was the slavemaster's standard issue for all his merchandise, her lips had been sharply defined but as plump and plush and red as labia, and having seen those lips he had had to see the rest of her. It was not the accepted thing to ask to inspect the merchandise of a certificated trader thus; but Tycho was a very persuasive man: half an hour and two dozen cantari later and he had made a very thorough, and very satisfactory, inspection indeed. That had, of course, been before he was known by the world in general, before he had come by his title and his lands; and by the time he had become Lord Tycho Issian, his beloved Alizon had been so highly trained in the social etiquettes of their adoptive country of Istria that not even the Duchess of Cera could have sniffed out her lowly origins.

'Selen: my dear.'

'I imagine if you have disturbed me at the hour before prayers, it must be for a good reason.'

So distant, so chill, he thought admiringly. Her mother had been a fine teacher. But if she was anything like Alizon, there would be a heart of fire beating beneath the cool flesh, a furnace of lava between those smooth thighs . . . He felt his member stir and collected his thoughts hurriedly.

'The Vingos came again to see me today.' She made no response, so he went on: 'Their offer is becoming extremely tempting.'

'For you, maybe.'

'For me, yes. They are very keen to join their estates to ours, and their political fortunes, too. The settlement sum they offer is . . . not inconsiderable.'

'It would clear your Treasury debts, then?'

That startled him. He had not thought she studied the ledgers with such a sharp eye. 'Oh yes, it would settle my obligations.'

'Which would leave you clear to run for the last remaining seat on the Council, would it not, Father?'

His eyes narrowed. It was just as well women had no public voice if they spent their time thus, spying and calculating and picking over men's characters and ambitions like vultures over carrion.

'It is time for you to take a husband, Selen, and I think Tanto Vingo will make you a good match.'

'And I have no say in the matter?' Her voice was icy.

Tycho smiled. 'None at all.'

'And what if I will not speak my vows?'

'I will have you whipped till you do.' The image of her on her knees, stripped to the waist with the lash curling its red tongue across her sweet skin was almost too delicious to contemplate.

'You would not dare—'

'Oh, do not dare me, daughter. It would profit you nothing.'

'Oh, but profit is all you care about.'

Tycho raised an eyebrow. 'Not the only thing, daughter; but, I grant you, one of the dearest to my heart.'

'Heart? You? When Falla made you she placed a spent coal between your ribs.'

He laughed. 'Ah, daughter, daughter. What a happy man young Tanto will be with such a viper to nestle to his bosom at night.' He sighed. 'Be sure, my dear, to paint your mouth nicely, won't you, when they come for the formal betrothal tomorrow?'

In the silence that followed he could sense the way her face tightened under the gauze; could feel the way her eyes went to slits and a muscle twitched in her cheek.

'So you would sell me like a whore, would you?' she asked at last. 'Why not have done and pimp me to the northern king?'

His hand struck her cheek so fast it shocked them both.

'Heresy!'

Her head came up defiantly. 'At least the Eyrans treat their women with a degree of decency, instead of hiding them away, wrapped like confectionery, taking them out only to service their lusts.'

'By Falla, you will be silent!' he roared.

'Or you will hit me again? But it would be rather a shame to spoil the merchandise, would it not, in the event of the Vingos requesting a closer inspection? They might not pay up the full amount for damaged goods.'

'You will present yourself at the appointed hour tomorrow,

Selen, mouth shut and painted prettily; or I will give you to
the Daughters, so help me Falla.'

And with that, he turned on his heel and left.

Selen stared at his departing back and felt hot misery well
up inside her. How could he treat her like a commodity, to
be bought by the highest bidder? Did he have no human
feeling left for her at all? When she had been a little girl –
before the Veiling – she remembered him watching her play
with the deerhound puppies in the courtyard. Then his face
had not been so stern. What had changed in him, that he
would cast her aside thus? It was no empty threat, of that she
was sure, giving her to the Daughters of Falla, for her father
was a man of violent passions. It was not just the pursuit of
wealth and power that made him burn: it was also his love
of the Goddess. He worshipped Falla with a fanatical love, an
extremism rarely seen even in the most devout of Istrian men,
an adoration that bordered on fetishism. Everywhere in the
villa there were figures of the Goddess – in ivory, in sardonyx,
in wood, in silver – her naked image, as narrow-waisted and
flat-chested as a boy, guarded the front door, twined about
by her companion cat; stood warriorlike in corridors, was
ensconced in niches with votive candles; hovered balefully
from the ceilings of the bedchambers; kept watch grimly
over the tiled bath; one hand tucked behind her, the other
covering her mouth. Her eyes, and those of the feline that
accompanied her, were on you always. And always, always the
brazier stoked with offerings, stinking with incense and death.
It was, Selen thought, an unhealthy faith, that demanded such
ostentatious observances. So, in this bargain, as in all others he
ever made, it seemed her father would be the winner; for he
would gain wealth and power by selling her to the Vingos,
or capital for his soul by selling her to the Daughters.

And whichever way she looked at it, she could only be
the loser.

Fighting down her panic, she began to consider her options.

She made careful investigations through the women's network and learned that the Vingos were not known as overly
zealous nor cruel people. But when she had brought up the
subject of Tanto Vingo, her maids had gone unwontedly
quiet, then had hurriedly made up for their hesitation with
chatter about his looks and his athleticism, as if that would
impress her. And as if she would not have noticed their pause.
Fools! So: parcelled off to be the sex-slave and heir-maker for
an empty-headed lordling; or delivered into the hands of the
dread Daughters of Falla, to devote her life to the cause of
the Goddess.

She sighed, her mind shying unhelpfully away from both
prospects. She forced it back mercilessly. The former, she
could not imagine enduring. Just the thought of a man's
hands upon her flesh made her nauseous. Almost, she was
tempted by the latter. At least she'd have her books and time
for contemplation; she could garden and live quietly with
other women; unless, of course, her faith was ever called
into question. And there lay the nub of the problem. Selen
had never felt the flame of Falla take fire in her heart and was
beginning to find the daily observances a meaningless chore.
Could she continue the charade under the watchful eyes of
the Daughters? It was said they made tests for their novitiates
which none but the truly faithful could succeed in. It was also
said that those who failed faced painful sacrifice . . .

'I wish I had been born a man.'

In her fury, without thought, she had said it aloud. Her
hands flew to her mouth. Such an utterance was the greatest
heresy of all: she could be burned for even thinking such
a thing.

'Falla, Goddess, Giver of Life: made in your image, I worship you for your generous gift,' she muttered automatically.

As if on cue, there came the sound of handbells being
rung outside the tent, as the Crier carried the call to prayer
around the Istrian quarter of the fairground. A few moments

later, where there had been the low murmur of chatter and commerce, there was nothing but a deathly quiet.

Selen stared in loathing at the carved sardonyx figure standing on its plinth in the corner of her own tent: its blind eyes, its pitiless smile; its flaunting posture; its inhuman companion creature.

With a wordless cry, she turned her back on the idol, sank to the floor and put her head in her hands.

Four

Vanity

The next morning Katla woke to the smell of foreign ground and pungent waxed cloth. She opened her eyes. Sunlight was bleaching through the tent: even at this early hour she could feel its heat and the promise of the hot and cloudless day to come. Her father and brothers had so often spoken of the wide blue Moonfell sky and the heat that made it hard to walk about without breaking into a sweat when they had recounted tales of their previous visits to the Allfair as the family sat steaming around the steading's winter fire with the wind howling and the rain thrashing down on the turf roof, and Katla had thought they exaggerated. Now, though, it was clear they had applied their usual understatement and lack of poetry to the descriptions.

She rolled over in her sealskin, found her boots and with a single quick motion rolled off her pallet and came to her feet. Tucking her boots under her arm, she crept from the booth, stepping over her silent brothers. Halli slept as always on his back, his dense black beard making an obscurity of the lower half of his face; Fent, in contrast, lay curled into the corner the booth with his skins drawn up around him, like the fox she often thought he resembled. In the next compartment, Tor Leeson lay sprawled across two-thirds of the available space, snoring, while Erno, having lost the better portion of his sleeping pallet to Tor, was tumbled uncomfortably against the tent wall, his head propped up on a sack of grain. Katla grinned: in sleep, as in life . . .

Just as she thought this, Erno's eyelids flickered open and he looked straight at her. Katla held her breath. His mouth began to move as if he might form a phrase, and when she saw this she shook her head, then bent to him and placed a single finger on his mouth. A second later she was gone.

Erno stared at the opened tent flap. He brought his hand out from under his fur wrappings and pressed it hard against his lips, as if by this action alone he might save the sensation of her cool, light finger on his skin forever in his memory.

Her father had told her to stay always in his sight. But since his eyes were currently fast closed, Katla reckoned this negated any such bargain. Besides, she thought, preparing against accusation, he could hardly deny her permission to visit the latrines.

The ablutions tents had been erected down on the strand, where a team of Empire slaves had the previous day dug a series of deep channels leading from the tents down to the shore, thus allowing waste to soak into the black sand, or be washed away by the sea's tide. A waste of good piss, Katla thought as she made use of the facilities: in the skerries they kept their urine in deep barrels: for fixing dyes, for fertilising the ground; for preserving whale meat, for quenching metalwork. When she ran out of the good oil they rendered from the sea-creatures they caught, Katla had taken to plunging her red-hot spearheads and daggers into the barrel outside the smithy. It didn't work quite as well as the oil, and the smell was appalling; but it was a thousand times more effective than water in the process, as she'd learned to her cost; for some reason there was a lot less steam and the metal hardened faster. Iron was not so readily come by in the islands that you could afford to waste it with impunity.

Outside again on the strand with the sun on her face, Katla strolled past the rest of the tents. Gulls cried overhead; out over the shining water a cormorant folded its wings, dived and vanished from sight. She waited for it to reappear, but even though she stood there for a moment or more, nothing broke the surface. More than likely it had swum a ways beneath the water and come up where she had not been looking. She smiled. Diving birds she loved to see: masters as they were of two elements at once. Scuffing the black sand, she walked further along the strand, past the other tents. At the last one, she stopped and listened. There seemed to be an inordinate amount of splashing going on inside it. Katla frowned. She waited, but the cascade went on and on, punctuated every so often with a groan, then a clatter. Unable to control her inquisitiveness, Katla poked her head through the doorflap. Inside, a woman in a pale Eyran tunic was crouched down with her head in a bucket.

Katla experienced a momentary glimmer of recognition. 'Jenna?' she enquired cautiously.

The bucket went over with a crash and a stream of yellow liquid washed out across the ground and all over the figure's kidskin-clad feet.

'Sada's tits!'

'Jenna, such profanity from such a well-brought-up young maid: you shock me!'

The figure squeezed her long tail of hair into a spill of cloth and straightened up, eyes reddened and blinking.

'What in Sur's name are you doing?' Katla stared at Jenna, then at the bucket, and back again. 'You'll never drown yourself like that, you know.'

Jenna Finnsen regarded her furiously. 'What I'm doing is none of your business, Katla Aransen.' She tossed her head imperiously, but the effect was somewhat lost as the turban slipped sideways and tumbled to the sand, releasing an acrid scent into the warm, close air of the latrine.

Katla began to laugh. 'Oh, Jenna! Surely my brother's not worth such an effort?'

'Halli!' Jenna retrieved her headscarf and wrapped it tightly over her sopping locks. 'You think I'd go through this for your stupid brother?'

'I'm not sure who's the stupid one in this affair,' Katla said cheerfully. 'Do you really think that bleaching your hair in piss is going to win the heart of King Ravn Asharson, Stallion of the North?'

Jenna shot her a venomous look. Then her face began to crumple. 'Oh, Katla. What am I to do? My father has said I may come to the Gathering, and even that he will introduce me – though he has not yet agreed to offer my hand: I am still working on that – but if Ravn chooses another . . . I think my heart will break.'

Katla could think of nothing to say. Jenna was a foolish girl, but she was quite fond of her all the same. Poor Halli: would he ever cope with her fanciful ways? She bent to retrieve the wooden bucket, her nose wrinkling as its fumes engulfed her. 'By Sur, Jenna, you must be most determined.'

'I am, truly.'

Katla shook her head. It seemed there *was* nothing to say. She watched the trickling liquid soak away into the dark sand.

'Come on,' she said, after a while. 'Let's get back before our families miss us. Perhaps if you wash your hair out now in clear water, you won't attract flies.'

But when they got outside, there were many more folk up and about. Quite a throng were even now gathering on the strand, shading their eyes and gazing out to sea. Katla followed their example. Out on the horizon, silhouetted against the glittering waves and pale-blue bowl of sky, unmistakably, were a dozen great square sails of Eyran longships.

'Oh!'

Jenna stared and stared. 'King Ravn's fleet! Oh, Katla:

we shall see him arrive!' She grabbed her friend about the waist. There were tears of excitement in her eyes. Then her expression changed abruptly. 'My hair – oh, Katla: my hair – what shall I do?'

'Silly goose: he won't see you amongst all this crowd. Wrap it up in your cloth.'

With deft fingers, Katla twisted the headscarf up and around Jenna's head and stood back to admire her handiwork. 'There: it looks really quite exotic.'

'Thank you, Katla,' Jenna said. Then she looked quickly away, abashed. 'I had meant to ask you about your own, you know, but I was too caught up with myself.'

'My own what?'

'Your hair, Katla. What has happened to it?'

Katla's hands flew to her head. Then she grinned: a flash of white teeth in her thin, tanned face. 'Oh, that! I'd entirely forgotten. My da cut it off yesterday, as a sort of punishment, and, in a way, for my own protection.'

'For what?'

'I climbed the Castle, and some Istrians saw me. They said they were on the Allfair's Ruling Council and that it's sacred ground. Men get fined for such a trespass; but for women it's a capital offence.' She laughed mirthlessly. 'And there I was tossing my hair around as if in defiance of their dearest-held beliefs!'

Jenna gasped. 'You mean, if they catch you they will have you executed?'

Katla's brow creased. Until that moment she had given barely any thought to the matter. To climb a rock was such an innocent pleasure. And almost religious, in its fashion: for her, the touch of rock and metal was the closest she got to worship, even if it were worship of Elda, and not some specific deity. Though there were those who said the hand of Sur lay on her work. But who was to say which deity owned such a rock? It all seemed so ridiculous. 'That's the general idea, I suppose.'

Jenna was aghast. 'But Katla, that's *terrible*. You shouldn't be out: you should be hiding.'

'That would look guiltier than anything. Besides,' Katla laughed, 'look at me: how could they possibly think it was me now?'

'I know, but . . .' She scanned Katla's face anxiously. 'But, oh, Katla, your poor hair: what will you do for the Gathering?'

'It's only hair, Jenna,' Katla said quickly. She did miss it, whatever she might say aloud. 'Better that than lose my head.'

'For myself, I'm not so sure.'

'Jenna: you are a vain and silly woman!'

'I am: it's true, and I cannot help it.' Jenna took Katla by the hand. 'Let's go to the nomads later and see what ribbons and braids we can find to bind into what's left of your hair.' She paused. 'And perhaps I can find something that will make the King notice me.' She dropped her voice. 'They do magic, you know, the Footloose – they make charms and potions and the like. Marin Edelsen went to them yesterday with Erno, you know, and she told Kitten Soronsen there was all sorts you could get.'

Katla felt a little chill go through her. Erno and Marin? She had thought he held an interest in his heart for her, not for scrawny little Marin Edelsen. The chill became a shudder. Was this what they called jealousy? Surely not, for she had no interest in Erno herself, did she?

'Oh, look,' she said quickly, turning the conversation away from such uncomfortable thoughts. 'See the raven on the leading sail—'

And there it was indeed, the great black bird spreadeagled across the striped sail of the first ship – the raven: bearer of tidings and guardian of wisdom; the mythical lord of the air and the pathways of the lost, who sat on Sur's left shoulder and croaked its thoughts into his good ear, and was the symbol and the name of their King.

'It's his ship,' Jenna breathed. 'It really is.'

'Good morning, sister. Very fetching headwear, Jenna: very Jetran.'

Fent grinned insincerely at the blonde girl, then ruffled Katla's uncombed mop. Behind him, Katla spied her father and Halli, deep in conversation, and behind them, Erno. She shook her brother's hand away.

'Must you always treat me like your mutt?' she asked fiercely, flattening her hair down again.

'You always had the heart of a mongrel, sister; and now you have the head of one as well.'

'See that I don't bite you for that remark, brother.'

'And make me foam at the mouth and scared of water?'

'You wash so little, I think you already own that fear.'

'Little wolfhound bitch—'

''Tis not just for your red hair that they call you the Fox, brother.'

'Katla!' Jenna was scandalised. 'Fent, you should apologise to your sister; Katla, you too.'

Katla grinned at both of them, unrepentant. 'I have no sister to apologise to, Jenna dear; but I am sorry if our banter has offended you. Still, you'll get used to it if you're to become a part of our family.'

At this, Fent grinned broadly, and Jenna looked furious. Then a shadow fell across them.

'Good day, Jenna. I'm glad to find you keeping an eye on my errant daughter.'

'She was giving me a hand with the washing of my hair, sir,' Jenna said, meeting Aran Aranson's stern eye fleetingly, then glancing away to catch Katla's alarmed expression.

Aran, watching the exchange, smiled cruelly. 'Aye, well she has precious little of her own to care for now, so I doubt she'd be foolish enough to go wandering alone again at this Fair, for fear of a higher price to pay.'

Fent said quickly: 'You know that if they took Katla,

every Eyran man here would fight for her, do you not, Father?'

Aran regarded him briefly. 'I had rather my witless daughter were not the cause of violent confrontation, Fent. And I forbid such talk. Especially with the Gathering ahead of us. King Ravn has enough matters of state to put his mind to, without our Katla adding to his problems.'

'You mean the choice of his bride?' Jenna piped up eagerly.

'Aye; amongst other considerations.'

'And will you introduce Katla to him at the Gathering, sir?'

Aran barked a laugh. 'In current circumstances, I think not.'

'And you, Jenna,' came Halli's deep voice. 'Will your father be putting you to the King?'

Jenna's cheeks reddened. 'I – I'm not yet sure.'

'Aye, well he's here to make a useful political alliance, I've heard, so it'll most likely be an Istrian woman he'll choose. Lord Prionan's daughter maybe, or one of the girls from the Altan Plain.'

At this, Jenna gave a wordless cry and took to her heels. In a moment, she was lost from sight, swallowed by the mass of folk who had arrived to watch the Eyran ships come in.

'So do you think Lord Tycho will accept your renewed offer, Father? Will he take our price?'

Favio smiled fondly upon his favourite son. 'How could he not, Tanto? How could he not? We can offer him the one thing he cannot buy: our good family name and all that goes with it. And, for his daughter, the prize of Istrian manhood, the lad who will win the Allfair Games and carry all hearts before him.'

'Have you seen her, though, Father? I would not want

an ugly girl, or worse, a cripple.' Tanto scowled at the very thought.

'Rest assured, my boy: I have heard she is a very rose among women. But you shall see her later on when we go to make our suit in earnest, and if you do not like what you see, we shall talk more about the alliance before making any settlement. How does that suit you, son?'

'Admirably, Father. I follow your judgement in this, as in all things.'

Such a hypocrite, Saro thought bitterly. *He will say all the right things and go his own sweet way, as he always does.* He watched his father give Tanto the cloying smile with which he only ever gifted his eldest child, and then looked away to stare instead out over the heads of the crowd at the fleet of longships drawing smoothly into the bay, the dip of the serried oars barely stirring the surface in their disciplined rhythm. *How elegant were these Eyran vessels*, he thought, *with their high prows and low, sweeping hulls.* It was no wonder the Eyrans had travelled so far and wide across the turbulent oceans: they looked at home in their element, like a flock of great sea-eagles biding the time for their strike. Little surprise, either, that so many of the southern lords might be thinking to ally their fortunes to these raiders and explorers by trading their daughters to the northern King, for who knew what treasures might be held in the Far West? He was certain that if he and Tanto had a sister their father would not have the slightest qualm at putting her case at the coming gathering, whether or not others might consider it an insult to the Goddess. He had been looking forward to seeing something of the barbarian court, though the ordinary Eyrans he had so far seen coming and going around the Fair were a considerable disappointment to him, seeming as they did very little different to the Istrians he knew. They wore their hair long, and Falla alone knew what was meant by those complicated knots and braids; but all in all, they seemed as self-interested and as hard-drinking, as grasping and as argumentative as any merchant or lord in Elda.

Except, of course, for their women. He had seen few enough of these around the Fair so far, except for the nomads – though the women of the Footloose were so entirely outlandish to him with their piercings and tattoos, their shaved heads, their freakish paint and scraps of wild clothing that he could barely even regard such beings as human; but he was still haunted by the sight of the girl he had seen on Falla's Rock yesterday: all bare golden legs and arms and that magnificent banner of hair. He had walked the Fair all the previous evening, in and out of the half-constructed stalls, down to the shore, slowly past the women's tents, even as far as the beginning of the nomad quarter, but there had been no sign of her at all. And small wonder at that, with the edict given out by the Dystras.

And there they were of course, Greving and Hesto, just in front of the Vingo family at the edge of the shoreline, ready to greet King Ravn Asharson as soon as he set foot on the sand of the Moonfell Plain, as if it were but the garden to their great hall, and they welcoming him in as their honoured guest. What was it they wanted? he wondered. Would they press their granddaughter, the Swan of Jetra, upon him at the gathering? Would they bargain for ships and sardonyx, for the advantage they sought that would raise them above their neighbours and enable them to annex more land? Was this all there was to the world any more: fair words and gestures, transactions made and alliances forged; all principle forgotten except where pride and power came into the equation, with double-dealing and treachery done out of sight?

'I do not think much of their ships,' Tanto was saying. 'See how open to the weather they are, and so shallow-draughted. I swear one big wave would have them over.' He laughed.

Saro stared at him, but Tanto was into his stride now, his

hand on their father's arm, pointing out the defects of the Eyran fleet.

'See – they have no shelter on board at all; and why, it looks as if they have no slaves to row for them! What a primitive people they must be indeed to make even their king journey in such a fashion!'

Privately, Saro was thinking what hard men they looked, these northerners, with their big arm muscles flexing with the movement of the oars and their long hair bound back from sharply-featured faces and beards that accentuated the powerful jut of their chins. Hard and warlike and afraid of neither ocean nor storm. He had, perhaps misjudged their countrymen, men who kept their muscles under their sleeves and spoke politely in the Old Tongue.

'Is that their king?' Tanto was asking now. 'That tall man in the dark tunic standing in the stern?'

'Yes, son, that's King Ravn all right.'

'He doesn't look much of a king. Do they have no pride, these northerners, that they have their king wear the same old clothes they wear themselves: no crown, no chain of office – no cloak, even?'

Uncle Fabel laughed. 'They set less store by trinkets, lad, that's true; but he's a kingly enough man, Ravn Asharson, as you'll see. A striking fellow, and taller than most.'

Two men were hauling aloft the great steering oar at the stern as the lead ship came into the shallow waters of the Moonfell Bay. Others took down the sail, but no one made a move to take down the fearsome stempost, with its gaping dragon's head. A deliberate insult, Saro wondered, or an oversight? His thoughts were interrupted by his brother's insistent voice:

'Why do they not ship their oars?' asked Tanto. 'They can surely come in no closer now.'

The answer came sooner than they had expected. The wiry-looking man in the stern whom Uncle Fabel had

identified as the northern king now sprang lightly up onto the
gunwale before the tiller and with a single word of command
to his men ran down the length of the ship jumping nimbly
from oar to oar until he had run all twenty on the steerboard
side, his feet sure and true on each slippery rounded shaft. The
crew of the raven-ship cheered and stamped at this feat of skill;
but when their king reached the last oar, instead of stepping
back over the side and down onto the deck, Ravn gave his
men a wide grin, then skipped back onto the gunwale, and
from there ran up the mighty stempost and vaulted powerfully
from the top, legs and arms cartwheeling.

It was an enormous leap. Almost it was enough to take him
to dry land. Almost but not quite: he landed in the shallows
with a loud splash, in the process drenching the elderly Dystra
brothers, and all those around them, with a huge white plume
of water, and rose, shaking himself like a dog, laughing all the
time as if at some hugely enjoyable joke.

From beside Saro there came a shriek of rage. He looked
around, the spell of this strange landing broken. Tanto was
hopping up and down, his face red and furious, his hands
making small, ineffectual rubbing motions on the rich purple
drapery of his tunic. 'Ruined! By the bitch: it's ruined! You
can't get salt stains out of silk velvet, everyone knows that.
The bastard. He did that on purpose! Now what will I wear
when we see Lord Tycho? I have nothing in my store that
will not make me look a pauper, and an embarrassment to
our family.'

It will surely not be your clothes that have that effect, Saro
thought drily. Meanwhile, Fabel and Favio, both equally
dampened by the arrival of King Ravn, but smiling indul-
gently at one of Tanto's familiar, if profane, outbursts of
temper, each took one of his arms and pulled him away.
'No point in shouting about it, lad,' Uncle Fabel was saying.
'We came for a bit of spectacle, and you can't complain too
bitterly if it comes a little close sometimes. Tunic's an easy

thing to replace, but you'll not forget the experience in a while, eh?'

He caught Saro's eye over the top of Tanto's furious head and winked.

Saro, surprised, grinned back.

That was more like it, Katla, contemplating the world from behind the boards of her stall: a bit of entertainment to enliven the Fair, and from their own king, of all people. By the time she'd trailed back to the Eyran quarter in which their tents and stalls were situated, everyone had been joking about it – that old running-the-oars-trick; the sort of thing drunken seamen did late at night when the ale ran out, to impress the women or to win a bet, though she doubted many would have the grace of Ravn Asharson. She could see – almost – why poor Jenna had gone weak at the knees for him. And the drenching of the richly-dressed Istrians had not gone amiss, either. She'd been surprised at the level of ill-feeling towards the southerners that appeared to underlie the normal courtesies of the Eyrans. It was apparent in the knowing looks, in the roars of laughter; in their eyes, in their secret delight at the wicked provocation of the erect stempost. Perhaps Fent was right, after all: perhaps hostilities were never far away. She'd heard him and Tor ranting on about the enmities shared between the two countries; heard the complaints of land stolen and ancient massacres; the older men's war stories, though her father said little on the subject. There had been peace all her life: it was hard to share the bitterness.

Ironic, she thought, to be laying out weaponry. But the pieces she had brought were such beautiful things! More like art, or jewellery, really, than the instruments of death and wounding. And indeed, when she was hammering the iron bars and folding the hot metal back on itself again and again, watching the fire turn it first to pulsing red and then to smoking white; when it cooled to sooty black and she could just make out the steely edges; when she polished it with the strop and watched the tiny bits of slag drop away; when she doused it and heated it and polished it again, with wood, then wire-wool and at last the sheepskin mitt; when she saw the secret patterns weaving their way across the metal as if they had always been there, under the surface, just waiting to be discovered by the hand which best knew the enchantment over iron; all she thought of was beauty, and balance, and a job well done – never of the killing thrust or the way a spearhead's barbs would hold fast in their target. Never that.

Unwrapping another piece from its protective waxed covering, she smoothed her hand down the length of its gently tapering blade. It really was fine work.

'A beautiful piece.'

Katla jumped, but it was only Tor.

'You startled me. What are you doing here, anyway? Shouldn't you be earning your keep elsewhere?'

In response, Tor shrugged a shoulder. He bent to the stall and ran his hands over the sword she had just unwrapped. 'Pretty thing, very pretty.' His fingers traced the patterns the overwelding had made in the metal. She watched them, wordless. His fingers were long, the tips broad and blunt; the knuckles covered with little coils of hair of a bright silvery-gold. 'Just like snakes, or tiny dragons, see: they swim the length of the blade ready to give their victim a nasty dose of venom.' He laughed, and with a single fluid motion, hefted the blade above his head and brought it swishing down to within an inch of Katla's head, but she stared him straight in the eye, determined not to flinch. His mouth quirked in what might have been fleeting disappointment at such a lack of reaction; then, still maintaining eye contact, he lowered the sword and ran his thumb down one of the edges. As the blood began to well, he gave her a feral grin. Katla found abruptly that she could not hold his gaze. Looking down, she watched the thin line of crimson flare across the ball of his thumb.

'Quite an edge on it,' he said approvingly. 'Take a man's leg off nicely, I'd say.'

She raised an eyebrow.

'You sound as if you have someone in mind.'

'I might.' He held the bleeding thumb out to her, leering. 'Kiss it better, won't you, Katla?'

Disgusted, she pushed his hand away.

'They say if a virgin tastes a man's blood, she'll be bonded to him forever.'

'Oh they do, do they?'

'Aye.' He laid the sword down with exaggerated care, then quickly turned and caught her by the chin. Furious, Katla sprang back, her eyes flashing, but Tor hung on, his fingers clenching on her jaw, trying to angle his head for a kiss.

When she dropped her head for a moment as if in defeat, Tor closed upon her. Under her spiky new fringe, Katla smiled wickedly. He obviously hadn't been paying too much attention to her wrestling bouts. She brought her head up sharply and dealt him a hard crack on the chin.

'Ow!'

His hands flew to his mouth. Blood was spurting from a split lip where he appeared to have bitten himself.

'Looks as if you've bonded with yourself there, Tor. Never mind; they say there's no better love than to love oneself, and I'm sure you've already had plenty of practice at that.'

Tor wiped his hand across his face, smearing blood grotesquely into his beard, then stalked off between the booths, Katla's laughter ringing in his ears.

How his brother could possibly claim to have 'nothing to wear', Saro could not imagine, standing in front of the enormous carved wardrobe the slaves had erected in Tanto's tent. He had never seen so many rich clothes – tunics and cloaks in fabulous brocades and plush in every colour of the rainbow; trimmed with silver; with copper wire; fine linen undershirts, soft leather boots in a dozen different styles; even a pair of jewel-encrusted slippers in what some exploitative Ceran designer had dubbed to be just like those worn by the lords of the Far West (though since no living man had set foot in that legendary land, let alone some fat merchant who could barely even walk up a flight of stairs, it was hard to see how anyone could have come by such arcane knowledge) and were now all the rage throughout the richer Istrian social circles. Personally, Saro thought they looked ridiculous, with their restrictively narrow toes and uncomfortable concretions of gems – it would surely be like wearing some gaudy crustacean on your foot – a cooked lobster, maybe, or a spidercrab.

Still, these slippers, plus a cerise tunic studded with pearls, a pale-green shift and a pair of pink hose, were what he had been sent to salvage, once his brother had calmed down enough to despatch him imperiously on this errand. Saro tossed the clothes down onto a goose-down quilt with disgust. Clearly, Tanto had no intention of helping with the horses today.

There was a short burst of swearing outside the tent and the sound of skin striking skin: clearly a slave had inadvertently stepped in Tanto's path, and then:

'Idiot boy: you'd think he'd gone blind in his other eye for all the care he was taking . . . Ah, excellent, brother: not quite as fine as the purple, but it'll have to do. Now help me out of these stinking rags: I am determined to make the best possible impression.' Tanto tore at the wet tunic, ripping the fine lace at its neck in his haste to be rid of it. Twenty-five minutes later, after much prinking and preening and poor Saro running around to find warm lavender-scented water and the right jewellery, Tanto stood ready.

Saro surveyed him with ill-disguised amazement: did he

really want to look like a stuffed flamingo in front of his future wife?

'Should make a fine impact, eh, brother?' said Tanto, seeing Saro's slack-jawed expression.

'Ah, yes, indeed. Not one she'll forget in some time, I'd say.'

'She? What do I care what the girl thinks? It's her father I want to impress, not some silly trollop.'

'Are you ready, son? We should be on our way.'

Tanto strode confidently out of the tent. If Favio thought his appearance a little unusual, he said nothing; but the one-eyed slaveboy who accompanied him gawped like a simpleton and almost dropped the pannier he was carrying.

Lord Tycho's pavilion was as far from the Eyran quarter as it was possible to be; clearly his people had arrived early at the Moonfell Plain with strict instructions, and had established the great tents on a grassy rise that gave a fine view of the fairground, and of the shining sea beyond. Here, too, the air was a little fresher; even a little cooler: down amongst the stalls and stock pens the midday sun had made for stifling conditions. None of this had improved Tanto's mood, which had been blackening steadily ever since they had set out. First of all, an Eyran urchin in a stained leather tunic and carrying an armful of knives had laughed openly at his appearance, and had called out to a rather plump girl with a towel wrapped about her head to come and see what the mummers were wearing this year; then a thin blond man with plaits in his hair and beard had run past them and stared at Tanto so hard he had run into a group of mercenaries and fallen over; they in turn had pointed and guffawed, and a small fat one had run along behind them for a while, aping Tanto's stiff-backed stalk; then, to crown it all, Tanto had lost one of the stupid slippers in the loose sand while they walked up the slope to Lord Tycho's tent, and Saro had had to scrabble around on

his knees to retrieve it for him and when he had tried to refit
the thing, Tanto had merely stuck his foot out, all resistant
and obstructive like a spoiled brat. By the time they reached
the pavilion, Tanto was scowling and silent: never the best
of signs.

A slave in perfect white linen with the Lord of Cantara's
mark on his cheek stepped smartly out of the shade of
the pavilion's awning and ushered them wordlessly inside.
Within, it was silky-cool. Two more slaves stood unobtru-
sively to the sides of the main room, wafting great fans; while
an ingenious flap in the top of the pavilion had been opened
to allow both the through-flow of air and a shaft of bright
sunlight, which fell, as though by intent or supernatural
power, upon the Lord of Cantara himself: a neat man of
middle-height with darkly burnished skin, a hooked nose,
and an impeccably understated style of dress.

'Welcome, my lords Vingo,' he said, bowing politely to
each of them in turn. Tanto nodded back with the barest
minimum of courtesy, and hurled himself down onto the
nearest cushion-strewn bench, legs splayed wide.

Saro waited to see what the Cantaran lord's reaction to his
bizarrely dressed and ill-mannered brother would be, but if
Tycho Issian noticed anything out of the ordinary in Tanto's
behaviour or appearance, he gave no sign of it.

There followed niceties of small conversation and the
serving of several goblets of attar-flavoured araque, which
Tanto and Uncle Fabel took straight, and which tasted sumptuous and powerful, though like nothing Saro had ever
previously encountered. He noticed, however, that Lord
Tycho watered his serving down almost to nothing and,
having seen this, Saro placed his own glass down on the
table, hardly touched.

At last, Favio said, 'We have considered the terms we
would wish to offer, my lord, for this excellent match. To
keep such matters plain and above board, my scribe has made

a note of them for your scrutiny,' and handed the Lord of Cantara an extravagantly ribboned scroll.

Tycho pulled the bindings apart with long, careful fingers, unrolled the scroll slowly and cast his eyes down the thick black figurings within. 'Twenty thousand: very generous; and the bloodstock, too. Also the fort and lands at Altea, in exchange for the castle at Virrey. An interesting location, if a little . . . remote . . .' He perused the rest of the document silently, his sharp eyes flicking across the complex marks and columns. Then looked up. 'There's no mention here of the land bordering the Golden River at Felin's Bluff,' he said softly.

Favio and Fabel exchanged an uncomfortable glance. Saro had the sense they had somehow been caught out.

Favio held his hand out for the scroll and ran his eyes down the listings. 'Stupid creature! – my scribe, my lord, I mean – such a foolish oversight. I knew the man was not paying attention.' He reached across the table, poured himself another glass of the smoky, rose-flavoured liquid, and knocked it back in a single gulp as if to divert attention from the lie.

Lord Tycho took the scroll back. 'As I thought,' he said smoothly. 'An unfortunate omission. But do not concern yourselves: I have my own scribe here: he shall make the correction.' He gestured minutely to one of the slaves, who melted away into the darkness at the back of the tent, returning a moment later with a thin young man with his head bound in the Jetran fashion bearing a goose-quill, a small pot and another, unornamented document.

Favio grimaced. As Tycho bent to take his seat again, Fabel shrugged minutely.

'And the land from the village of Fasal, extending to . . . to Talsea in the north and in the south bounded by the cliff at Felin's Bluff, with access to the Golden River, its toll-bridge and barge station,' Favio dictated, his voice flat and resigned.

'Excuse me, Father.' Tanto leaned across and gripped him by the arm. 'What about the woman?' he hissed, audible to all present. 'I want a good look at the baggage before you sign my inheritance away—'

Tycho's eyes narrowed then bored themselves into the side of Tanto's sun-kissed head. 'Let me call my daughter,' he said silkily. 'She is eager to see the young lord to whom she may be betrothed.' He paused to allow the veiled repayment of the insult to find its mark. 'Perhaps your lordships would like to peruse the terms of my share in our agreement while the Lady Selen is brought to attend our audience?' Taking the sheet of unrolled parchment from the scribe, he passed it to Favio Vingo, then turned and sharply called his daughter's name.

Saro watched as his father blinked: once, twice, then held the document at arm's length and stared at it. Oh Falla, Saro thought suddenly; he's drunk.

'Father,' he said softly. 'Would you like me to read it to you? I know your eyes have been paining you of late.'

Favio gave him a curious look, but did not relinquish the parchment.

'Don't interfere,' Tanto said loudly. 'You're just a hanger-on here: it's none of your business.'

As if she had been waiting in the anteroom throughout the preceding hour, the Lady Selen materialised suddenly at her father's side. She wore a sabatka of a dark hue – black with just a hint of aubergine to it – very plainly and severely cut, but of the finest linen. Entirely unornamented, it covered her from head to foot, and had the appearance more of funereal garb than a dress befitting what might by others be regarded as a joyful occasion. With her head held low, all that was visible of her at this moment were her hands.

She took a step forward, her hands held palm-out in the tradition greeting, and bobbed her head first to her father, then to the elder Vingos, and at last to Tanto and his brother.

Tanto leaned forward, his eyes keen to scrutinise.

In silhouette, her form was tall and slim, which in itself was pleasing enough, he noted; and when she moved it was with silent grace: altogether a good thing in a woman. But when she stepped into the shaft of light, his mouth fell open in wonder. From behind her came a hiss of disapproval: the first emotion Lord Tycho Issian had shown during the visit.

The single allowable slit in the sabatka's veil revealed that Selen Issian had painted her lips like those of a street whore. The shape – exaggerated to a more than generous bow – had been filled in with a rainbow of glittering colour. Sunlight played over gleaming yellows and purples, scarlets and greens, every opposition of the spectrum represented at once as though by the model for a cosmetics pedlar. Just to the right of her top lip – currently quirked in a humourless smile – a silver beauty-spot in the form of a crescent moon had been stuck to the pale olive skin: the universal symbol of those prostitutes who preferred to offer a very particular, and irregular, service.

Tanto's regard travelled hungrily across this palette; and came to rest on the beauty-mark. His eyes widened; then he beamed.

'She is a treasure, my lord,' he breathed, turning to Lord Tycho. 'A veritable treasure.'

Selen Issian's mouth became a long, hard line.

Favio Vingo looked surprised. Fabel seemed rooted to the spot. Lord Tycho's brows were drawn together in a single dark furrow. He looked as if he might explode. Saro stared from one to another, and back to the dark column of the girl. There was an electric charge to the air, a sense of challenge and sexual tension, but he did not fully understand its import.

Favio coughed, once, and returned his attention to the document.

'Ah, this all seems in order, my Lord Tycho. Shall we sign our respective offers and seal our bargain?'

From behind the veil there came a sharp intake of breath. The slim figure began to sway. Then Selen Issian crumpled to the floor.

When she came to the pavilion was empty. Except for her father, who was standing over her, his face grim and vivid with intent.

In his hands he carried a leather strap.

PART TWO

Five

Gold

Tycho Issian strode through the Fair, looking neither to right nor left until he reached the slave blocks which, appropriately enough, it seemed to him, were situated close to the livestock pens. By midday – barely even the start of the Fair – they were already thronged with interested customers thinking to make themselves a cheap deal. The smell from the nearby animals was lofting pungently into the windless air.

At the first blocks, a fat merchant from the south was showing off a mountain girl of nine or ten. Even shrouded by the seller's voluminous standard sabatka, she looked painfully thin, and one shoulder stood significantly higher than the other: hardly the 'sturdy scullery maid' he termed her. No one was bidding. Behind her were arrayed a motley collection of chained men, dark and wiry, all apparently from the same hill clan, no doubt captured and enslaved during the recent insurrections in the south, dressed to appeal to those looking for herdsmen or body servants, but such was not Tycho's goal.

He passed on swiftly.

The next seller had more likely merchandise: all women, all very properly dressed and presented. They huddled together on the raised dais. Two of them held hands, as if seeking some human comfort in the face of their inquisition. Tycho could just make out the glint of manacles on their wrists. He threaded his way to the front of the small crowd who had gathered to listen to the merchant's spiel.

'. . . ladies from the Farem Heights: beauteous, bounteous, housebroken and willing, and all from the same family. As long-limbed and finely fettled as their horses: and the blood of desert chieftains runs fiery through their veins: how can you resist their charms? Falla knows I couldn't!' And here he leaned forward to leer at his audience, many of whom roared with laughter; some surreptitiously counted the money in their purses, while others stood unmoved and stony-faced, ready to strike a hard bargain. 'I am content to sell the ladies singly or as a group. But imagine the pleasure, gentlemen, you could have from the whole job lot. Do I have any bidders for the group of five?'

Herded by the merchant's assistants, the women shuffled forward. Tears had streaked the cosmetics that had been so carefully applied to their mouths. Tycho turned his back on the scene and walked on . . .

It was not, he thought as he went, that he objected to such crude displays; rather that the obvious did not appeal to him, even aroused as he was at the moment, had been, indeed, ever since the shocking sight of his daughter's provocatively painted mouth. Had been, particularly, since he had beaten her for her defiance, quietly and painstakingly, not to leave marks that would last or be noticed, even by her attendants. The memory of her, cowering away from him, trying hard not to show her weakness, keeping her tears in check, made his loins boil with blood.

He must surely try to find a woman with whom to worship the Goddess, and quickly. He castigated himself silently for having left his favoured bed-partner behind in Cantara, but it had been necessary, given her current predicament. The foolish woman had thought to trick him, tried to hide the softness of her belly and breasts under sabatkas of a stiffer fabric that would not cling to her curves. But he did not pay his staff well for nothing: the housemistress had come to him as soon as she saw Noa vomiting one morning. Just in time: it became dangerous to abort the child beyond sixteen weeks; and while he was angry at Noa for trying to keep it, he would still not see her die under the chirugeon's knife. It would be a waste of resources: and, Falla knew, he had little enough of those to spare at the moment.

Always he hoped, when he visited the slave blocks, to find another Alizon: a proud, quiet, intelligent beauty, who would stir more than just his desire; who might even prove a stimulating companion for those soft, dark evenings by the lake, amongst the lemon groves. Not a wife from slavery: not again. His position, though weak, was too public now; and would be more so with the increase in status the Vingo alliance would bring him, and the place on the Istrian Council they would surely award him once he had cleared the debt. He had, by strenuous efforts, secured considerable respect amongst his peers and the elders of the Council; he was known for his oratory, and for his piety. Indeed, he had thought in his youth to combine the two and enter the priesthood; but events had conspired against that. He brushed those unpleasant memories swiftly away.

The women on the next dais were dark-skinned, and not to his taste. Impatient now, and with his member pushing insistently against his tunic, he turned for the nomad quarter.

Aran Aranson took a critical look at the position of the sun and, judging that he had sufficient time to spare before trading in the Eyran quarter started in earnest, set off purposefully. He knew exactly where he was going: Edel Ollson had mentioned seeing a Footloose man setting out a collection of maps and maritime charts and the like. Unusual, they were, Edel had said: parchment so old it was fragile to the touch, yellowed to the brown of a hazelnut around the edges, as if lapped by a tongue of fire. As to what others were made from, he had been less sure of: goatskin, maybe; or – and here he'd brought his head close to Aran's, his eyes darting apprehensively – perhaps even a man's skin!

Edel Ollson had a wayward imagination, Aran thought dismissively. He was a man who was always coming up with schemes and plans and never seeing them through. You could not trust the word of such a man; they might not even be maps at all; probably they were old love songs written for noble ladies; sheets of tabla music or even playscripts. Edel, like most Eyrans, had never learned to read, preferring to keep record with the traditional use of knots and braids, and Aran himself had hardly more than a rudimentary knowledge of letter-making. But surely even a man like Edel could tell the difference between music and nautical charts? It was certainly worth a brief investigation.

Aran Aranson loved a map. Maps were to him a marvel, with their rhumb lines and wind roses, their intricate coast-lines and stylised mountain ranges; their scattered islands and fantastically rendered monsters of the deep. But, most of all, he loved maps for all the promises they held out to him of journeys still to be made.

He walked briskly through the Eyran stalls, nodding to a man here, exchanging a greeting there, his eyes constantly watchful and intent: there seemed to be less sardonyx around this year – were supplies running low? It might drive the price up. On the other hand, the first two sardonyx stalls he passed – manned by Hopli Garson and Fenil Soronson – were deathly quiet. Halli might yet be looking elsewhere for the price of his longship, Aran thought ruefully. The third one, however, against the time and all the odds, was thronged. Aran craned his neck. Stacks of the dark, banded stone stood on each side of the display, ignored by the bystanders. Instead, they were almost falling over each other to lay hands on a small piece of glittering rock in the centre. Aran Aranson stood up on the balls of his feet. His heart skipped a beat. It was gold – or what looked like it – a great, gleaming lump of

yellow ore. Gold: that rarest of all commodities. They had
dug pits all over the Istrian plains in search of it on the
flimsiest of rumours; they had opened mines into the roots
of the Golden Mountains, only to find those dour peaks
once more misleadingly named. In Eyra, men had gone mad
skimming for it in glacial streams and moorland tarns. The
only examples of the lovely metal had been gleaned by the
brave and fortunate from the wrecks of ancient ships come
long ago to grief on the treacherous skerries of the Eyran
islands: ships that bore little relation to the simple vessels of
either north or south, bearing gorgeously-crafted artefacts that
spoke of a bygone age and a lost civilisation. He remembered
the fabulous sceptre he had once seen in the palace at Halbo,
massive and jewel-encrusted, so heavy it took two men to
carry it, found generations ago in the shallow waters off South
Island and now used for the investiture of the Eyran kings; and
once at the Allfair six or seven years since when one of the
Istrian lords had paraded around in a golden collar of bizarre
design that made him stoop under the weight. The next day,
the man lay dead down on the strand, his blood congealing
into sticky pats that drew the attention of the flies and skuas.
The collar, of course, was gone; and no one had seen it since;
it had surely been broken up, Aran thought, broken up and
melted down and incorporated in a hundred other pieces
of jewellery and dagger-hilts, sold, and most likely worn,
clandestinely. He frowned. Surely no one would have the gall
to display such unusual treasure so openly, unless he was the
wealthiest man in all of Eyra; yet Aran did not recognise the
man behind the stall; and in addition he was simply dressed,
and the two guards who stood behind him were clearly not
professionals: their gear was old and obsolete: the pommel of
the first man's sword finished in a rounded end, a style that
had been out of fashion two generations or more. Neither
did the weapon look so splendid that it would be a family
heirloom, passed from father to son down the years. Still,

you never could tell, and he knew well that appearances could deceive.

He watched proceedings at the stall for a time, while the onlookers touched the gold like a talisman and eventually filtered away to spread the word. No one bought any sardonyx. Aran approached the stall.

'May I see?'

'Of course.' The man made an open-handed gesture, as if he was well-used to such requests.

Aran reached out and put the tips of his fingers to the rock. It was cold and rough to the touch, though it drew the sun's rays to every shining, irregular plane of its surface as if it were a magnet. His fingertips buzzed and crawled at the contact.

He drew back: he had never touched gold before. The story-tellers said that gold was warm and sensuous; but perhaps that was just the licence of their poetry. 'Where did you come by this magnificent specimen?' he asked, carefully flattering.

'It was a trade I made, sir, a very fine trade.'

'Might I ask with whom?'

'A travelling man, and that's all I'll say, sir.'

A Footloose man, Aran thought. He felt a little shudder of excitement flicker through his chest. Uncle Ketil's tales of magic and treasure reignited in his mind as if he were suddenly nine and at the old man's knee once more.

'And was this man openly offering gold, in the nomad quarter?'

The seller looked suspiciously at Aran. 'There's no point in your going to find him: this piece was all he had,' he said quickly.

Too quickly, Aran thought. He bade the man farewell and walked swiftly to the nomad quarter, taking no notice of the rest of the Eyran stalls, the livestock pens, or the slave market. It would have been easy for a lesser man to have been distracted from his purpose, but Aran ignored the temptations that surrounded him. There would be more time to dally, to choose at least a small gift for Bera, later in the Fair. Now, his impatience drove him on, and while his face bore outwardly its usual stern expression, inside he was grinning like a child. Gold: he felt then that if he could take with him even the smallest ingot, it would be the talisman he was searching for in his life, the turning point that would take him from the drudgery of the farm, sailing into an endless blue horizon . . .

The map-seller took some finding, and he discovered him, eventually, only by asking a tall woman with feathers in her hair. She had cupped her hands to her ear and bent towards his question, which he repeated slowly, making signs with his hands to indicate a man unrolling a parchment. Then he showed her his windrose, the one he had got from the chandlery in Halbo, of the latest and most advanced design. She took it from him, then laughed raucously as if she had understood his purpose, and started to stow the windrose in her money-pouch. When she took him by the hand and patted his tunic where it covered his genitals, he realised in some horror that she thought he had offered it in exchange for her services. Hastily, Aran shook his head and retrieved the precious windrose. She stared at him in bemusement as he began to trace a design in the black sand – a coastline: he mimed a ship bobbing up and down to show her the wavy lines he had drawn indicated a sea. After some moments of this charade, she had smiled, showing off a mouthful of filed stumps – a prostitute, then, indeed; and one who had clearly once been owned by a slavemaster from the south – and clapped her hands together. She said something unintelligible, and then, realising he could not understand her, had walked with him for a way, her arm linked through his. Aran was beginning to think she had entirely mistaken his meaning and was about to pull away, when she drew him between two covered wagons to another all of wood, larger than most, with a lean-to stall in brightly-painted colours that had been erected on one side, and shaded with an awning. Beneath the awning stood a tall, thin, pale man, and before him, spread upon a gaudy cloth, was a pile of parchment scrolls. A pulse beat at Aran's temple and he felt his heart begin to race. He pressed a coin into the nomad woman's hands, and she bowed and smiled and walked on.

He was about to approach the stall when his attention was caught by a slight movement in his peripheral vision. On the steps of the wagon sat a black cat with slanted green eyes. A hand rested upon its neck, startlingly white against the black fur, the fingers tapering to pearl-pink nails in perfect ovals. Of the owner of this hand, no more could be seen; just the fingers moving rhythmically, hypnotically against the creature, whose purr he could hear from where he stood.

Almost, he could not tear his eyes away from the sensuous stroke, the beautiful hand. Almost: but the lure of the maps was too strong.

As soon as he turned back towards the stall, the tall man raised his head. Their eyes met and Aran felt a powerful jolt of reaction, but whether it was of anticipation or even of revulsion, he could not tell. The man, so pale as to be colourless, his features wide and flat, was a strange-looking creature, Aran thought, though he was not usually a judgemental man. He was of indeterminate age, the skin of his face entirely unmarked by the usual lines that life inflicted; but his eyes were not those of a young man. Nor could he place his provenance.

'May I look at your maps?' he asked quickly in the Old Tongue.

Without a word, the man dipped his head in what Aran took to be assent. Aran picked up the first scroll that came to hand and unrolled it carefully. Something about it – his own anticipation most likely – made his fingers itch and burn. It was, curiously enough, a map showing the islands just to the east of his own, meticulously detailed and divulging every

reef and outcrop of rock that revealed themselves only at
the lowest tide. Fishing areas had been marked with shoals
of beautifully drawn mackerel; and whales spouted in the
deeper seas to the north. A useful tool, to those who needed
such. Aran knew his fishing grounds. He smiled and rolled
the map away again.

The next one he picked up was of the Istrian mainland,
centring on the Golden Mountains and the lakes and rivers
that drained off them. Barges had been drawn at various points
to indicate the best navigable routes to the sea.

The third map he examined was sketchy in the extreme.
Mountains had been drawn like marching triangles across the
eastern quarter and stick-like yeka walked the empty area from
there to the sea. 'Terreta prion' he read, the words that spidered
the centre of the map, his fingers tracing their path. The desert
lands. Fascinating; but he was a sailor, not a horseman; nor had
he ever even sat upon a yeka. Disappointed, he put this map,
too, away from him.

'Are you seeking something specific?' the man asked in
unaccented Eyran.

Aran's head came up sharply from his reveries. He shook
his head. 'Not really.' He paused, then said softly, so that no
one else might hear: 'Though a friend of mine mentioned
a map he had seen of a certain treasure-filled island. And
another man I met showed me some of that treasure.'

The man smiled without revealing his teeth, so that his
long, pale lips stretched across his face. The smile did not
reach his eyes, which seemed as cold and pale as those of
a squid.

'Show me your hands.'

Aran stared at him.

'Excuse me?'

'Your hands.' There was, unless he was mistaken, a slight
impatience in the man's voice now: a touch of adamant.

Slowly, Aran held out his hands. The map-seller took hold

of them, turned them palm-up and began to scrutinise them silently, running the tips of his fingers lightly up and down their seamed surfaces. Aran felt intensely uncomfortable. No man had ever touched him like this before: he hoped no one he knew would walk past and see this odd display. After several long moments, he could bear it no longer.

'What do you see?' he asked.

The man did not lift his eyes. 'I see that you are a seafaring man, and have been so for some long while. It takes no great hand-reading skill to know this, for your hands are roughened by salt and rope, and you have rowing callouses across the pads of your palms and fingers. However, you also work the land, though maybe less willingly. And here—' he turned Aran's right hand over, to indicate a long white scar down the brawny, tanned wrist '—here is where you took a wound from a thin sabre of Forent steel, fighting Istrian enemies, maybe nineteen or twenty years since.'

Aran found he was holding his breath. He let it out in a great rush. 'That's remarkable,' he said at length. He found he was grinning at the man. 'What else do you see?'

'You have an adventurous streak, currently frustrated by your circumstances; but if you follow your instincts, and make use of those long years of hard-won skill, you will be afforded the chance to overcome the obstacles in your path and gain the treasure you seek, though it may be necessary to shed a little blood in exchange for such good fortune.' His finger traced a transverse line on Aran's palm, and where he touched his skin, Aran felt the cold of sea-ice in his veins. 'Another's blood. And the fortune is truly great.' The map-seller looked up, and was rewarded by a flare of light in the Eyran's dark eyes. 'For the right price,' he said, lowering his voice, 'I might be able to help you take the first step towards such a fate.'

'Yes?'

The map-seller cocked his head. 'Can you be trusted, I wonder, with such a secret?'

'Trusted?'

'I have in my possession the fragment of an ancient map, a map to a long-hidden island called Sanctuary, the fastness of a great magician who lies in a dream, wrapped around by sorcerous sleep. In this fastness is a fortune – in gold and silver, gems and coins; rare artefacts and magical implements. If I were to let you have this fragment, it would be for the price of my asking.'

Aran drew back, suddenly dubious. 'I have heard of this place: but only in stories. It is surely a figment of fairytale and fireside romance?'

The man grinned. From beneath the counter he produced a lump of the same bright, glittering ore Aran had seen on the sardonyx-seller's stall and placed it on the flat of the Eyran's still-outstretched hand. Then he pressed Aran's fingers down tightly over it. The ball of metal sat heavy in his palm. It was too large to close his fingers on. Aran opened them and raised the ore to his face. Facets of it sparkled in the sun, shot light into his eyes. His palm felt as though it cupped a hot coal.

'Gold!' Blinking, he lowered it back to the stall.

'Keep it,' said the map-seller. 'There's plenty more where that came from.'

'The fastness?'

'Indeed. Would you know more?'

'Let me see the map.'

The man turned away. As he approached the steps, the cat retreated, lips drawn back, fur on end, then shot into the recesses of the covered wagon. There was a scuffling commotion, followed by the sound of conversation, muted and brief, then the map-seller reappeared, clutching a leather bag. From this he extracted a folded sheet that seemed more supple than paper, though darkened by age, and one part of it was torn away. The side that came to light was unmarked. Slowly, the map-seller turned it over.

Aran gazed at it avidly. Though partial, it was clear that the map-maker, whoever he might have been, had lavished some care upon the draughtsmanship. A windrose sat in the top righthand corner, with its southern arm pointing diagonally down towards the missing lefthand corner. Around its decorated frame, where the directional points would usually be indicated, Aran could just make out the words 'Isenfelt', 'Estrea', 'Eaira' and 'Oceana prion'. The core of the rose bore the circled lettering: 'Sanctuarii'. He took a deep breath. The spellings were antique: even he knew that much. Intersecting lines had been ruled across the entire surface, radiating out from the points of the compass, and someone had marked in a different hand figures and illegible notations, as though calculations had been made for navigation. Aran bent closer, suddenly recognising a complex squiggle of coastline.

'Whale Holm! And there: the mainland of northern Eyra!' He scanned the map more closely, skewed it sideways and looked again. Cross-hatchings and erasings obscured a number of details in the top right quarter.

'This is amazing! What do you want for it?' He started to open his money pouch, but the man's hand shot out as swiftly as a striking snake.

'No money, sir navigator. No money.'

Aran frowned. 'What, then? I have good quality sardonyx, if you wish to trade; and my daughter makes the finest knives in all of Eyra—'

'Nor those, either. What I ask is far more precious. What I ask, sir adventurer is, can you be trusted? For if you can, I have a task for you, and if you swear to me you will carry out that task, then the map is yours, and yours alone.'

'I can be trusted: I am known as a man of my word.'

'Then come inside sir and seal the pact, and the map shall be yours.'

It was with a certain self-disgust that Lord Tycho Issian

discovered he was eyeing the Footloose women with interest. There was no question that they were handsome creatures, under their stained and patterned skin; beneath their feather and bone trinkets, their odd braids and bizarre clothing; but the sight of so much naked, unconsecrated flesh was hard for a man of his convictions to bear.

He wandered between the carts, the wagons and the stalls in a kind of daze. Jugglers danced round him; boys tried to press sticks of sweetsmoke upon him; musicians begged for coins; a female acrobat walked towards him on her hands, her bare breasts, revealed through strands of amber and coloured beads, balanced precariously above the ground, were covered with the volcanic plain's fine black dust. This detail stayed with him, unwanted but persistent, as he weaved between jewellery stalls and fortune-tellers, hair-braiders and charm-pedlars. He was just trying to sidestep a tall dark man coming away from a map-seller's stand with a roll of parchment clutched in his hand when he saw her, ducking her head out of a gaudily painted wagon to watch the dark man leave.

It was only a glimpse, but it was enough. A pair of sea-green eyes framed by a sweep of dark lashes; a long, straight nose; skin as fair as a swan's wing, and a pair of lips so pink and pale, they might have been a child's. The eyes, though, belonged to no child; and to no innocent, either. He felt his heart rise up; and not just his heart.

And then she was gone.

He pushed his way towards the wagon into which she had disappeared, only to be met by a man of middle years, who stepped out in front of him, making the odd little nomad bow.

'*Rajeesh*. Can I help you, my lord?'

He spoke with little intonation: certainly not an Eyran accent, that; nor Istrian either. He was too fair-skinned to be a desertman, despite his mannerisms; too wan and light-eyed to

have come out of the mountains. His hair and brows and lashes
were so pale as to be colourless. He looked like a plant kept
too long out of sunlight, that has grown etiolated and weedy
in some cold, dark place. Tycho regarded him curiously.

'Out of my way, fellow,' he said, his voice suddenly thick
with desperation.

The man smiled. It was a slow smile, and not entirely
pleasant.

'Ah,' he said, and winked.

Tycho bridled, insulted by the man's knowing look, his
confiding tone.

'There was a woman—'

The man inclined. 'Yes, my lord?'

'The woman. In your wagon . . . I want her.' The words
were out before he could stop them. A terrible cold wave of
dread flooded over him. Something wrong here, something
terribly wrong.

The albino cocked his head. 'All men seek a fountain in
which to quench their thirst. And the Rosa Eldi is the very
ocean. Every man seeks the Rose of Elda,' he said cryptically.
'Who would not?'

Tycho stared at him. 'What are you talking about? All I
want is a woman: the woman in your wagon. Is she yours?
Will you sell her to me?' He started to open the leather pouch
at his belt, but the man put up his hand.

'My business is maps and charts,' he said softly. 'Those I
sell. The Rose of Elda cannot be bought.'

'If she is a woman, then she can be bought. Surely all things
have a price?' Tycho was horrified to find himself wheedling,
plaintive.

The map-seller laid a hand on the Istrian lord's arm. Even
through the linen of his shift, Tycho could feel the man's
fingers were cold and clammy, like a sea-creature, a jellyfish;
some thing not fully alive. He felt himself quail away from the
touch. 'If I cannot buy her,' he said, more forcibly, 'maybe

we can come to some agreement whereby I can borrow her for an hour or so?'

'Borrow, my lord? What is borrowed and then lost can never be returned.'

Tycho frowned. 'Don't play games with me, map-seller. Why would I lose her? I'll give you two hundred cantari for an hour of her time.' Two hundred cantari: it was a small fortune: what was he saying? He must be addled. But the pale man made no reaction.

'Regretfully, lord, I cannot trade her: her fate lies elsewhere.'

The image of a white face and huge green eyes swam up suddenly in Tycho Issian's mind. His heart began to hammer alarmingly; he could feel the beat of his blood down every inch of his arms and legs. It prickled his back, pulsed through his skull, as if he were in the grip of a fever.

'Marriage, then,' he said hoarsely. 'I'll take her to wife.'

What was he saying? This surely was madness: a possession of the spirit.

This offer, at least, had sparked a reaction. A strange, quizzical light had appeared in the map-seller's eye. 'Marriage, you say, sir?'

Tycho took a deep breath, meaning to take back the foolish words. But instead: 'Yes: I'll wed her. Give her to me now and I'll wed her directly, as soon as the proprieties can be met and the rituals performed. By Falla, I swear it.'

The man shook his head slowly. 'Ah, I knew she was precious, sir: but maybe I have underestimated her true worth. Indeed, sir, I do not think I shall part with her thus. I bid you good day, my lord.' And with that, he brought the wooden blinds clattering down over the stall and retreated into the wagon.

Tycho Issian hammered on the door for ten minutes or more, but no one answered.

★   ★   ★

'Katla, Katla!' It was Jenna, and she had clearly been running. Her ample bosom heaved and heaved. It had made her cheeks rosy as apples. Her eyes sparkled.

'What is it, Jenna?' Katla laid down another of the chased daggers and stood back to admire her handiwork. They made a pleasing array, fanned out as they were against the rich red cloth, their steely edges glinting in the sunlight. Already she had sold two: to a rich Eyran farmer from the mainland, and another to a quietly-spoken Istrian with short silver hair and a patrician manner. She'd charged him extra: it looked as if he could afford it.

'Father will present me to the King: he will put me forward as a possible bridal partner!'

Katla's head came up with a start. 'What?'

'He has agreed, at last! King Ravn will see me tomorrow night, and he will choose me for his bride.' Her face was rapt, her eyes made sly and unfocused by the power of her dream; she looked like a farmcat slipping sated from the dairy. She leaned across the stall, clutched at Katla's arm. 'So you must come with me now, at once, to the nomad quarter. I must get charms and potions and ribbons and — oh, Katla!'

'I cannot come now,' Katla said carefully, thinking that Finn Larson must have lost his mind. Been nagged into insanity, most likely. And so much for poor Halli, after the family had encouraged him so. The venality of the shipmaker and the inconstancy of his daughter infuriated her, sharpened her tone. 'This is my living, selling this lot — I can't just go traipsing off round the Fair at your whim!'

'Don't fret, Katla.'

She turned around to find her father standing there, his eyes filled with the same dreamy rapture as Jenna Finnsen's. In his right hand he clutched a roll of old parchment.

'Go have fun with your friend — it is your first Fair, after all.'

'But, Da: my stall. I need every bit of the money I can make from it if I'm to recoup my expenses and have any left to myself—'

Aran waved her objections away as if they were midges. 'There'll be no problem with money: not now, nor ever.' He reached into his pouch, withdrew the lump of gold.

Katla's eyes went round.

Jenna Finnsen gasped. 'Oh, it's gold! How beautiful it is. Gold—'

'Where did you come by it, Da?' Katla asked, suddenly suspicious. There was something not right here, though she could not finger it; as if the world had bent slightly out of true.

Aran smiled and tucked the ingot carefully into the pouch once more. He patted it. 'Ah, now that would require the telling of a long, strange story. Run along, Katla: I will mind your stall myself. I know the price your wares can fetch, don't worry about that. And—' he pressed a coin into her hand '—have some fun.'

'But, Da: what about the sardonyx?'

'Halli's manning the stand. It was time he took some responsibility on his shoulders. He's a man grown, and will soon be making his own way.' He smiled at Jenna, who blushed and looked away.

Katla's sense of unease only deepened further as they forayed into the nomad quarter. Jenna babbled on and on like a river in spate – about dresses with embroidered facings, the latest Galian braid, slippers with a heart-shaped heel. The words washed over Katla, whose mind shied away from her ridiculous prattlings like a frog trying not to drown in the backwash. It was hard to know how best to serve your friend in such circumstances: to tell the truth – that King Ravn was surely here to make a strategic match, which meant lands and power; money and influence; and though Finn Larson might be Eyra's finest shipbuilder, he was hardly a noble; nor was his daughter such a beauty to sway a man's judgement beyond the rational – would just bring Jenna grief, and anger at the speaker: as Katla's grandmother always said: 'the bearer of bad tidings always bears the brunt'. So instead, she nodded and smiled and pointed out to Jenna as they passed the stalls on which lay pretty gewgaws: ivory buttons carved into snowdeer and ermine and strange, long-necked animals like malshaped cows; ribbons with a many-coloured sheen; pieces of lace so fine they looked like cobwebs. But Jenna knew what she was after, and these fineries, though they distracted her for a while, were not her goal.

'The charm-seller,' she said after they had wandered for the best part of an hour. 'Over there!'

She pointed to a coloured wagon above which a banner had been raised with a name spelled out awkwardly in the Old Tongue. Katla narrowed her eyes and scrutinised the banner for some moments. Her letter-reading was neither quick nor accurate: it had required too much sitting still as a child to learn it properly, and Katla had always been a fidget, always had other plans in mind than sitting quietly at Bera's knee, while the boys ran around in the yard, yelling their heads off.

'Fezack Starsinger?' Katla said at last. 'What sort of a name is that?' She scoffed. 'If you believe that to be a true name you are more simple-minded than I took you for.'

Jenna tossed her head so that the sun gilded it with every shade of gold. It seemed possible, Katla thought with surprise, that the urine might have done its work after all.

'The Footloose choose their own names: it's a mark of their freedom. Don't you know anything? Marin told me about Fezack Starsinger. She's a proper magic-maker, Marin said: sold her a potion to make her breasts grow, and already they are each a finger's width greater than they were yesterday.'

'When they are a hand's width greater, let me know and I'll send Tor to check them out.'

Jenna giggled. 'Now he's a proper man,' she said. 'Hate to think where his hands have been.' She glanced slyly at her friend. 'Though perhaps you know more about that than you're saying.'

'I do not! He's an oaf.' Katla shuddered.

'So would Erno be more to your taste then? All quiet and shy, and no need to brag about what's in his breeches?'

'Jenna! Anyway, what would you know about such?'

'Girls talk.'

'And which girl would know such a thing?'

'Marin says he's a fine figure of a man, Erno Hamson. That's why she's doing all she can to make herself more attractive to him.'

'And Erno likes a woman to be hung with cows' udders, does he?' Katla said furiously. She thought of her own small breasts, as firm as a boy's, and hardly any bigger. Not much for a man to get his hands on there. Perhaps she should buy Marin's potion. She grinned. Perish the thought, and be thankful to be able to run without getting a pair of black eyes.

'Come on, then. Let's go see your charm-maker.'

They were just about to knock upon the wagon's door – a work of art in itself; since it had been painted a rich dark-blue and decorated with a firmament of stars and the moon in all of its phases – when it was flung open and a young man came stumbling out, head turned to bid the charm-maker farewell. 'Wear it next to your heart,' the old woman was saying, 'and her love will keep you warm . . .'

Then he cannoned into Katla, who fell backwards down the steps, landing unceremoniously on the black soil, where she began to laugh uproariously.

It was Erno.

For a second he stared at Jenna, flattened against the side of the wagon, then down at the shorn girl, an expression of the utmost horror on his face. Then he stuffed something rapidly under his shirt.

All at once Katla stopped laughing and regarded him solemnly. There seemed to be something different about him, something striking; even impressive. Framed by the gloriously artificial welkin, all glowing golds and silvers against their dusky background, with the arch of the true heavens rising above him, Erno looked for a moment like Sur rising from the Northern Ocean to survey his newfound realm with wonder.

Then, with an embarrassed bob of his head, he was gone, running like a rabbit between the stalls. Katla watched him till he was out of sight, then shook her head as if disturbed by something and picked herself up off the ground.

Jenna, grasping her money-pouch eagerly, was already halfway into the wagon. Katla ran up the stairs to join her.

The Footloose woman was a sight to behold. It was not that she had not seen a bald woman before, Katla thought, remembering Old Ma Hallasen, whose hair had fallen out, they said, at the news of her husband's death at the hands of the raiders twelve years ago, and who had since that time gone simple in the head, and now lived in the little bothy down by the stream with no more company than a cat and a goat; it was just that Fezack Starsinger – her single weird decoration of feathers standing proud on the top of her skull – had a head the perfect oval and burnished brown of an acorn.

Jenna was already in full flood, so that the nomad woman started to wave her hands about frantically. She whistled and cawed like a jackdaw, and then, quite clearly, she said: 'Quiet now, girl. Slowly for Fezack, if you please. Old ears, slow mind,' and Jenna reiterated her request again, without all the embellishments about King Ravn and her heart, and her father's promise, and all the crowds of people who would attend the Gathering.

'Something he will notice me for,' she finished. 'Something that will draw his eye away from all others.'

The old woman leaned forward and fingered Jenna's hair. 'Such beautiful hair: like spun gold.'

Jenna grimaced. 'Lots of Eyran women have hair like this,' she said. 'It's not enough to make him notice me. Don't you have a potion or something?'

Fezack grinned. She had little red gems inset into her teeth which caught the light like tiny fireflies. Then she nodded vigorously. 'I have what you need. Not cheap, though.'

'I don't care,' said Jenna, recklessly. She poured the contents of her pouch out into her palm. 'Take what you want.'

The old woman bent her head over Jenna's outstretched hand and rooted around in it with a clawlike fingernail. At last she fished up two or three small coins and bit each one consideringly. Then she slipped them into a small ceramic pot on the shelf behind her and went off into the back of the wagon.

'I do hope you know what you're doing,' Katla whispered. 'I'm not sure I'd trust her.'

Jenna's chin came up obstinately. 'This is my one chance,' she said resolutely. 'I must seize it with both hands.'

Fezack Starsinger came back a moment later with a small glass vial. She pressed this item into Jenna's hands and, lifting the great golden curtain of her hair, whispered something in her ear so that Katla could not hear what she said. Then she straightened up and opened the door to usher them out. They each bobbed a courteous farewell, and then they were out in the blinding sunshine again, blinking and disorientated by the startling contrast with the dingy, stuffy wagon. The old woman stood on the steps, looking down at them. 'Not till he sees you,' she reminded Jenna, wagging her finger sternly. 'Remember.'

★　　★　　★

'You see the tits on that, Joz?'

'Mmm.'

'Did you see, Knobber? The big blonde one walking with the scrawny-looking lad over there by the pastries stall?'

'Aye. Very nice.'

'I wouldn't mind hiding me sausage in her box.'

'You've got a filthy mouth on you, Dogo.'

'Filthy hands, too, given half a chance—'

'You'll keep them to yourself when you're around me, that or lose them.'

'Yes, Mam.' A pause. Then: 'Still, I bet you've some tales to tell, eh, Mam, from your days as a pro?'

'They're not stories for *little* boys, Dogo.'

'Come round to my bivvy tonight and you'll find me not so little.'

A smack.

'Ow! What d'you do that for?'

'Little boys shouldn't tell lies.'

'Who's been talking, then?'

Six

A Gift

Fent Aranson and Tor Leeson strode quickly away from the sardonyx stall, leaving Halli shouting something inaudible, but in all likelihood obscene, after them.

'Well done, Tor. I couldn't have stood Halli for a minute longer. All he can talk about is Jenna this and Jenna that; and the longship he's got his eye on. He's been lecturing me all afternoon on the benefits of a settled life: taking a wife, earning enough money to buy a farm, putting a little aside every day, not spending all my money – all my money, I ask you – on drink and women!'

'I thought he had his heart set on voyaging to the Far West.'

'Only to win the price of the land and the stock: not for fun – not like me.'

'He's a prig, your big brother,' Tor opined briskly. 'Wouldn't know a good time if it bit him. Jenna Finnsen indeed. All flesh and fabric, that one. I'd rather have one I could get my teeth into, a girl with a bit of substance, a bit of imagination and a bit of muscle, ready to wrap herself round you for an hour or two, then just as happy to go her own way.' He grinned wolfishly, then shook his head. 'Women: they're nothing but trouble to men like you and me.'

Fent regarded him askance. 'Failed to win my sister's favour, did you?'

'She's a minx: tooth and claw. But I do love a bit of spirit in 'em.'

'True enough.' Fent chuckled. 'Nomad quarter?'

'Nomad quarter.'

'Women or wine?'

'Both!'

'Let's go and get horribly, uproariously drunk.'

'Let's go get horribly, uproariously drunk, and find ourselves a couple of Footloose whores to tup senseless!'

Saro Vingo slipped away from the family pavilion as soon as he could. He'd had about as much as he could take of his brother going on and on about his prospective bride. 'Once I've got that one locked away, she won't be able to stand up for a month,' Tanto kept saying. 'Did you *see* that mouth? She can't wait, and no mistake.' It made him ashamed to be a Vingo; to be Istrian even. Or perhaps this was what it was to be a man.

He walked through the fairground with his head down, avoiding the eye of all those he passed. Was this how all men talked about their wives? Surely his father had never spoken of their mother so? Illustria, so tall and serene, her mouth painted in restrained plums and violets, who talked so softly that everyone present in the room fell silent to hear her speak; had Fabel once called her a whore and boasted to others of what he'd liked to do to her?

Saro felt himself flush, implicated by his gender in even the potential for her debasement, and knew he was little better himself. The pictures he'd had in his head ever since seeing that barbarian girl on the Rock . . .

His money-pouch chinked as he strode along, prompting a thought: he would buy his mother a gift, something foreign, unusual, something no one else would think to bring home. With new purpose in his step, he headed for the nomad quarter.

The sun had just begun its long slow dip towards the

sea before he reached the first stalls, bathing everything in an indeterminate, chancy light. It was strange, and a little thrilling, to be wandering the fairground – especially this part of the fairground – on his own. Little tremors of anticipation ran up and down his spine. Who knew what sort of adventure he might encounter, what bizarre folk he might meet?

He threaded his way between innumerable stalls offering trinkets and fabulously-patterned fabrics, exotic-smelling foods and flasks of drink. Around one stall specialising in variously flavoured araques a large group of young men had gathered rowdily, drinking the samples and shouting down the distressed stallholder, a wizened old man without a tooth in his head. Saro walked quickly by.

He bought a spiced pastry and stopped for a while at a puppet theatre. On a gaudily-painted stage in a striped fabric booth which hid the puppeteers, three grotesque mannequins clacked up and down on sticks. They had long, thin fingers and pointed noses; spidery limbs and gilded clothes. He had no idea who the figures represented; and when the fourth character made an entrance: a smaller figure in a white robe whom the audience cheered as if he was the hero, he was still none the wiser. The small white-clad puppet led the three larger ones on a journey towards a board of painted mountains and into a dark hole in the backcloth. Then it clapped its wooden hands together and a great puff of green smoke engulfed the stage, much to the delight of the onlookers. When the smoke cleared, the three larger figures had vanished, leaving only the white one, with a tiny wooden cat at its feet, and everyone started to applaud. Saro found himself doing the same, since it seemed only polite.

A small dark-haired girl with a silver ring through her nose and another through her right eyebrow came scooting out from behind the screen and bowed, then with a flourish produced a large leather bag, which she held out before her. Folk started to throw coins into the bag, then to drift away. Saro was one of the last to leave. When the girl came to him, she placed her palms together and bowed to him.

'*Rajeesh, mina Istrianni,*' she said.

He made a clumsy copy of the bow and repeated the odd greeting, which for some reason made her laugh. Then he asked her, slowly and carefully in the Old Tongue, what it was he had just seen.

'Rahay and the Wizards!' she said in surprise. 'Don't you know anything?'

He grimaced. 'Apparently not. I arrived late to the performance and missed all but the last scene.'

'Come with me while I get the stall ready for tonight's performance and I'll tell you the story, if you'd like.'

'I would love it.'

She disappeared into the booth and began to sweep the dust from the explosion off the stage with her hands, then with a grin turned the palms up towards him. They were bright green. 'You want to smell some magic?'

Saro laughed. 'Magic? That's just green dust!'

'Maybe now it is: but in the play . . .' She held her hand out to him and he took it briefly in his own. Her fingers were tiny, like a child's. The dust smelled acrid and pungent and entirely unfamiliar to him: the smell of another country, another world.

In a singsong voice, she began her tale:

> '*Rahay, he was King of the West*
> *Keeper of peace, maker of gold*
> *Of all kings the wisest and best*
> *His folk lived well till they were old*
>
> *Word of the West spread far and wide*
> *Till wizards heard tell of the gold*
> *On their great ship they caught the tide*
> *Planning to steal all they could hold*

To his court they came from the sea
(Their ship lay broken on the rocks)
King Rahay smiled, a shrewd man, he:
Wise as an owl, wily as a fox

"To stay here in my land of gold
Just grant me three wishes, I pray."
The wizards laughed, for they were bold
And knew their promise they'd betray.

So King Rahay asked for the skill
To move rock, call fire from the sky
"That's two," they said. "You have one still."
Then the King's cat came walking by.

"Fill my cat with your magic charms,"
Was the third wish of the good King
And he placed the cat into their arms
"It is done," they said, "this strange thing."

For three days the wizards ran amok
They smoked, they drank, they defiled
They brought with them the worst of luck,
They killed a goat, a dog and a child.

The next day the King took them into the hills
Where caves of gold glittered and shone
And when they were in he called on his skills:
In an eyeblink the wizards were gone.

For he had called a thunderbolt down
To cleave the golden cave in two
And mountains moved across the ground
To cover the old caves with new.

Back at the court he stroked his cat
Till it gave up the spells to its lord

He used them to make his lands fat
And fine; and for this he was adored

Rahay, he was King of the West
Keeper of peace, maker of gold
Of all kings the wisest and best
His folk lived well till they were old.'

She dusted her green-stained hands down her tunic. 'The Old Tongue doesn't rhyme where the original did I'm told, but that's the version I was taught. And, to be properly traditional, I ought to have accompanied it with a cither, but mine's so out of tune at the moment, I think you'd thank me for the lack!'

Saro dug in his pouch and withdrew a silver coin. 'I thank you anyway,' he said, holding it out to her. 'I loved your tale.'

She waved it away. 'Don't insult me with your money: this was not a paying performance – I chose to tell you the story. Regard it as my gift to you, at your first Allfair.'

'How can you tell?'

He smiled at her and was delighted to see her smile back, her dark eyes crinkling in that smooth tanned face. Her very naked, female face. He felt a wave of shame rise up in him for seeing it so, and bobbed his head to hide his blush. When he raised it again, she was watching him intently.

'You stare at me as if you've never seen a woman's face before.'

Saro felt stupid. 'Sorry, no,' he stammered. 'It's just that where I come from women do not show their faces. They wear a veil that leaves just their mouth free to eat, and speak and—'

'You are Istrian.'

He nodded, though it had not been a question.

'Your people have odd ways with women.' She laughed, picking up the puppets and untangling the rods and strings where they had fallen at the end of the play. 'To hide them away so jealously. The men must be very afraid.' She handed one of the untangled puppets to Saro, who took it cautiously. He turned it over. It was beautifully made, he saw now: carved by a master's hand, each feature, each digit delineated with exquisite care. He moved one of the rods and saw how a limb jerked; saw that with a skilful puppeteer's art, the fingers could be made to move individually, so that the hand might beckon or make a fist.

He thought about what she had said, turning the puppet over and over. At last, he said: 'It is said that the power of Falla shines out of a woman's eyes. Perhaps we are afraid of that power.'

The girl laughed. 'So you should be! Now, give me that wizard before you rub all his gold off.' She replaced all four mannequins into a cleverly-made wooden box with compartments to keep the rods and strings separate. 'So, what are you doing here with the Wanderers on your first Fair, young sir?'

'I came to look for a gift for my mother.'

'Good boy,' she regarded him approvingly. 'Women like gifts. Did you have something in mind?'

Saro shook his head. 'Some jewellery, maybe,' he added lamely.

She clapped her hands. 'I'll take you to my grandfather, then. He specialises in moodstones – set into necklaces and bracelets, rings and brooches; or, even better, I think, on their own, just to hold in your hand. Your mother will be enchanted.'

'But why are they called moodstones?'

'They change colour to match your mood.'

Saro laughed. 'How can a stone do that?'

The girl shrugged. 'Ask my grandfather: he's the expert.'

'In stones?'
'No, silly: in moods.'

The old nomad's stall was situated just behind the one selling araque that Saro had passed earlier, but the crowd had grown since then: both in size and in volubility. Young Istrian men with their clean-shaven chins and elaborate tunics rubbed shoulders with Northerners in leather and braids, and while they appeared incongruous in one another's company, it seemed that the universality of a shared drink had bound them in great good cheer: one lad – who might have been Ordono Qaran from Talsea, had an arm around a young Eyran with white-blond hair and beard, and they were singing an old drinking song, each in their own language, but with more or less the same tune. Saro recognised others he had met – friends of his brother's a few years older than himself; sparring partners and hunting companions – Diaz Sestran, in a ridiculous silver and orange doublet, and Leonic Bakran; and, oh Falla, there was Tanto himself, stumbling, red-faced and bleary-eyed, upending the last drops from a violet-coloured flask into his gullet.

Saro sighed and walked faster.

'Do you know them?' the girl asked curiously, staring at their antics. One of the Istrians had picked up an Eyran and was carrying him around on his shoulders. The Eyran, all long red hair and wolfish grin, brandished a wicked-looking knife.

'My brother, for one,' Saro said through gritted teeth.

'And you have no wish to join him?'

'None at all. I came here to avoid him.'

The girl laughed. 'He's enjoying himself far too much to notice you. Come on.'

Her grandfather's stall was festooned with chains and glittering objects, all set with milky-looking stones polished to a high gloss. The old man himself wore them on his hands, in his ears, on bands around his arm. There was even a single large moodstone in the middle of his forehead, suspended from a thin silver circlet and looking for all the world like a huge third eye. And while those on the stall were a pale, cloudy white, those worn by the old man swam with shades of soft sky-blue.

'Grandfather!'

'Guaya, my dear.' The old man's black eyes were small and round, as shiny as a robin's. He cocked his head to look at her, then cocked it the other way to regard Saro, as quick and intelligent as a little bird.

'This is my friend—?'

'Saro,' Saro supplied quickly.

'My friend Saro wants something for his lady mother.'

Saro smiled at the old man. She – Guaya – had called him 'friend', and though she was a little foreign girl of hardly more than twelve or thirteen, it made his heart feel large and warm in his chest.

'Guaya—' he stumbled over the pronunciation: in the nomad tongue it seemed to have too many syllables to it '—Guaya said your stones can change colour to match a person's emotions . . .'

Without a word, the old man picked out a pendant, a long, pear-shaped stone suspended via a simple setting from a fine silver chain. It was elegant and understated, and when he touched it, the stone took on the cloudy blues like those on his own hand. He held it out to Saro, and at once the colours swirled and changed to ochre and mustard yellow.

'You are happy at the moment, though your happiness underlies a deeper emotion: of anger, maybe or even fear.'

Saro stared at him.

Guaya leaned forward and took the necklace from him, and the ochres gave way almost immediately to a translucent gold. The old man laughed. 'She is a simple child, my Guaya; and very serene.'

'It's a lovely thing,' Saro said softly. He scanned the display, but the old man had been unerring in his choice. 'How much would you like for it?'

He was about to open his money-pouch and tip out the contents, when there was a louder cry from the adjacent stall, followed by a great crash and a lot of shouting.

'Something going on over there, Doc.'

'Looks like a spot of trouble, Joz.'

'Shall we wade in, Knobber?'

'Aye, may as well: always enjoy a bit of a ruck at an Allfair.'

'Never know who you might thump!'

'Coming, Mam?'

'Don't be stupid: we don't get paid for this sort of thing.'

'Suit yourself.'

'I fancy hammering one of them Istrian louts right in the chuds, I do.'

'Best be careful, Dogo: they're a fair bit bigger than you.'

'Here we go down the slippery slope, slippery slope, slippery slope . . .'

Lord Tycho Issian was passing through the fair, having finally found temporary relief at the hands of a dusky woman with shells threaded through her hair (though all the time she worked upon him all he could think of were a pair of pale hands and sea-green eyes), when he noticed a commotion at one of the liquor stalls. A pair of young men were at each other's throats; but luckily neither of them appeared to be armed. The tall fair one drew his fist back and got the Istrian youth a hard blow just under the ribs. When the Istrian boy – dressed in a strangely familiar bright pink garb – doubled up, the Eyran brought his knee up sharply and his opponent crumpled to the ground, clutching his crotch and whimpering. There was a moment of quiet, when it looked as if the incident might just blow over; as if someone might make a timely joke and everyone would return to their drinking, but into this unnatural calm the blond lad shouted, 'Take that for your bitch-goddess, you scum! Falla would spread her legs before Sur and bless him for the opportunity!'

Tycho stopped still. The blood rushed to his face, then drained again, leaving his usually walnut features as pale as a northman's.

At the stall, all hell broke loose. Drinking partners and companions in horseplay they might have been but a moment before; but now they were Istrians and Eyrans to a man: goddess-worshippers and followers of Sur: history and religion separate them more surely than language, culture and learn-ing: enemies for more than a hundred generations, through the rise and fall of dynasties, the destruction of cities, the desecration of shrines, they now recalled with hot passion the side to which they rightfully belonged, and laid about them with swift and stunning violence. Grudges harboured for two hundred years boiled swiftly to the surface: slights recalled from family tellings round the fire; lost grandfathers and wounded parents; fortunes sunk in war and debts owed for ever.

The stall went over with a great crash, the little nomad who owned it running like a cornered mouse this way and that, desperately trying to avoid the raining blows. Then, with a bellow, four men in weathered armour leapt into the fray and began throwing punches in a haphazard fashion, not seeming to care whether their targets were Eyran or Istrian. For a while, it seemed as though their uninvited intrusion might defuse the situation; but then a wild-haired youth had his belt-knife out and there was suddenly blood on the silver blade. An Istrian youth in an absurd silver and orange costume fell to the ground with his hands clasped to his abdomen. Sestran's younger son, Tycho realised with a start.

His own hand went to the dagger at his belt, but even as his fingers brushed the pommel, the fighting had surged back and engulfed another stall. Two northern youths stumbled backwards, pursued by four or five of the southerners. One of the Eyrans was the tall red-haired lad who had wounded the Sestran boy. He raised his knife hand – a threat, it seemed – but two of the southerners fell upon him and wrenched it away. A tall Istrian with short dark hair and a thick nose yelled in triumph and went for the Eyran with his own blade. The northerner tried for frantic evasion, but in doing so, backed into the jewellery seller's stall, which had partly been sheltering him.

'Saro!'

Guaya clutched his arm in terror, for suddenly there were brawling men everywhere. There was a high, thin wail of despair, and Saro whirled around just in time to see the old man disappear from sight as his stall overturned in a great flurry of boards and fabrics. Moodstones flew all around, and where they touched human skin flared to deepest crimson and wild purple, before falling, pale and cloudy once more to the ground.

A pair of combatants came crashing towards them, their faces contorted with hatred, their fists swinging wildly. Saro grabbed Guaya and thrust her behind him. He could feel how she trembled in his grasp, and then someone caught him a savage blow on the temple and he was down on the ground, with the black dust of the plain in his mouth and eyes, and feet all around him, on top of him, kicking and stamping. Where he had been struck, it felt as though his skull had swelled to twice its normal size, and each beat of his blood there felt like a tide. He tried to raise his head and felt an appalling wave of nausea sweep through him. Someone kicked him hard in the guts and he doubled up reflexively, retching and heaving. With a tremendous effort, he managed to roll under the remains of the moodstone-seller's stall, only to find himself face to face with the old man, whose blood ran freely down his face from a rough gash on his forehead. The moodstone there shone clear and limpid, a blue so pale as to be almost white in the midst of so much crimson.

'Grandfather!'

Suddenly, Guaya was on the ground beside him, with blood in her hair and her tunic half-ripped from her. Tears poured down her nut-brown cheeks. She cradled the old man's head on her lap. 'He's badly hurt: we must get him away from here.'

Saro nodded dumbly: it was about as much as he could manage. He closed his eyes and swallowed down the bile that rose in his throat. Then he hauled himself upright, using one of the stall's struts for support. The sight that met his eyes was astonishing. It looked like a battleground: two men lay writhing on the ground – one was Diaz Sestran, he realised with a chill of recognition; but the other was a young Eyran with light-brown hair and a braided beard. Blood spurted from a deep wound in his thigh. All around the two wounded men, a dozen or so youths were fighting in earnest – knives out, or with sticks in their hands – impromptu clubs taken from the broken stalls – and the air was heavy with bellows of rage and bloodlust.

He reached down and hauled the nomad to his feet. The old man felt as insubstantial as a bird: all skin and clusters of thin bones that felt as though they might snap like twigs under his hand. Guaya ran around the other side of her grandfather, wedging her shoulder under his armpit, and together they began to drag him away.

They would have succeeded, had a small man in boiled leather armour not cannoned into them as he tried to flee a tall young Istrian in a bright pink tunic, who was coming after him with his silver knife outstretched. The small man caught Saro by the arm, swinging him round, so that the moodstone-seller was wrenched from his grip and flung forward. There was the sodden, crunching sound of an impact, followed by a terrible wheezing cry, and by the time Saro had recovered himself, he found Guaya, her face distorted by grief and loathing, laying about his brother, Tanto, with her fists, and the old man lying on the ground with the silver knife buried to the hilt in his chest. Tanto was holding the child away from him, his fingers splayed wide across her forehead, a look of pure disgust on his face; then he pushed her savagely, turned, placed his foot on the old man's chest, retrieved his knife, and walked away. Saro, rooted to the spot, stared after him in disbelief.

The small man Tanto had been chasing vanished into the crowd.

With a terrible wail, Guaya fell, sobbing, across her grandfather's prone body. The old man moved a hand slowly to her face and cupped her cheek. His eyes were dull. Saro knelt beside them, shocked into uselessness. Where Tanto had withdrawn the dagger, bright-red blood pumped inexorably out of the wet hole, staining the nomad's white robe. Saro watched it with something approaching fascination, then slowly, instinctively, he pushed his hand against the gaping wound, trying to stem the flow. It pushed up between his fingers, fountains of it, thick and unstoppable. So much blood. He could not imagine any body held so much blood, let alone the body of such a frail, elderly man. He could feel the quick, thin pulse of the heart beneath the heel of his hand, fluttering away like a tiny bird in a cage. He pressed down again, harder. As he did so, the old man turned his head. His dark eyes bored into Saro's and the nausea rose in him again; different this time, more like dizziness or vertigo, and then the nomad placed his hand over the one Saro held upon his chest and whispered something in a language Saro could not understand, a language punctuated with little pressures of air that in a stronger man might have come out as whistling sounds: and then he died. Saro could tell the exact moment the nomad's spirit passed from him; not just by the way his eyes went unfocused and his mouth fell open, as if in some expression of regret; but when the moodstone on his forehead gave up all its colour, falling away through the sheerest of pastel shades to an eventual bleak and unmarked grey.

Saro felt his mind become a cool, clear pool of calm: a glacier lake; a mountain tarn, untroubled by the movements of men, its surface unbroken by the slightest ripple. All around, there was a moment of the utmost quietude; and then came a hubbub of sound. Out of the distant crowd rose the high-pitched wail of a grieving woman; the shouts of men, angry or horrified; the weeping of a child.

Saro lifted his head. Tanto was standing some distance away, his eyes blank and unresponsive. Beside him was Lord Tycho Issian, his hand on Tanto's shoulder: an approving hand, it seemed to Saro then, in that moment of clarity, rather than a restraining one. An old woman came running towards him, arms outstretched, tears streaking the paint on her face. She fell on her knees beside the dead man and began to cover his face with kisses. Suddenly embarrassed to be witness to such pain and intimacy, Saro stood up, and the blood ran off him in streams. His hands dripped with it.

He turned and started to walk away: away from the scene of death, away from his brother and the curious onlookers; but suddenly there was a hand upon his arm. As it gripped him, he was engulfed by a hot wash of sorrow; sorrow, and despair: someone had killed her grandfather, needlessly, wantonly, and then had walked away; he had died in front of her, all the light going out of his eyes. Fear, such fear: for now Grandmother would break her heart, and who would look after them both now, now that Grandfather was gone, dead and gone?

He blinked, shook his head. The hand fell away, and with it went the chaos of emotion, leaving him feeling like a fish cast up on a stormtide, weak and struggling for air in an unfamiliar element. He looked down. Guaya, the child, stood there before him, her eyes huge and brimming. She held her hand out. In it sat the moodstone pendant that Saro had chosen for his mother. In the child's palm the stone had taken on the blue of a winter sky, streaked with pale strands of purple, like the premonition of a sunset, and he knew at once that it marked both her grief and her fear; knew not from the stone, but from something inside himself, something new and unasked for; something that had entered him like an uninvited visitor.

'He said he wanted to give you a gift,' she said quietly. 'I think he meant this.'

Saro shook his head slowly. 'No,' he said. 'Not the necklace, that wasn't what he meant.' He smiled, and felt the tears come.

The child stared at him uncomprehending, then pushed the pendant into his hand nevertheless, and ran away.

Seven

Rose of the World

From the safety of his caravan in the nomad quarter, Virelai watched the fracas with interest and not a little fear. He saw the moodstone stall go over with a crash, and the old man disappear from view beneath a trample of angry feet. He saw how a small, fat mercenary – trying to escape the fury of a young Istrian almost twice his height, dressed in a vile pink tunic that had no doubt afforded the mercenary ample ammunition for the insult that had engaged the southerner's ire – had cannoned into old Hiron, spinning him around to meet the thrust of his pursuer's knife. All this had been extraordinary enough to someone raised in the swaddling confines of Sanctuary, where his entire experience of violence had been restricted to an occasional cuff around the ear. But witnessing the casual brutality with which the Istrian had then retrieved his dirtied weapon – setting his foot on the dead man's chest for leverage – he had felt both deeply agitated and yet at the same time perversely excited. The action had spoken of something deeper and darker than mere ferocity. It was at once fascinating and repellent. It spoke of insouciance at the value of a life; a fixation with self to the exclusion of all else; a rampant, intemperate egotism. Virelai had not believed men capable of such aberrant behaviour; he found himself unable to take his eyes off the man.

He watched as the killer strolled through the parted crowd to stand beside a noble dressed in plain, dark silks. With a

start, Virelai realised he recognised the man as the one who
had that very afternoon come to his stand offering money,
marriage – almost his soul – for the woman (if such she could
be termed) who even now lay quietly on the bunk behind
him. A man who had gone away empty-handed, with murder
in his eyes. What peculiar extremities of emotion these men
possessed, he thought: and each reaction so inappropriate to
the circumstances that had provoked them. They seemed an
entirely different genus of humanity to the nomads – diverse
though they were – with whom he had travelled these past
months. The Footloose – as the foreigners called them – were
placid people, gentle with one another: gentle even with the
lowest of their animals. In all these months he had seen no
nomad raise either voice or hand to another. These others
seemed in contrast turbulent: unstable, as vicious as the wild
dogs which had set upon the yeka calf they had lost in the
Plains, tearing it limb from limb as if to do the greatest
violence to the poor beast's flesh was a kind of reward
in itself.

And where the nomads lived cheerfully moment to
moment and hand to mouth, these others schemed and
planned and dreamed of the wealth and the power they
could amass, the way they could control others, manipulate
and exploit them and the world they shared. Virelai had
watched and learned. Their greed and their gullibility had
taken him by surprise, as had his own ingenuity. If the Master
had taught him anything, it was how to use his mind; and
he had been putting that ability to ferocious use. Using a
parody of Rahe's tone of cryptic authority in combination
with the glittering lumps of ore he had – on a whim? By
premonition? – taken from Sanctuary and the maps he had so
painstakingly copied from the collection he had brought from
the library, he had already gulled half a dozen treasure-hunters
and glory-seekers to undertake the hazardous voyage north.
Surely one of them might make it safely through the floes

and storms to the fastness and there strike down the old man forever? The terms of the geas Rahe had laid on his head and repeated each year on what he referred to, with a mocking smile, as Virelai's 'life-day', prevented him from killing the Master himself, augmented as it was by the vile images the mage sent into his mind of tortures by faceless demons, howling wastes, endless agonies . . . Sending the old man into a long, long sleep, however, until someone else could complete the task seemed to circumnavigate the prohibitions of the curse nicely.

But what to do with the Rosa Eldi? There was profit to be had there; profit and power, if he could only think clearly . . .

As if his thoughts had brushed her mind, the figure behind him began to stir.

'What is it, Lai?' The woman rose up in a single supple motion, to peer over his shoulder out of the door. The cat, unseen somewhere in the darkness of the wagon, began to purr. 'What have you seen?'

Fronds of her white-blonde hair brushed his cheek, causing him to shiver. He could not help himself. The shiver went through skin and muscle, fibre and bone and proceeded to root itself firmly in his groin.

Time for another draught of the brome, he thought grimly, *to keep her diabolical attraction at bay*. He had found the oat-grass extract was the only remedy for the appalling burning he otherwise had to endure in her presence. It was lucky that the further he had gone from Sanctuary, the better his potions worked, as if the Master's grip upon him waned with every mile travelled. A pity that the Rosa Eldi's power had not followed the same pattern. The boat-trip had been the worst, for then he had no brome with which to dose himself. It was his own fault, he rebuked himself, for taking her away in the first place, and then for opening the damned box, rather than simply dropping it over the side, or trading it to the first merchant he happened upon when he came into port. In the end, he'd lifted the lid during a particularly bored period at sea: with magic fanning the sails and the yowling of the cat finally quietened by a twist of cloth about its muzzle, he had had nothing else to occupy him than to fantasise about the creature he had stolen.

One sight of those extraordinary eyes as they fixed themselves upon him, and he had been lost to her, overcome by unstoppable lust. The problem was, even if she had been willing – and oddly enough she had shown him no antipathy – his own body did not seem to be equipped to carry out the act he craved. This had been a strange discovery for him after such a long, isolated and innocent existence. For while the sight and the presence of her made his entire body flame with need, a fire that focused itself most precisely in his groin, the flesh there refused in the Rosa Eldi's presence to rise to his need, remaining pale and flaccid ever since he had first touched her in the Master's chamber. It was, he thought, a mystery: damnably odd, and damnably unfair. Even more unfairly, the cat had proved to be in this particular instance quite useless. Extraordinary, really, considering the quantity of magic it contained. If it had not been for the oat-grass, and the nomad healer who had sympathetically suggested it, he would surely have gone out of his mind.

'Nothing to see now,' he said, extricating himself with care to avoid further dangerous contact. 'There was a fight and someone was killed.'

The sea-green eyes went wide. Virelai looked quickly away.

'Killed?' She frowned. 'Made dead?'

Her understanding of such concepts was still remarkably limited, despite all his efforts to educate her; and even her ability to speak and understand the Old Tongue had been patchy, as if the Master had decided it not to be a valuable trait in one whom he used as he did.

'Yes, made dead,' he returned flatly.

'Who was it?' She was avid now: he could tell from the tone of her voice. It was odd, he reflected, that she had somehow learned the ability to intonate, while her teacher's utterances remained defiantly inflectionless, no matter how he tried to remedy the matter.

'It was Hiron Sea-Haar, the moodstone-seller.'

'How came he by his death?'

'He was stabbed through the heart by a young Istrian; or rather, he ran onto the knife.'

She considered this for a moment.

'Cannot you do something for him?' she said at last.

Virelai turned and regarded her curiously, mentally prepared for the jolt such a glance would afford him. 'I am not the Master,' he said softly. 'In case you had forgotten.'

She smiled then, and the upturned lips dimpled her cheeks sweetly. 'I had not forgotten that,' she said. 'How should I?' She picked up the cat and cradled it against her. Two pairs of lambent green eyes regarded him dispassionately.

'Look at the pair of you! Blood and tatters and stinking to high haven of araque and piss. You're a disgrace, to yourselves, and to the Rockfall clan.'

Aran Aranson strode up and down the booth, his face thunderous, his brows making a single black line across his forehead.

'Tor: as the elder and as my fosterson I expect you to have learned better than to behave thus while under my care; and as for you, Fent, I am pained to find yet again that I cannot trust you further than I can see you. I had thought after last year's Allfair you might have learned your lesson; but, no. Quite apart from your behaviour in the nomad quarter, you left your brother in charge of the sardonyx for the entire afternoon; and for that you shall forfeit your share in today's takings, small as they are.'

Fent, chastened, hung his head, which just made it throb all the worse, for the drink, and for the blow he had taken in the midst of the brawl, which had left a swelling the size of a puffin's egg on his temple. Tor, however, continued to stare at a point just over his fosterfather's left shoulder. His eyes gleamed. Katla had the sense that he was relishing this scene as much as he had the drink and the fighting.

'You do not seem to realise that conflict with the Istrians is the last thing Eyra can afford right now. Our resources are low: we are still recovering from our last bloody war, and our king is young and untried and surrounded by adventurers and politicians. And you charge in and start a fight with a group of wealthy Istrian youths. If we don't have blood-price to pay, we'll be lucky—'

'We didn't start the fight,' Tor said flatly, moving his stony eyes from the back of the tent to his fosterfather's furious face. 'It was already in progress.' He smiled, remembering with sudden pleasure the grunt of pain he had won from the Istrian boy in pink. 'We just waded in to help our friends.'

Fent, knowing this to be a downright lie, stared harder at the ground between his feet.

Aran held Tor's gaze for a few grim seconds. The air was full of menace. Katla found herself holding her breath: so when the voices came outside the tent, she was almost relieved.

Almost.

The doorflap opened to reveal a pair of Allfair guards, swords unsheathed. They wore the blue cloaks that marked them as law-keepers, but both were Istrian in appearance, with cleanshaven chins and dark eyes. All the guards at the Fair this year were Empire-born. In this, his first year at the Allfair as King, Ravn had failed to provide an Eyran contingent. There had been some muttering amongst the northern traders at such a lack, but to Katla's mind officials were officials, whatever their provenance.

'We are looking for three perpetrators,' the first guard intoned in heavily-accented Old Tongue, stepping into the tent. 'Two are believed to be Eyran. There was a fight in the nomad quarter and a young Istrian has been badly wounded. We are looking for the man who did it.'

'He had red hair,' the second added smoothly, staring over his colleague's shoulder straight at Katla, who sat closest to the door.

Fent, in the shadows, made a move to step forward, but Tor held his arm.

Katla stood up. 'Do I look as if I've been in a brawl?' she asked sarcastically. Bundles of coloured ribbons and pretty beads showered down from her lap. 'I've been buying trinkets for the Gathering.'

The second official coloured, but the first, unperturbed, declared with a thin smile: 'The second perpetrator we seek is a young Eyran who committed a sacrilege upon Falla's Rock.'

Katla felt her heart thump with sudden force. 'A sacrilege?' she repeated stupidly.

'A crime punishable by burning.'

Tor strode out of the shadows. 'Don't intimidate this young woman any further,' he said forcibly, stepping between the Istrians and Katla. 'She is not the one you seek, I am.'

The second guard looked him up and down. 'Your hair is yellow,' he said sharply. 'So you do not fit the description of he who wounded Diaz Sestran. And witnesses say the one who climbed the Rock was a woman.'

Tor made a gross curtsey. 'At your service.'

The officials exchanged glances.

'You waste our time with such mockery,' the first one said angrily, staring past Tor into the booth. 'It is not appreciated.'

Aran picked up a stoneware flask and came into the light. 'I regret young Tor's irreverence,' he said solemnly, extending the flask. 'As you can see, he fits neither description. Please take this flask of stallion's blood in recognition of your wasted time and as a token of fellowship at this Fair.'

The first man took it and sniffed suspiciously, and his head recoiled. He passed the flask to his companion. 'What is this?' he demanded. 'Horse piss?'

Tor guffawed.

'It is the best wine in the northern isles,' Aran said stiffly.

The second guard took a hefty swallow and choked. He wiped his mouth, shook his head, and laughed. 'If this is the best liquor Eyra can produce, then you have my sympathy, friend. For that and for your idiot son.' He turned on his heel and walked off. Light from the dipping sun shone suddenly, redly, into the tent and fell square upon Katla.

The first official regarded her curiously. 'Your hair is cut in a most barbarous fashion,' he observed rudely.

Katla swallowed. 'Indeed. But it is the fashion in our islands, especially in the hot season.'

The man continued to look at her. His eyes were dark and unblinking. Katla, used to the clear, light eyes of the men of the northern isles, found his gaze unnerving, but she held it all the same. At last he shrugged, then smiled crookedly. 'For all that, you have a pretty face. If there is to be dancing at the Gathering, perhaps you will share a reel with me.' Then he was gone.

Katla stared after him, speechless.

'Hot season!' laughed Aran. 'In Eyra? It's a good job the man's an idiot.'

'Aye,' said Tor. 'Pretty face, indeed.'

By the time Tanto Vingo returned to the family pavilion, he was no longer wearing the cerise tunic which would have marked him out so unmistakably from the other Istrians, but a doublet of midnight blue donated to him by Lord Tycho Issian in a gesture, Tanto felt, of true familial solidarity. Well, they were very nearly related now, and would be as soon as the Allfair was over and the bride-price paid over. Two good tunics lost in one day. Still . . . He fingered the fine silk. It was a rather sober garment for his taste, but it was excellently tailored and exquisitely finished. He imagined it in a lighter shade of Jetra blue, could see – as clear as day – how he would stroll through the Council chambers while the other nobles bowed and whispered their admiration. *Lord Tanto Vingo, heir to the Cantara estates.* It had a certain pleasing sound to it. Almost took his mind off the dull ache in his groin where that damned Eyran had kneed him so hard.

'Father, Uncle—' he greeted them with a wide grin, and was surprised to see them turn to him with anxious, strained faces. Oh Falla, he thought, they've heard about the old man. 'It wasn't my fault—' he started.

'Heavens, no, son, we know that. Not your fault at all.'

'Come and sit with us, lad,' Fabel said gruffly, patting the tapestried settle beside him. 'Best prepare yourself for a bit of a shock.'

Tanto frowned. Perhaps this wasn't about the old nomad after all.

His father leaned forward solicitously and touched him on the knee. 'I'm sorry, Tanto. There's been a bit of a setback. On the money front, you see.'

Tanto stared at him. 'What?' A suspicion started to seep coldly into the pit of his stomach.

Favio grimaced at his brother, then turned to his son. 'The Council have called in the loan they made us last year. It was supposed to run for five; but something must be afoot . . .'

'What your father means, Tanto, is that we don't seem to have enough money for the settlement—'

'We could perhaps trade him some more of the land, Fabel: perhaps the land west of Felin's Bluff—'

'But that would cut right into my breeding grounds, Favio—'

'I know, brother, I know, but what else can we *do*? This is Tanto's future we're talking of here: the future of the Vingo family, the future of our name carried on through the generations to wealth and glory.'

'You know as well as I do, *brother*, that it's not the land he's after, Lord Tycho: he's up to his neck in debt – he owes the Treasury a small fortune from what I've heard: why do you think he'd trade his daughter to us so readily? He's not just desperate to ally himself with our oh-so-aristocratic family: he needs the money! And if they've called in our debt you can bet on Falla's tits they've called in his, too. If he doesn't get the money from us, he'll sell his daughter to the next bidder who comes along offering him ready cantari, not some poxy patch of pine trees.'

'Excuse me, I *am* here: the subject of this rare discussion you're having. Me, Tanto Vingo, your nephew, *your* son. So don't keep on talking about me as if I don't exist.' Tanto glared at his uncle and father in turn. 'Are you saying you can't afford the bride-price for Selen Issian?'

His father nodded dumbly.

Tanto was outraged. 'By the bitch, how dare you put me in this position?' He plucked hysterically at the silk doublet. 'My future father-in-law has just given me this fine item of clothing as a token of goodwill, and you're telling me there's no *money*?'

His uncle lifted his arms in what was meant as a placatory gesture, but Tanto turned upon him as if to strike him. Fabel, a good hand's breadth shorter than his nephew, cowered away. 'We're very sorry, Tanto: really. If there was anything else we could do—' he shrugged.

Tanto lowered his fist. 'Well that's tupped it then, hasn't it?' he said viciously. 'No bride, no title, no future, all because of your total, useless bloody incompetence.'

At this ill-timed point, Saro entered the pavilion.

Tanto whirled around, eyes bulging. 'What do you want, you little bastard? Come to gloat, have you?'

Saro stared at him, uncomprehending. The last time he had seen his brother he had been wiping an old man's blood off his Forent blade, as if cleaning horse-shit from his shoe; but this argument did not sound like an interrogation of his brother as a discovered murderer; rather it seemed to be Tanto who was filled with righteous anger against their father and Uncle Fabel.

Favio took a step towards him. 'Best go for a walk, son, till we've finished this discussion,' he said, ushering Saro outside again.

Canvas was a poor barrier to sound: clearly it was for the sake of propriety and to prevent further outbursts of his brother's evil temper that he had been shooed away. From outside the tent, Saro could hear perfectly well what was going on, and he could not help but smile. Not enough money to complete the bride-settlement, an embarrassing situation indeed. There was a sudden lull between the raised voices, then the doorflaps were flung outward and Tanto emerged, his face red and his eyes bulging with fraught emotion.

Saro sat quickly down and gave his attention to a broken strap on his shoe. Uncharacteristically, his brother pitched himself down beside him.

'Incompetent fools! Do they had no financial foresight at all?'

Saro glanced up, but the remark seemed to have been cast into the air, rather than at him. Tanto tugged with preoccupied fingers at his choker of sardonyx and added: 'There's seven thousand cantari still to be found, so now I shall *have* to win the swordplay, and you, brother, will need to ride that colt as if your life depended on it.'

Saro stared at him. 'What?'

'The yearlings' race. There's a big prize resting on it, and I'll need the money.'

'But—' Saro's thoughts raced faster than any horse. Night's Harbinger certainly stood a fine chance: he was fleet and well-schooled, but rather than race him they had planned to breed him, so his schooling was for treading imperiously round the ring with his head held to show off his best points, rather than for fighting it out with a field of other stallions. He'd heard tales about the races they held at Allfair, too: horses dead of stampede, wounded from gouges and bites; riders with broken limbs and crushed ribs – not that the riders mattered in such a race; it was the horses that were counted victors. He shook his head. 'Sorry, Tanto. If you want to race him, that's your business – you can discuss it with Father.'

He had expected bullying bluster at his refusal, but instead Tanto's tone was wheedling. He craned his neck up at Saro and made his voice like honey. Saro had seen him use the same trick, over and over, on the slavegirls. Sometimes it worked.

'For me, brother, please, for all of us. The future well-being of our entire family rests on this one alliance. Think how proud mother will be, how delighted to see me married and with estates of my own—'

He reached over and grasped Saro's arm. All at once, Saro found himself infused with emotions not his own: rapacious greed, a barely-quelled fury, a seething unarticulable, childish violence, and something darker still, and deeper buried. He looked away from his brother's handsome, intent face and his glance fell to the object he still clutched. The moodstone glowed in his palm, an unperturbed and steadfast golden-green. He shook Tanto's hand away and stood up before his brother could spy the gem.

'I'll do it,' he found himself saying, and was surprised at his own decision. 'But only in exchange for a promise.'

'Anything, brother.'

'If I win the prize for you, you may take one half of the money for the bride-settlement. The other half you must take yourself to the old nomad woman whose husband you killed and give it to her as blood-price.'

Tanto stared at him in disbelief. His mouth fell open. Then he began to laugh. 'You cannot be serious, brother. For that old man? A blood-price, as one would pay for a fallen warrior? For some wizened old beggar with no family name? I'd be a fool.'

You are a fool. The thought went unspoken, but all the same Saro knew it to be true. A cruel, wilful and selfish fool: he had seen the turmoil of his brother's mind, all focused on a single, shallow intent.

'Even so, this is my price for riding the race for you.'

Tanto's eyes narrowed. His little brother, whom he had bullied successfully for so many years, standing up to him thus, all steely faced? It was insupportable. His mind made furious calculations. Two and a half thousand for the swordplay; one and a half for the archery, if he won both events. Take only a place, and he was in trouble. Falla damn them all, he needed the little bastard to win the horserace, and to have three of the four thousand that prize afforded. To the fires with the old man's family . . .

Tanto Vingo looked his brother directly in the eye and grinned.

'I promise,' he lied.

Lord Tycho Issian lay upon his cushion-strewn couch, staring up into the heights of the coloured taffeta hangings. A glass of cloudy araque lay on the carved wooden table beside him, untouched. Eyes opened or closed, that woman's face was always before him now, pale and delicate, her mouth as full of promise as a flower bud. Her hair, the fairest gold. Her hands, those long, tapered fingers, would feel so silky and cool upon his—

The fires flooded through him again.

He had tried prayer, to no avail whatsoever: each time he conjured the goddess into his mind, it was with the nomad woman's face, and sacred turned disturbingly, heretically profane. He had tried cold baths: but even the rough towel had raised his passion again; even the air evaporating off his skin became in his inflamed mind the brush of her mouth upon him. He had never known such torment.

At last, he flung his cloak over him, and, without a word to the slaves who stood guard at the door, strode out into the darkness and headed for the nomad quarter once more.

King Ravn Asharson reclined upon his sea-chest, his head resting uncomfortably against the frame of the booth and listened to his earls bickering. His men were out in the field, helping to erect the great pavilion ready for the Gathering. He had much rather be with them, hauling ropes and calculating angles than bored out of his wits by politics. Succeeding to the throne after the death of his illustrious father this last year had provided little in the way of benefit and much of tedium and what others referred to as 'statecraft', in which he found himself barely interested and not at all gifted.

'But I tell you we cannot trust the word of these Istrian lords,' the Earl of Stormway was saying heatedly. 'They have reasons for selling their daughters to the King – and that in itself is strange enough, and entirely against their own custom, for they regard their women so highly it is the men who pay the bride-price in Istria. Something's going on, mark my words. My theory is that they're after using us to forge a passage to the Far West: they need us only to brave the seas and chart the navigations for them, then they'll turn upon us like dogs. An empire's a hungry beast to feed: no doubt they've burned all their spare slaves to their bitch-goddess by now. Ravn needs a good Eyran wife, a strong, straight-speaking woman like Queen Auda, not some tricksy southerner.'

'The Lord of Jetra's offer is very fine, though,' countered Earl Forstson. 'Bales of silk, and gems, and those fine ceramics—'

The Earl of Southeye laughed. 'What a woman you are, Egg. Fine ceramics! All beakers shatter when thrown in the fire, say I.'

Egg Forstson, Earl of Shepsey, rubbed his bald head miserably and applied himself to the wine. It was foul stuff, in comparison with the mellow reds of the south, but it was all they had. Money was tight in the northern court: he had better supplies in his own tent, having come to the Allfair largely to savour the luxuries Istria and the travelling folk had to provide: it took a lot to persuade him to undertake that sea-crossing these days.

'I notice none of them are offering Forent steel as part of their trade,' observed Stormway.

'Aye: keeping that for themselves, as ever.'

'I'd welcome another chance to show them what a bit of iron can do,' said the Earl of Stormway dourly. 'Only a spring lad, I was, when Forent steel took this.' He hefted his left arm, which ended in a stump of leather. 'Always keep an eye out for the man who wielded that blade.'

Egg Forstson frowned. Talk of the old war was agitating, the memories still ached like a fading bruise. He'd been wedded only two years when the call-up had come: two years and two bonny babes, a third on the way (for what good Eyran would wait for the marriage rites before bedding his maid?) and he'd been off onto the high seas with the old King's warfleet. He'd survived sea-sickness and starvation, storm and shipwreck; arrow and spear and sword and a dozen minor wounds, and had returned to Eyra four years later feeling fortunate to be alive. Fortunate, that was, till he'd arrived back at the steading to find it long deserted, the roof all burned off and the skeletons of slaughtered animals littering the farmyard. They'd never found his wife and children: gone

for slaves in the southern markets was the favoured opinion,
and ever after the uneasy truce had been agreed he had
scoured the slave blocks each year at the Allfair in the hopes
of finding his beloved Brina again. But how to tell, when the
women were all so swathed? And the children would now
be fully grown, if they still lived. He imagined his baby girls
as adult women, but the image slipped away. As for the third
child, he had not even known its sex. Yet at every Allfair, his
eye would be drawn by a chance movement, a sway of hip, a
gesture of hand, a tilt of head, and his heart would rise; every
year his hopes would be dashed. He imagined, over and over,
how they might live now, in a foreign country with a warm
climate and fair houses, away from the storm-wracked strands
of the north with its turf-roofed houses and sturdy keeps, and
over the years as the pain passed to memory he came to look
upon the trappings of Istrian living with a proprietorial eye,
rather than that of a man who had lost all he loved. Had Brina
touched this plate, this glass? Had she marvelled at the fine
blue glaze of Jetra's pottery as he did? Did his children retain
any memory of Eyra at all, or did they speak like natives of
Istria, all lilting accents and soft sibilance? He wondered what
he would do if he did find any of them, remote though that
possibility now seemed. Would he bargain politely with the
blockmaster, haggling for the best price? Or charge into the
fray in a bloodlust, to take back what was his own by main
force? Or, he sometimes pondered, would he simply close
his eyes on the sight, and walk away?

'—Egg?'

It was the King's voice. His head came up with a start.

'What think you to the daughter of Earl Fall Herinson?'

'A very comely maid, my lord.'

Ravn laughed at this careful avoidance. He knew Egg's
opinion already: that Ragna was a pretty, opportunistic little
minx, and that he, Ravn, bore poor comparison in either
character or potential to his deceased father, King Ashar

Stenson, and was a fool when it came to the wiles of women. 'Aye. She is that. Still, it wouldn't do, I suppose?' Ragna's father, Fall Herinson, was an ineffectual drunk who had pissed away his noble inheritance and was unlikely to create difficulties, but equally unlikely to have anything more useful to offer than his daughter's maidenhood. And that was long lost . . . He looked hopefully around the gathered lords. Stormway looked as grim as ever. Ravn knew he still harboured hopes for his own daughter, a twenty-three-year-old brute of a girl unfortunate enough to be saddled with the square chin and beetling brow of her father, but he hadn't had the heart to tell Stormway he had rather wed his prize mare than take the old man's daughter to bed. There were other nobles jockeying for position, he knew that well enough – his cousin Erol Bardson, for one, hoping to marry his blood back into the royal line; his dead father's adviser, Earl Keril Sandson for another, a man with eyes too close for comfort; and any number of others who'd no doubt present their warm and willing daughters and dowries to him at the Gathering in exchange for some preferment or advancement at court. It was a dangerous game, this marriage business. Dangerous, yet dull: all the women – at least, all those he had not yet had – were sows; their male relatives rutting boars waiting to tusk him at an opportune moment and take the throne for themselves.

'No, sire,' Southeye said firmly. 'The coffers need filling. Bed her if you must; but wed her, no.'

Ravn sighed. This was going to be a tedious process. Not helped by the fact that the Istrian women were so wrapped about with fabric that you could barely tell whether they were fat or thin, keen or chaste. He liked the touch with the lips, though, all painted up to high heaven: that slash of colour in the midst of all the sombre robes. Did the Istrians have any idea how suggestive was that gesture, how lewd in its implications? He doubted it: they were a dull lot, too, more interested in commerce and their grim religion than the real pleasures life had to offer. Their women could probably do with a taste of the north: a bit of rollicking good fun, instead of the pained, pretentious pawings of their insipid husbands. He hadn't yet bedded a southern woman: it was almost worth taking one to wed just for the novelty value . . .

'My lord—'

There was a ruckus at the door.

He looked up to find that two young men had entered the tent, one, tall and flaxen-haired, supporting the other, a thin young man with long light-brown hair that had come free of its braids, whose entire right leg, though wound with makeshift bandages, was drenched with blood.

At once Southeye was off his bench. 'Thuril! By Sur, lad, what happened?'

'A scratch with an Istrian pin, Father, that's all,' the wounded boy replied, smiling weakly, and promptly fainted.

'Istrians . . . drunk . . . in the nomad quarter,' the flaxen-haired lad offered, short of breath. 'A fight . . .' he added, unnecessarily.

The Earl gathered his son into his arms. Ravn, roused at last by the prospect of something practical to do, was already out of the door and shouting for the royal ship's healer.

The remaining lords exchanged anxious glances. Uncharacteristically, it was Egg Forstson, rather than the superstitious Stormway, who recalled the old saying: 'Blood shed at the Fair marks the pattern for the year: lose one life, and there's strife: more and there's war.'

Aran Aranson, in the privacy of the curtained part of the Rockfall booth late that night listened to the regular breathing of his clan-members, then removed the map he had come by that afternoon from the interior of his tunic and turned it this way and that under the wavering light of his taper. It was, he concluded again, a most beautiful piece of work. It was not just the unusual use of the various coloured inks – violets and blues for the ocean depths, greens for the coastlines and scarlet for the landmarks – that commanded his admiration, but the extraordinary precision of the letters and the lines the map-maker had drawn. The handwriting was tiny, barely even legible, especially to one not well versed in reading; but each tiny indentation in the coastline promised a secret bay, each jagged line an outcrop or reef. But it was the rather vaguer markings towards the top of the map that drew his eye most seductively, for there, marked by the broken lines that suggested a shifting seaboard, amid an ocean labelled at intervals with the single word – 'ice' – lay the prize itself: '*Sanctuarii*', the land of gold.

Almost unconsciously, his fingers went to the lump of mineral weighing heavy in the pouch against his hip.

Despite the late hour, there were still many revellers abroad in the nomad quarter: it seemed to be the place where all those seeking recreation had come, for the rest of the fairground was still and quiet. Recreation, and re-creation: Tycho Issian had made a momentous decision about his life. He would gamble all he had on one throw of the dice, in a single reckless gesture, and as long as he achieved the outcome he craved, he cared nothing for the rest of the world.

Desperation drove his stride. He elbowed his way through a tangle of folk watching a Footloose woman swallowing, in a particularly lewd fashion, dozens of flaming daggers tossed to her by a tattooed man in vast pantaloons, averted his eyes from a brace of painted prostitutes who were cackling and whistling at him through the gaps in their teeth (one of them, he realised in dismay, seeing the glint of white shells in her hair, was the woman whose services he had availed himself of earlier that day), then was diverted from his crow's path by a large crowd gathered about what appeared to be some kind of freak show. Horrified (for those who devoutly worshipped Falla believed

in the perfection of the human form – deformed babies in the
far south of the country were routinely given to the Goddess,
left out by night on the high, cold hillsides, where inevitably
they gave up their ghosts to the starlight) he found himself
suddenly transfixed by the sight of an armless child balanced
precariously upon a two-headed yeka calf. Gripping the beast
with its knees, it manoeuvred the yeka in neat, swift circles,
stepping in and out of a course of red ribbons laid in devious
patterns upon the ground, all the while grinning delightedly
as the crowd erupted in enthusiastic applause. A small, round
man in battered leather, with a silver ring through one ear and
a gleaming stud in his nose, laughed loudly and laid claim to
another pile of his companion's coins.

Tycho looked away. To gamble thus on such a freak of
nature seemed at best perverse, at worst a deadly affront to
the Goddess. Not the best omen for his own venture.

It was with some trepidation that he arrived at the map-
seller's wagon. The money he had brought as a token of his
good faith clinked against his thigh. The wagon, however,
was in darkness. He walked around it, tried to peer through
the curtained windows, but there was no sign of life. Except
that, when he returned to the front of the wagon, having
made his circumnavigation, there was a large black cat sitting
alertly on the steps. He stared at it. The cat, unblinking, stared
back, but when he put a hand out to it (he did not know why:
he did not like cats at all) it stood away from him on its toes
and all the fur on the top of its head rose into a fearsome-
looking crest, which then proceeded to extend down the
length of its back – now rounded into a tight arch – and
spiked its long, snaking tail. It began to hiss.

Tycho took a step backward, and collided with the map-
seller, who had appeared, as silent as a spirit, behind him.

'I do not think the cat likes you, sir,' the map-seller said
in his peculiarly flat voice.

Tycho bit back the retort that formed behind his teeth.

'No. It seems not,' he said instead, giving the man a curt nod.

'It is usually a good judge of character,' the map-seller went on, reaching to pick the cat up and for once it was cooperative, lying in his hands as limp as a towel, but its ears twitched with annoyance and it regarded Tycho warily. The man opened the door to the wagon, and shooed the cat inside. It disappeared into the darkness without a backward look.

Tycho cleared his throat. 'I have come to make a bargain with you, map-seller,' he said, somewhat portentously.

The pale man observed him wordlessly. Then he smiled. The smile made Tycho feel uncomfortable. It was like watching a slick of scented oil spread across the surface of water in a bowl: something which floated on the skin, but had no deeper connection.

Tycho hastily untied his money-pouch and extended it to the map-seller. The man's glance dropped to the pouch, but he made no move to take it from Tycho's hand.

'A down-payment,' Tycho said quickly, before he regretted his decision.

The man quirked an eyebrow. 'Ah, yes?'

'For the woman,' Tycho hurried on. 'I will give you twenty thousand cantari for her at the end of this Fair. Take this as a deposit upon the full sum: there's five thousand in the bag.'

Five thousand cantari was a huge sum in itself: you could purchase a herd of yeka for five thousand cantari; build a villa; buy a stretch of prime land. For twenty thousand, you could raise a small castle, keep a standing army. Tycho had never had twenty thousand cantari in his hands, or even with his banker, at any one point in his life. It was a large fortune. It was exactly the sum he expected to acquire by the end of the Allfair, having traded his daughter to the boorish, but very rich, Vingo boy. Once the Council had been repaid, he would have cleared a comfortable thirteen thousand . . .

He pushed the debt from his mind, and it fled willingly. Madness: this was madness, but he could not help himself.

The map-seller's face had become oddly blank. Was it the face of a card-player judging the odds, Tycho wondered, or was he shocked into stillness? Either way, he decided to press home his point.

'It is a very great sum of money, map-seller,' he said, pointing out the obvious. 'You could not make so much in a hundred Fairs.'

The man cocked his head. 'Where is your land, Istrian lord?' he asked.

It was an impudent question from a nomad. Outrageous, even. But Tycho cared little for etiquette now. 'In the far south, bordering the mountains.'

The map-seller's face became even more blank as if this consideration used all his reserves. Then he gave a little nod as if confirming something to himself. Then he took the pouch from the Istrian's outstretched hand, weighed it consideringly, peered inside, and slipped it into his voluminous robes, where it disappeared without a sound.

'I will accept your offer,' the man said tonelessly, and Tycho's heart leapt, 'but on one condition.'

'Anything.'

'For your twenty thousand cantari you win yourself not only the most beautiful woman in the world, but also the services of myself and my cat—' The man swept a low bow. 'We cannot be separated, you see.'

Tycho frowned. What did he want with a map-seller, let alone his flea-ridden animal?

The man smiled again. 'I can see the question framing in your mind,' he said softly. 'But we have our uses, Bëte and I. And I could not let the Rosa Eldi slip out into the world unaccompanied. It would be most . . . dangerous.'

'I would protect her with my life.'

'That, sir, is not what I meant.'

The man held his gaze in a disconcerting fashion until Tycho looked away. 'As you wish then,' he said briskly, doubts crowding in upon him. 'You have the money as a token of my good faith: may I see the woman for a few minutes in token of your own?'

'A moment.'

The pale man opened the door and slipped inside. There was a creaking sound, a rustle of fabric, then the low murmur of voices. A light came on in the interior of the wagon. The man reappeared, then turned and made a beckoning motion to the figure behind him. Tycho, who had rather hoped to be allowed to enter the wagon and share some minutes with the woman in its privacy, felt acutely disappointed, but all traces of regret vanished as the woman appeared, her eyes as round and black as the cat's in the fitful light. She turned her head slowly towards the Istrian lord and regarded him, for the first time, full on. He thought his heart would burst the bounds of his ribs, it thundered so hard. His blood boiled in his ears, his face, his chest. He tried to smile at her, to allay her anxieties at such a bizarre situation, but found he could not. Instead, he found himself walking towards her like a man in a trance. When he was but a step away, his hands reached up and cupped her lovely face. He found it easier to kiss her with his eyes tight shut. As soon as their mouths met, her tongue flicked between his lips, as if she knew his whole desire. The sensation was so unexpected, so beyond description, that it turned his knees to water, his groin to fire, but when eventually he pulled away, he found her gaze upon him, full and intense, and knew that her eyes had been open all the while.

Eight

Rumours

During the next day or so, the Fair was lively and for the most part well-tempered. Business went on with alacrity in the Istrian and Eyran sectors, deals were done and transactions completed, family alliances were sealed and goods were sold. As ever, folk took their pleasure in the nomad quarter; but everywhere you went there was a sense of indefinable tension in the air, as if strong words were about to be spoken, fists might fly, or tears might flow.

For those with sharp ears and the curiosity to listen, there were also many snippets of interesting conversation to be overheard:

'They say the northern king will take the Lady of Jetra to wed—'

'Many would see that as a sacrilege, to send one of the Goddess's own into pagan lands—'

'Aye, well maybe it won't come to that.'

'How do you mean? Everyone is saying he'll take the Swan . . .'

'Ah, well when he comes to take her,' the voice drops to a whisper, 'there may be soldiers waiting.'

'To do what? Surely even the Empire is not so arrogant it believes it can murder the northern king on sacred ground and come away unscathed?'

'Not murder, no. Not from what my sources tell me.'

'Then what?'

'Have you noticed how the Council is calling in its debts at this Fair?'

'I had: truly I was far from pleased when they came to me with their request. Early repayment, indeed. We settled on fifteen thousand now and the rest at Harvest month; but I had another two years to go on the loan, so I am not a happy man. But what has this to do with the northern king? Surely he does not expect us to pay him a bride-price, when he is stealing away our finest and best?'

'Ah, no, I think not. Let's just say the temptation of reaching the treasures of the Far West may be proving too much for our beloved Council.'

'And the northern king is putting together an expedition . . .'

'Exactly.'

'If Ravn takes Keril Sandson's daughter, we shall have to move fast.'

'I have spoken with the leader of a band of freeswords: his price was most . . . reasonable.'

'I've heard tell of a place where even the chamberpots are made of purest gold.'

'I do not know why everyone is so ridiculously fired up by all this talk of the Far West. We'd do better to mine the ores out of our own mountains.'

'Oh ho, you don't want to venture too far into those. Monsters up there, I've heard: someone saw a giant with the head of wolf up there only the other week; aye, and huge flying lizards, too.'

'The stories you believe! Truly, you are a gullible man, Pasto. You'd believe tin was silver and brass was gold.'

'I would not.' The voice was indignant. 'But I do believe there are great riches to be had by those who are adventurous of spirit.'

'Someone's been putting words in your mouth. For all we know, the Far West may be as poor as the rest of the world by now.'

'Who said anything about the Far West?'

'Oh, there's another legendary land of treasure, is there? Another wild-goose chase for you to take us all off on? Haran, your eyes have gone as sly as a stoat's—'

'I have a map.'

'Some of these Istrian lads are fair to look upon.'

'They are beardless wonders.'

'I liked the dark one with the choker of sardonyx.'

'They're all dark, idiot. Which one do you mean?'

'The one who took the archery prize. He looked like Great Horin the Hunter when he pulled that bow. His skin was like polished cherrywood. You could have seen the definition of every muscle in his torso when he flexed his arm—'

''Tis time you took a husband, Fara, and no mistake.'

'I had an odd one a couple of days back, Felestina.'

'An odd man: now there's a wonder.'

'Truly, though: he was so hard that I was quite concerned for my well-being. Hard as a rock, and just about as responsive. And what was really strange was that within a moment of our finishing, he was ready for more . . .'

'Some of these Istrian lords are as horny as goats. It's their religion, you know. Stifles their natural urges till they're mad for it.'

'What are you wearing for the Gathering, Jenna?'

'The green, I thought.'

'They say green is unlucky.'

'But it brings out the best in my eyes.'

'You think you'll get close enough that King Ravn will notice your *eyes*?'

'I thought I'd start by unlacing the top three eyelets of my bodice.'

'It certainly won't be your eyes he's looking at if you do that . . .'

'Gold, he said. Gold everywhere.'

'And all we have to do when we reach the island is to kill the old man?'

'That's what he said.'

'We'll need to get a crew together.'

'Aye, but quietly, or you'll have a fleet to contend with.'

'That's most odd.'

'What is, Fezack?'

'You see the little girl over there, the northerner who came to see me a few days ago?'

'I see her.'

'Look more closely, fool. Her chest—'

'It's certainly a goodly size.'

'When she came to me, she was as smooth as flatbread. The potion I gave her was to encourage her own body to start its womanly processes; but this sudden excess of bosom is unnatural—'

'She has, perhaps, stuffed smallclothes into her bodice . . .'

'Perhaps. I might think the same were it not for other things I have noticed of late.'

'Such as?'

'Have you not noted the blessed silence from Lornack's wagon?'

'That's true, he's not coughing any more. Perhaps it's the dry air here—'

'Dry air, indeed! You think the dry air can explain why Feria gave birth to a child with two heads?'

'But it did not live—'

'Or the babe with scales down its arms and claws like an eagle in Talsea Town?'

'Shush, Mother, not so loud—'

'There's magic at work: true, strong magic. I can feel it in my bones.'

'Do not say such things, Mother. The Istrians may tolerate a few harmless charms and potions, but the burning times for those like us were not so long ago that they do not remember their fears. None of us would wish to see those fires rekindled . . .'

'We shall have to be careful. Water down your prescriptions my dear: offer only the most anodyne fortune-telling, even if you see the whole fate. There is a power at work, and it's getting stronger.'

'Would you do me a favour, Doc?'

'Depends what it is.'

'Have a look at this for me, will you?'

'Ugh. Put it away, Dogo. Why in the name of all the Furies do you think I should want to see your ugly todger?'

'You know about these things, Doc: I seen you treat wounds and the like. Look: it's growing. It's been growing ever since yesterday when I bought some stuff from one of them nomad charm-sellers . . .'

'Looks like you need to go see my Felestina, you do. She'll soon make it dwindle.'

'A healer is she, Doc?'

'Healer, my arse. She's my favourite whore, Dog-boy.'

The Games had been drawing huge crowds – on the first day for the marksmanship events – the archery and spear-throwing – then for the heats for the swimming and sword-play; but especially for the wrestling event, where hundreds of young men – the flower of Istria and Eyra – had stripped down to their breeches and rubbed their bodies with oil to repel the grip of their opponents. The Eyran and nomad women had gathered at the rope boundaries, whistling and cheering as their chosen combatants won their bouts; cat-calling and hissing at those they deemed culpable of foul play, or those they thought less attractive. A particularly thickset Istrian boy with a thatch of dark hair had been pelted with fruit when he had beaten the Eyran favourite – a tall lad from the Black Isles whose piercing blue eyes caused many a young woman to swoon – in the final round.

Katla had looked on, unmoved. Halli, useless lump that he was, had gone out in only the second round. Of all the Rockfall clan, the wrestling was *her* event, the one at which she excelled in the island Games. She might even have given the Istrian a run for his money: not for strength – for he was fearsomely muscled – but certainly for agility and technique, though she doubted she'd have been able to pin him, even if she'd got him down. Here, though, they wouldn't let women participate, and without the opportunity for disguise: even with her flat chest, she reckoned they'd notice the difference, stripped to the waist. As it was, even to come and watch the sport, she'd had to wind a length of coloured fabric about her head, on her father's orders, after the officials had visited their booth. 'It's either that or dye black what's left,' he'd said grimly. Fent, meanwhile, drew glances wherever he went – though the charge for affray had long been dropped by the wounded Istrian boy, who was recovering well. No, it was the red hair – in conjunction with his finely cut features and slim build – that drew their eye. The sacrilege of a woman setting foot atop the Rock had struck some atavistic chord in the more fundamental southerners: now that word had spread and still the offender had not been caught, they were all talking about it. Fent noticed how many Istrians watched him sharply as he passed, as if determined not to be taken in by his mannish clothing or masculine stride. Twice, he'd been stopped, but one close look at the rough red stubble on his chin and he'd been waved on his way. Tor, accompanying him on one of these expeditions, had suggested that Fent don one of Katla's tunics and affect a provocatively sway-hipped gait in order to really give them something to talk about, and had earned a sore jaw for his trouble.

More seriously, the previous morning two flame-haired sisters from the Fair Isles had also been stopped and taken into custody. At only twelve and fourteen years of age, and having no skill in the Old Tongue, they had been kept in the holding cells for the best part of a day, crying out piteously in Eyran while stern-faced southern officials fingered their hair and asked them unfathomable questions in the musical Istrian language they had been admiring only that morning, as they listened to a pair of southern swordsmen exchanging pleasantries between heats.

At last, the family had noticed they were missing, and after scouring the fairground, had gathered themselves quite a large group of searchers, who had eventually converged upon the Allfair officers' booth, more to report the girls' disappearance than out of any suspicion they might be held there. The furore that had ensued had resulted in somewhat greater circumspection from the officials since then; even so, the incident had sparked brawls that night, and even now the mood was tense.

'Did you see me, Saro?'

Tanto Vingo leapt the rope and clapped his brother on the back so hard that Saro yelped.

'I was magnificent, even if I say so myself. Did you see how I wrong-footed him at the last? Feint, feint, block, turn—' he mimed out his win for Saro's benefit '—let him catch me a glancing blow on the dagger, then bam! Straight in under his arm. If it wasn't for that stupid competition button they make you put on the point, I'd have skewered him nicely.'

Saro stood there, swaying, his eyes unfocused, feeling the

triumph and bloodlust sweep through him from Tanto's touch; and then it ebbed away as abruptly as it had come, leaving him feeling empty, stranded.

'Wrecked the dagger though.' Tanto pulled the blade from its sheath and waved it under his brother's nose.

The blade, albeit slightly notched, was otherwise undamaged, though little spatters of blood had dried along its length and Saro found himself wondering whether it had come from his brother's opponents in the swordplay, or from the old moodstone-seller Tanto had so needlessly killed. It was typical of his brother that he would not bother to clean the weapon properly: that was a job for a slave to do, if he had thought to make the instruction.

'Have to buy another before tomorrow's final: can't afford to get some bastard's weapon caught in the nick.'

'But Tanto, you can't afford a new dagger, not if—'

'I shall win the swordplay, and you, my dear Saro, will win the horserace, and then I shall have the bride-price and plenty to spare, so don't give me a hard time over one small dagger.'

And with that he grasped Saro by the arm and marched him towards the Istrian quarter.

'I have seen the Vingos, my dove, and we shall complete our alliance tomorrow evening. I had hoped it would be today, but for some reason, they appear to be delaying. No doubt they're juggling their money, as are we all!'

Selen Issian observed with some distaste that her father appeared to be in an unusually jubilant mood. She supposed he was already counting the money, was already deciding exactly how to split the payments to the Council in order to keep as much of the dowry for his own uses as he possibly could.

Tomorrow evening. This would be her last day and night as a free woman: then she would be bundled off to some

cushion-strewn tent and – how did they so delicately put it?
– initiated into womanhood. She felt the rage rise up in her
again and had to stare hard at the floor, for if her father saw
the resistance in her eyes, she knew he would beat her again.
It was no surprise that he'd taken the strap to her after she had
painted her lips so crudely, but clearly her act of defiance had
rebounded upon her.

Knowing she had made the Vingo boy so avid was somehow worse than the beating.

'I've bought you something special, my dear, for the
ceremony.'

Tycho clapped his hands and two of the slaveboys came
running in: Felo and Tam, Selen noted with a little flutter
of emotion. She would even miss them.

They had been captured three years ago in the raids on the
hill tribes, she recalled suddenly, feeling for the first time a
twinge of empathy. What were they now – seven or eight
years of age? To be only four or five and see your family
killed, your village burned, to be sold into slavery: worse,
to be sold to foreigners whose tongue you could not even
speak, and be whipped until you could: it was a terrible fate.
She tried hard to feel better about her own in comparison,
and failed.

They laid a bundle at their master's feet, and with clever
hands untied the multitude of knots that held it all together,
then rose without a word and stepped obediently backwards
and out of the door.

Tycho quirked an eyebrow at his daughter.

'Don't you want to see what it is?' he invited smoothly.

Selen stared at him, then at the bundle. Her feet felt rooted
to the ground.

Tycho made a moue of disappointment then himself bent
to the package, grasped the contents, and, with a flourish,
rose and shook out a robe of the most perfect orange silk
Selen had ever seen. She caught her breath.

'Beautiful, isn't it?'

She nodded tightly, feeling the tears well up. Her marriage dress, the orange symbolising Falla's holy fire, the generative force of the world, which would be invoked at the ceremony. There were embroidered slits at breast and hip level, the top one horizontal, and lower vertical, for now held closed with ribbons of fine satin. She knew what they were for. Her women had been most specific in their descriptions.

King Ravn rolled his shoulders, stretched and sighed. His eye passed wearily over the charts and maps they had been perusing for the last two hours, amid heated debate (between his nobles, at least) as to the finer benefits and disadvantages of possible alliances with the south. The words on the maps, and in the air, had long since stopped making any sense to him. He had found some while back that if he relaxed his focus, the parchments, sandy and faded, became muzzy and indistinct, stretching across the table in their rolls and folds to become a kind of desert, the inky details upon them shimmering as if in the midst of a heat haze or Fata Morgana. He yearned for the days before he became king, when he could take to the high seas at will.

'Aran Aranson of the Rockfall clan is here to see you, sire.'

Ravn's head came up. 'Who is he?'

'A Westman Islander, sire.'

'An interruption, at last.' Ravn grinned. 'Send him in.'

Stormway and Southeye looked annoyed at this sudden intrusion into such crucial political discussions; but Egg Forstson was on his feet with alacrity at the sound of his old friend's name.

'Aran, my dear fellow!'

As the tall Westlander ducked under the canopy, he found himself engulfed in a bearhug, encompassed by smells both musty and animal, though whether they emanated from the man himself, or from the vast, yellowing fur he insisted on wearing even in the height of summer, it was impossible to tell.

Egg stood back, still gripping Aran by the arms, and regarded him with delight.

'It's been a long time, old friend.'

'A year, almost to the day, at the last Allfair.' Aran grinned back, his dark, stern face creasing suddenly into a rarely-used expression. Against the weatherbeaten skin and dark beard, his teeth gleamed as white as new ice. The Earl of Shepsey, on the other hand, looked tired, Aran thought, tired and grey, as if in the intervening year time had been running at different rates for the two of them, as if the older man was willing himself towards the grave, while he, Aran, was running as hard as he could in the opposite direction. They had fought together, side by side, back to back, in some of the bloodiest fighting of the last war, lads thrown into one another's company when the ship Aran had been on had been set ablaze and sunk as they made their raid on the Istrian port of Hedera, and he and the survivors of the *Dragon's Tooth* had been taken onto the *She-Bear*, Egg's father's fine old vessel. The Istrians had managed to blockade the harbour entrance behind the *She-Bear* so that they had been hemmed in, flaming arrows raining down on all sides, setting alight the sail, the deck, items of clothing; grappling hooks coming over the side and howling men hurling missiles from the swarms of little boats crowding around them, waiting for the fire to catch and the crew to jump. From their diverse armour and weaponry it had been clear that the larger part of them were hired freeswords. He could even have sworn some of them had once been Eyran. It was curious how the Empire always had enough money to pay others to fight for them, Aran remembered thinking, as the first mercenaries began to board them; and then there had come a great roar from behind them and the old King's ship – the *Seafarer* – had broken through the blockade and come crashing through the lightweight Istrian vessels, scattering them like chaff to the wind.

Great days, Aran thought, *and now we are reduced to diplomacy and deal-making with the old enemy.* How he longed to set out on a great quest again. He touched the map beneath his tunic, like a talisman, and stepped forward.

'I have a request to make of you, sire.' He bowed his head with all the deference due a liegeman to his king.

Ravn regarded the top of Aran's dark head. 'Out with it, then, Westlander. Tell me what it is you would ask of me.'

Aran looked askance at the other men present. 'It is a private matter, my lord.'

'These are my most trusted advisers: surely you can speak your suit before them?'

Aran looked uncomfortable.

Ravn grinned. 'Perhaps it is something too personal for an audience.' He turned to his lords. 'Go and fetch wine, lads: my throat feels like the bed of a dried-up lake! Go to Sorva Flatnose's stall and make sure he gives you his best cask of stallion's blood: he'll swear he has no such thing, but you'll find he's got it stashed there somewhere: I heard him boasting to Foril Senson. And if he demands payment, remind him he still owes me duty for his last two shipments. It'll be a big cask, if I know Sorva: it'll likely take the three of you to carry it!'

The three lords exchanged glances. None of them looked entirely happy with their chore. Stormway gave Aran his hardest stare and Southeye groaned as he rose from the table; but Egg Forstson clapped the Westlander on the back and wished him luck.

'He doesn't say a lot,' he said over Aran's head to the King, 'but what he does say is usually worth listening to. The keenest edges whistle least.'

When they had gone, Ravn motioned Aran to a settle and regarded the man curiously. He thought he might have encountered Aran Aranson once before: at the court at Halbo when he had first taken his throne and the lords and landowners had all come to pledge their loyalty. If this was the man, he'd thought him dour, hard and dour, looking ill at ease in his fine clothes, out of place amidst the luxuries and merrymaking; but all the same, impressive, in his own way. One of the old breed, though he was not an old man. He recalled that his father had spoken highly of him.

'So what is this secret request, Aran Aranson?'

After a moment's hesitation, during which he searched for the words that would convey his desire, and failed entirely, Aran reached into his tunic and withdrew the map, as if it had the power to speak where he had none. Unrolling it with infinite care, he spread it over the other charts that papered the table. Then he took up four of the stones the men had been using to weight down the corners and shifted them to his own map so that it lay as flat as he could make it. His fingers traced the outlines of the landmasses lovingly. He knew each line, marked reef, each indentation of the coast, by heart now: he had spent his last three nights awake, a lit candle for illumination, going over and over every beautifully-drawn detail – the windrose, the decorated margins, the navigation points and projections.

The King looked on boredly. Yet another map. He was sick of the sight of them all. The only map he was interested in was the one that would finally chart a passage through the Ravenway and into the Far West. *But perhaps*, he mused, *if he were to take the wife they wanted for him and got himself a swift heir, he'd be able to join the expedition force himself* . . .

Aran looked up expectantly and was shocked to see the glaze in the other man's eye. 'I got it from a nomad mapseller,' he said quickly, trying to catch Ravn's interest. 'It is a most wondrous thing. See here—' he indicated the outline of an island '—Whale Holm, most accurately drawn. And here—' he moved his finger south and east '—your capital, sire: Halbo.'

The King bent to peer at the mark on the map. 'Ah, yes,' he said listlessly. 'Though it appears to be spelled wrongly.'

Aran stared at the familiar letters. The map-maker had put a cross through the 'o', but that seemed to be all that was unusual about it. He said nothing. 'And up here, sire—' his fingers flew to the top of the map, amidst the words 'Isenfelt' and the repeated mantra 'ise', and then swept to the right '—look at this extraordinary windrose.'

'Very nice work,' the King said flatly. 'Most accomplished, I'm sure. Why are you showing me this, Aranson? Can't you see I have plenty of maps of my own?'

'Look more closely, sire,' Aran insisted. His finger touched the word inside the directional legend. 'There, lord.'

'*Sanctuarii*,' the King read. He looked up. 'Sanctuary?'

'Yes, sire.'

Ravn laughed. 'Fairytales for children! The last resting place of King Rahay and his cat!

> "*Rahay grew weary of the land of gold*
> *He took his cat and put to sea*
> *Into the north where winds are cold*
> *To the island known as Sanctuary!*"'

Aran bowed his head. 'Yes, sire.'

Ravn thumped his leg with delight. 'And you have the map to the magician's secret land?'

Aran looked up, hope gleaming in his eye. 'Yes, sire.' He thought for a moment. 'Also, this—' he dug into his tunic pocket and fished out the lump of metal the map-seller had given him. It glittered in his hand, brazen and gaudy in the noon light. It felt weightier than he remembered, too; heavy and urgent.

The King stared at it, then took it gingerly from the Westlander's grip. It seemed to vibrate in his hand like a live thing. Ravn frowned; tried to concentrate.

Without the gold in his possession, Aran felt suddenly dislocated, at a loss. He watched Ravn hold it up to the light, squint at it; weigh it in his palm. Then he handed it back, almost reluctantly. A pained expression crossed his face. 'Pretty enough,' he said at last. 'But a treasure only to those who wish to believe in it.'

Gripping his little piece of treasure once more, Aran felt charged with energy. Fury churned inside him, but he kept his face still and unreadable. Without the King's support he could never raise the funds he needed. He stowed the ingot carefully in his tunic pocket. 'I would ask you for a ship, sire. To make the passage. I would dedicate the region to you, once I set foot upon it, claim it in your name. King Ravn's Land.'

'And bring me all its treasures?'

'Aye, sire, that too.'

Ravn laughed. 'A ship, in exchange for a cargo of shining rock?'

'Gold, sire,' Aran said mulishly.

The man was so adamant: it would be easy to be carried along by his fervour. Ravn brought to mind the royal sceptre, remembered how the ancient artefact seemed freighted with magic in his grasp on the occasion of his crowning. He'd been drunk with funeral wines and barely steady on his feet; but even so, he recalled how the sceptre had had a lustre of a different order, like a piece of the sun held in the hands. The ingot, though had made him feel suddenly imbued with power . . . He felt his certainty waver, but only for the briefest moment. A king must be resolute in what he believes and show no indecision. Brushing the pebbles from the map's corners, he rolled the thing up roughly and thrust it back at Aran Aranson.

'Give up this foolish idea, man. Join my expedition to the Far West instead. At least we know it exists! And in the meanwhile, enjoy the Fair. Are you trading?'

'Sardonyx, sire.'

'Good, good.'

Aran watched the King's eyes lose focus again, as if he were terminally stupefied. 'So,' he said at last, rather stiffly, feeling the rage and disappointment welling up inside him. 'I'll take my leave, sire.'

Ravn's head came up. He saw the desperation in the other man's eyes and smiled. 'Not so fast, Aran Aranson. Now that you have had the benefit of my wisdom, at least do me the courtesy of giving me your own good judgement.'

Aran stopped in his tracks, the old fury rising.

'Who do you think I should I take to wife, man? It's a tedious business, this political marriage thing, and the women they offer me are all so dull. Moreover, it seems everyone who holds a view has an axe to grind.'

'I have neither view, nor axe.'

Ravn shrugged. 'You must have some thought, surely?'

There was a commotion outside the tent, the shuffling of feet and muffled voices as if someone were trying to manoeuvre something awkward through a narrow space. The Lords Stormway, Southeye and Forstson had returned, it seemed, with a cask as big as an ox.

King Ravn leapt up, filled with sudden energy. 'My stallion's blood! Excellent!'

The lords manhandled the cask with difficulty through the tent's opening, where it thudded onto the ground with such force that the table bounced, and all the charts and maps – no longer carefully anchored by their stones – cascaded onto the floor with a clatter. Southeye, who owned many of them – charts made in his grandfather's day and earlier – fell to his knees and began to gather them frantically.

Aran, seeing his chance to leave in the midst of this chaos, took it, stepping round the monstrous cask and past the lords, and headed for the doorway without making his farewells.

'Which one shall I choose, Westlander?' the King called at his departing back. 'Shall I take a good northern girl or a strange southern one?'

'Take a troll to wife, for all I care,' came Aran Aranson's reply, low but entirely audible, as he disappeared through the doorflap.

Nine

Deals

It was early evening by the time the Vingo brothers found their way to the blade-stall, though they had set out some hours before. Tanto had been diverted by jewellery and clothes stalls, by innumerable stands selling araque, spiced wines and nuts baked into cakes that made you oddly light-headed, and finally by a group of exotic dancers travelling with the nomads, but purporting to come from the southern desert tribes (and everyone knew the strange practices *they* specialised in). Wearing nothing but a thousand thin strips of cunningly tied leather, which they invited onlookers (for a small consideration) to untie and unwind as they spun and leapt like dervishes, these hard-muscled, hard-eyed women had mesmerised Tanto for the last hour, and Saro was getting seriously infuriated. Added to which, he had found that walking through crowds now carried its own difficulties. He had bumped against one man's shoulder, and been assailed by a sudden terrible anxiety about his ailing wife's health; another man, watching the desert women, had brushed his arm, and from him Saro had learned the lewdest possible thoughts of what might be done with a naked dancer, some strips of leather and a group of men. Saro had stepped aside briskly, feeling filthy himself, only to be nudged by another man feeling wretchedly nauseous. At last, exhausted by these unwished-for intrusions, he had pulled Tanto away by the arm.

'The swordplay starts at quarter-sun tomorrow: do you want to get your dagger or not? Besides which, if you spend any more on the dancers you'll have nothing left to spend.'

Tanto shrugged him off angrily. 'If I'm soon to be wedded I deserve a bit of entertainment first.'

'But I thought you wanted this marriage?'

'I *want* the castle. I *want* the title. I *want* to be my own man at last. And if I have to marry some lord's tight-arsed daughter to get it all, I will. What I *don't* want is my prissy little brother making my ears ache in the middle of a crowd.'

Saro sighed, tempted to turn around and head for the family pavilion and leave Tanto to stagger drunkenly round the fairground on his own for the rest of the night. But the truth of it was, he'd be glad to see his brother wed and off the estate, and the sooner the better, for the sake of himself, the slaves, the cats, the horses, the surrounding wildlife . . .

'We passed a blade-stall back there and on the left, between the sheepskin-seller and the ropemaker.'

And so here they were now, peering over the shoulders of a number of customers clustered around a stall offering a large array of beautifully-crafted weapons shown off to their best advantage against a cloth of rich blue velvet. It was the velvet, in fact, that had first caught Tanto's eye. It was the girl behind the stall who had caught Saro's.

She was tall and wiry, with bare arms in which each muscle was clearly defined as she lifted the weapons and passed them, pommel-first, to interested buyers. Her face, downcast as she pointed out the intricate inlays and forged patterns in the blades, was mobile and intelligent; her nose was long, her cheekbones sharp and her eyebrows like the wings of a kestrel – tawny-dark, and up-tilted. But that hair! It was as red as the embers in a dying fire, but a fire that had been carelessly kicked over and trampled by a dozen feet. Locks of it fell this way and that, and much of it stood on end, as if someone had taken the sheep-shears to her. It was the hair of a kitchen-lad, a stablehand: a street urchin. And the tunic she wore – grubby boiled leather mottled with foodstains and seasalt, and clearly both too short in the leg and too tight under the arms – served only to emphasise the image of chaos. Who would employ such a creature to show such expensive wares? The weapons were clearly of the finest order: even from where he stood, Saro could tell from the way the would-be customers handled them that the swords were perfectly weighted, the daggers deadly sharp. And yet she spoke with some authority, and clearly knew enough to answer the keen questions that came her way. She bent to retrieve a carved wooden scabbard from a box on the ground, and Saro was treated to a view of smooth, tanned thigh that had his heart beating like a trapped rabbit's. As she straightened up again, she caught him staring. Their eyes met – hers mocking and with a hint of laughter in them that suggested she knew his thoughts entirely – and he felt his own go wide. Something about this girl, something nagged at him. He searched those grey-blue eyes for a clue, but now she was talking to a huge man at the other end at the stall about the knotwork that had been incorporated into the design of the sword he was interested in. It was shorter and broader than a Forent blade, heavier than a southern sabre, and in the man's big, scarred hands it looked entirely lethal.

Saro leaned closer to catch their words.

'And this,' she was saying, 'is the Dragon of Wen.' She pointed to an intricate sweep of silver that curled about the hilt. 'See, this is his tail, wrapped around his opponent, the Snowland Wolf, and his wings here and here, braced along the guards.'

The grizzled man bent his head and traced the pattern approvingly.

'And then his head comes right up into the pommel: I countersunk the red gem – see, there – for his eye so that it would feel smooth in the hand. See what you think.'

The fighter hefted the sword in both hands to feel the

balance of it, then stepped backward and made some complicated passes with it. Folk moved aside to give him room. Despite his age and his great size, he was remarkably nimble on his feet: he danced to his right and lunged, fell back with a supple twist of the spine and brought the sword about in a sheeny arc so that the blade came cutting down through the falling twilight in what in combat would likely have been a killing blow.

'It's a beauty, Katla Aransen,' he conceded. 'The best I've tried.' He handed it to the woman who stood beside him: no wife, this, but a tough-looking islander with a square chin and skin the colour of seasoned pine. She wore the same outlandish gear as her companion: a jerkin of leather and mail, bright metals discs interspersed with dull iron, strung across the torso. She wore three knives in her crossbelt, and another strapped to her thigh. A sword was slung across her back. 'What do you make of it, Mam?'

The woman took the blade from him, switched it from hand to hand, then lifted it closer to examine the knotwork. 'Very fine,' she pronounced at last. 'Very fine, Joz.'

'Aye, it's a beautiful thing,' he said, taking it back from her, 'and hard as adamant. You've outdone yourself, Katla. Light it is, and keener of edge than any of your competitors' weaponry. Makes your fingers tingle, too. You sure you've not been using magic in the forging?' He grinned at her.

Katla grinned back. She shook her head. 'Falko, he uses whale oil for the quenching, and Trello Longhorn swears he uses blood, though I know different. Me, I have my own method,' Katla said, tapping the side of her nose. She laughed. 'I'm not sure I'd call it magic, though.'

Saro gaped. The girl – Katla – had *made* these weapons? Surely he had misheard?

But Tanto was way ahead of him.

'Hey, you, yes, you! Are you a woman, or a northern troll, to be claiming to have forged these weapons?' He stared around at the onlookers, eyes wide and slightly unfocused. 'Women can't make swords: it'd be like—' he searched doggedly for an analogy '—like men embroidering smallclothes!'

A guffaw from the back of the crowd, followed by a certain amount of shuffling as folk got out of Tanto's way.

Saro could smell the araque fumes coming off his brother. He looked at the old fighter and his companions: the woman, two other tall men who looked hard as iron, and a small round one who looked bored and alarmingly distracted. They might once have been Eyran in origin, but their gear hinted at a dozen foreign influences; and to have a fighting woman with them, that was an oddity in itself. Sell-swords, then, and probably thoroughly dangerous. He held his breath, but the one the woman had called Joz just stood there grinning, watching Katla, his hand at his belt.

Katla's eyes narrowed dangerously. 'As I'd heard it,' she said tightly, 'in the south embroidering smallclothes is all the men are good for.'

A great bellow of laughter this time, and not just from the mercenaries.

'No need to fight your battles for you, eh, girl?' said Joz.

'Got her mother's tongue on her, has Katla Aransen,' said the tall, bearded man beside him.

'Aye, I recall feeling the sharp edge of Bera Rolfsen's tongue a time or two in my youth!'

'That was how you lost your hand, eh, Knobber?'

'Nay, that was to some dog of an Istrian not much older than this young whelp at the battle for Hedera Port.'

Tanto, somewhat lost for words, was reduced to sneering, but luckily the sell-swords were in a good mood. The tall man called Joz started to haggle with Katla on the price of the blade, until at last she brought out a fine leather scabbard lined with oiled wool and sealed the deal with it. The old fighter counted a stream of coins into her hands, which Katla immediately transferred into an iron box behind the stall, looking immensely pleased with her sale.

With the purchase concluded, the other buyers began to drift away, until only the two Istrians were left behind.

Tanto, however, started to fiddle in a desultory fashion with some of the decorated daggers near the front of the display. 'A child's paring knife,' he declared disparagingly of the first he examined. 'Cheap rubbish.'

Katla cast him an unfriendly look, then, deliberately ignoring him, began to pack the larger items away. Clearly it was the end of the trading day: the light was fading and she had just these two idiots left to deal with. Not much chance of a major sale now, particularly to a callow, loud-mouthed youth who couldn't tell the difference between a glaive and a toothpick.

Tanto stared at the back of her head, annoyed at her obvious dismissal of him. He picked two daggers up and started to tap the edge of one on the edge of the other, gently at first, then harder and harder, like a wilful child smashing its toys together. The metal rang out, clear and true. Saro nudged him.

'What are you doing?'

'Testing the blade,' Tanto answered sulkily, staring at Katla's turned back. 'No point shelling out for a weapon that might shatter on me in the final.'

Katla whirled around and stared at him. '*You've* made the finals of the swordplay?' Astonished contempt sharpened the mellow vowels of the Old Tongue.

Tanto raised an eyebrow. 'I'd soon take out *that* old fool,' he said, indicating the northman who bought the sword and was now tarrying at the ropemaker's stall.

Katla laughed. 'Joz Bearhand? I truly doubt it! He's fought his way around the world and back again, that one. You wouldn't stand a minnow's chance. Look at the pair of you,' she included Saro in her gaze, then reached quickly across the stall and caught each of them by the hand, turning their forearms this way and that as she scrutinised their dark skin. 'Not a scar on either of you. Never seen a day's genuine action in your lives.'

Saro was swept through by a wave of warmth: cheerful good humour filled him, the confidence of a young woman who felt at home in her hale body, unperturbed by the brags and threats of a drunken youth, with the muscle born of hard work in the forge and years of cliff-climbing to see her through. *He'd* never have the nerve to do what she had done. A sudden vivid, unforgettable image jarred itself into Saro's mind.

'It was you,' he breathed, pulling away from the northern girl's disturbing touch. 'You I saw up on the Rock—' And then he stopped, aghast.

Time slowed. Saro watched the blood drain from Katla's face; and saw Tanto's dawning realisation. He could even tell the exact moment when his brother remembered the bounty that had been offered that morning for the perpetrator's capture; before Tanto started to shout.

'Guards! Here!'

And then Saro hit him. It was a movement so reflexive, so intuitive that his fist connected with the side of his brother's jaw with unerring, astounding force. Tanto dropped like a stone.

Katla came round the stall at a run. She stared at Saro, then down at his brother, who lay as if poleaxed, arms flung wide, one hand still grasping the dagger he had been toying with. His jaw had slipped to one side. Saro wondered, with a moment's profoundly guilty pleasure, whether he had broken it. Several folk looked round from other stalls at the commotion, saw Tanto lying on the ground and his brother smiling, and drifted back to their conversations.

'Why did you do that?' Katla asked flatly, her grey eyes almost black with some unreadable emotion.

Saro regarded her gravely. 'I— I don't know. It just seemed to happen.' He paused, then poked his brother with a careful toe, but there was no response. 'It was you, wasn't it? Up on the Rock?' he asked softly. 'Though your hair was long then.'

Katla gave him a knowing look. 'You're an Istrian,' she stated grimly. 'I'm hardly going to admit it to you.'

'I am. But I'm not the most devout believer.' And as he said it, he knew it to be true. He remembered long mornings under the instruction of the priests, harsh in their black robes, quick with a rod. He remembered their grave intonations of the observances, the dire warnings of the torment that awaited those who displeased Falla, or even her blasted cat. How could he believe their lurid stories, all those grim threats? Why should a volcano erupt just because you hadn't made the correct sacrifices to a deity? Why should your house burn down because you had made an offensive remark? He'd never seen a volcano; but he'd seen enough fire to know it was a natural force, not some magical property; and as for Falla herself: how could he believe in something he'd never seen with his own eyes? The worship of the Goddess had never meant more to him that an excuse for punishment, for control; a way of keeping you in line. Suddenly, faced with this new actuality, this possibility of mad, unnecessary death, it all came into clear focus. 'To give someone to the fires for climbing a rock, it's . . . well, stupid, barbaric.'

'Would they really do it?' Her face was curious, intent.

Saro laughed. 'Oh yes, in an instant. It's a cruel religion. It thrives on suffering.'

Katla was indignant. 'But all I did was climb a rock: no harm in that. Besides, this land was ours, and not so long ago: in my great-great-grandfather's day, and before him for generation upon generation. It was Eyran territory, the Moonfell Plain, the Skarn Mountains, the Golden River all the way to Talsea. Your people stole it from us, drove the settlers off their land, murdered and raped anyone not quick enough to run. Or made them into slaves to work for their bloody Empire. It's not forgotten, you know, even now.' She gave him an angry glance.

'I know. The last war's not so long past. My father fought in it.'

'And mine.'

'My grandfather died.'

'So did mine.'

She barked out a laugh then, and he noticed how long and sharp-looking were her dog-teeth, how like a wild animal she could look when animated thus. 'So who's to says it's Falla's Rock anyway? If it's anyone's, it's Sur's. We call it Sur's Castle.'

'That's just as bad, though, isn't it? That's just substituting one god for another.'

'At least ours doesn't demand we kill people in his name.'

Saro shrugged. 'Fair point.'

Katla smiled. It changed the whole shape of her face, he saw, and the colour of her eyes. She looked less . . . wolfish. Then she leaned forward and gripped him by the arm again, and again a wave of heat travelled through him. This time, however, it was not just the gratitude of the girl he felt, but a heat all his own, spreading quickly up through his abdomen and into his chest.

'Thank you for not giving me up,' she said simply. 'Tell me your name. I like to know whose debt I'm in.'

Saro told her and she nodded briefly as if storing it away for future reference.

'But what if he remembers when he wakes up?' Saro said suddenly, agonised at the thought.

'He'll find a different person on the stall, with no knowledge of a girl with hair like a broom's head.' She laughed. 'Anyway, I think I'd best keep it hidden for now, don't you?' She picked up a piece of oily cloth from under the stall and wrapped it quickly about her skull. 'There. A Jetran princess!'

Saro smiled. Whatever did these northerners think of them? 'I'll pay you for the dagger,' he said, picking up the weapon Tanto held in his outstretched hand. It seemed hot to his touch, as if it pulsed with some sort of life. Disconcerted, he held it out to her.

Katla waved it away. 'You won't. It's my gift and my thanks; and it'd give me great pleasure that you should keep it, rather than your vile brother have it.'

Saro smiled uncertainly, then slipped the dagger into his tunic, where it lay, pulsing gently: or was it the thump of his own heart he could feel? It was hard to say: this girl made his senses spin. He tried to focus on what she had said. 'Tanto thinks no woman can resist his charms.'

'He's obviously not much travelled, then,' Katla said, regarding the unconscious Istrian. 'Rather better company when he's like this than when he's awake, I'd say.'

'You'd better go before he comes round.'

'Indeed.'

She gave him another of those miraculous smiles, then with expert hands began to fold each piece of weaponry into its own twist of oiled cloth and stow it in a huge iron box. Saro turned to inspect his recumbent brother and was confronted by a tall young northerner with a white-blond beard and hair braided into complex knots threaded through with scraps of coloured fabric, shells and pieces of silver who had appeared silently behind them.

'Are you having any trouble here, Katla?'

Katla whirled around, hands up to her mouth, but when she saw the newcomer, she smiled. 'Hello, Erno,' she said, and her voice was warm with affection. 'No trouble: not any more.'

Saro felt his heart constrict and looked quickly from one to the other. Let this be a brother, he found himself thinking;

a brother, no more than that. But the look in the tall man's eyes as he watched Katla stowing away her wares was far from fraternal.

A groan brought his attention back to the matter of his brother. He looked down. Tanto's eyelids had begun to flicker. Saro bent to him, feeling a sudden mixture of remorse and dread.

'Tanto? Can you hear me?'

Tanto's hand flexed convulsively and for a brief moment, Saro thought he would swing wildly up with it and hit him, but the movement seemed to be no more than a reflex action, for then Tanto kicked out once with both feet and sat bolt upright, much too fast for one who has been struck unconscious. He grasped his head and groaned again.

'Wh— what happened?' he said groggily, struggling to focus on Saro's face.

'Can you not remember, brother?' Saro asked carefully.

Tanto frowned, the effort to dredge his thoughts clearly producing a mental pain that complemented his physical distress. 'I remember—' Saro held his breath '—I remember . . . the woman . . . the foreign woman . . .'

Saro's pulse thumped in his head. He looked quickly around, only to see Katla, having locked her strongbox with a great iron key, saying something in a low voice to Erno, then turn and disappear between the booths. Suddenly, he felt very empty.

'What foreign woman?' he said sharply.

Tanto glared at his tone of voice. 'The dancer, dolt . . . the one with the . . . ribbons of leather . . .'

Saro made his pent-up breath escape as normally as possible. 'Oh, that one. Nothing more?'

'How did I get down here?' Tanto stared about him in an accusatory manner and seeing no one else to blame, glared at his brother.

Saro, trying desperately to avoid an outright lie, shrugged.

'You did have a lot to drink,' he said gently. It was, after all, at the root of the problem. Had Tanto not raided every araque stall between the Vingo tent and the knife-stall, he might have been less confrontational, and unlikely to have provoked Katla into mocking their lack of battle-scars. Saro remembered the thrill of her strong fingers on the skin of his forearm, and knew it was a memory he'd return to again and again.

'Do you need help returning to your family tent?'

The tall Eyran, Erno, had returned. He held out a hand to Tanto, who stared at it as if he had been offered the aid of a shit-covered stick.

'Not from you,' he said rudely, shoving himself awkwardly onto his knees. He grabbed Saro's belt and hauled himself upright.

Erno regarded him consideringly until Saro wondered whether he would punch Tanto. In many ways, nothing would give him greater satisfaction, he thought grimly. Then the blond northener said curtly, 'Have it your own way,' turned on his heel and melted into the crowd.

Saro watched him go with a sinking heart. The northerner was all he would never be, it seemed to him then: tall, muscular, athletic in his stride; clearly a man of action and few words, a warrior, most like, and probably Katla's lover, to boot. The thought made him cringe.

Katla made her way across the fairground as if in a trance. Saro Vingo. Who had struck his brother unconscious to save her from discovery. Saro Vingo, with eyes like black velvet and a tentative smile that scored lines into the smooth plane of his cheeks. Saro Vingo: a foreign name for a foreign man. Even the way the syllables caressed her tongue was a fascination. She remembered how she had caught the southerner by the arm, how the skin had felt alive with heat beneath her fingertips and her memory – sharp as hallucination – lingered on the curl of the fine black hair on his forearm, silky as cat's fur; how the opening of his tunic below the hollow of his throat had revealed a glimpse of hard-muscled chest. The colour of that skin was seductive. Something shivered in her, deep and low.

'Katla?'

She started guiltily and found herself standing as if by magic on the threshold of the family booth with her brothers regarding her curiously, their attention momentarily distracted from the wooden chest that lay open between them. Whatever was the matter with her? She caught herself up with a rueful grin. First, she was mooning over Erno, of all people, and now over an Istrian boy she'd met once and would likely never see again. She'd become as bad as Jenna if she wasn't careful. She dropped her own strongbox onto the floor with a crash.

Then, quick as a snake, he wrapped an arm around Halli's neck, gave it a playful squeeze. 'What's up, little brother?' He was her senior by some seven years, and twice her size into the bargain, but this had become their jest. 'Playing bankers with fox-boy, are you?'

Halli looked around and grinned slyly at her, his slow, teasing grin. Then, quick as a snake his right hand came up and grabbed her arm, at the same time rolling his shoulder under her armpit, and thus pivoted her up and over and flipped her onto the ground in front of him. She hit the floor hard, missing the stout wooden chest by a finger's breadth.

'Ow!'

Fent creased up with laughter. 'That'll teach you for laughing at Halli when he went out of the wrestling in the second round.'

'She laughed at me?' Halli looked hurt. Then he buried his hairy fingers in Katla's midriff and ran them over her like a great spider.

Katla shrieked and giggled, returned to a lost childhood by this assault, and soon her heels were hammering the floor like a three-year-old's. Before long, Fent had joined in, too, till the three of them were rolling around the floor, tickling and thumping each other, howling like animals. At some point, inevitably, the money-chest went over, spilling its contents everywhere. It was this scene that greeted their father as he returned from his unsuccessful audience with Ravn Asharson. Somewhere between the King's tent and his own, Erno had found him. They both looked grim.

'What in seven hells is going on here?' Aran bellowed. 'I could hear your ruckus halfway across the Fair.'

Silence fell at once. The combatants disentangled themselves and stood up, looking sheepish. The coins lay glinting around them like an accusation of wrongdoing.

'Where did all this come from?' Aran bent and raked through the coins, picking out a twenty-cantari piece and a couple of tens and waved them in the air.

'We sold Tor into slavery,' Fent ascertained, face straight.

Aran's hand came out of nowhere and cracked his younger son sharply across the top of his head. Fent stepped back, looking shocked. His fists balled. For a moment it seemed as if he might charge at his father, but then he dropped his head.

'We found a buyer for the whole lot,' Halli said quietly. 'A stonemason from Forent with a commission for twenty statues of their goddess. He said they wanted only the best, and ours is the purest he's found, so he made us a good price. We're going to see Finn Larson tomorrow to talk about our ship.'

Aran's expression became closed. His mind worked furiously. Perhaps a solution to his dilemma had just been offered. Nothing happened in this life but for a reason, it was said; and Sur was clearly smiling on his venture. 'There'll be no more talk about expeditions to the Far West in this family,' he said briskly.

'But Da!' Halli was furious. 'It's been our plan all along to join the King's expeditionary force. You said you'd see it financed from the sardonyx sales, that you'd throw in your and mother's shares—'

'Enough! I won't talk about this further. Katla: you'll be dyeing your hair black tonight: Erno told me what happened earlier—'

'Erno!' She glared at him, her eyes hot with betrayal. 'You said you wouldn't mention it: you promised!'

Erno looked uncomfortable.

'He did it because he was concerned for you. Use this—' Aran tossed a small glass bottle at her '—and when you've done it, keep your head under wraps. We don't want any awkward questions about why your hair's suddenly changed colour; but at least if guards come looking again, they'll find no red-haired girls here. Leather and mail is safer than leather and silk. Better sure than sorry.'

'And what about the guard who claimed a dance?' Katla asked mutinously.

'You could wrap it up in this,' Erno suggested shyly. He held out to her a piece of gorgeous fabric. He'd found it on one of the nomad stalls, and it had cost him a small fortune. He'd picked it up for the colours: wild blues and greens, the grey of stormclouds, and Katla's eyes – like them it had just a hint of purple to it – and when the woman who had woven it had smiled and told him the piece was charmed, he'd misunderstood her and said he also thought it charming. 'No, no,' she'd corrected him gently. 'Charmed. Against the elements: hence the hues of sea and sky; and this, here against fire.' She'd taken it back from his clumsy hands and unfolded it carefully. 'See?' Along one hem ran a line of woven flame. It was the fire motif that had decided the purchase for him: it seemed a good omen, for it was the very colour of Katla's hair, even though he believed not one whit in the magic the nomad woman claimed.

Katla, holding her breath, unfurled the material, and a cloud of colour billowed out into the gloomy tent – greens and blues and grey swirling in subtle whorls and spirals; the soft white of a sea-mist wreathing through the whole, and all along the bottom hem, a riot of hot tones – orange and crimson, gold and vermilion – curled like eager flame.

Fent whistled. 'That must surely have cost you a queen's ransom, Erno.' He couldn't imagine liking any woman so well as to spend so much on such a gift, but Erno's only response was to blush and push past him into the depths of the booth.

Later that night, when Saro took the moodstone bracelet out of the pouch around his neck and held it in the palm of his hand, he found that the stones in it had gone the lurid shade of green of a tomcat's eyes.

Early the next morning, Fent and Halli found themselves outside Finn Larson's tent, the wooden chest slung between them. They were nervous: they had never gone against their father's express wishes before.

The shipbuilder had clearly been up for some time: he had his lads running this way and that on errands, and his son, Matt, rolling parchments into rolls of waterproofed hide. Larson was a burly man, wide of frame and thick of muscle. His shoulders, revealed by the sleeveless jerkin he wore, were as hairy and powerful as a bull's. Fent found himself wondering whether his daughter had inherited the same characteristics, under all her lace and frippery. If so, Halli was going to be in for a surprise on his wedding night.

As it was, the surprise was not just Halli's; nor did it – directly – concern Jenna Finnsen.

'Hello, lads. How are you this fine morning?' Finn twinkled at them, clearly in the best of humour.

'We're well, thank you, sir,' Halli replied politely, setting the chest on the ground at the shipbuilder's feet. 'And we have a proposition for you.'

'You do, do you?' Finn was clearly enjoying himself. He sent one of his lads for three stools and a jug of bier and would let them say no more till all three had downed a jar of the bitter stuff. 'Now what could you be offering me that your good father has not done already?'

'Our father?'

'You know, lad, Aran the Ogre; Aran the Bear – that's what we called him when we all fought side by side in the last war.'

Halli leaned forward, his face grave. 'What deal has my father offered you?'

'Why, lad, he's commissioned from me the finest ship I'll make this year: clinker built and of the best seasoned oak from Keril Sandson's own plantation, no less; a stempost of yew carved by the great Gunnil Kerrson himself (I salvaged it from Ravn's father's old vessel, you know, but I believe it will fit our purpose well); and an icebreaker of hardened iron. I shall have fifteen of my men assigned to the task of assembling it.'

'An icebreaker?' Fent said, bewildered.

'To be sure, that was one of his first requests.'

'But there's no ice in the passage to the Far West by all accounts, none at all. Storms and maelstroms, yes, indeed; but no need for an icebreaker.'

Finn Larson shrugged. 'I take the commissions I'm given, lad; and if your father wants an icebreaker—'

Halli cut in: 'What my father wants from you is no concern of ours. We have our own commission for you: sixty oars, back-curved stern and prow; fast and clean: that's all we ask. When last we spoke you said such a ship would cost in the region of six thousand cantari. We have the best part of that sum here for you now.'

The shipbuilder looked bemused. 'It seems that the Rockfall clan is high in funds at the moment,' he said, then rubbed his hands together cheerfully. 'Well, let's see the colour of your money, then I can start my calculations. There's a lot of work coming through at this Fair; rather more than I'd planned for. I hope you won't be needing your ship as quickly as some of these others?'

'For the autumn,' Halli said carefully. 'Autumn, this year.'

'Ah,' said Finn. 'Well, stranger things have happened. Of course, to find the right wood for the back-curves is harder than for straight. I can only do my best.'

'It is all I ask.'

Fent picked up the chest and upended it onto the ground. There was a clatter, harsh and dull, and a stream of broken sardonyx tumbled out, sending up a plume of dust. The brothers stared at the pile of stone in disbelief.

Finn Larson started to laugh, his teeth shining through the vast thatch of his grey beard. 'It's the . . . dawn wolf . . . takes the rabbit!' he wheezed delightedly, clutching his huge belly and rolling from side to side on his stool, his stubby hands flexing and tightening on the folds of his jerkin. At last he got enough air to be able to gasp: 'Well, I see you boys appear to be rich in semi-precious stone: while your father's suddenly rich in coin; but as far as I know, you're less rich in sisters?'

'Sisters?' Halli's usually gruff voice rose an octave as the fiasco became yet more surreal. 'We have but one, as well you know: Katla, Jenna's friend.'

'Aye, soon to be Katla, Finn's new wife. The coin Aran had was shy of the price, so we came to a slightly more creative arrangement. A pretty lass, she is, too, if a bit wild. Still we'll soon knock that out of her.'

The brothers stared at him. Then they stared at one another.

'By heaven, what has he done?'

PART THREE

Ten

Insights

Later that morning, Jenna Finnsen, having overheard a bizarre
and bewildering conversation outside the family booth, came
looking for Katla in order to try to make sense of it. But when
she reached the stall, her friend was nowhere to be seen:
instead, Erno Hamson was standing behind the glittering
display, looking large and muscle-bound and distinctly out
of place in his homespun tunic against the rich blue velvet.
In his big hands, the small dagger he was showing to a
wealthy-looking Istrian man looked like a brooch-pin. Jenna
grinned.

'A fine craftsman,' she overheard him saying to the lord.
'Yes, one of the finest in the northern isles.' He glanced up
then and caught her eye, and looked away again at once,
embarrassed.

'You won't find Katla here.'

Jenna whirled around. Behind her stood little Marin
Edelson. Except that she wasn't so little any more. Even
camouflaged by the intricately embroidered stole that she had
wound about her shoulders and knotted at her breastbone,
Marin's chest was unmistakably huge. As she greeted the
younger girl, Jenna found it almost impossible to tear her
eyes away from the fantastic sight. Almost, but not quite.
She dragged her regard reluctantly upward.

'Erno says she's unwell,' Marin said. 'She may not even be
able to come to the Gathering.' She added this detail with

a hint of triumph, it seemed to Jenna. 'So I'm waiting here until he has a break to ask him whether he might spare me a dance instead.'

'Marin!' Jenna was scandalised. 'You can't ask Erno to dance with you. It's not right. Not right at all.'

Marin looked wary. 'What is not right about it? He doesn't belong to Katla, whatever she may think,' she added with some spite.

'You can't ask *him* to dance with *you*: that's not how it's done, not by grown women, at least; and Sur knows, you look pretty much a grown woman to me now, Marin: by heaven, you do.'

Marin folded her arms close about her chest, but the irrepressible bosom refused to be thus contained. As soon as pressure was applied to it from below, it flowed upward and burst joyously out of the shawl like an independent creature. With a yelp, Marin hurriedly readjusted her dress. 'Oh, Jenna,' she wailed, grabbing the older girl's arm, 'whatever shall I do? They just won't stop growing!'

Jenna allowed her gaze to fall again. On Marin's thin frame, the size of her new appendages did seem inordinate. 'You should thank the Fates for such bounty,' she said, as kindly as she could manage. 'After years of being as flat as a flounder you should be pleased your womanly growth has at last come upon you. A goodly-sized bosom is no bad thing. I certainly intend to make the most of my own in the dress I shall wear for the King. What are you wearing tonight, Marin?'

The girl looked even more miserable. 'I . . . I don't know. The dress I was going to wear – you know, the blue one with the fur trimming—' Jenna nodded '—is too tight now. I tried it on last night, and split the seams. Today I cannot even pull it up past my waist. It's not natural, Jenna, truly it's not.'

'Of course it is, my dear,' Jenna said in her most comforting and matronly voice. 'It's the most natural thing in the world.'

'But it *isn't*!' Marin leaned confidentially towards Jenna. 'You must promise you won't tell anyone, for they will surely laugh at me for my stupidity; but I went to the Wandering folk.' She looked guiltily around, and her voice dropped to a whisper. 'It's magic. Magic gone horribly wrong. I bought a charm. To make them grow. To . . . to make Erno notice me.'

Jenna gasped, remembering her conversation with Kitten Soronsen, and how that catty little madam had gleefully (if erroneously) reported that Marin had taken Erno to see the Footloose people to buy him a love potion, an idea Jenna had at the time thought preposterous. *How pathetic*, she thought now, *that the childish, scrawny Marin should have been driven to such lengths to make a man notice her. And to have had such unfortunate results for all her trouble* . . . She had to stifle a laugh, it was so ridiculous. And all for Erno Hamson, too, that dolt. Besides, anyone with eyes could see it was Katla Aransen he burned for. She sighed. Poor Marin.

'Magic?' Unconsciously, Jenna fingered her hair. 'Well,' she said brightly, 'that's easily dealt with then.'

'It is?'

'Of course. We'll just go right back to wherever you bought the charm from and ask them to give you something that will reverse the effect.'

Marin stared at her, mouth open, as if at an oracle. 'Oh, Jenna, you're so clever!' Then her face fell. She dug in the pouch tied at her waist, tipped it up into her palm. Two small silver coins dropped out with a tinkle. 'Oh dear. Not nearly enough.'

'How much did the first charm cost you?'

'Twelve cantari.'

'*Twelve* cantari?'

'It was all my savings,' Marin said defensively.

Twelve cantari. Jenna had at least thirty in her own purse, but there was no way she was giving it to Marin

Edelsen. Then a thought struck her. She grabbed Marin by the hand and began to tow her away from Katla's stall. 'Come with me!'

'But—' Marin cast an imploring look back over her shoulder at Erno, who, by the set of his head and carefully downcast eyes, was very deliberately taking no notice of the pair of them. 'But where are we going? The nomad quarter's in the other direction. I don't understand—'

'There's absolutely no point in going to the nomad quarter until you've got the money to pay for a new charm. So we're going to get you that money.'

'But how?'

Jenna did not respond. Rather, she hauled on Marin's arm so that the girl lost her precarious balance and had to run after her to keep upright.

'Jenna,' Marin cried, her voice rising to a wail so that Erno's head came up sharply. 'The Games are that way—'

'I know, silly. That's exactly where we're going. Where there's competition there's betting. There's this young Istrian everyone's talking about, Fara Gilsen said. Handsome as a hawk and with a wonderfully exotic name: Tanto Vingo.' She elongated the vowels luxuriantly. 'Bound to win the swords, that's what Fara said. We'll bet your silvers on him and that should double your money.' She clapped her hands, delighted by her own ingenuity. 'Easy!'

Marin followed, confused as to how a lady should behave if she was not allowed to ask the man she liked for a single dance at a formal Gathering, yet could cheerfully mingle with the rogues and sharps at the betting stand. If her father saw her there, he'd surely give her a good clout. Fearful, but driven by her desperation, she trotted meekly in Jenna's footsteps, her bosom wobbling unhappily with every step.

Tanto Vingo was at that moment throwing a tantrum. His final bout started in less than half an hour, and yet here

he was, having found yesterday's damaged dagger still in its
sheath and no chance of ameliorating the situation in the little
time there was to spare. And yet he had a vague memory that
somewhere between wandering the Fair with his brother the
previous afternoon and the araque binge in which his father
and uncle had encouraged him last night, he had had in his
hands another weapon; a wonderfully balanced blade that had
fit in his palm like a deadly caress. He could feel it still, in his
memory, like an amputated limb.

'It's not so bad, Tanto, truly,' said his father soothingly.
Saro watched him retrieve the blade Tanto had thrown on
the ground in his fury, and dust it off. 'See: the nicks are
very small.'

'It's ruined!' Tanto howled. 'Just like everything else. How
by the Goddess's tits am I supposed to win the swordplay with
a broken blade? Even against that scruffy old man? And if I
don't, then Saro better win the bloody yearling stakes, or his
life won't be worth living.'

And it wouldn't, Saro knew that for a fact. He excused
himself and went to attend to the horses.

He'd awoken that morning from a fitful sleep. All night
he had been visited by dreams in which none of the import
was clear, and even those that seemed to start well would turn
suddenly to show him their dark underside. In the dream he
recalled most clearly he had been on horseback, riding hard
across an unknown moorland. Overhead, the clouds scudded
across the sun behind his shoulder, so that while they galloped
they remained always in the warm, but if they slowed, he
knew the shadows on the ground that mirrored the racing
clouds above would creep up and engulf them. It became
imperative that they outrun those shadows. Whatever the
reason might be, it evaded him. His heart had thundered in
time with the horse's hooves. When the lake had suddenly
loomed up before them, he had known they were lost. And
then the horse had vanished and he was sinking, down and

down, fighting for breath, until he was swallowed by the darkness and knew he must drown. But just as he was thinking this, a sea creature had come to him – out of nowhere, it seemed – propelling itself powerfully through the water, a sea creature with familiar storm-grey eyes. He had embraced it gladly, and together they had spiralled to the surface, where the clouds had passed harmlessly overhead, leaving them bobbing in a pool of golden sunlight.

A sea creature, he had thought on waking, in a freshwater lake? He must be losing his mind. He had extricated himself from his twisted covers and sat on the edge of the couch, slowly recalling the events of the previous day. And then he had felt beneath his pillow, and there was the dagger he had stowed there, the dagger *she* had made, all silver knotwork and fiery patterns where the metal had been folded back on itself, forged and reforged in the flames until its natural dragon emerged, to mirror the elaborately worked one that coiled up the hilt. He had picked it up, cradled it in his hand like a living thing; and like a living thing it had thrummed against his palm, sending warm vibrations up the bones of his arm.

'Katla,' he said now, remembering again. 'Katla Aransen.' The sound of it was like a spell to him. He finished grooming the bay's mane and laid his head on its fragrant shoulder. As he did so, he felt the horse tremble beneath his cheek, and then his mind roiled and opened. There was comfort there in the touch, a sense of companionship; a recognition that here was one with gentle, rhythmic hands who moved the brush with the grain of the hair instead of deliberately forcing it through knots to tug and pull; a recognition, moreover, that this was the one who carried delicious food inside his outer skin, where the other brought only pain and fear: the stone that stung, the foot that bruised . . . Saro pulled away from the bay with a start, and contact with the beast's mind ceased abruptly. He felt himself go hot, then cold. It was bad enough that the old nomad's so-called gift should bestow upon him unwanted access to other people's buried thoughts; but to suddenly be a party to the unfamiliar geography of a horse's mind was disorientating indeed.

Night's Harbinger whickered and nosed at him, but Saro dodged away, his own thoughts in turmoil. Surely to ride the horse now would be some sort of an intrusion, a violation? But then, to ride any horse would prompt the same response. How, then was he to go about his life, if he could touch neither man nor animal without this unwelcome flow of feelings? The subject was too huge: it shied away from examination. For now, he thought, trying desperately to focus on the smaller scale, on the manageable, there was the matter of the race to be decided. He dropped the grooming brush there in the dust and turned on his heel. He would tell them the horse was lame, that it could not run. Perhaps his father and uncle could find another way to make up the bride-price and save him from a beating. But what then of Guaya and her poor grandmother? Without the money he had determined to collect for them, how would they manage? His thoughts ran on and on, mercilessly tangled. The problem grew, took on further implications and consequences, became insoluble. His thoughts were as knotted together as the eight arms of the mythical Sucker of Ships after the hero Sirio the Great had vanquished it, so that he could find neither beginning not end to them. By the time he reached the sword-ring, he still had no idea of what he would say or do.

A considerable crowd had gathered for the bout and blue-cloaked officials had trouble keeping the onlookers behind the ropes that marked the edge of the fight arena, for still they kept coming, more all the time, as if word had spread far and wide across the fairground that this was the main event. Of the two contestants, though, only one had so far arrived: Tanto, who strolled nonchalantly about the ring as if it were his own, smiling and pressing the hands of the prettier women who leaned over the ropes to give him a word of encouragement, a touch for luck; a favour. He kissed one on the cheek, another (more voluptuous) on the lips. They giggled and blushed. The second tied an embroidered ribbon about his bicep, where it fluttered in the light breeze like a pennant. A nomad woman threw him a flower, and, laughing, he caught it in mid-air and tucked it behind his ear. The women loved that, Saro noticed bitterly. It was as if Tanto held them somehow in thrall, for the shyer ones fluttered and blushed if his eyes fell on them, while the bold plumped up their bosoms and made lewd remarks. Saro realised, with a jolt of envy, that this was what it was to have outer beauty and arrogance: the women cared nothing for the man beneath the handsome surface, for the cruelty and pettiness that he knew so well, so long as they were able to flirt and be teased. He wished with sudden vehemence that he could transfer to each of them the gift he had received from the old nomad. Then perhaps they would be less keen to attract his brother's attention.

Across the far side of the ring, the crowd began to move apart to make way for a tall man, wearing the wound cloth headwear of the desertmen. He came striding through the throng, followed by a half dozen of his followers, all clad in the same outlandish fashion. When he reached the ropes, instead of ducking beneath them in the usual fashion, the first man scissored his legs and cleared them neatly. A momentary hush quieted the crowd, then everyone started talking at once.

'The Phoenix, they call him,' Saro heard a man in front of him say to his companion, 'the carrion bird that rises from the embers.'

Saro studied the desertman closely, intrigued. He was, for all his imposing appearance, no taller than Tanto, he realised, slightly disappointed. It was the headcloth that had made him seem so; but still he was impressive: being lightly built, but wiry. A deceptive sort of man, Saro thought; one who did not wear his prowess like a peacock. Indeed, the Phoenix's gear was old and filthy. His undershirt, where it showed at hem and cuffs, was of stained and indeterminately coloured, crumpled cloth. Over this he wore a plain jerkin of tanned leather, cinched with a plaited rag belt and over this a breastplate of thicker leather covered with a hundred overlapping rounds of dented iron. His breeches were of the same dun hue as the jerkin and bound tight from knee to ankle in the barbarian fashion with strips of crossed hide from which not all the hair and flesh had been successfully flayed. Black and brown tufts stuck out this way and that where the bindings met, but Saro could not even begin to hazard a guess as to what sort of hideous creature had donated its ugly hide to the purpose. With the folds of the headcloth obscuring all but the Phoenix's eyes, it was hard to put an age to him. From his bearing – experienced, confident, fluidly fit – Saro could imagine him anywhere between thirty and fifty or more years of age. And the eyes did not help, either: they were dark and gleaming, but the crow's feet that fanned from their corners were, when the man stopped frowning (or smiling: it was hard to tell which) pale against skin that appeared dark with years of sun and wind. A tough one, Saro thought: hardly the 'scruffy old man' his stupid brother had dubbed him. The phrase 'a seasoned fighter' came unprompted to Saro's mind, as if the very definition of the words stood there before his eyes. And indeed it fit the man well: he did look as hard as seasoned yew or oak – left out in the elements to harden or rot. And when he rolled the sleeves of his undershirt up, Saro saw a maze of white scars criss-crossing his forearms. What chance did his brother stand against such a man?

Yet Tanto seemed entirely unconcerned by the forbidding appearance of his opponent. Everything about him was insouciant as he soaked up the admiration of the crowd. A woman cried out, asking if he had a wife.

'Today I am single!' Tanto declared, throwing his arms wide as if to embrace them all. 'But tomorrow?'

The women all seemed to flower beneath his gaze. Saro noticed a well-made girl with a flag of blonde hair dragging her companion, a creature with thin arms and a huge chest with her to gain a position at the ropes; how some nomad women with shaved heads and jewel-studded teeth whistled at his brother. Two Eyran beldames in homespun dresses and garish scarves remarked loudly on the fine length of Tanto's legs, so well displayed in the violet hose he had chosen to complement his bright-green embroidered tunic; his white teeth and glittering eyes so bright against the darkness of his skin. He looked, Saro had to admit, like a fine-bred colt turned out for a state parade: all sheeny and agile. But if Tanto was coltish, then the older man was a desert stallion, Saro thought, and went to place his own bet. When he got to the bet-collector he was surprised to find that the odds had shortened on Tanto, four hits to three. It was the work of the women, he realised.

It had taken Jenna and Marin longer to reach the sword-ring than Jenna had planned, since there had been so many distractions on the way. Marin had been particularly fascinated by the boulder-throwing competition, in which giants of men – almost without exception Eyran, it seemed – were hefting enormous rocks and casting them with huge, explosive cries only inches away from their own feet. A man with a measuring rod then marked the distance each man had achieved, but it did not seem to Jenna – whose taste did not run to the massy or muscle-bound – to be much of a spectator sport.

The horse-fighting, in the next enclosure, was too bloody for words. They had hurried past quickly, averting their eyes from the shrieking beasts, from the ripped flesh and thrashing hooves; and then past the wrestling rings, where it had been Jenna's turn to want to stay and watch: for where else would you have the chance to stare at men's unclothed bodies so freely and for so long – except maybe at the swimming contest, and they were now at some distance from the beach. Besides, she reminded Marin, grabbing her arm as if it had been the younger girl's idea to tarry at the wrestling, there was betting to be done, and her tip to be followed. And in fact they barely had time to place their coins on their chosen swordman and find their places before the officials called the contestants together for the examination of their weapons and the reading of the rules.

'He's very handsome,' whispered Marin to her companion as Tanto flexed and stretched. 'But I think he has a cruel jaw. I quite like look of the desertman, though.'

Jenna looked at her askance. 'What do you know of men? A cruel jaw, indeed! If my heart was not given to King Ravn, I would cast it down at Tanto Vingo's feet without a second thought.' She laughed recklessly. 'Because other than the King, he is the handsomest man I ever saw. Besides, what can you see of the desertman? Nothing but his eyes and hands. That's hardly enough to go on, is it?'

'It's more than the Istrians have to see when they choose their brides,' Marin pointed out with a certain petulance, 'for they see only their lips and hands. And when King Ravn chooses the Swan of Jetra, that's all he'll see of her, too, until the wedding night.'

Jenna looked furious. She stared wildly about the crowd in case anyone had heard their conversation; but the folk who surrounded them were intent on the contestants, as the blue-cloaks patted them down for any concealed weapons.

Marin spotted Saro, and took pity on the blonde girl. 'Look,' she said quickly, to turn the subject. 'Look at that one there, behind the man with the huge beard.'

Jenna followed Marin's gaze. There was certainly something about the young southerner on the far side of the enclosure. Like the man in the ring, he was well made and darkly complexioned, but his features had a less delicately chiselled look to them, and his hair was longer and less sleek. She marked how he moved carefully out of the way of the spectators, without ever once taking his gaze – black and intense – off Tanto Vingo. Perhaps they were lovers! She'd heard, from the sort of scurrilous gossip you picked up from the court-servants in Halbo, that in the southern states sometimes men lived with men as they would with wives. There was even a version of the story of the mage Arahaï which told how he had quarrelled with his lover, himself a powerful magician, and been forced to entomb him beneath the earth, in a cave all of crystal and gold, and that every day for the rest of his life he had visited him there, and mourned; how his magic had fled him, leaving his heart like ashes. It was all very poetic, she thought. And then there were the ancient hero tales which told of how lovers would go to war together – both men and men, and men and women; and sometimes, unimaginably to Jenna, even women and women – fighting back to back, each protecting the other or dying in the attempt, but no one she had asked in Eyra would even speak to her of such things, as if it was in some way shameful, a subject to be avoided. She was visited by a sudden, wonderful vision of herself as a shield-maiden, like the Fyrnir of Slitwood, in shining mail and helm, a gleaming sword in her hand, standing back to back – she could almost feel the warmth of his sunny skin through the layers of cloth and leather and mail – to defend her lord and lover, King Ravn . . .

The clash of metal brought her sharply from her reverie, and suddenly the crowd came alive with shouts and whistles.

The Phoenix, having made the first move, appeared to have driven the young Istrian back against the ropes to their left with his first charge, so that the lad was forced to step quickly away, turning and countering as he went, his feet dancing neatly over the ashy ground. As he came round to face them, Jenna saw that the southerner nevertheless was grinning wildly and his face was flushed with excitement.

Her betted silvers seemed suddenly very safe. 'Come on, Tanto!' she called, and heard the shout taken up all around her. The desertman, for all his mystery and expertise, was not, it seemed, popular on this side of the ring.

Again, the turbaned man came at him, and again Tanto turned him. The thick northern sword the desertman wielded sliced through the air with all the finesse of an abattoir axe. Tanto caught it on the dagger he held in his left hand and flicked it upward, then ran beneath the man's upraised arm and swept his fine Forent sword around in a gleaming arc, tapping the front of his opponent's breastplate as he passed.

'A hit!' cried the arbitrator, and 'A hit! A hit!' echoed the crowd.

Jenna clutched Marin's arm excitedly. 'You see?'

The desertman watched Tanto withdraw to the opposite side of the ring. He scythed his sword from side to side, shouting as he did so, in some guttural version of the Old Tongue: 'I'll cut you down to size, pretty boy! I'll take those purple legs home with me and feed them to my wolves.'

In response, Tanto flicked his dagger at the man in a gesture that in any culture was clearly insulting.

The Phoenix roared an oath and charged across the ring. Again, Tanto side-stepped; but when he tried the same manoeuvre that had won him the point, the desertman, quicker and lighter on his feet than Jenna could believe possible, feinted and dodged, so that Tanto over-balanced. A snaking foot helped him on his way, and all at once the young Istrian was face down in the dust. The desertman's eyes became bright with feral cunning. His sword came rushing down as if – had the edges not been blunted in line with the competition rules – he would slice Tanto in half; but he pulled it short at the last moment, stepping back a half pace so that the flat of the blade smacked the Istrian sharply on the buttocks. It must have stung, for Tanto yelped like a kicked dog.

'A hit!' cried the desertman's swathed supporters.

'A hit,' conceded the arbitrator.

Tanto threw himself upright. Every line of his body spoke of fury, and when he turned, the excited flush with which he had begun the bout had become an ugly, livid purple. Not so handsome now, Marin thought, feeling somewhat vindicated.

Tanto ran at the Phoenix, sword arm as stiff as a spar. Even with the button on the point, Saro thought, disquieted, such a charge, met head-on, could run a man through; but the Phoenix merely brought his guard-hand up and pushed the slim Forent blade off his dagger as if it were a meat-skewer. Again, Tanto rushed him, and again the older man caught his sword and turned it neatly. This furious charging and rebuttal went on for some minutes, until the crowd were screaming themselves hoarse.

And then the tide turned.

The Phoenix, in the guise of passing off Tanto's assault onto his dagger, now stepped smartly within the Istrian's range and, allowing Tanto's sword to pass harmlessly under his arm, turned, brought his shoulder up so that it met squarely with Tanto's chest, and flicked the lighter man over and onto the ground.

Had Katla been watching, she would have recognised it as an Eyran wrestling manoeuvre, one of her favourites, designed to use an opponent's weight and momentum against them, so that they hit the floor with twice the impact.

The crowd howled. 'Unfair!' screamed a woman to Jenna's right.

'Unfair!' cried the Istrians watching.

The Phoenix stepped back with a shrug. He looked to the arbitrator, but the man's mouth was pursed in disapproval.

Tanto, glimpsing his chance, vaulted to his feet and charged the desertman with all his might. Despite his exhaustion, Tanto's training had not gone to waste. He crossed the ring in three vast, leaping strides, arm extended, and his swordpoint − button and all − drove itself between the discs on the older man's breastplate before the Phoenix could even think of countering. The desertman roared and leapt backward, but Tanto's blade was firmly lodged; as the man stepped back, he had no choice but to go with him. The brutal northern sword came sweeping down at Tanto's head. It was a blow that − had it landed − would have split his skull in two: competition edge blunted or no − but Tanto's reactions were extraordinarily fast. His left hand came up in a blur of motion, catching the big blade in a life-saving parry. There were sparks, the ear-splitting screech of metal on metal; and then Tanto's dagger shattered. Pieces of it hurtled away from the impact like a shower of falling stars, raining out across the ring. One shard caught the desertman in the face, between the folds of the headcloth. Blood spurted, but Tanto, with his dagger hand numbed and his swordpoint still wedged in the other's breastplate, stood shocked and motionless. The desertman hurled his own dagger away and brought his swordpoint up to Tanto's throat.

'A win!' his followers bellowed.

'A win.'

The arbitrator stepped in to separate the combatants, and the crowd erupted. It took two of the blue-cloaks to extricate the Istrian's weapon from the overlapping iron rings of the Phoenix's breastplate, and when it was released, Tanto tore it angrily away from them, slammed it back into its sheath and stormed from the ring without bothering to retrieve the jewelled hilt of the broken dagger. He did manage, however, to gracelessly grab the purse his second place had earned him. A Footloose lad, quick-eyed, slipped beneath the ropes while everyone else's attention was still on the two contestants, and pocketed the hilt with a triumphant smile. A few moments later, a scuffle broke out between him and a big Eyran man, who was then confronted joined by a group of angry Istrians.

The Phoenix wiped blood from his eye–slit and, holding a wad of loose material against his face, claimed his prize and silently disappeared into the crowd.

Marin went to collect her winnings. Annoyed by Jenna's manipulations, she had backed the desertman. The bet-collector paid out a stream of silvers into her hand. Behind her, Saro was the only Istrian in the queue. When he got to the front, the bet-collector regarded him curiously, then tapped the side of his nose and winked at Saro. Saro had no idea what he meant by this, but he took the money the man paid carefully into his hand, pocketed it and made his way to the enclosure where he had left Night's Harbinger. Now he would have to win the damned race.

As he was walking through the crowds, his eyes focused on nothing in particular, he was hailed by a familiar voice.

'Saro, wait!'

When he turned around, he saw his uncle running to catch up with him. Saro's heart sank, but he needn't have feared for all Fabel said was: 'I just came to wish you luck, lad.' And he reached out with a grin and tousled Saro's hair.

A bizarre mix of sensations flowed through the skin of Saro's scalp: anxiety and despair; concern that he would lose the race, for it was hard to have confidence in the lad, who was not a natural athlete, and not hard enough on the beasts, and Night's Harbinger, which had little respect for anyone, would surely just kick up its heels and send the boy sailing out over the ropes in seconds; fear that they would never raise the bride-price if he failed; and Falla knew what Tanto would do then, for the boy was clearly unstable, for all his handsome looks and physical abilities; and Favio, Favio would be disappointed, too, and he bore enough guilt not to wish his brother further cast down. All this Saro felt in the time it took for the flat of Fabel's hand to ruffle his hair, and withdraw; and as the fingers abandoned his head, he was left with a single, discomfiting image: a woman's eyes, widened with surprise and some delight as a man mounted her. He heard her voice, like a whisper through time: 'Oh, Fabel, Fabel.'

It took him all the time from arriving at the enclosure, to saddling Night's Harbinger and leading him into the starters' pen, to realise – through the low-level nervous anticipation of the horse – that the voice he had heard had not been his aunt's, but his mother's.

'Fezack! Fezack! Look – I can see the horserace!' The boy was gleeful, his grin stretched from ear to ear. 'Look, Gramma, in the rock.'

'Child: don't be foolish, the race is not to run for an hour or more.' Fezack Starsinger was weary: it had been one long round of customers today: men wanting potions to give them prowess they were unable to earn by other means; women wanting beauty they could never naturally achieve; those who sought knowledge of the future, interpretations of omens and dreams; a blight on a neighbour or competitor. These last she turned away angrily. 'The Wanderers never do harm: it is not our way, know you better than to ask!' The last two customers to have knocked on the sun-and-moon door were those who had bought charms from her that had inexplicably worked too well, and were now seeking another potion to reverse the effect of the first. The girl, she had remembered, though her poor chest was unrecognisable. It had been a chastening experience, for both of them.

The old woman came to stand over her grandson, though she was barely taller than he was. She peered over his shoulder at the crystal, but could see not a thing. The child was not usually fanciful, but it was true that there had been a number of odd occurrences at this Fair. And not just at the Allfair, either, she corrected herself. No: she had noticed something – something intangible, like a tension in the air, a stirring in the blood – some weeks before, as if the fundamental nature of the world was undergoing some strange and subtle metamorphosis . . .

'Look: see there, in the midst of that great cloud of dust, two horses fighting – a brown horse with a big man on its back and a dark one, ridden by the boy who saved Guaya – oh! see, the chestnut horse has blood on its teeth and the dark horse has a wound on its shoulder—'

Fezack frowned. She pushed her grandson gently aside and leaned over the great polished rock – a piece of pinkish grey crystal that had been excavated with some difficulty from a cave in the western mountains, at that juncture where the Golden range met the sweep of sharp volcanic peaks known by the hill peoples as the Dragon's Backbone. It had been her parents who had dug it out, with great exclamations of delight at its purity and size, for it was a valuable piece, and they believed still in the old magic, that such rocks channelled the earth magic that had waned almost from memory, all but inactive these two hundred years and more. Time blurred so much for her now: but she could remember that day with remarkable clarity – how they had been travelling away from a gathering of the hill tribes, celebrating their victory over an Istrian lord and his soldiers who had tried to take them into slavery, all of whom now lay shattered and dead beneath the boulder-fall the hill-women had engineered as their men led the unsuspecting enemy below the cliffs. The Wanderers did not condone such violence; but neither did they believe in the enslavement of others, so they had joined the celebrations without too many misgivings, and yet it had been with a sense of dread that Fezack had headed up into the mountains the next day with her parents and the other nomads, and the finding of the crystal had done nothing to alleviate her sense that there was something out of kilter. And indeed, they had met a troop of Istrians later that night as they came down through the col; soldiers who had found their slain comrades and heard tales of nomads who had caused the rockfall with their magic. Her parents were both killed; as were seven of the men. The women who survived were raped. Her daughter, Alisha, had been one result. She had no love of the southern peoples.

Placing her hands on either side of the great crystal, she felt its power thrum through her: a faint tingling in the palms and wrists, a slight numbing of the arms. She was used to this feeling, this faint hum of energy the rock generated – enough to cure a mild headache, to absorb the pain from a sprain or bruise. Far-seeing had always seemed beyond its capability though: so it was with some amazement that she felt the crystal take hold of her, reach through her, seeking its outlet. Waves of warmth began to travel up through her bony arms. She felt them suffuse her chest, her neck, reach up through the bones of her skull, where it powered through her like a pale white light. Where it burned the backs of her eyes. She saw: a chaos of fighting horses, their hooves churning the lava of the plain up into swirling dark clouds of dust; the terrified face of a man, not much older than a boy, his dark eyes wide with panic and something else – a knowledge, a horror – as another man, bigger, older, bearing a wicked-looking whip, reached out and caught him by the shoulder and brought the whip around in a swingeing blow. Other riders charged by in a whirl of movement and when their dust cleared she looked for the dark boy again but could see him nowhere. The man with the whip was on the ground, getting trampled by his own horse. She tilted the stone for a better angle, but as she did so, the scene blurred and changed and then everything went dark and she smelled the tang of blood.

She shrieked and withdrew her hands from the crystal.

'You must not touch the stone,' she said to her grandson with unaccustomed severity. Her voice was shaking, and not only her voice. She took down a woollen blanket from the shelf where she stowed her sleeping things during the day, wrapped the crystal tightly in its folds, hefted her burden and staggered down the steps of the wagon.

When she reached her daughter's wagon she called her name.

'Alisha!'

There was some commotion in the confines of the wagon, muted voices, a hurried rustling of fabrics. Then came the sound of footsteps and the door came open by half a foot. Her daughter stuck her head out. Her shoulders were bare down to a hastily-wrapped sheet; her cheeks glowed, and her hair was in disarray.

'Mother?'

Fezack took in Alisha's state of undress, the sudden conscious silence in the wagon, and smiled thinly.

'Think you I would criticise your choice of man that you look so guilty, daughter?' she asked gently, arms and back sagging beneath the weight of the great rock.

'You might. He's not one of us.'

'Who he is, I know well.'

They both fell quiet. Then Fezack groaned. 'Daughter: will you leave me struggling with this thing?'

Turning the end of the bedsheet tightly into the band she had made above her breasts, Alisha padded barefoot down the wagon steps and carefully transferred the weight of the crystal into her own arms. The sheet trailed behind her like a train as she followed her mother behind the wagon to the place where the low eating table was set up.

'The crystal has begun to work, suddenly and with no warning. Falo used it to far-see. And then I looked, too. A shock, it was, Alisha: truly. I do not think I can bear to look again at what I saw there, and I know not whether my vision is true-sight, or false. Another opinion I would welcome.' Gingerly, she unwrapped the rock, allowing the corners of the blanket to fall back over the table-edges. The crystal glowed still, even without a human touch, its gleaming facets still milky with the remnants of the vision.

Alisha pulled a face. 'I have never seen it like this before. I'm not sure I want to have anything to do with it. Anyway,' she folded her arms, looking mutinous, 'I'm sure I don't have the art.'

'My mother, her sister, my grandmother and great-grandmother, and her mother before that, they all had the art. It was said that Arnia Skylark could true-see across two continents with the aid of a crystal far smaller than this one.'

'Tales and nonsense, Mother! That sort of magic hasn't worked for centuries.'

'Something has changed. Please look, for me, Alisha.'

With a sigh, Alisha hiked the sheet up about her and sat crosslegged before the table. At the little round window in the back of the wagon there was a movement as a drape was twitched and Fezack glimpsed a white face and a shock of pale hair before the figure disappeared. Alisha, too, stared at the window, then looked away quickly as her mother's attention came back to her. Dispassionately, she grasped the rock with both hands. And then her expression changed. Her eyes widened. The blood began to drain from her face and she started to shudder.

When she finally dragged her hands away from the crystal, she was shaking all over.

'We must spread the word. We must pack up and leave, Mother: now, as soon as we can.'

Fezack Starsinger gave her daughter a wan smile. 'You saw what I saw. Murder and blood and flames. The old ones are waking, daughter: I can feel them stir. The magic is back, and it brings death in its wake.'

Eleven

Affiliations

'You've done *what*?'

Too stupefied to do anything else, Katla sat down on the bench with a thump. It was as if her knees had absorbed the shock of her father's pronouncement before any other part of her had had a chance to.

'Finn Larson is a good man, and a wealthy man, to boot.'

All the colour had gone from Katla's face, except for two burning spots just upon each cheekbone. Her eyes were as black and hollow as two fishing-holes in ice. All she could manage was: 'But he's an *old* man.'

Aran bridled. 'He's a couple of years younger than me—'

'Why would I want to marry a man as old as *you*?' Katla stormed. Against her will, tears started to well up. She gulped them down, furious at her own lack of control. 'When I asked you if you'd brought me here to marry me off, you said you had other plans for me,' she accused.

'I did. I was going to take up Finn's offer to foster you, have you attend court classes with Jenna. Your mother and I discussed it. We thought it might teach you to be more of a lady—'

'So that you could marry me off for a better deal?'

'For your own good, Katla. Take a look at yourself: you're no better than a hoyden. You run and climb and fight with the boys; you can't cook or sew even wear a decent dress. It was Finn himself who made the suggestion to turn the fostering to a marriage offer, which certainly surprised me. But he seems remarkably keen.'

'I won't do it. I'll run away.'

'You'll do nothing of the sort. I gave him my word. The promise is shaken on.'

'Your word? What care I for your word? I'll give you *my* word!' Now Katla was on her feet. 'And my word is NO. Never.'

She tried to run past him, out of the booth, but he stepped into her path and pushed her back down onto the bench. 'Listen to me, Katla. It's a good offer. He has three greathouses, the shipworks at Fairwater, and high standing with the King. And we'll do it all properly. He'll bring betrothal rings to the Gathering tonight and we'll make a formal announcement. You'll sail with Jenna back to Halbo on the *Mermaid*, and he'll join you there for the blessing and bedding on the first full moon of Shoaling month.'

The bedding. Katla shuddered. Shoaling. She made a quick mental calculation. Less than thirty days away. She turned wildly to Halli, standing behind their father's left shoulder, looking almost as stricken as she.

'Halli – you can't let him do this! You were to marry Jenna and now you won't be able to, for I'd be your wed-mother. Can't you stop this?'

Halli dropped his head, would not meet her eye. 'I'm sorry, Katla. Father's pledged the honour of our clan on this. It cannot be gone back on.'

'Honour? Is that all you care for? What about your *heart*, Halli? I thought you loved Jenna, that you were going to commission a ship and sail to make your fortune so that you and she could marry?'

At that, Halli looked up. His eyes were bereft. 'All that's gone now,' he said flatly. 'Father has other plans.'

Katla turned to Fent. 'And what about you? You'll stand by and let him do this to me, will you?'

Fent shook his head slowly. 'He's our father, Katla. He's made the trade, and his word is law. I'm sorry.'

An uncomfortable silence fell over the group. No one looked at anyone else. It was Tor whose voice broke the lull. 'Whatever Finn's offered you for Katla,' he said to Aran Aranson, 'I'll match it.'

Katla's head shot up. 'So now I'm a prize cow to be bargained over, am I?' Her eyes shot sparks at him.

Tor shrugged. 'I thought you might rather have a younger man than old Finn Larson. One with no belly and a bit of fire still inside him.'

'I don't want *you*!' Katla spat back. She hugged her arms about herself as if feeling a sudden chill. Her entire family, it seemed, had betrayed her: those she thought would defend her to the death. Where, she wondered all at once, was Erno? Perhaps he'd rescue her. Surely he couldn't love little Marin Edelsen: she couldn't believe that. No. He loved her: she was sure of it. He could help her run away. The thought came out of nowhere, roiled around in her head, then took firm hold. Erno: he was the answer. She'd wait until the Gathering and amidst all that social chaos they could slip away unnoticed before the betrothal was announced. Erno could take an oar with her on one of the faerings: they'd row down the coast. She'd wear her breeches and tunic under her dress, pack her things and leave them somewhere convenient. She began to make a mental note of what she'd need: the dagger with the topaz set into the hilt; her best short sword; her leather jerkin – too heavy to wear beneath the dress – her boots . . .

Seeing his daughter with her face downcast thus, Aran felt his heart contract. He'd expected the fiery outburst, the denial, the fury. What he hadn't expected was this sudden resignation, this surrender. She was a good girl, underneath all the high spirits and horseplay, and she was his favourite. It had been hard to make the trade, whatever she might think, hard emotionally, despite the potential rewards. He found he could not let himself think too closely on how she would fare with Finn. For all he seemed a decent man, there had been rumours about the demise of his first wife: in childbirth, for sure; but there were those who said she'd come to bed earlier than her full term as a result of a fist in the belly. She'd lost the baby first; and then her life when the blood refused to stop, for all the women could do with their lichens and hawkweed. Some said she'd made up her mind to go, and that the will was stronger than any herb in such cases . . .

He dragged his mind away. Katla would have Jenna there with her for some of the time at least, and they were such good friends.

But in the back of his skull the thought nagged on: that in promising Katla thus, and denying Halli all he had dreamed of, he had done a wrong thing indeed. His hand strayed to his tunic pocket and his fingers curled for a moment around the lump of gold he kept there until everything seemed right again. With a bark of command to his sons, he pushed back the flap of the tent and strode out into the light. Halli and Fent exchanged a brief, uncomfortable glance and went after him. Tor made a half-step towards Katla, but when she didn't look up, he turned and followed the others.

It was only some minutes after they had gone that Katla realised she had not asked about why it was she had been traded. What on Elda could be so precious to her father that he would sell his only daughter?

Saro leaned his hand against Night Harbinger's glossy neck and felt the pulse beat there, hard and strong, eager for the race, excited by the presence of the other horses against whom he would race. He would outrun them all, for none were as fleet as he; he was lord of the wind and all the mares wanted him. The boy on his back had no more weight than a flea: nothing could stop him. He expelled the air through his nostrils with a great snort and tossed his head with impatience.

Saro found himself smiling. If only he had the stallion's confidence . . .

But it seemed all he had to do was to let Night's Harbinger have his head, for here they were now, the rope holding them all back – Leonic Bakran on Filial Duty; Ordono Qaran on a great white beast with its mane all plaited with red; Calastrina's eldest son on a neat piebald gelding with a rolling eye and a twitchy gait; and a dozen or more others, northerners and hillmen, even a desert-rider on a horse that was gold from ears to tail. Saro thought of Guaya. He thought of a home without his bullying brother in it. He had to win. He had to. He reached down and touched the bay's neck and tried not to let his own feelings of panic intrude themselves into the stallion's mind.

Lord Tycho Issian smoothed the front of the robe he had donned for the Gathering. It was his finest, though he planned to attend the event for only a short while. Just the time it took, in fact, to obtain the dowry from the Vingos and go find the nomad map-seller and make his trade. He had the priest standing by: he would marry the woman before he bedded her, sanctify their union in the eyes of the Goddess. What could be more proper?

He snapped his fingers and one of the slaveboys appeared promptly, dressed neatly in the velvet suit Tycho had bought the lad for the occasion, his unruly black ringlets sleeked down with scented oil. Which one was he? Felo or Tam? He really couldn't remember. His thoughts were befuddled: all he could think of was the woman. 'What's your name, boy?' he said sharply to the child.

The boy stared up at him in surprise. He'd worked in the lord's household for over four years, ever since the lord had acquired him and the others at the blocks in Gibeon. For the last two he'd been the master's personal attendant, along with Felo, his cousin, a member of the same hill tribe. It was the first time the lord had ever forgotten his name. 'Tam, lord,' he said hurriedly.

'Tam: you will walk directly behind me at the Gathering, and when we collect the coffer from the Vingo family, you will carry it for me, without stooping or stumbling, no matter how heavy it may be, and follow wherever I take you, as quickly as you can. Is that clear?'

'Yes, lord.'

Tycho nodded. They would have to get the money away to the nomad quarter as swiftly and smoothly as possible if he was to secure his bride; for only that morning a Council official had come to his pavilion asking for an audience. Tycho knew what that was about: other lords at the Fair had been complaining about the recall of debts, and he had no intention of paying over the money he owed them at this time. He had sent a boy to turn the man away – with all the correct observances, of course – and only after a glass of rose-araque and an almond wafer; and then had slipped silently out of the back exit of the pavilion.

He let his mind stray to thoughts of the Rosa Eldi. It was a peculiar name, even for a nomad woman, he mused, for the thousandth time since that fateful kiss; though she had not the dark looks of most of that rabble. Rose of Elda, Rose of the World, he translated from the Old Tongue. It suited her well enough, he had to concede, with her fragile colouring and graceful neck. Ah, Rosa Eldi. I shall soon fold back those petals and bury myself in your scent. Soon you will be mine . . .

'It was a stupid thing to do. Mad. Irresponsible. What your father would have said, I cannot imagine. And now look at you: how will we explain this to the lords who come to do you honour this evening?'

Stormway had been ranting on in like vein for the last two hours or more, and that was after the Earl of Shepsey had had his say and stalked out.

King Ravn Asharson sighed, took the bandage away from his face, examined the latest outpouring, refolded it to expose a slightly less bloody section, and pressed it hard against his cheek again. The damned wound just would not stop bleeding, and the blow had also caused the skin around his eye to blacken and swell. He would indeed look a sight at the Gathering tonight; but for that he cared not a whit. It had been sheer bad luck that the boy's dagger had shattered so: he'd made damned sure otherwise the Istrian would not damage him, for all his fancy footwork and that furious charge.

'And whatever will your prospective bride say to see you thus, all bruised and bloody? You're lucky you did not lose that eye.'

'For Sur's sake, man, stop your nagging. You sound like my mother when I fell down the castle stairs chasing Breta at the age of seven.'

'Sire, you'll forgive me, but even a seven-year would have had more sense than to do what you did this afternoon.' Stormway sat down with a thump, as if all the energy had suddenly run out of him. He looked old, Ravn thought, a tedious old man.

'It was only a bit of fun. I'm going out of my mind with the boredom of this place. I can't wander the Fair, for fear of being assassinated by some shadowy villain, just because one of your so-called spies has picked up a rumour; I can't take part in the Games for fear someone will run me through or break my neck; I can't tup any women for fear of the scandal—'

'You're our only king,' Stormway said more gently. 'You have no heir, yet. If we were to lose you, there would be civil war in the north. You know this, sire: you must understand our concern.'

'And if I marry Keril Sandson's girl?' Ravn regarded his chief adviser challengingly. He knew it was the last thing Stormway wanted. Or perhaps the next-to-last thing . . .

The Earl of Stormway rubbed his remaining hand across his face in a weary gesture. 'In the end it will be your choice, sire; but you must know that that is exactly what Sandson has been planning for these last few months. Why do you think he's been seen at court so frequently? It's not for love of you, sire, whatever you may think. I have seen him whispering in corners to the Earl of Fall's Head, and to that snake Erol Bardson, too. And we all know Bardson's spent the last few months adding to his private army—'

'Ah, my beloved cousin. Also trying to push his girl at me. It's a shame, she's quite a pretty little heifer, that one. Which is more than I can say for all the rest. Well, if it's any consolation, Bran, I don't think I shall pick any of the beauties they are trying to force upon me.' He watched the old man's face relax. 'But do not think that means I shall choose your Breta, either.' He pictured her now: a sturdily-built young woman, which he did not mind in itself – a bit of flesh to hold onto in the midst of the deed was no bad thing; nor the softness of a woman's inner thighs to pillow you as you dozed – but, Sur, her face! Even as a child, when he had chased and teased her all around the palace at Halbo, she had been as ugly as an elk. Give her a beard, and it would be like tupping her father . . .

'You know our advice,' Stormway said stiffly. 'Take one of the Eyran girls – Ella Stensen or Filia Jansen, or the Earl of Ness's daughter; or even Jenna Finnsen, for all her father's only a shipmaker, he's still a damned fine shipmaker, and I believe the girl herself is not unattractive. Take one of them, no matter what the south offer. We cannot trust the Empire lords, as those of us who remember the last war will remind you.'

Ravn rolled his eyes. Why were his advisers all such old

men? All they could think of was the old wars, the old ways. 'Have you no adventure in your spirit, Bran? Do you not sometimes hanker for change, for surprise in your life? Could you not fancy finding out what one of those southern girls have under their robes?'

'I had enough of "surprises", as you term them, Ravn, twenty-two years ago,' Stormway said sourly, waving the stump of his hand in the King's face. 'And I'll wager the southern women have exactly under their robes what the northern ones do.'

'You cannot tell me, Bran, that you never found out for yourself when raiding the southern ports? That you didn't indulge in a little defilement and depredation, a bit of rape and pillage?' Ravn eased himself back against the pillar and watched the Stormway's face cloud over with some enjoyment. If it served to deflect the old boor from his ranting, and embarrass him into the bargain, it was time well spent. And the truth was, he *did* rather fancy finding out what the southern women were hiding, whatever his lords might advise. The idea of a foreign girl in his bed, one who smelled and looked different to the big blondes and redheads he was so used to, one who might have unusual practices in her armoury, and who wouldn't prattle on at him in endless Eyran platitudes, was an attractive proposition – and damn the consequences. If it meant stirring up the pot and letting old enmities and new conspiracies float to the surface, then so be it.

It was not that he did not understand the theories and counter-theories his lords rehearsed so endlessly before him: how the different factions would side with one another; how an alliance here would bring strife there; how the choice of a bride from the Western Isles would inflame the Earl of Ness; how taking Ness's daughter would prompt hostility from Erol and his schemers; how taking any of the southerners' women would turn his traditional supporters against him and leave him open to dissent and uprising in his own country, and possibly to some unseen machination in the Empire. It was that he truly didn't care. Life had been dull for a long time in the northern court. He'd bedded every woman he liked the look of, and a few he didn't, he'd fought duels and started blood-feuds that had all but bankrupted the coffers to bring conciliation between the clans, and the only prospect that held out any spark of interest to him was the chance to take passage to the Far West. Which his lords would not allow him to do until he had safely got himself an heir to secure the damned kingdom.

So a wife – any wife – was now his first priority. Perhaps he'd take the Swan of Jetra, after all; so long as she didn't look like a walrus underneath those all-enveloping robes.

The Rose of Elda lay on her bunk in the map-seller's wagon, with the black cat stretched out beside her and a dark green shawl artfully deposited over the damp patch where she had poured the greater part of the sleeping draught that Virelai had given her before he left. A huge rumble rose from the cat, where her hand travelled its silky fur. When Virelai was not around, she noticed that the cat was happier, more relaxed. Now, it lay on its back with a line of drool falling like a spidersilk from its mouth, with all four paws splayed under the touch of her fingers. Did she, she wondered, regarding the slit-eyed creature askance, have the same effect on beasts as she did on men? Was the cat also captivated by her? Her hand stopped its rhythmic course as she pondered on this, not knowing quite how she felt about such a proposition. It could be troubling to see men reduced to slack-mouthed wonder, to see their pupils flood with desire; to watch the stirring in their breeches, and know that they responded only to her aura, to the sight and the sense of her, not to the woman she was.

And who was she? The Rosa Eldi's beautiful brows knit themselves in frustration. Her recollections were so vague, so recent. She sometimes wondered whether the Master had deliberately induced a kind of memory-loss in her, with all his potions and charms, to keep her from straying. To prevent her from feeling any sense of loss, or displacement, or wishing to return to her own folk, wherever they might be.

She thought these things without forming words into sentences; another gap in her education in Sanctuary, with Rahe as her only tutor. Only now was she beginning to pick up any knowledge of the languages of Elda, as Virelai did his best to teach her. But even as she learned, she had the sense there was a deep chasm between the words and what they stood for in the world of men; for the world of men she understood not at all. What she did understand was desire and its currency. The Master had been very thorough in his tutelage of all aspects of *that* subject.

When Virelai returned to the caravan some minutes later, he found the Rosa Eldi rather more alert than he'd expected, given the particularly strong dose he had administered to her earlier that day to prevent any trouble arising between then and when he completed his bargain with the powerful southern lord. He was tired of travelling with the foul-smelling yeka and this broken-down wagon, with its creaking wheels and damaged rear axle, currently held together only by a binding spell he'd finally managed to coax out of the cat, though his fingers had swelled from its bite for two days, and he'd had to seek the ministrations of the old charm-seller's daughter to cure the poison. Still, that episode had had its consolations . . .

He kicked the rotting wood of the doorframe as he came in. The worthless thing probably wouldn't even hold together for the trip back over the Skarn Mountains. The prospect of travelling south with Lord Issian had been giving him some intensely pleasurable fantasies, based on the ancient books the Master had kept in his library, with their brightly-inked, hand-drawn pictures and delicate sketches. Virelai could feel a palace beckoning, a palace of warm golden sandstone set in the lush, rolling valleys of Istria, a palace fragrant with the scent of lemon trees and olive groves; a palace strewn with silk draperies and soft cushions and dusky maidens.

When he'd first encountered those passages in the Master's books that told how the Istrians swathed their women and kept them locked away, he'd thought them mad. If he'd had a palace full of women, he'd thought then, he'd have them running naked through every room. Now, in the thrall of the Rosa Eldi, he could better understand why they might try to limit the power of the creatures.

He sighed.

'What is it, my dove?' crooned the Rosa Eldi in that strangely toneless voice.

The cat gave him the evil eye and sat up. He noticed that it kept itself close to the woman's side, as though proclaiming her its territory.

'I was thinking of the luxuries that await us in the rich southern lands,' he said, smiling. 'When you are the lady of the palace, and I the court mage.' Though he knew this was not the only reason; and that she would be lady there for only so long as it took for him to put his plan into motion. It would be strange, at the very least, to return to the land of his birth, perhaps even to see folk from the hill tribe who had left him out according to the Master's tale – an unlucky albino baby – in the caves above their settlement for three cold nights in the hope he would die. He supposed he should be grateful to Rahe for saving him, but it was hard to feel gratitude after nearly thirty years of torment.

She regarded him expressionlessly, though he could have sworn that the colour of her eyes had changed since last he saw her. She sat up and swung her legs from the divan, so that the cat was displaced. With a yelp of protest, it jumped down onto the floor, dodged past Virelai and shot out onto the steps, where it started washing itself vigorously, as if this had been its plan all along. When Virelai looked back, he found himself gazing at a long expanse of smooth white flesh where the Rosa Eldi's robe had parted, as if by accident.

'Why is it that you wish to give me to the southern lord?' she asked curiously, though her intonation did not rise with the question.

Virelai stared at her legs so hard that it seemed to him as if her skin shimmered. 'I have my reasons.' It was a phrase he had picked up from Rahe, when the Master did not wish to explain himself, which was most of the time. He strode past the woman to the medicine cabinet on the top shelf of the wagon, and took down his cache of powdered brome. When he turned back to fetch some water with which to mix it, he found that the Rosa Eldi had spread her legs so that he could see every detail of her female parts. Rose of the World, indeed. One of her eyebrows quirked at his anguished expression.

She leaned forward, and the silk of her robe slipped down from her shoulder. Virelai bit his lip until the pain drove his hopeless desire underground.

'Cover yourself,' he said roughly, flinging the shawl at her. 'I know your game.'

In response, the Rosa Eldi merely stood and drew the robe up over her shins and thighs, all the while engaging his eyes. When she pulled it up further to reveal her hips and pudenda he found he could not bear not to look, and when he did, he was lost. She was hairless there and as white as milk, save where the central fold was pinkened by a blush of blood and slightly parted, as if she, too, was filled with desire—

Even though one part of his brain reminded him monotonously of the futility of the venture, the animal part of him could not help but pull off his clothes. By the time her robe had reached her breasts, he stood naked from toe to waist, exposing to her merciless view his recalcitrant member, as uninterested now as it might be if confronted by a pitcher of milk or a summer moon.

She leaned to kiss him, enfolding his lips in her own as he had seen her do with the southern lord. Fires ran through him at her touch. No wonder, he remembered thinking incongruously in the midst of this embrace, no wonder the southerners worship a woman who makes them burn. Perhaps this time, he thought, it would be different. Perhaps a miracle might occur and his unwilling part might suddenly unfurl itself, push its way upwards like the head of a fern growing into the light, so that he might at last penetrate the heart of her mystery and know the truth of her.

But he knew even as the thought left him that no such miracle had his name on it, and he felt his heart wither inside him.

Even so, they lay together and he took some comfort from the touch of her cool hands upon his overheated skin. After a while she said: 'Will you take me with you to the Gathering tonight?'

Virelai sat up, shocked. The sedative he had administered earlier must be wearing off. He stared at her suspiciously, but her pupils were as wide and black as ever, her whole face languid and composed. 'Why would you ask me this? You know it cannot be.'

The hands never ceased their rhythmic caresses and soon he lay back against her, hypnotised as the cat had been. For some minutes the Rosa Eldi said not a word, then she shifted so that her face came looming over his. Just the rim of her eyes flared with that extraordinary sea-green, but golden stars flecked the black. He watched them dance and stream, like sunlight on deep water, for an unknowable length of time and when he came to himself it was many hours later, the wagon was in darkness and the Rosa Eldi was gone.

Twelve

Temptations

Saro had known the whip was coming at him before the man made to strike, for when the other rider had caught him by the shoulder he had 'seen' his cruel intentions as clearly as if watching them played out in front of his eyes. And Night's Harbinger, intuitive beast that he was, knew too. The two of them had swerved deftly away leaving Saro's attacker out of balance and flailing wildly. The switch came down hard into thin air, carried through its vicious trajectory and struck the man's own horse so sharply that the chestnut stallion reared with a shriek and pitched the man to the ground. Other riders came racing past them, kicking up a great storm of dust, and Night's Harbinger, his blood up, his whole frame vibrating with adrenalin and fury, charged after them, ears flat and his neck outstretched. Saro was reduced to hanging on for his life to the bay's knotted mane as Night's Harbinger forced his way between a pack of horses just behind the leading group, blood and sweat streaking off him in pinky-white suds.

A big Eyran with his long blond hair and beard flying out behind him, mounted on a huge dappled grey beast, was contesting the lead with an Istrian on a magnificent black and the desertman on one of the famous golden horses of the southern plain. The two southerners appeared to have formed some sort of pact, for they seemed to be trying to cut the Eyran off, wedging him between them, trying to foul his mount's legs with a discarded cloak. The Eyran snarled

and raised his arm to retaliate, and the man on the golden
horse reined in hard. As he did so, Night's Harbinger lurched
forward into the gap. The Eyran looked puzzled as this
unfamiliar horse and rider surged into view; then he swept
his fist down like a hammer into Saro's side, and the next
thing Saro knew was a deathly pain under his ribs, the scream
of a horse that he knew to be Night's Harbinger, a great
rush of air and finally the uncompromising impact of the
ashy ground. Hooves thudded all around him. Instinctively,
he drew himself into a tight ball and waited for the race to
pass him, his heart beating as loudly as the hooves as he took
stock of his injuries. A broken rib, maybe, from the Eyran's
fist; a pain in his right knee where a hoof had caught him
a glancing blow; aches in his hip and arm from his fall. An
unknowable time later, the sounds of horses and riders faded;
distant cheers could be heard from the crowd. The worst pain
Saro felt was that of keen disappointment. All his plans were
in ruins; and now he would face his brother's wrath, too.

He sat up, every bone and muscle complaining. At the
far end of the field, a dark horse, garlanded with braids of
safflower, was being paraded around the victor's enclosure.
Of its rider, there was no sign. Saro stood and shielded his
eyes against the glare of the sun. The horse was dancing
around in an agitated state, throwing its head up in protest
at being handled by the race officials. The horse was a bay,
and on its forehead it bore a white star . . .

Saro frowned. Had someone managed to vault onto Night
Harbinger's back in the midst of the chaos and ride him to
victory? It was unthinkable. Was it another horse entirely?
He began to run; but with each step he took, the stallion
came into better definition: finely boned, with a long, arching
neck, the wound upon its left shoulder barely visible between
the winner's garlands.

Now, belatedly, he remembered his uncle's tales of previous Allfair races. He had pushed them from his mind, with

all their grim details of ripped flesh and broken limbs, horses that were so badly damaged in the course that they had to be destroyed. But it was the *horse* that was feted in this race, not the rider: you rode the beast to keep it on course, stop it fleeing the whips and goads – but if the animal came in ahead of the field without its human burden, it was still the worthy winner; regarded by purists as the best win of all, for it required a horse with spirit and aggression to prevail without the urging of a rider.

Saro grinned. He ducked under ropes of the enclosure and a moment later found himself accepting the heavy bag of cantari and the compliments of the race officials as if he were in a dream. In fact, it was rather like being in a dream, this bizarre state he found himself in as he walked through the gathered crowd with people thumping him on the back and clutching his arm, touching his hand for luck and in congratulation. It was like walking down an endless dark tunnel onto which a hundred doors opened at random, offering him flashes of others' existences, sometimes visual, often inchoate, all blending together in the end to a sea of colour, floating faces, jumbled emotions. The pain had subsided where the Eyran had struck him, so he concluded the rib was bruised, not broken, by another stroke of luck. By the time he made it back to the Vingo family pavilion, having hobbled Night's Harbinger and paid one of the slaveboys to groom and feed him, he felt as wrung out as an old rag, and he ached from top to toe.

There was no one there. He weighed the prize money in his hand – five thousand cantari: a huge sum; and along with the two thousand Tanto had won as his second prize and the money his uncle and father had managed to pool together, just enough to buy Tanto his bride, his castle, his alliance with Lord Tycho Issian. And he, Saro, would at last have the family villa to himself, and all his father's attention, too . . . He put the pouch down on the table and sat crosslegged on the silk floor cushions regarding it. No doubt Tanto and their father were even now wandering the early evening stalls together in a jubilant mood, looking for more gewgaws to add to their already-gaudy costumes for the Gathering that night: he knew they had seen him win, for he had seen them in the crowd as he led the bay on its victory lap, though there had been no sign of Uncle Fabel.

He had pushed the unwanted glimpse into his uncle's consciousness down to the deepest, darkest part of his own mind for the duration of the race; but now it came shooting back up to him, as brightly coloured, as clearly focused, every scent and moan as tangible as if it were he participating in the horrible act of incest, and not his father's brother. Mother! he thought, anguished. How could you do this? She had not been forced, that much he knew as truth; and not only from the desire in her eyes.

Impossible to know when the act had taken place, or whether it were an isolated incident or a long-running affair. Casting his mind back, he tried to remember an occasion when they had been in public company with one another, whether there was a clue to their deception in the way his mother had watched Uncle Fabel, or if his uncle had gravitated to her when others were not looking; but he could recall nothing that would impeach their honour. Had he perhaps made a terrible error, to believe his own mother to be capable of such a thing? To sleep with another man was a burning offence: surely his mother, that silent, deferent woman, would never risk her life so?

But he knew the image had come to him unbidden, entirely independent of his own buried thoughts. It was a form of true-sight, a sort of magic, to be able to see into men's hearts like this; and if anyone knew of it, he was liable himself to be subject to the Goddess's fires.

It was clear he didn't know the first thing about his mother, had merely built up a picture of her in his mind,

a picture made up like a child's piece-puzzle of goodness
and compassion, meekness and compliance: all those traits
the Istrian men so valued in their womenfolk. Valued, or
enforced?

For a moment, Saro felt almost as disgusted with himself for
his stupidity as for his mother's transgression; but the moment
soon passed and with it came anger and a sense of betrayal, and
at the same time the notion that this knowledge now placed
him somewhere outside the very family whose hidden drama
he had been witness to; that this very act of discovery had
somehow set him apart from them forever. Who was he
now, if not his father's son? A Vingo, maybe; but a Vingo
tainted with sin and deceit.

Something nagged at him. Was he, in fact, his father's son?
Or was he a product of the liaison he had observed? Part of
him was already working on a frantic calculation: for surely
it was twenty-one years ago that his father had been called
away to war, leaving the estate in his brother's hands. What
more perfect opportunity? Saro had even been born while
his father was on the campaign to hold the northern ports
against the Eyran foe, hadn't even seen his youngest child
for a year and a half after he was born. This had been the
reason, in Saro's mind, why his father had never loved him as
well as he loved Tanto. It all fell into place, the child's puzzle,
with a terrible inevitability. At last he knew, with a certainty
that made his heart as cold and as heavy as iron, that it was all
true: Fabel Vingo was his true father, and, moreover, Favio
Vingo had known it all along, and had decided to lay his
disappointment and animosity at Saro's feet rather than his
beloved brother's. Rather than lose his wife to the fires. It
explained a lot about his father's bitterness, Saro thought; but
it was hard to forgive him his coldness even so.

An outsider, he thought again. *I have been made an outcast
from my own family; have been one, indeed, for over twenty
years: a cuckoo in the nest.* He picked the bag of coins up and

tipped the coins onto the tabletop. Then he counted them, stacking them in two separate piles: one for Tanto, as he had promised; and one for Guaya – an outsider, like himself.

Tanto would have to scrape together the shortfall in the bride-price as best he could, or go beg Lord Tycho's indulgence for the rest. He would, he knew, never have persuaded his brother to make the apology he'd said he would; but making him promise had at least been a small satisfaction in itself. He shovelled the coins he had piled up for the nomads back into the pouch, rose and fetched a parchment, quill and inkpot and left his brother a note to accompany the depleted pile of money that remained on the table. Then he wrapped himself in a cloak, attached the pouch securely to his belt, and left the pavilion. What would be would be.

The criers were calling the early evening observances to Merciful Falla and the light was fading as he made his way out of the Istrian sector and headed west, towards the nomad quarter.

Here, there appeared to be fewer stalls than he remembered, and some of the wagons looked well-laden, almost as if folk were packing up to leave. He threaded his way through the last of the day's customers and stallholders and eventually found himself in clear space. He could see before him where three or four carts had mysteriously vanished by the dark impression they had left on the otherwise guano-spattered ground. The Fair was not due to end for another two days, he mused. But perhaps they had somewhere else to go, or wanted a head start on the rest of the caravan.

It only occurred to him now that Guaya and her grand-mother might have been in one of the wagons that had gone; and that even if she were still here, he had no idea where her wagon might be situated.

He was still thinking this, and staring out across the nomad quarter, when a boy ran into him.

'*Na-gash!*' exclaimed the lad, sitting down on the ashy ground with the force of the collision, and rubbed his head, which had collided with Saro's hipbone, and the pouch of money that hung there. He looked up at Saro with an expression of the utmost confusion, and all Saro felt from him was how bewildered he was that anyone might have such a hard and bumpy frame. Then the boy's expression changed to one of cheery delight and he cried out: '*Jeesh-tan-la*, Guaya!'

Saro whipped around, and found himself staring at the nomad girl, struggling to carry two immense stick-puppets whose limbs kept tangling with her own.

'*Tan-la*, Falo,' she said softly, looking past Saro.

The boy jumped up, apparently none the worse for his fall, and went skipping back the way he had come.

Saro felt the relief flood through him. He grinned at Guaya. 'I found you: how amazing!'

But Guaya stared back at him, unsmiling.

'I was looking for you,' he said, feeling awkward now.

'So. You have found me. What do you want?'

She didn't look now very much like the joyous child he had been so delighted by, Saro thought. She looked as if she had neither eaten nor slept since her grandfather had died, and as he reflected on this, he realised it was probably so. He had been looking forward to giving her the money, to seeing her pleasure and gratitude at the gift; maybe to sitting with her for a while as she told him of the significance of the changing colours of the moodstones, and particularly what that peculiar shade of green in the pendant had meant last night.

But her grandfather's death now loomed between them, making all of that impossible. Now she was a Footloose girl, one of the despised, the unregarded folk of Elda, and he was the son of an Istrian nobleman. (The son of which one, he realised now, hardly even mattered.) They were worlds apart and even the money would never change that fact, though it might help her family in more practical ways. He tugged at the strings that attached the pouch to his belt.

'I am sorry for your loss—' he started in formal style, but she interrupted him vehemently.

'Sorry? Your people have no knowledge of what that word means, in any language, be it Istrian or the Old Tongue. The Empire has burned and slaughtered its way through every bit of land between here and the southern mountains. It burned my mother for her magic, and killed my father when he tried to save her. And now it has taken my harmless old grandfather too, it is so greedy for our blood. The Empire will not be content until it has killed us all.'

Saro was shocked into silence. What she said was out of kilter with the randomness of the events he had witnessed – the brawl, the chase, the stumbling man and Tanto's careless sword-stroke – yet it held an ineluctable truth. His people were arrogant and ruthless: they forced their will on others. They forced their laws and their religion on them, took their freedom and gave them to the Goddess for the slightest offence. He hung his head.

'Here,' he said thickly. He thrust the pouch at her and when she made no move to take it, he dropped it at her feet. 'It will never make up for what my brother did and it will not give you back your grandfather. But it's something. It's the best I can do. I'm sor—' He bit the word off. Tears had begun to form at the back of his eyes. He rubbed at them fiercely with his hand, but still they persisted.

The nomad girl watched him curiously. She had never seen a grown man weep before, except in joy – at a child's birth or his first view of the ocean – and that was certainly not the emotion that held the southerner in its thrall. She watched as he turned from her, embarrassed, and walked away. And when he had gone thirty feet or more, she saw him look back, and so she tucked the recalcitrant puppets under one arm and picked up the pouch, because she hated to see him hurt as much as she did, and it was the only thing she could do to make him feel better.

In the Rockfall tent, Katla Aransen was surreptitiously collecting her most useful belongings. Under an unwontedly magnificent red gown, she had already put on a thin pair of soft yellow pigskin leggings and a close-fitting tunic of white flax-cloth. Already she felt as if she were being roasted. Footwear was somewhat more of a problem, though: she was fairly sure her father would remark on her battered old leather boots if she were to keep them on, for even if she walked more decorously than usual and avoided the dancing, she doubted she could keep them hidden. In the end, she opted for a pair of elkskin slippers, flat enough to run in, which laced about the ankle. She would persuade Erno to take her boots along with the pack she was putting together, and stow them in one of the faerings. She had wrapped her shortsword and dagger in a shawl: now she added her flints, a lump of hard cheese and a small loaf, and a flask of wine she had filched from among Tor's belongings. Water would have been preferable, but her father was sitting with Halli on the water-butt outside the tent, making sure she did not slip away. How Halli could relinquish all his plans at their father's whim, she still could not understand. She felt almost more aggrieved at his spinelessness than she did at their father's betrayal.

She finished tying up the bundle, plumped it down in the middle of her sleeping pallet and scattered a jumble of clothes over it for camouflage.

The red gown had been a betrothal gift from Finn Larson, brought back by her father, who had gone with the shipmaker to the stalls to purchase it. Red, to go with her hair, Fent had laughed, before seeing his sister's stricken face. She hadn't wanted to wear it: to do so seemed a defeat, an insult; but in the end she had taken it meekly, thinking to put him off the scent, make him believe she was acquiescent to his plans. It was, as he had pointed out, a handsome garment, hand-stitched and embroidered by the King's mother's own seamstress. It was finished with silver lace, and the stiff, embroidered panels of the low bodice hugged her so tightly that it pushed her breasts up so firmly that even she almost had a cleavage. With the tunic underneath she could hardly breathe: as it was, she'd had to open the neck of the shirt with her belt-knife so that it wouldn't show.

With her shorn hair now dyed an ugly, piebald black under Erno's silk scarf (for she had given little care to the process, and her palms and nails were still stained by the stuff even after intense scrubbing) she was hardly a catch to be shown off on a rich man's arm, she thought savagely. Serve him right: he'd have little enough time to display her.

'Katla!'

It was Jenna's voice, shrill with excitement. Oh gods, Katla thought. That's all I need.

'Katla, are you ready?' Jenna's head came round the tent flap. She was wearing a lurid green dress, cut so low Katla could almost see her nipples through the froth of silver lace. Quite how it managed to stay up, she couldn't imagine. What a sight they'd make together: Feast and Famine personified. She laughed.

'Oh, Katla, I'm so glad you're not upset!' Jenna came scurrying in, beaming all over her big round face. Her hair was completely hidden by some ornamental turban affair. Perhaps the nomad woman's charm had gone horribly wrong.

'Why ever should I be upset?' Katla turned an uncharacteristically beatific face to her friend. 'My father's sold me to your father and I'm to be your wicked stepmother. What could be finer?'

Something in Katla's tone gave Jenna pause; but since she could not possibly spare more than a moment's thought on anyone but herself, she started to babble.

'What do you think?' She twirled lumpenly about the tent

till Katla had to rescue the candles before they set her alight. 'Isn't it gorgeous?' She crossed her arms beneath her bosom so that it rose alarmingly. 'Surely this should catch King Ravn's eye?'

'If it doesn't, he'll be blind as a mole.'

'Oh, Katla, I *know* he's going to choose me. I can *feel* it, in here.' She pounded her well-cushioned ribcage. 'Everyone's saying I'd be a safe choice for the King, what with no one trusting the southerners and Erol Bardson's scheming. He likes a generously-proportioned woman, too, I've heard: so that's one in the eye for the Swan of Jetra.'

It'll be two in the eye for the poor woman if she gets too close while you're dancing, Katla thought darkly. 'Oh?' she said, instead, in polite enquiry.

'Thin as a spear-shaft, my brother says, and with about as much appeal, all wrapped about in those shapeless robes.'

Katla had seen but two of the mysterious Istrian women at the Fair, hurrying between pavilions, accompanied by a train of similarly-dressed, tiny slavegirls. They looked so bizarre, so literally outlandish, that she had been fascinated by them. Now, if she had robes like that she'd easily have been able to hide her clothes away, boots and all. And most likely the faering, too.

'The sum we're offering is five thousand cantari.'

'Apiece?'

'For the job.'

Mam stood with her hands on her hips, her feet planted foursquare on the ground. No preened and scented Empire lord was going to overface *her*. 'For my troop, twenty-five thousand.' Five was already a decent sum, if not quite a king's ransom, she thought, with some irony.

The man laughed. He was tall for an Istrian, with a hooked nose and a receding hairline. His skin was like polished walnut, and on his right shoulder he wore the badge of the Supreme Istrian Council. Behind him stood four other lords, looking uncomfortable in the presence of this foreign woman, with her sun-bleached hair all in knots and rags and threads of shells and feathers, her battered war-gear and efficient-looking weaponry. The business they were engaged in was both clandestine and perfidious; to reveal such plans to a foreigner was risky at best; but to involve a woman so – and such a woman – was quite outrageous, tantamount to sacrilege. Nevertheless, the lord persisted.

'Six.'

'Twenty, or we leave.'

'Eight, or I'll have you incarcerated.'

'Fifteen, my Lord of Forent, or I'll skewer you where you stand.' Mam's smile was evil, her mouth full of gaps and smashed teeth.

The smile never left his face. He placed his hands palm-down on the table that separated them, leaned forward. 'You won't get far enough to unsheathe your sword.'

'You think so, eh? I'd be willing to wager high on it, and I'll take your four fancymen, too.'

One of the other lords stepped forward now, his face grim, and gripped his leader by the shoulder. 'The woman's a barbarian, Rui,' he said, not caring if she heard. 'You're mad to trust our strategy with her.'

'Be calm, Lord Varyx. She comes highly recommended.'

Another of the lords stepped forward and whispered something in Lord Varyx's ear.

Mam grinned. 'He means we were the ones responsible for firing the Duke of Gila's palace.' Mam leaned forward conspiratorially. 'No one escaped: we were very thorough.'

Lord Varyx looked appalled, but Rui Finco, Lord of Forent, was unmoved. 'Remember, it's exactly because this lot are led by a barbarian woman that we need them. What Eyran would suspect a woman like this of presenting her compliments to her King?'

'But not looking like that, surely?' Lord Varyx's haughty regard swept across Mam, taking in her horny hands and big knees, her calves as hard and knotted as tree roots, the leathery skin and broken nose.

'Well, we'll dress her rather better, and her companions, too.'

'If we come to terms, you can dress me how you like,' Mam interrupted impatiently in fluent, if horribly accented, Istrian. She grinned at their obvious discomfiture as if she could see them working hard to recall all their rashly unshielded words. 'Though I'm not sure even Galian lace is going to make Knobber a pretty woman.'

The leader of the lords gave her a thin smile. 'You'd be surprised. Ten thousand, and that's the final offer.'

'Fourteen.'

Rui Finco gnashed his teeth. 'Twelve.'

'Give me thirteen and we'll shake on it.'

'Twelve and be damned; I'll not touch you.'

'Six up front.'

He glared at her.

Mam winked back. Then she hawked, opened her fist, gobbed copiously into it, and grabbed the lord's hand, engulfing it entirely. He tried to pull away, but she was far too strong for him. The look on his face was almost worth the rest.

'Done.'

She released him. The lord opened his cramped fingers and inspected his palm with a look of the utmost disgust. He waved a slaveboy over. 'Clean that.' The boy scurried off, returning a few second later with a dampened rag with which he proceeded to scrub the spittle and mucus away. It was bad enough that he had to hire a barbarian woman for the job, but to have her foul fluids on him . . .

'Indeed. Now remember: if things go awry and he ends up dead, the six is all you'll get.'

Mam made a face. Then she grinned. 'Still, six thousand's more than my lads have seen in a while; with six more to come they'll wrap him in silk and deliver him to you with a bow on.' Idiot man, she thought. Were they really so desperate they'd overpay so? She'd only been testing him: they'd have taken eight, and happily, for the fun of it.

'The violet is a fine choice, Tanto: I swear you'll look like the young Alesto.'

Tanto frowned and put the robe back down on the display in a crumpled heap, which made the stallholder tut and fuss. Even from the little attention he had paid in his classes he knew that scriptures told that Alesto had been Falla's lover, the man she had chosen to couple with from among all mortal men for his beauty rather than his brains. His father had clearly forgotten that Alesto, as a result, had come to a rather unfortunate and crispy end . . .

'We must get back, Father,' he said impatiently. A doubt about Saro and the prize money had been nagging at the back of his mind this last hour.

'Ah, yes, preparations to make for tonight. And we must congratulate young Saro on his win.' It was a shame they'd missed the actual race, Favio mused. It had seemed so unlikely to him that Saro would ever triumph in anything that he'd allowed himself to be distracted by some exotic dancers Tanto seemed keen on watching, and as a result they'd arrived at the course only in time to see Night's Harbinger making his victory progress. 'It was a fine performance, by all accounts. I always said the boy had it in him.' He knew this to be an untruth even as he said it, but he was feeling generous, in the circumstances. 'And lucky for us, too, though I doubt we'll be making much of it to my lord of Cantara: we don't want him thinking he's got the wrong son-in-law, eh, Tanto?'

But his elder son was in a world of his own. Tanto's mind had strayed yet again to the beauty mark Selen Issian had worn; the beauty mark, and those lips . . .

'How long before we can have the wedding, Father?' he asked suddenly.

Favio Vingo smiled. He remembered how eager he had been to take Illustria to wife. Ah, Illustria . . . the thought stretched away into the distant past, became uncomfortable, and was pushed away. 'Well, my boy. It'll need some planning, that's for certain: a lot of nobles and their retinues to be taken into account; a suitable date; auspicious omens; the right sacrifices, all that sort of thing. I suspect we'll not be able to secure a date that suits all before Harvest.'

'Harvest?' Tanto almost howled, it was such a shock. He'd been expecting to bed the woman tonight, tomorrow at latest. Harvest was still four moons or more away, and though passing up on a lavish ceremony in which he would be the centre of all attention was hard to do, to find out whether Selen Issian would perform the perversion that beauty mark actually denoted was worth the renunciation.

Favio saw his son's dismay with some amusement and took pity on him. 'But of course, that's just the Goddess's ceremony, Tanto. No need to wait so long to bed your bride: we'll find a priest this very night to consecrate the match, if her father's willing. We'll soon have you fornicating away like a pair of mountain cats! It's praise to the Goddess herself for a girl to make the Joining with her belly full of her husband's seed.'

Tanto felt a fire in his groin. He might still have her tonight! Even though he'd groped his way through a hundred prostitutes, he had never experienced the sort of anticipation he felt now for the act, which before had been impersonal, perfunctory. No, this would be different. This would be *ownership*. He felt himself a larger man already.

They left the stalls behind them and made their way back to the Istrian quarter. Even as they did so, the criers were beginning their evening observances, a mournful wail that rose into the twilight air. Favio, a pious man, dropped immediately to his knees and started to chant. Tanto rolled his eyes. Yet another delay! Even so, he followed suit as dutifully as he could, and hurried through the prayers so quickly that he finished his incantations a good half minute before his father. As soon as Favio pronounced the final 'safe in your fires forever', Tanto had leapt up, grabbed him by the elbows and hauled him upright. 'Come along, now, Father: the evening's drawing in and I'd not want you to catch a chill,' he announced with false solicitude.

Back at the Vingo pavilion the sconces were burning brightly, and they could smell the sweet safflower incense from twenty feet away. 'They are wasting that stuff,' Favio muttered crossly. 'Do they have no idea how expensive it is?'

It was the only occasion on which Tanto had ever heard his father complain about the cost of anything. Obviously the calling in of the Vingo debt had made a significant hole in their family finances, that he would complain so. For the first time he realised just how important this alliance must be to his father, that he'd stake so much on the settlement. He smiled. It would be worth it, he knew. The joining of the estates would make them a formidable force in the power-play of the provinces, and he and Selen would found a dynasty to be remembered down the centuries . . .

Inside, a pile of money glittered on the table, the candle-light sparking off its curves of shining silver. Propped up against it was a note in Saro's workmanlike hand. Tanto took in the scene at a glance. The pile of coins clearly amounted to rather less than the sum Saro had won.

Favio picked up the note and read aloud:

'*Dear Tanto,*
Here is the half I promised you. Since I know you treasure your honour more highly than silver, with the other half I will fulfil your obligations. I will no doubt see you at the Gathering later.
  Good wishes from your brother,
    Saro Vingo.'

Favio stared at Tanto, who had gone white. 'What does he mean by this?'

Tanto tore the note from his father's unresisting hand and scanned it desperately as if in the three intervening seconds the words might somehow have changed their import.

'It means I am lost.' He sat down heavily on the cushions and buried his head in his hands. The note fluttered to the ground.

Favio, bemused, sat down beside him. 'Lost? Nay, it is I who am lost, my boy: what's this bit about "obligations"? And why isn't he coming with us to the Gathering, rather than saying he'll meet us there?'

Tanto shoved himself to his feet. 'I'll find the little bastard and wring the bloody money out of him, I will!' And so saying, he ran from the central chamber to the side-room where Saro slept, ripping open the door-flap so violently that it tore. His father stared after him with a pained expression on his face, then retrieved the note from the floor and read it again.

Saro was gone: his cloak was missing. Tanto stared furiously about the room for places where his brother might have cached the money. First he flung open the chest in which Saro stored his belongings, but all he found inside were some neatly folded smallclothes, some hose, a plain pair of doeskin slippers and some candles and flints. Beside the chest, on the rush-matted floor, the inkpot and quill had clearly been discarded in some haste, for a single drop of black ink had stained the matting, spreading out like a canker across the delicate green surface. Saro kicked at the chest viciously and it went over, taking the inkpot with it, spattering the white linen and pale suede beyond salvage. Tanto surveyed the damage grimly, then went to work on Saro's bed. He stripped the cover from it and slung it across the room. He felt under the pallet with desperate hands: to no avail. He was just rising when a glint of something silver caught his eye. Grabbing up the pillow, though, he found not coins, as he had for one ecstatic moment anticipated, but a pattern-bladed dagger. He picked it up and weighed it in his hand, his brows knit in confusion. The pommel fit his palm with a rare and perfect balance. Something about it tugged at his memory. He'd been looking for such a blade as this, knowing the other flawed. Damn Saro: if he'd had this blade, he'd never have lost to the desertman – instead by now he'd have had a further two thousand cantari in his pouch and no headache. He rubbed at his temples. Why would his pathetic, unwarlike weed of a brother have a superb weapon like this? Why would he have any weapon at all, let alone *under his pillow?* Was he so very afraid of him? The thought almost made Tanto smile. He was right to be afraid; for if he ever caught up with him, he'd soon be sorry he'd ever bought the thing, sorry that its blade was so sharp. He could exactly imagine the sort of cut he could inflict with an edge like this. The sort of cut that would leave a scar, somewhere none too visible – a buttock, maybe, or the sole of a foot. And if Saro had given the money to the nomad girl, then she'd soon be joining her grandfather. Tanto stabbed the dagger down into the pillow and ripped it sideways so that a cloud of white goose feathers came billowing out into the air. They spiralled lazily, then drifted down to cover the room in what appeared to be a light covering of snow.

At this point, Favio came in. He stared around in dismay.

'By Falla, what chaos! I have never seen such a disgusting sight. The boy must have run mad with the headiness of his win. I always said he was not strong of spirit, but this! This is a disgrace. That pillow alone cost me a cantari, and what is this?' He bent to pick up the white linen shirt, now covered in patches of dark, sticky ink. 'The Goddess abhors a sloven. Saro should be ashamed of himself for mistreating the good things he owns in such a way, and he shall be sorry when next I see him.'

'Sorry for what, brother?'

Fabel had appeared at Favio's shoulder. He peered around the chamber, gave a short whistle.

'Dear oh dear. Bit of a mess. Still, he's not a bad lad, our Saro, not by a long stick. What a ride, eh? Fine ride, I'd say. And I've had two very decent offers for the beast, too. Should make a good sale tomorrow.' He tapped Tanto on the shoulder with the piece of parchment. 'I see he's going to meet us at the Gathering with the rest of the money. Good lad, eh? Saving you from yourself.' He winked. 'Might spend it all on women and wine otherwise, eh Tanto?'

Tanto gave him a wan smile. 'Ah, indeed, Uncle.'

Favio looked suddenly relieved. 'Of course, of course. He'll meet us there with the money. What a good lad he is. Come on then, Tanto, hurry along. Let's get you looking your best, make Lord Tycho proud to give his daughter to you.

'Fabel: those gifts for the northern king—'

As Tanto left, he distinctly caught the words, 'sold, brother, and at less than we paid for them,' and his father swear in a most impious manner.

Thirteen

The Gathering

Even preoccupied as she was by her plans for escape, Katla was wonder-struck by the crowds at the Gathering. It was not just the sheer number of folk, though there were more people here than she had ever seen in her life, crammed into the grand pavilion, with its rippling fabric roof and tall mast-pillars, but the riot of colours, the phenomenal display of finery. Everyone, it seemed, had overdressed for the occasion. Or rather, she corrected herself, every Eyran had done so; for while the Empire men wore their rich robes with a nonchalance that bespoke a complete unconcern with the evening's proceedings, the northerners by contrast had bedecked themselves with all the jewellery and decoration they could ladle on, as if to show the old enemy they were not such barbarians after all.

The fabrics you usually saw in the north were coloured by the natural dyes of the islands, from the lichens and pulped weeds that produced soft shades of green and yellow and pale mallow-pink; and from the summer berries, lilacs and reds that promised much, then faded to a dull brown. But it was clear that everyone here tonight had cast their Eyran-bought clothes aside in favour of the gaudiest colour clashes they could manage. For many folk it had clearly been a good Fair, for such fabrics did not come cheap. She saw Falko and Gordi Livson in quartered tunics of crimson and yellow, standing next to Edel Ollson and Hopli Garson in doublets of violent green and orange. Edel Ollson had also treated himself to a hat trimmed with the most ridiculous feathers – vast green things with great blue eyes bobbing at the ends. They could not possibly be real, she thought: no bird could hope to survive with such flamboyant plumage.

Jenna's eyes were shining. As were her cheeks and her nose. She was already on her third goblet of southern wine, Katla noticed, still nursing most of her first. She would have to eke it out if she were to keep a clear head; but Jenna had no such inhibitions. Now she was pointing across half the tent, her voice shrill. 'See that man there? He must be *vastly* wealthy.' Katla followed her finger and saw an Istrian nobleman of middle height and dark-brown skin. His black hair was held back from his face with a simple silver circlet, so it was clearly not his jewellery that had attracted Jenna's attention. 'That purple cloth is terribly expensive. They say it's made from sea snails.'

Katla stared at her in disbelief. 'Snails? I can't believe that's so: Gramma Rolfsen and I experimented with snails. The dye came out a horrible, watery brown.'

Jenna clicked her teeth impatiently. 'Not ordinary snails, you dolt; sea snails. They're found only on a remote stretch of coast bordering the eastern ocean, and each one has to be squeezed by hand.'

Katla made a face. 'Can't fancy that much. Doesn't the cloth stink?'

Jenna laughed. 'Do you think a man like that would wear it if it did? Anyway, I don't know what you're so disgusted about, considering that dress you're wearing.'

Katla coloured. 'It was not my choice, you know. It was your father's.' Jenna seemed to have taken this new development remarkably well in her stride, Katla thought. But more likely she was so absorbed with being presented to King Ravn, she could hardly concentrate on anything else. Katla knew how she felt. It was all she could do to

make conversation herself. There was still no sign of Erno,
and she was beginning to feel decidedly edgy.

'Don't you know how they get the crimson so bright?'

Katla picked up a handful of the cloth and examined it, as
if by doing so she might divine the answer. 'I dare say it's
something horrid.'

Jenna smirked. Her teeth and gums were all stained to
an odd greyish-purple by the wine, Katla noticed. Grinning
away like that she looked like an afterwalker, one of the
perambulating dead of the northern islands, who, unless you
buried them securely under the porchstones of the house,
would wander your lands after the sun went down keeping
their semblance of life by sucking the blood out of animals.

'Lice,' Jenna said cheerfully.

Katla grimaced.

'They crush a million shield lice to gain a cup of dye.'

'No!'

'They do.'

If Jenna had thought to disgust Katla, she had reckoned
without her friend's robust constitution.

'Sounds expensive, that,' Katla said thoughtfully. 'The dress
should fetch a decent price, then.'

Jenna looked at her oddly, but then Katla cried: 'Oh,
look!'

A bevy of Istrian women had appeared in the doorway,
surrounded by a great crowd of Empire men. There were
maybe half a dozen of the women, all dressed from top to toe
in their voluminous sabatkas. Katla saw the paleness of their
hands fluttering like moths as they spoke, and their lips were
bright through the slits in their robes. The men ringed them
about as if, like her, they might otherwise escape. Katla stared
at them, wondering if their trammelled lives were really any
more confining than the one that awaited her, if she failed to
get away this night. There was a peal of tinkling laughter and
one of the women waved her hands around as if in delight at

what another had said. She saw a tall woman's mouth work, and then there was another gale of laughter.

'Which one do you think is the Swan of Jetra?' Jenna asked rather belligerently, as if annoyed by their good spirits. 'They say she's tall and thin, but they all look much of a muchness to me.'

'I don't know.' Nor did she care. Where was Erno? Now that she thought about it, she hadn't seen him all day. Could he have given up on her so easily? Perhaps it really was Marin Edelsen he liked. The thought made her cold. She had never really thought what she might do without his help. It would be hard to manage a faering on her own: they were wide boats and needed two at the rowlocks, one oar apiece. Katla fought her panic down determinedly. She'd find a smaller boat if she had to. She balled her fists. Damn it, she'd *swim*!

She stared out over the crowd. Somewhere to her side Jenna's voice was buzzing on and on like a gnat, describing the folk coming in – Kitten Soronsen and Fara Garsen, big Breta Bransen; the Earl of Ness and his daughter; Earl Sten and his daughter Ella; Ragna Fallsen – reputed to be the King's mistress, a statuesque woman with a magnificent fall of black hair and uptilted grey eyes; and the Earls Stormway and Southeye; Egg Forstson, the Earl of Shepsey, with Filia Jansen, his great-niece, on his arm.

Katla watched them stream into the already-crowded tent, take wine and pastries from the long tables, gather into small groups to gossip. She watched an odd-looking woman in a gigantic green dress stride in, followed by a small man looking deeply uncomfortable in a close-fitting doublet and tight breeches. Behind them, three more Istrian ladies bobbed in and stopped at once, no doubt finding it hard to adjust to the low light of the candles through the thick gauze of their veils. And then she held her breath, for there was the nobleman's son who had come to their stall; she'd forgotten his name now, if she'd ever known it. He was in the company of two older Istrian men, both dressed very finely, one a head shorter than the other and sporting a bright silk turban rather like her own. They entered the pavilion and stared around. The taller man suddenly narrowed his eyes and pointed, and they all gazed towards the back of the crowd. Katla turned to see who they were looking at, and found herself staring straight into the eyes of Saro Vingo. She felt a powerful thrill run through her, but she put it down to the wine. In contrast to the rest of what she took to be his family, Saro wore an ordinary-looking tunic and carried a cloak over his arm. He looked uncomfortable, Katla thought, apprehensive, almost.

And then they began to move towards him through the crowd like a small flotilla through a choppy sea.

'Where is my money, Saro?' Tanto arrived first, his face grim.

Favio and Fabel appeared in his wake.

'Yes, come along, lad,' Favio called from a few paces behind. 'We're keen to get this done.'

Saro looked from one to another and finally focused on his brother. 'You know where the money is, Tanto,' he said quietly. 'I thought you'd thank me for not spelling it out for all to see.'

'You little bastard.' Tanto's hiss was inaudible to any but the two of them. 'You know I need every coin. How could you put a worthless nomad whore before your own family?'

Time stilled. Saro could feel the beating of his own blood in his ears. He could feel his heart beating, with a steadily rising pulse. He could feel his shoulders squaring, as if to withstand a blow. He had known it would come to this: to a denial and the furious argument that would follow. Perhaps he had even sought this confrontation for the excuse it would afford him; for the clandestine punch he had so satisfyingly landed on his brother's chin the day before had somehow freed something in him, made him stronger. There was a mottled red swelling on Tanto's jawline, he noticed now, for the first time, but Tanto had clearly not made the mental connection. Still he said nothing.

'The money,' Favio prompted, standing at his elder son's shoulder, his face now looking pinched and anxious. 'We're still considerably short of the bride-price, son, and our family honour rests on this agreement.'

Saro surveyed them all silently. Then he gave them a long, slow smile. His gaze lingered a moment longer on 'Uncle' Fabel, met a new wariness there, a sudden shrewd calculation. 'I am sorry, Father, Uncle, brother. I no longer have the money. Tanto knows why and if you question him hard enough I am sure he will tell you one tale or another. Whether you choose to believe it or not is up to you. I no longer care. It seems that to save my family's so-called honour means acting with cruelty and deceit, and I like that not.' He shrugged. 'So, I have made a decision, and it is not one *you* will like. I bid you farewell.'

He gave them a cursory bow, shook out the cloak he carried over his arm, and donned it as he might a second skin. Then he turned on his heel and vanished into the crowd.

Favio and Tanto exchanged stricken looks. Fabel stared after Saro, his eyes gleaming with some unreadable emotion. At last he addressed his brother: 'Favio, I'm afraid Lord Tycho is even now bearing down upon us. I hope you have your excuses at the ready.' And he ducked away, leaving Favio and Tanto to face the Lord of Cantara.

'My lord, greetings.' Favio tried to hide his consternation beneath an extravagant bow.

'My lord. Tanto.' Tycho's eyes were unnaturally bright, expectant. His face was flushed, the colour visible even beneath the darkness of his skin. Perhaps, Favio thought, clutching at a desperate thread, he had been drinking hard; perhaps they might yet negotiate a lower rate, or a day's grace.

But the Lord of Cantara was in no mood for time-wasting. 'Do you have my bride-price?'

Tanto's gaze scanned the gaggle of Istrian women by the musicians' dais. One of them must surely be Selen Issian. He could feel himself hardening at the very thought.

'My lord—' he started, but Lord Tycho was staring intently at his father.

'Twenty thousand cantari, this night, I believe was our agreement, Lord Favio.'

'Indeed, my lord. However—'

'I must have it now.' Tycho's eyes narrowed, boring into the older man's with a frightening intensity.

Favio Vingo laughed nervously. 'We do not have all your money here, my lord; but we will have it for you tomorrow.'

A dark hand snaked out and grabbed the robes below his chin, tightening the cloth to the point of asphyxia.

'Now, or never!'

Favio tried to speak, but no words would come out. His eyes began to bulge.

'My lord, I beg you.' Tanto put his hand upon Tycho's arm. He was sweating, and looked almost as desperate as the Lord of Cantara. 'Let my father go. I swear we will get the money to you this very hour.'

Tycho shrugged the boy's hand away angrily, but he let go of Favio's robe. Favio Vingo's face had gone the colour of a mandrill's arse. He shook himself, cleared his throat, rearranged the cloth, and the circlet that had slipped down over one eye, and took a hasty step backwards, away from the madman. People were starting to take notice, pointing out the scene to others and muttering excitedly.

He stared at his son. Tanto looked appalled; terrified – but whether at the prospect of his father being throttled before his very eyes, or at the thought of losing his bride, it was impossible to tell.

'One hour,' declared the Lord of Cantara. 'A moment later and I will sell her to the first man who bids me well for her.' He barked an order at his diminutive slave, and strode off in the direction of the dais. Folk scattered before him, like a sea parting.

Favio wiped his hand across his face. 'The man is deranged,' he said, quite loudly. He stole a look at the people closest to them, but they would not meet his eye. 'We must call the whole arrangement off. What the Lord of Cantara just did to me cancels any obligation we may have had. We can do better for you, my son.'

'No, Father.' Tanto was aghast. 'We cannot do that. I must have her: I have set my heart on it.'

But Favio was adamant. 'I will not have our family allied to that man. He is clearly unhinged; and they say madness runs in a family. You will find yourself with a crazy wife on your hands, Tanto, with crazy children to plague you. I suspected something of the kind already, from the mark the creature had applied to herself, when her father presented her to you. No sane noblewoman would dream of disporting herself thus; and no sane father would allow his daughter to treat her future family with such disrespect. I will not have it, and that's an end to the matter. You will go after him, Tanto, and tell him that the Vingo family has decided against this match.'

'I . . . cannot—' Tanto began, but his father had already turned his head away and was striding in the opposite direction.

Erno lagged behind Aran Aranson and his sons, his feet weighing like lead. In truth, he had not wanted to attend the Gathering at all. Why come to such a public event just to see the woman you loved given away to another man? The hair amulet, dangling on its thong beneath his tunic, itched against his skin as if to remind him of the futility of it all. He had never believed in magic, and now here was his conclusive proof. Katla clearly had no thought of him at all – for there she was with Jenna Finnsen, laughing and drinking wine as if she had not a care in the world. It was hardly any consolation at all to see that she had bound her head in the scarf he had bought her. His eyes swept over the crimson dress, with its panels of lace and embroidery, its wide skirts and fashionably loose sleeves, and came to rest on the swell of brown flesh cresting the top of the tight bodice. *A beautiful woman*, he thought suddenly, *for all her skinniness and her wicked eyes. Her beauty will now be as clear to other men as it always has been to me.* The realisation came as something of a shock. Katla's beauty – for him – had revealed itself in unconventional details: in the silver intensity of her gaze as she watched a mackerel line; the way bright sunlight softened the hard planes of her face, the way the lost red hair, tangled and threaded with pine needles, had bobbed like a horse's mane when she ran. It revealed itself in the way she chewed her lip when examining a weld; or the sweat that sheened her upper arms in the orange fires of the smithy. He loved that she could make a sword, and wield it as well as any man; he loved her for her unpredictability, her sharp tongue and her savage delights: in short, for being so very different to the other women he knew. But this orthodox elegance made it clear that her old wildness was gone, put away so that she could follow the traditional path of every other young woman – to be packaged up and traded away by her family for what he could never offer: money, prestige, a useful clan alliance. To see her so made him want to weep; or to run mad through the crowds, dagger drawn, to carry her off into oblivion.

And now she had seen them. He watched her smile fall away, her lips fold themselves grimly. As they approached, he noted, too, how her knuckles whitened from gripping the goblet.

'Daughter.'

'Father.'

'Finn is a little delayed. He had some last-minute business to attend to.'

Was it a flicker of relief Erno saw cross her face? When Aran turned to say something to Fent, Erno found Katla's eyes upon him, bold and urgent. He returned her gaze as steadily as he could manage, but felt the telltale blood flushing up the fair skin of his neck. What did she want of him, now, when it was too late? He tried to order his scattered thoughts. Her eyes were huge, the pupils so dark they had almost eclipsed the irises. The silver-grey coronas blazed at him.

'I'm hungry,' Katla enunciated very clearly.

'Ah, so am I,' said Jenna, taking Katla's arm.

Katla shook her off. 'Stay here, Jenna. I'll bring something back for you. Erno, give me your arm and accompany me to the tables.'

Jenna stared at them, speechless, then turned as Aran offered her a compliment on her dress. Erno mutely offered Katla his arm and her fingers settled upon it like a hawk's talons into a rabbit, the nails digging into his flesh. He could feel her trembling, feel the pulse of her blood – fast and strong – through the pads of her fingers. Somehow, he managed to coordinate his feet and move away from the family group towards the provisions tables. Katla seemed to float beside him, the red dress gliding across the floor, all her weight, it seemed, in the electric touch of the fingers on his arm. When they were ten feet or so away from the trestles, she broke the contact and turned to face him.

'Erno, I need your help.'

'You have only to ask. Anything.'

'I have to get away from here. Tonight. Now. Before they affiance me.'

Erno looked around quickly, but Jenna and the Aransons were engaged in various conversations. No one seemed to have noticed that his heart had suddenly become such a beacon of hope that his whole body was aflame with it. He caught Katla by the elbow and ushered her quickly through the crowd towards the entrance. They paused to allow a tall woman go by, a woman wrapped so well in a long robe and silk shawl that only a glimpse of her pale face and a flash of green eyes was visible as she ducked past them, and then they were outside the grand pavilion in the darkening air.

'This way.' Now it was Katla who stepped in front of him, picking her way neatly between the guy-ropes to circle the pavilion and head towards the Eyran quarter. They walked silently like this, not touching, for some minutes until the sounds of voices became muted and distant. The moon sailed overhead, veiled by high cloud. Its silver light limned Katla's face.

'I have everything packed,' she said breathlessly. What she had to ask was an enormity, she knew: and all she could think was to blurt it out: 'Erno, will you help me escape? I thought to take one of the faerings, but I can't manage it on my own. Will you come with me and defy my family?'

'I will.'

He gave it no more thought than that. It required no more.

'It'll mean a blood feud, you know.'

'I know.'

'We can never go back.'

'This I know, too. Where will we go?'

Katla hung her head. 'I never got that far,' she admitted. 'All I could think of was rowing away, down the coast.'

Erno nodded, silent. Two fugitives from Eyran law: her father was sure to declare him outcast, his goods – such as they were – forfeit. His life, too. He laughed.

Katla stared at him. How could he laugh when she asked so much of him? He looked slightly mad, but wonderfully so, his skin so dark and his blond hair almost white in the moonlight, his sharp teeth gleaming like a wolf's. And then she was laughing as well: it was a ridiculous situation — for here she was, in a dress dyed crimson with crushed lice, her hair shorn and blackened and her life at risk because she had climbed a rock, about to kiss a man she had known all her life, a man she had never till recently given any thought to, a man who was willing to risk everything for her . . .

About to kiss—

It was Erno who made the first move. He caught hold of Katla's shoulders, tilted her head back and smothered her lips with his own. For a moment all she could feel was the blood pulsing between them and she surrendered to it as if there was nothing more in the night than their mouths, joined, and all else in the world fell away in a long, thin thread that spiralled down and down . . .

And then she began to feel dizzy, disorientated.

A vile, pungent scent rose into the air.

Something was burning. Something was burning *her*, burning the exposed skin just above the low neck of her dress.

'No!'

She pushed Erno away. A patch of his tunic, in the middle of his chest, had begun to smoulder, turning the pale linen to a dull, rusty orange. Tendrils of smoke started to wisp from the neck of the tunic, sparse at first, then in a thick coil. Erno looked down, bemused, opened the neck of his tunic and stared in. Realising what was burning, he stepped quickly away from Katla, turning his shoulder from her as he did so to block her view. It was the amulet the nomad woman had made for him, glowing a dull ember-red as if it would suddenly take flame and burn them both to ashes. Magic! He drew in a hiss of breath. Damn it, that was why she had kissed him . . .

He snapped the thong and drew the accursed thing out. As soon as it lost contact with the skin above his heart, the unnatural glow went out of it. Much of the hair had smouldered away and as he pulled at it the rest lost its form, the weave disentangled. Strands of burned hair floated to the ground.

Katla stared down. Then she bent and snatched up some of the remnants. The burning had darkened it, but she knew her own hair. The implications of why Erno would wear a plaited round of her hair beneath his shirt, a weaving that would burst into flames so, ate at her like acid, etching a course through her thoughts.

'Magic,' she whispered at last. A charm. A love charm? A trick . . .

Even as she thought it she felt emptied out, hollow, all her emotions drained away. It was as if her skin had been stretched tightly about her ribs like hide across a drum. And after a few moments, when she looked at Erno again, she found she felt nothing for him at all, nothing but a terrible disappointment.

Erno, however, could not meet her eye. He was gazing at his shoes as though they fascinated him, the knotted braids of his hair, with their remembrancing rags and shells swinging forward to obscure his darkening face.

Katla forced the last shreds of magically-enhanced emotion out of her head, forced herself to think clearly. It changed nothing, she decided, nothing of the practical circumstances; whether Erno still wished to help her now, without his love reciprocated by artifice, was up to him. She smiled sadly.

'If you're coming, we'd best hurry, before they miss me.'

He hesitated, as if trying to think of something to say that might improve the situation. Eventually he merely nodded and started to walk purposefully towards the Rockfall booth.

'Two thousand cantari, Fortran. It's all I ask.'

Fortran Dystra regarded his friend curiously. 'What on Elda do you want two thousand cantari for at this time of night?' Then comprehension struck him. He grinned, punched Tanto on the arm. 'It's a woman, isn't it?'

Tanto forced a smile. 'You might say that.'

But Fortran shook his head. 'Lost it all on the horses,' he said affably. 'Didn't expect your runt of a brother to win at all. Put it all on Filial Duty, didn't I?'

Tanto's face fell.

'Never mind,' Fortran said. 'Tomorrow you'll realise I've saved you a fortune. No woman's worth two thousand cantari for the night.' He laughed. 'Have some more wine to clear your head!'

Fortran had been Tanto's last hope: not one of his so-called friends had been able – or willing – to lend him the money. He downed the goblet of warm Jetran wine Fortran had offered him in a single draught. And then he said: 'Have you seen Lord Tycho Issian?'

Fortran raised an eyebrow. 'I wouldn't go asking him for it,' he said. 'Came storming past some while back with his face as black as night.'

'Did he have his daughter with him?'

'Selen? Oho, what's up there, Tanto?'

'Did he?'

'No. I don't believe she was here at all. What do you—'

But Tanto had already turned rudely on his heel and was ploughing his way through the crowd.

Bëte was being most uncooperative. Virelai had managed to trap the creature in the wagon, where after some panicked forays back and forth, searching for an exit, it had at last shot under the bunk. He could see it there now, its green eyes gleaming defiantly in the gloom. Reflexively, he licked the bleeding striations on the back of his hand. The blood was sharp and salty, the welted edges rough against his tongue. So much for the blasted calming spell he'd tried on it . . .

His first thought on waking to find the Rosa Eldi missing had been to run after her, and indeed he'd gone as far as the end of the nomad quarter before giving up on his mission, for there had been an immense throng of folk coming and going at the twilight hour; packing up stalls, carrying goods, leading yeka back from the compound. He'd climbed onto an abandoned stall and searched across the heads of the crowd for her shining flag of hair for ten minutes at least before remembering that the dark green shawl that had been strewn across the bunk beneath them had gone and that his eyes might therefore have flicked over the disguised Rosa Eldi a dozen times as he stood there. Damn. He would have to use the cat to lure her back.

Which was why he was down here now on all fours with his arse sticking out at an undignified angle, his head jammed under the low bunk and his hands all raked and smarting, trying to tempt the little demon out. Food and cajoling had failed utterly. Main force was all that remained. He rolled onto his belly and began to insert himself beneath the bunk. The cat, however, determined to maintain a safe distance between them, backed itself into the furthest corner. Its black lips peeled back – he could tell from the sudden gleam of pearly white fangs – and it started to hiss. The last time this had happened it had struck out, not wildly and in fear, but with the utmost calculation for maximum damage. Suddenly his exposed face felt horribly vulnerable. Slowly, Virelai withdrew again. There was an old cloak of his hanging on the back of the door. He took it down, wrapped it about his hands and went in after the cat again. It was a cloak of thick serge, but even so when he managed to get the thing in his hands he felt its claws – or its fangs – meet like hot needles in the soft webbing between the thumb and first finger of his left hand. He howled with pain and rage, and then his right came in hard over the top, found the cat's head (ah, so those were its fangs, then) and clamped down on its neck. The loose skin there filled his fist, beneath the folds of cloth. He felt the little beast release its death-grip on him, unable to resist the kitten instinct, even though it was aware with the clever part of its head that what gripped its neck so tightly was not, in fact, its mother. If it had ever had one.

Virelai squirmed backwards, came to his knees and held the thing at arm's length. It hung there, unrepentant, ready to do more damage as soon as he let go.

Able at last to focus his skills on it, he stared it squarely in the eyes and muttered an incantation. Against its will, the cat went lax. Virelai sat on the edge of the bed and, pressing his thumbs hard against the sides of its jaw, forced its mouth open. There was blood on its teeth, he saw. His blood. He felt abruptly like dashing its head against the side of the wagon. It was a peculiar sensation, this rage. Peculiar, and unaccustomed: he had never felt anything like it in his life. Even when poisoning the Master, there had been no hatred there, only a cool decision based on his best chance of escape with the Rosa Eldi and what was left of the magic. He felt the hot anger drain away.

'Now then, Bëte: give me the spell to draw back the Lost, and I'll let you go. Do you hear me?'

In response the cat's eyes flickered with hatred. The fight might have gone out of its limbs, but it still knew its enemy. Virelai pressed his mouth against its silky muzzle, felt the warm air from its nose against his lip.

There came a soft, whooshing sound, then he felt (rather than saw) bright lights in his head. The lights shattered and spun, then coalesced. He saw the Rosa Eldi enter a vast pavilion all candle-lit and stuffed with people. The Gathering. He watched her, thinking herself hidden, under the dark shawl, looking this way and that, the sea-green eyes darting around at all the humanity present, in its velvets and silks, its trinkets and jewels, all drinking and grazing like so much prey. She made a sudden half-turn and he saw her eyes widen in shock. Then she ducked her head away from his probing gaze and vanished into the throng.

'What in fiery heaven are you doing with that animal?'

Virelai's head shot up. The cat, sensing a weakening in the holding spell, took its chance. Becoming a single hard, twisting muscle, it wrenched itself from the map-seller's hands and tore around the vertical walls of the wagon like something whirled on a string. At last it dropped into the space between the ceramic stove and the clothes trunk and went to ground.

Lord Tycho Issian filled the doorway. Virelai stood up slowly, smoothing his hands over his breeches. Little tufts of black fur drifted to the floor. The lord, he noticed, was making strange gestures with his hands, as if to ward off something unpleasant. The spell had left the slightest tang of sulphur in the air. That, or someone had farted.

'Ah,' said the map-seller, trying to appear unruffled. 'You've come for the Rosa Eldi, I presume?'

'Where is she?'

'She awaits us at the Gathering, my lord.' He watched Tycho Issian's gaze fall to the scratches on his pale hands, no doubt wondering, Virelai thought, whether it had been the cat or the woman that had put them there. 'Do you have my money?' he said to distract him.

'I do not. Yet. But I shall. Soon.'

'Well, let us pursue our respective quarries then, my lord, and make our exchange at the Gathering.' He ushered Lord Tycho Issian before him down the steps of the wagon, following close behind, and brought the latch down sharply to keep the cat at bay. Let the lord drag the Rosa Eldi away: from the light in his eyes and the colour of his face it looked as if he would brook little hindrance to his plans for the rest of the night.

From his vantage point on the dais, Ravn watched all the folk come and go as if in a haze. It was true that he had fortified himself for the wretched occasion with as much good southern wine as he could lay his hands on, but even the wine could not take the edge off his restiveness. He watched his scribe desperately trying to keep track of all the tributes that had accumulated at his feet: enough Circesian rugs to carpet the entire great hall at Halbo, and lay a path three miles to the sea; urns and vases and goblets that in all probability would shatter at the first hint of a storm on the homeward passage; pots of spices and mounds of herbs from the southern plains and the eastern hills, which would at least mean that this winter's food would taste of something other than salt and smoke; bales of silk, which also meant that his lady mother would be well catered for, if only he could persuade her to give up the drear greys she had affected ever since his father's passing. The fine aquamarine would suit her well, he thought, bring out the blue lights in the still-black hair. It was Sur's own colour, which might persuade her: the colour of sun on the god's own sea. It would suit Ragna Fallsen, too, he thought suddenly, catching her eye across the room as she danced with Erol Bardson's eldest son, Ham. Ham by name, and nature too: for the boy was as pink and fleshy as any pig's haunch. Lord knew what Ragna thought she was doing by encouraging him so: for it was hardly going to spark a moment's jealousy in her lover of a hundred tumbles to see her fondled by such a lout. And if truth be told, he was becoming rather bored with Ragna, for all her beauty and inventiveness. She had, he had found recently, a nagging tongue on her, having suddenly discovered in herself sufficient gall to complain if he came to bed unbathed, or in his cups. Insupportable, since both were frequently the case . . .

His eyes strayed to the group of southern women, seated calmly on the opposite side of the pavilion by the musicians' dais, where they had been all night, their servants at their feet, their menfolk at their backs. He watched the way they daintily nibbled their pastries and sipped their wine: white hands and dark mouths, and no morsel else to be seen of them, and he felt his cock stir for the first time that day. Quiet, docile, and fiends in the bedchamber: so he'd heard. He remembered the tale one of his oarsmen had confided to him that morning, that he'd heard from a friend of a friend, a mercenary captain currently keeping the sea-wolves at bay off the Istrian coast: how one Empire whore had apparently brought off an entire crew of longshipmen – thirty at least and no callow youth among them – in no more than an hour, and yet still managed to give each of them such intense pleasure with her cool hands and hot mouth that when it came to his turn, the navigator had shrieked his climax and then lost his mind for the best part of three days.

He'd heard similar tales of the Footloose women, too. Indeed, he'd been planning to visit the nomad quarter in his guise as the Phoenix after the swordplay, had it not been for the damned wound the Istrian's splintered dagger had afforded him. A shame, he thought to himself now, refilling his goblet from the flagon at his feet, for the Wandering Folk had a well-earned reputation for their creativity and imagination, even if it was not so many years ago that the south claimed to have burned the last of the true magic-makers. Sex with a sorceress: now that was a thought . . .

Still, they were all now rendered down to ash and bones in the name of the Goddess – entire tribes, they said, whole caravans gone to the salt-pits, their severed heads put out for the carrion birds – the lammergeyers and vultures of the far south. No wonder they had ceded those desert lands to the Lord of Cantara, he thought, recalling the dull schooling he'd received on the Empire and its provinces from Stormway and Southeye before this year's Allfair: they must be crawling with the spirit-dead, with ghasts and afterwalkers, for as any Eyran knew, to sever a head from its body and consign them to different locations left the spirit free to wander. And burning was no good: you had to weight the body down well, whether on land or at sea . . .

He shivered, despite the closeness of the night, the thousand burning candles, the proximity of so much live humanity. His mind had been turning in such bizarre directions for
the past half hour or more. It was not like him to ponder such
matters: it made him feel uncomfortable, somehow outside
himself. His hand went for a moment to the chain he wore
about his neck, to the charm nestling in the hairs of his chest.
Sur's anchor wrought in silver, there to provide safe harbour
for the souls that sailed life's ocean.

'You look perturbed, sire. Is there ought I can fetch you:
another flagon of wine perhaps?' Southeye was at his elbow,
his grizzled old face anxious.

Ravn laughed. 'I've already drunk enough to float a
ship. Bring the girls on, Southeye: perhaps they will lighten
my mood.'

'Aye aye, my lord. The girls it is. Remember what we
said.'

'Just bring them.'

There were ten of them, he knew: an auspicious number
in itself – exactly the crew of Sur's own ship, the *Raven*, his
chosen companions who rowed those who had died in the
sea-god's name to the Shores of Peace – *ten for the god*, so
the saying went; so *ten for the king* had a splendid resonance
to it. Perhaps he'd take them all: wasn't there some record in
the annals about randy old King Blacken taking fifteen wives?
Ten was positively conservative.

Southeye stepped away to confer with Egg Forstson,
who nodded, then threaded his way through the knots
of folk to find the Earl of Stormway, who appeared to
be entertaining with some grim tale or another a gaggle
of Eyran girls in bright dresses and outlandish headgear.
Ravn watched as Bran's daughter, Breta, coloured and put
her hands to her face. Silly woman: surely she knew her
presentation was no more than formality? Egg touched heads
with his grand-niece, and passed her on to Breta's arm.

The two girls gave one another petrified looks, then began to giggle.

The Earl of Shepsey was now on his way to a group of tall men talking with a girl in a low-cut green dress and silver turban-affair, and as Egg arrived and said something, they all swivelled to regard the King. Ravn's eyes narrowed as he marked the older man to be Aran Aranson, that arrogant bear of a man who'd been so rude to him the day before. He was pleased to see him looking away, slightly discomfited now, staring over the heads of those around him as if he'd lost someone. The burly, bearded man beside him Ravn recognised as the royal shipmaker, Finn Larson. So the big girl in green must be the daughter they'd mentioned. He sighed and lost interest at once.

On the far side of the pavilion, the robed women had begun to rise from their benches, their servants scattering before them. He watched as they glided across the floor in such a fashion as to suggest they had no visible means of conveyance, and it made him remember the old saw about swans: how you could see nothing but their grace above the water, while all beneath was frenzied flapping. Perhaps the same was true of the Swan of Jetra. Perhaps he would find out later . . .

The first to be presented, however, was the daughter of Lord Prionan. Ravn paid little attention to his flatteries and the overblown description of his overblown daughter, since the man had already tried to buy his favour earlier that night with a group of chained slaveboys, children so gaudily dressed that at first he had thought them a troupe of tumblers, until the Empire lord had clarified their purpose. It had been impossible not to show his disgust. The northern isles had no system of slavery, he had explained to the man; they found folk worked more effectively for decent treatment and some form of payment, rather than trained to perform unnatural acts in very fear for their lives; but Lord Prionan had clicked his teeth and shaken his finger at Ravn and said something unintelligible in his sibilant tongue. Now, Ravn waved him away impatiently: sheltered coastal lands or no, he wouldn't ally himself to this man.

The Earl of Ness came promptly on his heels, trailing his daughter, Lian. The Earl was a tall, stick-thin man in his early fifties, and his daughter looked as spare as her father. No meat on her, Ravn thought irritably, imagining how her hipbones might grind beneath him, and dismissed the offer of men and the stronghold at Sharking Straits. The old fortress might hold a strategic position, but Ravn knew from his information network that it was in ruins, Sharking Straits overrun by brigands and outcasts. He smiled.

'I thank you for your fine offer, my lord of Ness. I shall consider it further.' He inclined his head to Lian, who dipped a low enough curtsey to confirm her lack of assets to his trained eye. Ravn sighed.

Earl Sten's daughter, Ella, by contrast, was remarkably well-endowed, and remarkably plain, her face so freckled she looked mud-spattered. Still, at least she looked keen, Ravn thought. The beauties of the court were liable to take too much for granted: the plainer ones were often more eager to please.

'Lovely girl, Sten,' he said as cheerfully as he could manage. The Earl, one of his father's closest friends, veteran of a hundred scraps, returned the smile with a gap-toothed leer. Clubbed hard on the head at some point, Ravn thought: not too many wits to spare.

The arrival of the Duke of Cera caused something of a stir. Ravn watched the crowd part fearfully before him in some bewilderment, until the cause of the hush made itself known: two huge-pawed beasts with fangs like scythes and fur of a delicate, heathery hue that gave way to a deep, stormy grey where the muscles moved in their giant flanks. Rosettes that were almost-purple in tone mottled their fine coats, and their eyes were as great and as gold as those of the snow owls that were sometimes to be spied in the far northern wastes. Around their necks they wore collars of solid silver studded with an unusual blue stone.

'Mountain leopards, my lord,' the duke pronounced proudly. 'All the way from the Golden Mountains. They are the only pair in captivity in all of Elda. I caught them as cubs and raised them myself: they will eat from your hand; or run down prey for you faster and more surely than any hound. Imagine hunting through your northern forests with such a pair! Nothing can withstand their swift grace and mighty jaws.'

In his head, Ravn could see the scene clearly, could hear the hunting horns and the sound of horses' hooves muffled by the snow. He could see himself running out ahead of his men with these glorious beasts on their long leashes, pursuing the stag he had missed last winter. It was seductive, the picture it made; but in the end he found he did not have the necessary surfeit of vanity for two wild cats to sway the balance: besides, to transport them back to Eyra on a longship would likely costs the lives of crew, if not the beasts themselves. He thanked the duke profusely then graciously refused the offer. The palace at Halbo was no place for such wild creatures, he declared: it would be like confining eagles in an aviary. The Duke of Cera shrugged. He did, in fact, have several eagles in his collection, so he was not entirely sure what the northern king might mean by this. Secretly, though, he was relieved the bid had failed; it had been the Council who had prevailed upon him to offer his beloved Caramon to the barbarian king, sacrilege or no. At least, he'd thought, if the northerner had taken her, she'd be protected by the finest examples of the Goddess's sacred beasts he could find.

Lord Sestran offered jewels and casks of wine and a share in his prosperous spice fields, but his daughter stood at less than half Ravn's height and was almost as wide, a fact undisguised by the cerise sabatka she wore.

Two elderly Empire men in deep-red brocade, with identical sagging jowls, tufted grey eyebrows and elaborate chains stepped forward next: the Lords Dystra, joint heads of the Istrian Council. And behind them stood a slight woman in deep blue silken shrouds.

'My lord of Eyra—' one started, and,

'—we bring you greetings,' continued the other;

'—our terms are generous.'

The first lord flourished a scroll, from which the pair proceeded to read in turn, voices so eerily similar that if Ravn closed his eyes, he'd have thought them one and the same. He had little need to pay attention to their bizarre double-hander: he knew what they offered was what the north needed – passage through the Circesian Straits via the wide Golden River, passage for barges of grain and ore and wood; all they were beginning to lack in the northern isles. But now came the interesting part.

'—we are honoured to present—' the first declared,

'—the most fabled beauty of the Empire—' the second continued;

'—the Swan of Jetra—'

Ravn sat forward, his elbows on his knees and his chin cupped in his hands and surveyed the swathed blue shape they ushered forward. These damned robes, he thought; here's one that looks worth examining and I can see nothing of her but that demure little mouth and those pretty hands. How on Elda they could possibly claim her to be a fabled beauty when none could assess her charms, he could only imagine. But the mouth was exquisitely shaped and lacking in those fine downturned lines he had learned denoted sourness and bad temper: Ragna Fallsen seemed to be developing such day by day.

'My gracious lords; my Lady of Jetra; a very fine offer and one I must think on further, if you will bear with me.'

The old men nodded and smiled and bowed, and nodded

and smiled and bowed again, and took away with them into the crowd their most prized possession, the fabled Swan.

And now he must politely embrace his treacherous cousin, Erol Bardson, as he presented his ward. Erol avoided his eye; but for her part, the girl gazed insolently back at Ravn, completely unawed. Her pupils were a dark violet, fringed by long, fair lashes. It was an unusual combination in that pale, finely-boned face. Her chin came up as he regarded her in unspoken challenge. A bit of spirit there, he thought. She's angry that her guardian should parade her like this, and not afraid to show it. Erol had played his gamepieces well, Ravn thought, grooming this girl to the occasion and presenting her thus; even so, the offer was far too dangerous to consider, for all Erol's inherited power and influence. Once the girl had spawned a boy, they'd find a way to dispose of him and set the babe on the throne, with Erol, his protector, as the effective king. Stormway had been most insistent on the necessity to avoid this pitfall.

Breta Bransen knew even before her father presented her that Ravn wouldn't choose her. She'd loved him since she was seven, even after he'd pushed her in the horse-trough to see if she'd drown. 'Your mother was a sorceress!' he'd taunted her cruelly. If my mother was a sorceress, she remembered thinking, even then, she'd have done better to make me in her image, pale and dark and willowy; and gone from this place. So now, when he smiled at her and praised her dress, Breta smiled wanly and at once made way for her prettier cousin.

'Sire, I have the honour to present to you my grand-niece Filia Jansen, a girl of seventeen summers and most accomplished with a needle. She has made a fine tapestry for your hall, in token of the honour in which she holds Your Grace.'

Forstson urged the girl forward. Timidly, and peeping up at him all the while with her pale-green gooseberry eyes, she unrolled the tapestry. By any standards, it was a fine piece of work and she had clearly laboured on it for a goodly time: the figures were intricately stitched and artfully coloured. The scene portrayed, though, was one from a story he had always hated: the Black Mountain. A tragic tale, it told the story of good Queen Fira, whose beloved husband, King Fent, had been captured by trolls and taken into the Black Mountain. Every year they demanded tribute – barley and corn; cows and sheep; whales and herring – and every year they reneged on their promise to release the King, until, fifteen years later the kingdom faced famine and there was no tribute spare to pay. So the Queen had gone herself to the Black Mountain and begged for her husband's life. Out they had come, the trolls, tall as a ship's mast, wide as a sail, each tooth a cairnstone; and they had laughed at her plea.

'We ate the King fifteen years ago, woman. We toasted him with honey and played jacks with his bones: so if there is no more tribute forthcoming, we must make do and mend.'

And then they had roasted and eaten poor Queen Fira: the lesson being, as the Earl of Shepsey had delighted in explaining to the young Ravn he dandled on his knee, that it pays to be pragmatic, to take what you can rather than to wait on empty promises. Ravn had always thought it a stupid story: if it had been his father the trolls had taken, he'd have carried fires and an army to the mountain and razed it to the ground. He waved Egg and the grand-niece away wearily. He was bored now. The mountain leopards had provided an interesting distraction, but he could feel his choices narrowing to the inevitability of the Empire's Swan or the shipmaker's daughter.

He nodded to Finn Larson; and when he did so, Jenna thought she might faint.

'Sire,' Finn swept as low a bow as his great belly would allow, 'I give you my only daughter, Jenna, whose attributes are all you could ask for.' And the burly little man had the temerity to wink at his king.

Ravn, caught somewhere between irritation and amusement, cast his eyes over this last wench. He knew the
advantages the match brought: the priceless new fleet to take
the Ravenway by storm, the convenient political neutrality –
but the girl was more of a surprise: big but as well-structured
as one of her father's ships; her face shining with heat and
wine (so at least she took a drink).

Jenna stepped forward. She had rehearsed this moment for
months – how she would curtsey low to afford the King the
best possible view of her bosom, then look up at him through
her lashes while she seductively undid the headcloth and let
down her sheet of golden hair – her best feature, she knew,
and sure to win his heart.

His dark eyes upon her now, with their heavy, sensual lids,
made her so weak and foolish that untying the infinity knot
she had made for luck became problematic; but at last she
fumbled it free and the fabric slipped at last from her head.

The crowd gasped.

Wave upon wave of shining hair tumbled from the confines
of the silk, transformed by the nomad charm even as it escaped
its bindings. 'If you really want him to notice you,' Fezack
Starsinger had said, 'you must wait till his eyes are upon you
and you have his sole attention.'

'I want it to look like a sea of corn,' Jenna had said,
imagining a cascade of gold, a gleaming, textured sea.

Now that phrase came back to plague her.

Had she stipulated ripe corn, it might at least have ameli-
orated the colour; but she had not paid sufficient thought to
the wording of her wish: green it was, her hair; as green as
any new crop. And the magic had not stopped there. Out
of the sheeny green tumbled fieldmice and bees; earthworms
and loam. People close to her swatted at their faces, picked up
their feet. A lark burst from her mane and soared up among
the mast-pillars, where it trilled in panic.

The King began to laugh, until he realised this was no mere

prank designed for his amusement, for the girl was shrieking
hysterically and beating her head with her fists.

And then a tall woman stepped out of the throng. She
wore a long pale robe and a dark-green shawl covered her
head. Her skin, when she stretched out her hands towards
the girl, was as white as milk, the fingers long and fine; the
nails as pink as nacre. She touched the shipmaker's daughter's
head and as she did so the illusion – if illusion it was – ceased
abruptly. Jenna sank into her father's arms, her long hair –
blonde, inanimate once more – covering her shame. Of the
creatures that had fallen from her, there was no sign.

A trick, after all. The King sat back on his bench, irritated at
the deception, the stagy histrionics of it all. A man as practical
as Finn Larson should know better than this. He waved the
tall woman away, but she did not go. Instead, she took a pace
towards him. Her hand came up to touch his damaged face.

'You've taken a wound,' he heard her say, as if from a
great distance.

The dark shawl she had worn over her head had fallen
back. Ravn's gaze was drawn to her face. A perfect pale oval
awaited him there, and a pair of sea-green eyes.

Her cool fingers brushed his skin.

He felt his heart stop.

Somewhere, in the rafters of the tent, a lark sang.

Fourteen

Madness

Tanto helped himself to another goblet of wine from a passing server's tray. The good stuff had run out now, he noted, his thoughts as sour as the wine. Even so, he threw it down his throat and reached for another. His head had begun to take on the familiar dull ache that presaged an almighty hangover for the next morning, but right now he did not care.

Damn his self-righteous little brother. Damn his stupid father and Uncle Fabel, too. And as for Lord Tycho Issian: he hoped the Goddess's hottest flames would devour the man. But not until he'd accepted Tanto as his wed-son, whatever that might take. He drained the goblet in a single gulp, barely even aware of the tart, spicy liquid burning its way down his gullet.

He was just about to find the serving-boy for another refill when he saw the Lord of Cantara making his way through the entrance to the pavilion. Beside him was a tall, thin man with almost no colour to him at all. Despite himself, Tanto stared. The man's hair was so pale as to be white, and against the pallor of his face, his features were indistinct. He looked like a lamprey, Tanto thought, a sickly, slippery eel of a man. The two of them walked quickly into the midst of the throng, heads inclined towards one another as if they were deep in conversation.

I will sell her to the first man who bids me well for her. Lord Tycho Issian had been true to his vile word: he had found his bidder. Tanto felt a fury rise in him. So he'd strike a deal for his daughter with this . . . this . . . *slug*, would he? He hurled down his empty goblet, and began to push his way through the crowd towards them, then changed his mind. What would he do: confront the Lord of Cantara; knock down the slug-man; have everyone here know his family didn't have the money for the bride-price? No. He thought for a moment, his befuddled mind spinning. No, indeed. He smiled. He had a much better idea.

Outside, the stars were burning brightly and the moon was mantled by drifting cloud. The cold air soon sobered him, but rather than deter him from his plan, it stiffened his resolve. He stared out at the canvas city that had spread itself across the barren black plain, and struck out for the Istrian quarter. He passed the great tents of Lord Prionan's retinue, deliberately pitched close to the grand pavilion as if to gain authority from their very proximity. The coloured family pennants hung lax in the windless air.

He walked past the pavilions belonging to the Qarans of Talsea, and the Duke of Cera's huge complex of tents. As he went quickly by, a deep, rumbling growl rolled out through the darkness towards him. It was a sound like none he'd ever heard. For a moment, it stopped him in his tracks, thinking that the Goddess had seen his thoughts and had sent her great cats to rend him; but then he remembered the two mountain leopards the duke had presented to the northern King. Clearly the Duke of Cera's bid had failed, and the big cats been sent away in disgrace. What cared the Goddess for his plan? He laughed and hurried on.

Soon he found himself walking in the moonshadow cast by the great Rock, towering into the night like the Castle the northerners called it; and there, on the slopes below it, was his family's own pavilion. No sconces were lit: the slaves must be abed, he thought, or enjoying themselves elsewhere in their masters' absence. This was not his destination. He passed silently onward. ·

Beyond Falla's Rock, the land rose more steeply. Tanto quickened his pace to compensate for the incline, his feet sinking into the dry volcanic ash. Up the hill he went, past the Sestrans' tents and those belonging to Leonid Bakran and his family. A great cluster of pavilions came up before him now. Heedless of his trespass, Tanto pushed through the circle of tents and found himself in a quiet enclosure. It had been laid it out in the form of a Jetran contemplation garden: all ornamental stones and terra cotta; alternating pots of water and scented powders; garlands of safflower around a little shrine – a brazier piled with still-glowing embers. Someone had sacrificed to the Goddess not many hours past: the rancid, sweet smell of burnt meat and hair invaded his nose as he went past. So much effort, and all for the stupid Allfair. Fancy carting all those pots and stones all the way from the Jetran Plain. They'd have done it for the Swan, he thought. To give her a last taste of her beloved south before she got carted off to the Eyran isles with the bastard northern king. This thought enraged him further. A noblewoman sold into barbarism by her greedy, scheming family, rather than saved for the deserving men of Istria. Men like himself. It was an insult to him and to every able-bodied southern male. He kicked out viciously at one of the terracotta pots and watched it smash with a satisfying clatter. Shards of fired clay skittered out across the garden. Then he kicked over the altar, too. The garlands of safflower broke apart, showering him with their fragrant petals, and the ochre pollen from their loaded stamens. *Alesto*, he thought. *Alesto: the Goddess Falla's lover, brought to her in just such a cloud: the fragrance of heaven, to bless the union between mortal and deity.*

It was all he needed to spur him on. With renewed determination, he took the last few hundred yards at a run, and the smell of safflower followed him all the way.

The Lord of Cantara's pavilion was in darkness, as he had expected. But the smaller tent annexed to it glowed from within with a faint rosy pink. From where he stood, Tanto could make out the silhouette of two forms inside the tent: a seated figure, and another, much smaller. One of these must surely be Selen. The other, probably a slavegirl. Tanto's heart raced with anticipation.

At the entrance to the pavilion, he stopped. There was a low murmur of voices – no, one voice – coming from within. Tanto took two big calming breaths. He ran his hands over his disordered hair, smoothed his fabulously-embroidered tunic, tugged up his wrinkled hose and adjusted his undergarments. What he would say to her, he did not know; but what he was about to do was so natural, so *right*, that he knew he could trust the words to come to him when he needed them. He hovered outside the doorflap and peered in.

Selen Issian was seated on a low couch. A robed slavegirl sat at her feet. Selen's head was bowed over a sheaf of parchment pages bound together with ribbon, and from this she read aloud to the girl. From the tilt of her head, the child was clearly enthralled by whatever it was Selen was reading – by the sound of it some ancient tale of gods and monsters, fair ladies and brave princes ready to battle through and carry them to safety. Tanto found himself smiling. It was such an idyllic scene. Tanto could imagine Selen sitting thus in a few years' time, with their own child at her feet and himself with his feet up on a stool by the brazier, a flask of araque by his side. He could see all this so clearly that when he stepped through the doorflap and into the pavilion, he did so as if he were indeed walking into his own house.

The sound of his entry was masked by the turning of a parchment page, but even so the slave's head turned sharply. These hill girls, Tanto thought, amused: as jumpy as cats they are. The child said something he could not catch and Selen's head shot up from her reading. She was not wearing the traditional sabatka, Tanto realised with a sudden thrill; just a flimsy silk shift and a shawl about her head and shoulders. His eyes devoured her face. His wife: this was his wife. And how blessed he was, for she was lovely, as he had known she would be, with her pale olive skin and those startled black eyes – as wide and dark as those of the doe he had brought down with his best crossbow on the hillside above their villa last year. The mouth – oh, the mouth he remembered well from a dozen steamy dreams – though it was bare of paint now, and none the less appealing for it.

She rose awkwardly, hampered by the slavegirl clinging to her legs. 'Get out,' she managed, her voice low with rage; but Tanto had already closed the distance between them, eyes blazing.

And Alesto crossed the marble floors of the summer palace and called for his love to take her mortal shape that they might share their desire.

'Selen, my love. Let us share our desire—'

With a wordless cry of horror she thrust her arm out to keep him away; but all he could see was the pale flesh emerging from the golden shawl, the perfection of the limb foretelling the lovely sleekness of the rest of her smooth body.

From between the pillar of flames she came walking with her cat, Bast, by her side, but Bast she dismissed, saying that she needed no protection now her love was come. And then she took him by the hand . . .

He took another step forward. 'Send the girl away, Selen. Now I am here, you need no other.'

He reached out and pulled the shawl from her. It slithered down the silken shift, fell to a heap amongst the cushions on the floor. The slavegirl stared at it, then at the exposed shoulders of her mistress, her mouth open in shock. For a man to see a woman thus was sacrilege, a sin in the eyes of the Goddess; and she, Belina, would surely be punished for it. And not by the deity, either: no, she was far more worried about the lady's father and his propensity for using the lash. She should call out, summon help from Sharo and Valer in the next chamber, or run for Tam—

She began to form the word 'help', but nothing came out except a tiny gasp. The man looked away from her mistress's naked arms and fixed his eyes on her. She could feel the weight of his gaze on her, even through her veil. He is so handsome, she thought, wildly, disconnectedly. He smiled at her, and she found herself smiling back. How could anyone so handsome bring harm—

Tanto stared at his dagger-hand in surprise. The beautiful northern blade glinted at him, its silver sheened with red. He hadn't planned to stab the girl, but suddenly there she was crumpled among the bright cushions on the floor, her blood flowing out onto the golden shawl in a great, dark stream.

Selen Issian began to tremble. She stared at the corpse of her body-slave in utter disbelief. Then she turned her face to Tanto Vingo. 'No,' she said, almost inaudibly. And: 'No!'

Committed now beyond retreat, Tanto kicked the body of the slavegirl out of his way. He dropped the dagger and pushed Selen roughly down onto the couch, his hands ripping at her shift. There was a shearing sound and the fabric parted at her neck, the tear following the line of the weft right down to the waist. Tanto stared at her breasts. The aureoles – dark and round – stared back at him accusingly. Suddenly, Tanto found he did not possess enough hands. His first thought was to cup both breasts in his palms; but he needed one to stop her mouth and another to free his cock. Brute instinct took over. He fell upon her, his mouth on hers, but his probing tongue met a bar of gritted teeth. With one hand he ripped the shift clean away from beneath them both, while with the other he eased himself from the constrictions of his hose and smallclothes. A couple of blind, desperate shoves and he was in and grunting like a hog.

A storm of agony and outrage – furious, howling – rose

up in Selen Issian. She wrested her head away from him
in disgust. 'Goddess help me!' she cried. She flailed at her
invader, but Tanto, glassy-eyed, ploughed on, heedless of
the fists pummelling his back, his climax building.

At last one hand fell away from him, to scrape upon
the floor. Something chill met her warm skin. Her fingers
closed upon it. The hilt of the dagger fit her palm like an
answered prayer.

Erno had insisted, with some odd and misplaced chivalry,
Katla thought – or some sort of guilt – on carrying the
bundle she had packed before the Gathering as well as his
own bag.

'I do not have much to my name,' he said with a rueful
grin as Katla looked sceptically at the largely empty leather
sack with which he emerged from the booth.

Even as he said this she realised his gaze had inadvertently
gone to her fabulously-coloured headcloth, and then slid away
again. She coloured. Most of what Erno had owned had gone
into the purchase that now shielded her patchily-dyed hair
from public view. 'Here,' she said quickly, starting to unwind
the fabric; but: 'No,' he insisted. 'I bought it only with you
in mind. There is no one else in my life to give it to, and I
doubt it would suit me well.'

So she wore it still, though it was oddly in contrast with
the knocked-about leather jerkin she had retrieved from the
tent, and slipped on over the linen tunic. The red brocade
dress they had bundled up as best they could and stuffed
into the top of Erno's bag. 'We can sell it down the coast,'
Katla said mulishly when Erno had suggested they might
more honourably leave it folded neatly for Finn Larson as
a apology, as well as a rebuttal of his offer. 'Besides, if they
find the dress, they'll know for sure I've fled – and where
would any good Eyran head for if not the sea? At least if
they're looking for a girl in a long red dress, they're not

necessarily searching for a fugitive. It may slow them down just long enough for us to round the first headland.'

Now they ran swiftly and quietly through the Eyran quarter, heading east towards the Istrian sector and the strand on which the boats were pulled up. There was, it seemed, no one about, as if every living soul was ensconced in the great pavilion. Even in the usually more populous southern quarter, they came upon no other folk. They passed a group of southern-style tents clustered about the foot of Sur's Castle, and here, Katla stopped. She cocked her head, staring up at its great dark mass, silhouetted against the starry sky. She wet her lips.

'If we had the time, I'd climb the Rock again, now,' she said with a grin.

Erno gave her a peculiar glance. 'So it was you?'

Katla laughed. 'Of course.'

'When he cut off all your hair, I thought your father cruel and unfair.'

Katla shrugged. 'When he took Halli and Fent's money and gave it to Finn Larson I thought so, too. To lose your dreams, as my brothers did, is surely worse than to lose your hair.'

'But he traded you to the shipmaker.'

'Aye. But not for long, eh?' Katla was gleeful. She looked around, then up at the Rock again. Her eyes gleamed in the moonlight. For a moment she looked as fey as a changeling; then, before Erno could say anything more, she undid her sword belt and sprinted to the foot of it, located the crack system she had ascended before, and started to climb. The white charge of energy she got from the rock was stronger this time, if anything. Perhaps it was the peril of the situation that enhanced it.

Erno flung down the bags in exasperation. 'What in seven hells do you think you're doing? Have you gone mad? One minute you're concerned about buying time for your escape, and now you're climbing the thing that got you into trouble in the first place!' He paused, as if expecting a response. When he got none, he called up, as loud as he dared, 'If the Istrians don't kill you for it, I bloody well will.'

A low chuckle floated down to him, followed by: 'It's such a nice crack-line, Erno: how can I resist?'

All he could do was to stand there, helpless, his hands balled into fists, his eyes flicking constantly back and forth from the quiet fairground behind them to the nimble figure ascending the Castle. He watched her moving with quiet intensity, saw how she placed each foot with careful precision before putting her weight on it, how she tested the rock above her head with her reaching hand before pulling up on it. Where the crack became choked and bulged outward near the top he watched with his heart in his mouth as she swung herself up with both feet in the air for a second or two before making the move that took her over the obstruction. Moments stretched into what seemed hours. He heard a dog howl, its eerie sound oscillating through the still air. A horse whinnied somewhere to the west, then fell silent again. No folk appeared. A single gull, defying its natural sleep patterns, ghosted overhead to wheel above the Rock, saw Katla up there and banked sharply away.

At last she reached the summit. He saw her running about on top of its flat surface, waving her arms in the air in some private paroxysm of celebration and his heart swelled with a perverse pride. The wildness was back with a vengeance, he thought, and he loved her all the more for it.

Then, abruptly, she dropped her arms and ran to the western edge of the Rock. She peered down towards the landward side, then vanished from his view. The next moment she was back, gesturing furiously. Erno's heart skipped a beat. Had she been seen? Had pursuers come after them already? He cursed the wasted minutes of the climb, the sheer, mindless stupidity of it: for there was Katla, marooned upon Sur's Castle like a treed cat, with nowhere to hide or run to. Katla, for her part, looked not panicked, but galvanised. He saw her begin her descent, hand over hand, down some rope contraption set up for the less nimble on the far side of the Rock, and in a remarkably short space of time she was safely on the ground and running towards him.

'Erno, Erno, quickly!' She bent down and grabbed up her swordbelt and pack and started running uphill past the western side of the Castle.

He had no choice but to follow her, even though they were now heading in the opposite direction to the faerings and their planned escape. Even with the pack, running uphill on shifting ash, she was fleeter than him. Head down and puffing, he did not see what Katla had espied from the top of the Rock until they were upon it.

Katla threw herself down beside a kneeling, naked figure, a figure covered in blood, with a dagger in its hand. Long tangles of black hair spilled across narrow shoulders but did little to disguise the swell of breasts. A woman . . .

'Are you all right?' Katla asked her in Eyran, and when this received no response other than a bewildered frown, she repeated the question in the Old Tongue. The woman nodded slowly. Runnels of tears had left pale channels through the gore on her face. Sobbing, she tried ineffectually to cover herself with her hands.

Katla looked back at Erno. 'Stop gawping at her and give me the dress!' When he hesitated, for a moment unsure of what she meant, she snatched his bag from him and hauled the brocade robe out of it. She took the dagger from the girl's hand and cast it down. With a sleeve she wiped the worst of the blood away from the girl's face and hands. 'I knew it would come in useful,' she grinned at the woman. 'Red on red – it won't even show.'

She put a hand beneath the woman's elbow and eased her to her feet. There were smears of blood on her legs and in her pubic hair. Erno looked away, acutely embarrassed but at once Katla rounded on him. 'For Sur's sake, Erno, help me. Don't tell me you've never seen a woman naked before.'

He hadn't. But he wasn't going to tell her that. Reprimanding himself for seeing the girl as a female before he saw her as someone in need of his help, he took an arm of the dress from Katla, gathered the thing up from the hem and helped her pull it over the woman's head. Together, they adjusted the neck, laced the back. She was a different shape to Katla, he could not help but note, a different sort of woman altogether. There was no muscle on her, though her skin was smooth and her limbs neatly formed, and she was narrower in the waist and shoulders, though wider in the hip, so that the dress hung loose upon her upper body even with the laces tight.

'Thank you,' the woman said at last in the Old Tongue. 'By Falla, I thank you.'

Katla and Erno exchanged glances. An Istrian woman, then, as they might have judged by her colouring, if nothing else: for whoever had seen one of the southern women run naked and bloody across the Moonfell Plain?

'What happened to you?' Erno asked slowly in the Old Tongue.

The woman looked distressed. She started to cry. Erno felt more helpless now than he ever had in his life. He put a hand out to her, but she flinched away. To cover his confusion he bent to retrieve the dagger from the ground. Though it was mired by blood, there was something familiar about it . . .

'Isn't this one of yours?' he asked Katla softly in Eyran.

She stared at him, then at the blade. A moment later she took it from him, hefted it in her hand, then, heedless of the mess, wiped it across the thigh of her breeches. She held it up to the moonlight, and gasped. It *was* one of hers. Not only that, but it was the dagger she had given to the young Istrian man but two days ago at her stand. She looked at the woman again, her mind working. Surely the mild-mannered Saro had no part in this? She felt a chill run through her. 'Who are you?' Katla said urgently, reverting to the Old Tongue. 'Tell us how you have come to this.'

The woman rubbed her tears away roughly, then pushed back her hair. Her chin came up. This is hard for her, Katla thought, recognising the pride there. She tucked the dagger into her belt and took the woman's hand encouragingly.

'My name is Selen Issian,' the woman said. 'A man murdered my slave, then forced himself upon me. I think—' She fought down another rising sob, then gathered herself again. 'I think I killed him.'

Compelled by a nameless dread, Katla tightened her grip on the hand. 'Tell me who he was—'

Selen Issian frowned. 'The Vingo son,' she said. 'We were to be betrothed tonight, though I did not want it. He would not wait.'

Katla felt dizzy. Saro Vingo – a rapist, and dead? Nausea rose up inside her, followed by an equally disorientating wave of pity, but whether it was for the woman – due to be betrothed, like herself, this very night to a man for whom she had no love – or for herself, she could not tell.

'I have to get away,' Selen Issian went on. 'My father . . .' She turned to Katla, her black eyes huge. 'Help me. If they find me they will surely burn me for his death.'

Another woman escaping her family and the fires. This was all too strange. Katla took a deep breath. She looked at Erno. He gave a single nod: how could they possibly turn her away?

'As luck would have it, we are also leaving this place: you are welcome to come with us.'

Selen Issian smiled wanly. 'I have nothing to offer you but my thanks.'

'No time even for that,' Katla grinned. 'Come on.'

They were just nearing the western edge of Sur's Castle and had begun their downhill descent towards the shining sea, when there was a shout. Katla stared around. Behind them, in the Istrian quarter, torches danced in the darkness. The shouting grew louder.

'Run!' cried Erno. He grabbed Selen Issian by the arm and dragged her along with him. Katla heaved her pack up onto her back and ran behind them, turning every third step to assess the pursuit.

They dodged between a group of tents, fled through some sort of pebbled enclosure scattered with flowers and stinking of death. More tents, and a small group of drunken folk weaving their way back from the nomad quarter, who stared at them as if they were some sort of impromptu entertainment, and then they were out on the strand. Here, the ashy ground was rough and sharp. It cut into Selen's bare feet so that soon there was fresh blood spattered up her legs. She bit back her whimpers of pain, but it was impossible to keep up with the long-legged northman and it was not long before she stumbled on the long hem of the dress and fell headfirst. Erno ran back, took one look at her ruined feet and stopped dead.

Katla turned and looked for their pursuers. A line of firelight marked their position. They had come the long way round the Istrian pavilions, but now they were heading fast in their direction. She turned back to Erno, made a swift assessment. 'Pick her up and get down below the crest of the rise,' she said. 'Head for the faerings. I'll draw them off this way.'

'Why should they follow you? If they're looking for Selen, they'll hardly be seeking someone in Eyran clothing—'

Katla lost her patience. 'Look, just take her and run: it's her only chance. I can't carry her as fast as you can, and if we split, they may at least become confused. I'll meet you at the boats. Just launch one out and get away: I can always swim after you.'

He stared at her, wordless; but there was no time for further discussion: the first of the torches came at a run around the last of the tents. Instead, he grabbed Katla's chin and kissed her once, hard, on the mouth. Then he hauled Selen Issian over his shoulder and dropped down over the rise and out of immediate sight.

Katla waited until the pursuing group gained a clear view of her, then took to her heels, running uphill away from the sea. She heard shouts behind her, as shrill and avid as a pack of huntsmen sighting quarry and knew her ruse had worked. Up amongst the Istrian tents she ran again, doubling back on herself. The pack soon became a burden now that she was running flat-out. She thought quickly, then cached it behind a pavilion with a long line of flags on a pole out in front of it, so that she could locate it easily again, and ran on. The shouting got close enough that soon she could make out individual voices, but not the words. It took her a moment or more to realise this was because they called to one another in Istrian, and she grinned. Perfect. Even if they caught up with her, they'd have to let her go.

A few minutes later she had managed to lose them again amid the welter of tents and pavilions, and shortly after that found herself back in the pebbled enclosure. Here she stopped, the air sawing painfully in her lungs. Not so fit after all, she chided herself ruefully. Still, this should have given Erno sufficient time to reach the boats. She bent over, feeling the blood run into her turbaned head, and tried to catch her breath. A strong smell of incense rose up to meet her. It came from a garland of crushed orange flowers that lay on the ground beneath her feet. Curious, even in the midst of the drama, Katla picked one up and examined it. Flecks of its dark pollen tumbled out onto her hands. It was like no flower she had ever seen: some exotic southern species that would never survive in the windy north. She discarded it with a certain disgust, wiping her hands off on her tunic. She looked up at Sur's Castle rising before her. If she were to run back up around the Rock and come down to the sea from its landward side, that should throw them off the scent. But then she remembered her pack. Damn. She ran quickly through its contents in her head and knew with a sinking heart she couldn't afford simply to abandon it. Slipping out of the garden the way they had originally entered it, she cut between pavilions and looked around. Unrelieved darkness. No sign of the pursuit; nor of the flags. She ran a way downhill again, dodging between the tents. When she came to the last of the pavilions she stopped and peered carefully around its seaward side. Nothing but the volcanic strand and the moonlit sea rolling into the shore on line after line of silver surf. She felt her breathing steady itself. Looking back west, she saw the topmost of the pennants she had noted previously hanging from its flagpole maybe thirty lengths to her left and a little further up the slope. Excellent. She slipped into the open space between two pavilions without a second thought.

A voice terrifyingly close behind her shouted in the Old Tongue: 'Halt!'

Another declared: 'Move and we will kill you where you stand, Eyran scum.'

It took a moment to realise the significance of that last utterance. She whirled around. Three Allfair officials stood there, two of them training sturdy crossbows upon her. She recognised one of them. Her heart started to beat very fast. She gathered herself for action: if she were to dive and roll, then run back towards the tents, she might lose them again. If she could get to the Rock, she could shimmy up the crackline before they got anywhere near her. It was surely the last place they'd expect to look, and by now the line was firmly in her head: she could climb it blindfold—

She hurled herself down and heard the first bolt whistle over her back. She rolled and came to her feet running. Head down, she hurtled sideways towards the westward tents, and straight into an obstruction. She hit it so hard, she fell down, winded. When she looked up she found it was another guard, and he had the point of his sword at her throat.

'Can you see her?'

Virelai, a head taller than most of those present, stared out across the crowd. This time he knew what he was looking for: that damned green shawl. Splashes of green kept drawing his eye – a headcloth there, a tunic here; a robe of deepest forest-green; a blocky-looking woman in an emerald dress, a man's mossy cloak, a pale young woman in a virulent green and gold dress.

His eye strayed beyond her to a dark man seated on a dais, surrounded by a great tumble of coloured rugs and crocks, trinkets and flasks. A scribe sat beside him, quill poised over his parchment, staring and staring as if his eyes were no longer his own. Virelai knew well what that look meant, and he had learned to keep the Rosa Eldi well hidden from the public gaze as a result. He took a step to one side and peered around the group who had been blocking his view, and there she was, seemingly in deep conversation with the dark-haired man.

'Ah, what are you about now?' Virelai breathed, taking in this scene with some curiosity.

'What? What did you say?' Lord Tycho Issian grasped the map-seller's shoulder with fingers of iron. 'Did you say something?'

Virelai swivelled his head. He regarded the hand on his shoulder, then turned his pale, unblinking stare to the southern lord's desperate face. As Tycho's eyes narrowed in a prelude to fury, the map-seller quickly returned his gaze to the Rosa Eldi and began to plough a furrow through the crowd towards her. Nearer the dais, the throng grew more dense. Cleanshaven, dark-skinned men in rich clothing, attended by their respective retinues, had gathered on one side of the man on the dais, bearded men with their women on the other. Virelai cast a curious eye over them. They were all chattering away like jackdaws, he noticed, though they could not drag their eyes away from the scene that played itself out before them.

Behind him, there was a gasp. His lips quirked. So the southern lord had seen her at last. This should prove interesting.

Lord Tycho Issian shouldered past the map-seller with a curse. He barged through a group of Eyrans, who turned and regarded him with open hostility. One of them, young and red-headed, shouted something and tried to step in front of him, but nothing could stop Tycho now. He pushed roughly past Lord Prionan without a thought for the delicate political manoeuvrings he had been making towards the man for the past two years, and drove a shoulder between old Greving and Hesto Dystra likewise. Of the Swan of Jetra – rumoured to be the most beautiful woman Falla ever created – he took no more notice than the momentary irritation of finding her foot beneath his sole. Without a word of apology he forged on, until there were none left between him and his goal but the woman in the green dress.

The dark man had risen now and, taking the Rosa Eldi's hands in his own, lifted her lightly up onto the dais beside him. Not once did his eyes leave her face.

Tycho felt the blood pumping about his body like surging flows of lava. Its incandescence flooded his limbs, his torso, his face, his groin. There she was – his prize – just three feet away, the Rose of the World, the heart of his life, the woman he would this very night wed—

Sound diminished all around as if he stood in a bubble of air. And then:

'Wed her? My lord, you cannot!' The voice was outraged, shrill with consternation. Tycho spun around to answer the speaker with his fist, then realised with a dawning horror that he was not the one addressed.

Confusion fell upon him, followed by an awareness that he

had just missed something crucial in the exchange between the Rosa Eldi and the dark-haired man.

A tall, bearded man parted the crowd and came striding towards the dais. 'Sire, I say again: you cannot take this woman to wife.'

A second northerner followed, grizzled as an old bear, his beard a bush of grey. 'Ravn, what can you be thinking of? This is madness.'

Ravn. King Ravn Asharson. Stallion of the North. Heathen lord of the Eyran isles, here to choose his wife. Tycho felt the madness roil over him.

For her part, the Rosa Eldi let drop her shawl, revealing her silver-blonde hair, as straight as a waterfall; the perfect white skin and sea-green eyes. A hush overtook the room, washing out across the crowd like the ripples made by a thrown stone in water, or the destructive spiral of a typhoon. In the silent eye of the storm, the Rosa Eldi took the northern king's hand. She parted his fingers, placed the index finger of his right hand inside her pink mouth, then withdrew it and blew softly upon it. Then she leaned towards him.

'Say it again,' she urged in that low, uninflected voice. 'For them.'

Ravn Asharson drew himself up. He roared something in the guttural language of Eyra. Then: 'I have chosen my Queen!' he cried out in the Old Tongue.

And the Rosa Eldi smiled.

Virelai stared. He had never seen her change expression before. He had not thought she knew how.

Aran Aranson watched all this play out with some bewilderment, but his mind was not entirely on the royal choice. He appeared to have lost his daughter. And some while back he'd realised that Erno Hamson was nowhere to be seen, either, which two facts taken together gave him genuine concern. He'd known young Erno was sweet on Katla, as Gramma

Rolfsen would say, for the last couple of years at the least, but he'd paid it no mind, for Katla would never choose for herself a man as good-natured and taciturn as poor, shy Erno: he knew his noisy, wayward daughter too well. Or he thought he did. Most likely Erno was playing the maiden-aunt, he told himself, calming her nerves, walking her about outside. He had been trying to put a polite face on his growing anxiety for the past twenty minutes or more since he had first noticed her gone, and determined also, that Finn Larson should not know it. For his part, the master shipmaker had been bent on Aran witnessing Jenna's triumph with the King and kept clutching at his arm, which meant that Aran had not been able to slip quietly away. 'See what a fine family you are marrying your girl into,' Finn kept saying. 'And soon with a royal connection, too.' He winked. 'Who else can Ravn choose but my beautiful daughter? Istrians may offer tawdry temptations to gild their offers, but Ravn's a proper man: he'll choose a red-blooded northern girl. I am eternally grateful to you, Aran, my friend, for putting your good son to one side to make this match possible.'

And now here they were with Jenna weeping over her embarrassment, and no doubt over the King picking some unknown beggar-girl like the complete fool that he was; and Katla – on whom his trade with Finn, and hence all his dreams and plans were founded – had vanished with Erno Hamson. Aran Aranson was not by nature a anxious man, but his skin was crawling now. There was something not right here, not right at all. His superstitious mother, who claimed to be able to see the future, and had on occasion been unnervingly prescient, would have said he was feeling the skeins of the web-makers brushing his skin, as the strands of his fate were woven. His fingers found the nugget of gold in his pouch, caressing its cold brilliance. The tingling sensation it transmitted travelled through his palm up his arm and into his chest, where it suffused him

in a wash of warm comfort. It was his talisman: all would
be well.

Relaxed now, his head light with relief, he gazed around,
his eyes coming to rest at last on a tall man, towering pale as
a lily over the crowd to the right of him. It was, he realised
with a certain surprise, the map-seller, the man who had
entrusted him with the quest that so enthralled him, and
with the ingot in his pocket. As if recognising its erstwhile
master, the rock buzzed in his hand, so unexpectedly that his
fingers came off it as if burned. As they did so, a connection
struck him. He focused for the first time on the woman with
the King. Something about her. Something . . . magnetic . . .
He watched her pale hand move rhythmically on the King's
arm and remembered that same hand, that same gesture, upon
the black-furred cat on the steps of the map-seller's wagon.
Puzzled now, he stared back and forth between the two. Was
this some sort of trick, some mummer's play? He looked
about more widely; saw how a big woman in a hideous green
dress moved towards the dais with great strides that kicked out
the front of the fabric as a woman more used to such fashions
never would; he saw a small man bobbing in her wake; more
oddly, he watched a small group of Istrian matrons in their
voluminous sabatkas detach themselves from the anonymous
group by the musicians' stage and begin pushing through the
crowd in a most unladylike manner.

The hairs on the back of his neck began to rise.

He was still watching this strange convergence of paths
when there was a great hubbub at the entrance to the
pavilion and a band of uniformed men came rushing in,
shouting something about murder and abduction.

In the midst of them was his daughter, Katla, bound and
blood-stained.

Fifteen

Prisoner

'Katla!'

He heard his own cry emerge as an anguished, keening howl, high and tortured, like nothing he would expect to issue from his own throat. And then he was pushing forward, careless of the folk between him and his daughter. Behind him, he could hear, as if from afar, Fent screaming obscenities at the Istrian guards; Halli, his voice lower, as ever more temperate, apologising gruffly to the families they trampled in their passage.

A clamour rose from the Eyran families close enough to see the guard troop and the figure they held as the perpetrator.

'Who did you say it was?'

'Katla Aransen.'

'Aran Aranson's pretty daughter? Never — it's surely a lad.'

'Would it be Fent Aranson?'

'No, stupid, look, he's right there behind his father, threatening bloodshed.'

A laugh. 'That'll be young Fent all right: little firebrand he always was.'

'It's Katla Aransen, I tell you: I heard her father call her name.'

'But I saw her earlier: she wore a red robe — very grand.'

'It *is* Katla Aransen, I swear.'

'By Sur, so it is. But why?'

'They've got one of our girls—'

'Take your hands off her, Istrian bastards!'

Word burned like wildfire around the Eyran clans. Every-one started to push towards the front of the Gathering, where the guard troop were marching their captive. Distinctive and official in their crested helms and blue cloaks, by now they had their swords out and looked ready to use them.

Ravn tore his eyes away from his chosen bride, distracted by the noise. Released from that piercing green gaze, he felt his head clear, as if he had just come up from a deep-water dive. Down on the floor of the Gathering he saw a chaos of movement: an Allfair guard troop hustling a prisoner along, the crowd behind them parted by a group of furious Eyrans, shouting and waving their fists in the air. Of a sudden, the mood had turned dangerous and he had not even noticed the transition. Chill touched his heart. He was a king and this his Gathering, these people his subjects; yet somehow he had been unaware of the drama. He felt confused, disorientated. He had drunk a lot of wine; but this sensation of detachment was not the warm familiar haze incurred by too much drink; rather it was like emerging from a dream, a dream not entirely his own. He shook his head, stared out into the crowd. The silver of the guard troop's swords glinted in the candlelight. Swords: that was something he did understand.

'Hold fast!' he bellowed into the din. 'Put away those swords: this is a peaceful Gathering, I'll have no weaponry here.'

The guard captain was staring at him, uncomprehending.

Ravn glared back, infuriated by the man's insolence; then realised he had spoken unthinkingly in Eyran. He repeated himself in the Old Tongue.

The guard captain drew himself up, affronted. He gave no order for his men to disarm, and instead of presenting himself to Ravn Asharson, bypassed the northern king and pressed on towards a knot of Istrian nobles. They were, he reasoned, the men who paid his annual stipend, now that Rui Finco, Lord of Forent, headed the Allfair forum that ruled on such matters.

'Falla's greeting to my lords this night,' he intoned, in formal Istrian. 'I bring before you a prisoner whom we took by force running from the scene of a crime.'

The Lord of Forent – a handsome, wiry-looking man with a plain silver band set upon his burnished temples, and the nose of a predator – had at first looked flustered by this turn of events, but he rose to the occasion admirably. Raising an elegant eyebrow, he regarded the guard captain with interest. He turned to Lord Prionan beside him. 'A theatrical presentation to enliven the evening, my lord?' he enquired smoothly.

Prionan shrugged. 'I know nothing about it, if so.'

Rui Finco addressed himself to the guard captain in Istrian. 'I fear we have not been rehearsed in our lines, sir,' he smiled. 'But carry on, for I'm sure we're up to the task of improvisation.'

The guard captain looked uncomfortable. 'It's no mummery, my lord,' he said. 'It's a grave matter. There's been a death—'

A hush fell over those who understood the sibilant southern words.

'*Grave* and *death* – a clever wordplay: bravo!' Hesto Dystra clapped his hands. Nearing seventy now, his wits were not always as sharp as they'd been.

'This is not a play!' the guard captain bellowed at last, his temper frayed beyond manners.

The Lord of Forent looked from the guard captain to the captive behind him and saw a scrawny-looking lad with a swelling black eye, wearing a stained and bloodied tunic and the most garishly coloured headcloth. As if aware of his regard, the prisoner's head came up and he began to shout something at him in the guttural northern tongue. The Lord of Forent regarded him with greater interest. His knowledge of Eyran was rudimentary but functional.

'Excellent,' he declared, in Istrian. 'We shall have our entertainment after all: for the captive declares himself innocent of all charges!' His gaze enveloped the milling crowd. He switched to the Old Tongue. 'We have a trial!' he called. 'We need quiet to hear both the charges and the prisoner's response.'

At this point, three Eyran men burst through the ranks of the throng with murder in their eyes.

'What in Sur's name is this travesty?' roared Aran Aranson.

The Istrian lord eyed him warily. 'The prisoner is held on suspicion of a crime,' he said steadily in correct but stilted Eyran.

'What crime?' demanded Fent, over his father's shoulder.

The Lord of Forent consulted briefly with the guard captain. 'The man under arrest is suspected of abduction, sacrilege; and—' he paused to watch the prisoner's response '—murder . . .'

'Murder?' Aran cried, aghast.

'Katla?' Halli looked dumbfounded.

'Man?' howled Katla. She laughed. In a perfectly inflected Old Tongue she said: 'I think you've got the wrong girl.' With a flourish somewhat constrained by the ropes that bound her wrists, she pulled away the rainbow-silk that confined her hair. Or what was left of it. Damn: that little detail she had forgotten.

Shorn and patchily-dyed, damp with sweat, her hair stood up in little peaks and spikes from her skull, accentuating the sharp planes of her face, the preternatural brightness of the unswollen eye. Revealed thus, she looked even more the desperado they claimed her to be.

There was a general puzzled silence as those nearest to the scene tried to make sense of the captive's odd gesture, and others craned to stare. The elderly Dystra brothers put their noddles together and began to mutter furiously. One of the soldiers in the guard troop cocked his head and regarded Katla speculatively.

The guard captain stared at his prisoner as if making mental note.

The big, dark Eyran was shouting again. Something about a daughter . . . Rui Finco regarded him dispassionately. 'Speak more slowly, Northerner: I cannot follow your gibberish.'

Aran Aranson's eyes flashed dangerously. 'I said, this is my daughter: a daughter of Eyra, and as such she should questioned according to Eyran law, which demands the highest-ranking Eyran lord hear her case. I call for King Ravn Asharson to hear this matter, for I know my daughter Katla to be truthful, and I will not trust her life to the enemies of our people . . .'

Lord Rui Finco held Aran's gaze for several heartbeats, then he turned to confer with the Lords Prionan and Dystra and repeated the northerner's request. Hesto Dystra shrugged. 'He is within his rights.'

Lord Prionan acquiesced. 'The Allfair is held on neutral territory.'

The Lord of Forent nodded. 'As you will.' He turned away from his peers, glanced towards the dais, only to find that King Ravn Asharson had once more been captivated by the pale nomad woman. He stared at this tableau, his mind working furiously. All was not going to plan. Giving a swift glance back at the Gathering, he took in the various positions of the mercenaries, poised as they were at different points around the pavilion in their bizarre guises. He caught the eye of a big woman in an ill-fitting green dress, gave her an imperceptible shake of the head, and watched as she melted into the background.

Vaulting onto the dais as smoothly as a leaping cat, Rui Finco bore down upon the northern king, who stood motionless and perplexed, the mer-creature's pale hand upon his arm. *How bizarre*, he thought, *that it should come to this, on such a night*. As he approached, he saw how Ravn Asharson's head came up, how his eyes were as vacant as a sleepwalker's. Perhaps opportunity would present itself once this new matter was dealt with; and the woman could be useful, too, given this uncanny effect she had upon him.

'My lord king,' he said quietly in the Old Tongue, 'we have a situation here that demands your immediate attention.' He took Ravn's arm to draw him along the dais towards the guard troop, feeling at once elation and repulsion at the ease with which the northern king gave himself into his command. The side of his face felt suddenly chill. He turned, to find the mer-woman staring fixedly at him, her eyes as hard and green as malachite. 'Never fear, my lady,' he found himself saying to her, 'I will return him to your care shortly.'

'You will,' said the Rosa Eldi softly. 'You will.'

Katla was unceremoniously bundled up onto the dais, where she stood awkwardly, one knee bent, blinking at all the unwanted scrutiny. So much for an inconspicuous getaway, she thought bitterly: she'd have a fair few miles to swim after Erno if she ever got out of this one. She watched King Ravn Asharson being detached from the arms of a tall, pale woman and led towards her by an Istrian lord wearing a plain silver circlet. *So the King didn't pick the Swan of Jetra, then*, she thought inconsequentially. *At least that's some consolation for poor Jenna.* The pair of men looked well-matched: both tall and dark and well made, even if one was bearded and the other, in true southern fashion, was not. The flickering light of the candles played off similarly high cheekbones, reflected in two pairs of dark eyes. As they came closer she could see that there the resemblance ended, for the Istrian lord was older than her king, harder about the face, too. A moment later, her heart pounded as she realised that this man to whom the others deferred and called by a strange foreign name was the one who had come to their stall the first day of the Fair. *Oh, Sur,* she thought, *he already had me marked down as a miscreant.* A dangerous fanatic, he had seemed then, ranting about the woman found on top of what he called *Falla's Rock*, then appalled at the very idea Aran would allow a woman to touch a sword, let alone have forged it herself.

The guard captain manhandled her roughly into position, facing her king. Someone, she noted, had carried his throne to this part of the dais, where he now sat in isolated splendour, his crown a little skewed, his eyes bleary. He looked, she thought, like the play-king from the mummer's theatre who had entertained them at Rockfall last winter: tawdry and rather the worse for drink. Her heart fell. For the first time since they had taken her, she felt afraid.

'Your name, prisoner,' declaimed the guard captain.

'Katla Aransen.'

King Ravn regarded her with a little more focus, trying to place the name.

'Sir,' the guard prompted self-importantly.

Katla stared at him with a queer light in her eye. She would 'sir' no one.

The guard captain glared at her, but he recognised stubbornness when he saw it. Just let him have five minutes with this chit in a quiet place, he thought, she'd soon learn some deference. He drew himself up, filled his lungs with air and began to bellow out the charges:

'Katla Aransen: you have been apprehended on the suspicion of carrying out murder—'

'Who has been murdered?' someone cried from down on the floor.

The guard captain halted, irritated by the interruption. 'A slave,' he said, addressing the crowd. 'A slavegirl has been cruelly slaughtered and her mistress abducted. And the Lords of Jetra's shrine for the Swan has been horribly desecrated—'

Oh seven hells, Katla thought then, looking down at the safflower stains on her tunic. *All I did was pick some of the damned flowers up: it's hardly what you'd call desecration . . .*

A few of the Istrian faces in the crowd looked at once rather less interested in the proceedings: a slave – well, that was something of an inconvenience, and an expense when it came to replacement, to be sure, but at least it was not one of their own. As for the desecration of the shrine: was it not a showy gesture to make a contemplation garden in the midst of the Allfair? Asking for trouble. But the abduction – that was the intriguing thing . . .

Seeing how Ravn Asharson was guided away along the dais by Rui Finco, Lord Tycho Issian had felt a small hope rise in him. It seemed that Falla – the champion of all true lovers – was offering him a chance at last to claim his bride, to save her from desecration at the hands of the barbarian king. Trying to force his way to the dais through the crowd of voracious onlookers – all intent on the forthcoming trial as spectators at a bear-pit – was like swimming against a strong tide. Yet to see her standing there, pale and silent, as beautiful as her name; perfect in every detail, he knew he would risk all – reputation, fortune and daughter – for this woman. He longed to take her in his arms, to make her sacred to the Goddess by all the laws of holy Istria, to take her home to Cantara and hide her away from defiling eyes forever. The thought of the northerner's hands on that cool white skin, of his mouth investigating her most secret places, was too much to bear. This was not merely a marriage bargain he was upholding, he thought: it was a sacred mission to save a soul.

So when the guard captain loudly announced the charges against the captive, he was not, at first, paying any attention to the man's words.

It was only when folk started to stare at *him* that he stopped fighting his way through the crowd.

'What?' he asked angrily of the man blocking his way. 'What is it?'

The man in front of him was a rich merchant from Gila. He knew Lord Tycho Issian from a few hard business dealings, and also by reputation: a cruel man, it was said, cruel and . . . strange; but one whose star was rising rapidly. 'Your daughter, my lord,' the merchant said hesitantly. 'They are speaking of your daughter.'

Infuriated, Tycho whirled around. Those nearby quailed at the look in his eyes. 'What of my daughter?' he cried.

'The prisoner is charged with involvement in an abduction,' the guard captain returned loudly. 'The abduction of the Lady Selen Issian. My lord.' He inclined his head towards Tycho with a chill in his stomach. Not to have come to this lord quietly and immediately with the news of his daughter's disappearance was something he might well come to regret.

Tycho felt his heart grow still and cold. Selen abducted . . . How could that be? His face worked uncontrollably. He moved towards the dais, and the crowd melted away to let him through.

The guard captain lowered his voice when Tycho was close enough. 'My lord, I fear Eyran raiders have ruthlessly murdered your little slavegirl and stolen away your daughter. We caught one of the perpetrators running from the scene.'

'Why would . . .' Tycho's voice broke. He stared at the prisoner, uncomprehending. Without Selen all was lost – the bride-price, the Rosa Eldi – everything. 'Why would this . . . thing . . . conspire to take my daughter?' He returned his gaze to the guard captain, his eyes black with rage. The official quailed. A moment later, the Lord of Cantara had leapt upon the dais and was running at Katla, arms outstretched, fingers like claws. Even with guards coming at him from all angles, still he managed to grasp her by the throat, careless in his desperation of the unclean touch. 'Why?' he shrieked, and: 'What have you done with her, you whore?'

The soldiers pried Tycho away, handed him back down to the ground, where, as if from nowhere a tall, pale man appeared to lay a comforting hand on his shoulder and say something quietly into his ear. The Lord of Cartara subsided, as if distracted.

'Continue!' King Ravn called above the hubbub.

'We found this . . . woman . . . running from the scene, my lord,' the guard captain declared pompously. 'And we may, if the Goddess smiles upon us, also have a witness to the atrocities committed. In the meantime, we have this—'

He produced a wicked-looking dagger and brandished it at the crowd. It was a dagger in the northern style – pattern-welded and beautifully ornamented. Dull red had been smeared down the silver blade, had set in thick courses down the dragon-wrapped hilt.

King Ravn took the dagger from the man's hand and regarded it thoughtfully. A fine piece of work: beautiful craftsmanship, as elegantly functional as a good Eyran longship.

Seeing the knife, Aran Aranson's face grew still as stone. Beneath the wind-dark tan, his blood fled away to leave an ashy pallor. He recognised the blade of course: it was one of her best.

Other Eyrans sighed and whispered: Katla Aransen's work was well known in the northern isles.

'I have killed no one; wounded no one; abducted no one,' Katla said loudly into the hush. 'I swear it in Sur's name.'

'And this dagger?'

Rui Finco's voice was smooth and detached. He took the weapon from the northern king and turned it over in his hands, careful to avoid the still-tacky cross-piece, then passed it back to the guard captain, wiping his hands fastidiously on his doublet. 'It's an unusual-looking blade,' he said. He thought of the weapon he'd sent the mercenaries to purchase;

so much more sensible than his original idea of selecting it himself. 'Most distinctive.'

'It's one of mine.' Katla's chin came up defiantly. It gave her a certain pleasure to look this southern fanatic square in the eye and declare her trade to his face. 'I made it: the forging of fine weaponry is a certain skill of mine.'

Someone called out, 'Aye – and no mistake: she's a craftsman of the finest order, and that's the truth.'

'Best blades in Eyra,' another called gruffly.

Katla narrowed her eyes: this last seemed to come from the direction of a shrouded southern beldame, which seemed surreal, to say the least.

'However,' she went on, 'it was one of many that I have . . . sold during the course of this Fair.' (It was almost true, she reasoned: 'twas a barter, after all – payment for Saro's saving blow.) 'Someone had discarded it amongst the tents and I picked it up.'

'A likely tale,' Lord Prionan scoffed. 'And that you should have this very blade back in your possession if such was the case seems to me too great a coincidence to overlook.' He beamed around at the crowd, as if revelling in the powers of his logic.

'And what were you doing, to be running away from the scene?' King Ravn asked.

Katla felt her father's regard upon her. There was nothing for it.

'I was running away – indeed – when I came upon the dagger, and thought it a waste to see it cast aside so. But I was running away not from the scene of a crime, but from my imminent betrothal,' she said. 'Which is why I am dressed like this.' She indicated her stained and battered jerkin. 'I did not wish to marry the man my father had chosen for me, and had determined to escape such a fate.' She searched out her father's anxious face and held his gaze. His eyes showed nothing but anguish: no rage, no accusation. Katla smiled. Her voice softened and dropped to barely more than a whisper. 'But I still won't marry Finn Larson, Father—'

'Finn Larson?' echoed the King. He brought to mind the shipmaker: a barrel of a man well into his fifties: no fair match for this fiery girl. Better dressed and unshorn, she'd be worth a tumble, he thought, but Aran Aranson's harsh voice broke in on this pleasant reverie.

'Katla, I had not realised you would take it so ill that you would run away from here, from your clan, from me,' he pleaded from the ground. 'I will cancel the betrothal plans, I swear I will.'

People started to murmur, curious now, rather than appalled. 'Who's she marrying?' someone from the back cried.

'Finn Larson,' returned a leathery-looking Eyran matron.

'Finn Larson is an old goat!' someone else shouted and there was laughter

'Let the girl go,' someone cried in Eyran, and the cry was taken up.

Ravn Asharson called for quiet. 'You have blood on you,' he pointed out to Katla.

'I wiped the knife off,' Katla said truthfully. 'But only to examine it the better.'

'You lie!' It was a feeble cry, but compelling nevertheless.

Heads turned as one. From the back of the grand pavilion a litter was being borne through the crowd. Upon it lay Tanto Vingo, wrapped in a cloak donated by one of the guards, his head shrouded in its folds so that he peered out, ashen, like one risen from the dead.

'It was you and your Eyran friends who killed the slave and took the Lord of Cantara's daughter!' he spat. 'You who attacked me when I threw myself between your murdering blade and the Lady Selen.'

Tanto's face was white from blood-loss. Beneath the cloak, someone had bandaged him roughly about the hips, but already blood as dark as wine was starting to seep through the thick, unbleached linen. He pointed a trembling finger at the bound figure on the dais.

'That's the man: the very one who stabbed me!' He stared around at the assembled faces, saw their greed for the drama, their avid eyes.

Katla stared in disbelief. This was a scene from nightmare, a hag-ride from the seventh hell. The world had taken on surreal perspectives, an unfathomable new system of rules. 'I did not! This is utmost madness!'

'Madness indeed: to steal away a woman so; and a noble Istrian woman at that.' Tanto propped himself laboriously on an elbow, eyes blazing. Such fortune, he had thought when the guards who carried him told him the news: that a foreigner had been so propitiously apprehended – red-handed with the dagger and all, and that another man had been seen running away with a woman who sounded suspiciously like Selen Issian. The Goddess was surely smiling on him. He had known his union with Selen was blessed. Even the wound he had taken did not seem so bad now, though he was beginning to feel a little chill about the waist . . .

As they bore him closer to the dais, he took in the man who would go to the fires in his stead. He was a ruffian, clearly, in that appalling tunic, all stained and filthy; and that vile shag of hair. But there was something about the man – something about the eyes, the long nose, the scathing expression—

His eyes flickered from the northern king to Lord Rui Finco, and then to the blade the guard captain held in his hands. His dagger – or at least the one he had removed from beneath Saro's pillow. Something stirred deep in his skull, like an itch, or the small buzz of an insect . . .

'May I see the weapon, sir?' he asked the guard.

The crowd parted silently to allow the litter through and the guard captain placed the dagger carefully into Tanto's outstretched hands.

It was as if the blade were communicating with him. Something about the way it weighed in his hand, how the dragon's head fit the curve of his palm— Sensation triggered a memory, jolted into a searing connection. He stared at the prisoner's face again: took in this time the fine bones, the lips, the slight swell of the tunic as it passed to the narrow, belted waist. And then recollection flooded back: he remembered the knife stall, the feisty *woman* showing the weapons – *this* weapon – his brother, for no reason, punching him cold . . .

Not for no reason; no. What was it Saro had said? *I saw you up on the Rock . . .*

And he remembered the reward.

Sacrilege. The word snaked smoothly through his mind.

He laughed.

'My lords, I think you are going to owe me a debt of thanks, as well as two thousand cantari . . . This person you have arrested is . . . a woman!'

He waited for indrawn breaths, but there were none. He stared about him, then shook his head as if to clear his thoughts and continued: 'She is the very same woman you have been seeking throughout this Fair. She is the one who climbed our sacred Rock!'

The Istrians in the crowd gasped.

Rui Finco frowned. Forgetting in the heat of this moment that the trial had been put into the hands of the Eyran King, he addressed the captive direct. 'Did you climb Falla's Rock?'

'She did, she did!' Greving Dystra was almost beside himself with emotion. He pulled at his brother's sleeve. 'We saw her, didn't we, brother?'

Hesto peered myopically at the prisoner. 'The one we saw had long red hair,' he said doubtfully.

One of the guard troop stepped forward. 'May I speak, lord?' he asked Rui Finco. The Lord of Forent inclined his head. 'While I was making my rounds with Nuno Gastin here—' he indicated another guard '—we went into the Rockfall clan booth on routine questioning,' he said. 'They seemed inordinately anxious to be rid of us, and I noticed then that the daughter of the family had had her hair shorn most barbarously. She said it was for the hot summer in Eyra—' He coloured. 'But I have been assured since then that the northern isles do not tend to enjoy such weather. I thought, my lord, that she might have been jesting with me; but now I see my error.'

'It is not red, though,' persisted old Hesto Dystra. 'My eyes may be bad, but I'm not colour-blind—'

Ignoring the protests of the northern king, the Lord of Forent stepped up to the dais. 'Lower your head,' he said roughly to Katla.

In response, she glared at him. She would not submit to this. Instead, she thrust her head up and stared defiantly into the crowd. 'I climbed the Rock,' she said. She focused on the elderly Dystras. 'It was me you saw,' she added, almost kindly. 'The first time.'

'The first time?' Rui Finco stared at her in amazement.

'Oh, yes,' said Katla. 'I climbed it again just now.'

The din started with muttering, then with electrified discussion. People started to talk loudly to one another over the noise. Some began to shout. Amid the clamour an Eyran voice yelled, 'That's no sacrilege – it's Sur's own Rock!' while an Istrian shrieked: 'She has defiled the name of our Goddess. She must burn!'

This last voice came from close to Tanto, and it sounded familiar to him. He stared around, and found himself but feet away from Lord Tycho Issian. The southern lord's eyes were bulging with fervour, his hand jabbing the air. Beside him stood the tall, thin, pale man Tanto had seen earlier. Unlike the Lord of Cantara, his face showed no trace of emotion.

Rui Finco turned to Ravn Asharson. 'It seems, my lord

king,' he said smoothly, 'that this matter is now out of
your hands. While it concerned common criminal matters
on neutral territory, we could submit the case to Eyran
judgement; but I fear this desecration of Falla's Rock is
another matter entirely.'

'But it is our Rock,' King Ravn declared. 'And all she did
was climb upon it.'

'It is Sur's Castle,' confirmed the Earl of Southeye from
the floor. 'It has been so for all time.'

The Lord of Forent laughed. He turned to stare down at
the Eyran lord. 'Old man,' he said, and his eyes were like
obsidian, 'times change. The Moonfell Plain we may share
equally with you; but Falla's Rock was ceded to us by your
old king – King Ashar Stenson, the Night Wolf, the Shadow
Lord; father to King Ravn here – in return for – how shall
I put this? – a favour. Or perhaps I should say, our silence
on a certain embarrassing matter.' He stared back coolly at
the present king, who held his gaze unblinking. 'They say
blood will out, my lord,' he said to Ravn so softly that no
other save Katla could hear his words.

Ravn's eyes narrowed. His chin thrust out mulishly. 'I do
not know what you are talking about, southern lord,' he
hissed. 'But I mislike your tone.'

Rui Finco shrugged. 'As you will. Perhaps you and I will
discuss these matters later, somewhere a little more . . .
private.' He raised his voice. 'In the meantime, I think
you must concede the girl to Istrian law. She has admitted
to sacrilege, and you can see the wound she has given this
brave young man. Surely this is enough for you? We do
not wish for further violence here tonight.' There was silky
menace in his tone.

Ravn Asharson wavered. He turned to look back at where
the Rosa Eldi still stood like a statue. Their eyes met, and
again he felt that extraordinary wave of heat shock through
him; heat, and something else. He turned back. 'I am not yet

convinced of the degree of her guilt,' he said slowly. 'And until I am, I insist at least upon a shared ruling: Eyran justice to match Istrian justice.'

Rui Finco cocked his head, then turned back to the crowd. 'What say you, my lords of the Council; will you allow the woman a shared judgement?'

'I have no objection,' declared Prionan.

The Dystra brothers conferred briefly. 'In the spirit of goodwill on this Gathering night, we agree with Prionan.'

'No!'

A scandalised cry. Tycho Issian, Lord of Cantara, had pulled away from the tale nomad and was clawing his way towards the dais.

'You cannot do this!' he howled. He heaved himself up onto the dais and addressed his fellow Istrian lord. 'My lord of Forent − Rui − it is my daughter who has been taken; my soon-to-be-son by law who has been so cruelly struck down in her defence; my slave who has been evilly slaughtered. Do you not think I should have a say in this case?'

Rui Finco inclined his head. 'Have your say, Tycho, and then we shall make our ruling.'

Tycho turned to face the crowd. Breathing deeply, he felt time slow. Now was his chance and he must seize it with both hands. *Oh, Falla, Merciful One*, he prayed silently, *Falla, Lady of Fire, I implore you to aid your abject worshipper. Help me to gain my goal and I will sacrifice to you for all the days of my life. Just let me secure the star of my heavens, the love of my loins, the Rose of the World and you shall have blood aplenty before this day is through.*

His only chance of taking the Rosa Eldi away from the northern king would be in the midst of confusion. Violence and confusion. He must play the situation he had been handed like a gift with the utmost skill. So what if his daughter was missing? If he could bring the Istrian crowd to a sufficient pitch of righteous fury, he'd have no need for a bride-price

anyway: for who knew who might fall to their death in the
heat of battle? His eyes snaked once from Ravn Asharson,
sitting there like the stuffed and useless king he was, to the
tall, pale map-seller, his face upturned to the figures on the
dais as a flower turns its head to the sun. He felt nothing but
contempt for them all. *Play the personal card first*, his inner
voice told him; *win the crowd to your side, and then press home
your argument.*

His voice breaking as if under the strain of his shock, Tycho
Issian began:

'My daughter,' he croaked in Istrian, 'my beloved Selen.
A more beautiful, loving, pious girl you could never wish
to find. She came here with me to the Allfair, that most
wondrous of events, with hope in her heart. She hoped
for a wedding, my friends; to dedicate herself to Falla in
the service of a husband. Like any pure maid, this was her
dream. She was to have been married tomorrow, to the
man I chose to wed her to, a young man from a fine and
upright family. I have never seen her so happy, my lords, my
ladies—' he gestured to the crowd '—as when she opened
the parcel I had brought her and found her wedding gown
within.'

A woman sobbed.

Tycho wiped his dry eyes. He gazed into the throng.
'It was to have been the happiest moment of my life –
and of my beloved Selen's too – to stand with her at
the shrine tomorrow and join her to young Tanto Vingo;
but that happiness has been cruelly snatched away, by this
– creature—' he gestured at Katla, who stared at him through
narrowed eyes, understanding nothing of this foreign rant –
'and her co-conspirators, no doubt to ravish her virgin body,
to violate the Goddess's own handmaiden! And in their
attempt, they have slaughtered the girl who was dearest to
her in all the world – a slavegirl she helped to raise from a
babe-in-arms, rescued from a plague-stricken hill tribe—' (an

outright lie, but he could feel the crowd swaying towards his
fervour) '—and wounded this fine, brave young man here, a
man from an upstanding noble Istrian family, the Vingos –
whom you all know – a young man, who, careless for his
own life tried to stand in the way of their barbarism!'

Tanto raised a hand modestly to the crowd in acknowledgment of his heroism. 'It was nothing, my lord,' he managed
with a wan smile. He was beginning to feel decidedly faint.
'For the virtue of the Lady Selen, I would do the same and
more again.' He swung his legs from the litter and laid his
feet carefully upon the floor. He would walk to the Lord
of Cantara, take his hand, pledge his allegiance. When they
retrieved his bride again, how could Tycho turn him away,
bride-price or no bride-price? It was hard to position his
feet as he wanted: they seemed like lead weights, cold and
unfeeling. Bracing his hands on the litter, he levered himself
upright. His legs, uncooperative as the unstrung limbs of a
puppet, crumpled at once beneath him, spilling him outward
in a flurry of fabrics.

'A hero!' cried a man in a sumptuous black costume. 'A
true Istrian hero!'

'A hero?' This southern word Katla knew. She also knew
the man on the floor. *It was the Vingo son,* the Istrian woman
had said. But it was not Saro Vingo. In all the panic and fury,
she had forgotten his disgusting brother. She raised her voice
above the clamour, and addressed the crowd in the Old
Tongue: 'Hear my tale!' she cried, using the time-honoured
story-teller's opening: 'This man is no hero: he is a rapist and
a murderer! I found the woman of whom you speak – Selen
Issian – naked and bleeding as I was making my way from the
Gathering, on my own flight for freedom. She told me she
had stabbed this man – this Tanto Vingo – when he killed her
maid and attacked her, and then she crawled away for help—'
By now she should be clear away, Katla thought, and Erno,
too. 'And my friend and I gave her that aid. She will be far

from here now: far from the man who ravaged her; far from the father who sought to marry her against her will.'

'Silence!' Tycho Issian rounded on her. 'Not satisfied with your evil deeds, now you make foul allegations against those who loved her most. Is there no end to your ill-will? Do you have no shame?'

Behind him, he could feel the mood of the crowd sway; the Eyrans calling out for the prisoner; the Istrians against her. He smiled coldly at Katla. She stared back, chilled to the bone. *It was like looking into the eyes of a viper*, she thought suddenly. For all the avowals of heartbreak and misery, she saw no emotion in them but a calculating, deathly will.

He turned back. 'Can you not see?' he appealed in High Istrian. 'My lords of the Council, my ladies of the Empire, you who are the flower of the southern lands, representatives of all that is most precious in Falla's hallowed country: how we are surrounded by such hatred?

'These northerners are barbarians who even after they have carried out the foulest of deeds will deny all: will lie in the face of the Goddess herself. They have no honour. They have no faith. All they wish for is to damage and destroy us, by whatever means they can.

'The deeds this woman and her band of reivers have carried out may seem to you to be a personal attack upon me; and indeed my losses are grave: a daughter, whom I loved with all my soul, is missing,' he ticked the points off on the fingers of a raised hand. 'My sweet servant, a second daughter to me, has been horribly murdered. My friend here—' he indicated Tanto Vingo '—terribly wounded in her defence.

'All these things I feel deep in my heart: but you should feel them, too: for these are attacks not just upon me and mine, but upon Istria.'

He allowed the words to drop into the silence like stones into a well; watched the ripples of reaction spread out across the Gathering.

'The people of the north are men and women of foul
manners and vile habits. Murderers, abductors, desecrators
all. They have hated the South for half a thousand years;
hated and envied it. How many wars have we fought in
that time with this same enemy? Twelve and more; and
each time the Goddess has smiled upon us and enabled us
to drive them further from her fruitful shores, away from
the heartlands of fire and purity, deep into the northern seas
and rocky wastes where they belong with their barbarous
religion, their mooncalf of a god, their eating of whales and
horses and other vile practices. Some two score years ago
the Rock was made sacrosanct to the name of the Goddess;
washed with blood, cleansed with fire it was dedicated to
Falla the Merciful, saver of souls. But what have we seen
at this Allfair but disrespect and defilement? The prisoner
– with an insouciance you might expect from her impious
origins – has desecrated the Goddess's Rock not once but
twice – such is the contempt in which she, as a typical Eyran,
holds our dearest beliefs. Not content with that, she destroys
a holy place – a shrine made with loving hands to honour a
brave and upstanding woman.'

He bowed to the Swan of Jetra and her grey-haired
grandfathers.

'Desecration against the men and women of our Empire;
a violation of the Goddess herself. Sacrilege: the most despic-
able sin of all.'

'Sacrilege . . .' murmured the Istrians in the crowd. 'Desecration . . .'

The Lord of Cantara grew contemplative. He began to
walk the stage, all eyes upon him. He looked down upon
where the Duke of Cera stood with Lord Sestran, disappointed men both. 'And what have we all witnessed here
tonight?' he looked around the crowd as if expecting them
to answer his question. They hung upon his every word,
hungry for the next damning statement. 'Not only have

we seen they have no respect for our faith; but they have nothing but contempt for the generosity and sacrifice of our most noble families.'

He turned back to regard King Ravn Asharson.

'There are many amongst us who believe it a sacrifice too great to bestow upon such a barbarian one of our finest and best, and we may rejoice that such an oblation has proved unnecessary given the man's own mad and insulting choice . . .'

There were cries of 'Shame!'; 'It's Falla's own truth!' and 'Barbarian!'

Tycho paused, waiting for the murmuring to reach a crescendo and die away. 'This woman has he chosen, above the extended hand of peace, the offers of shared bounty, marriage contracts with the flower of our land: offers made by our greatest lords, men who had rather see their precious daughters borne off into foreign lands and a life of torment than keep Falla's fair gifts confined to our own treasury. Moreover, to add outrage to injury, this woman he values above Istria's finest is a woman who can be bought and sold, a loose-moralled creature come here uninvited from the wagons of the Footloose!'

The Istrian crowd began to roar, though no one thought to enquire of the Lord of Cantara just how he might have come by such information. The Eyrans, meanwhile, unable to understand the sibilant hisses of the ranting southern lord, were growing restive.

Rui Finco frowned. He was unconvinced that matters were quite as clear-cut as Tycho Issian suggested; but even so, this anti-Eyran passion might yet be turned to good effect. He then waved his arms and called for quiet in the pavilion.

'Thank you, my lord of Cantara, for your eloquent and impassioned speech.' He turned to King Ravn. 'Tycho Issian has had his say, and his argument has been most . . . persuasive.

It is the feeling of the Istrian Council that if justice is not seen to be done upon this woman, there will be ugly scenes. What say you?'

Ravn looked annoyed. 'I couldn't make out more than one word in five of what the blasted man was shouting; but it seemed to me he was whipping up a ferment. However, if you turn the girl over to my authority, I can promise she will be suitably punished – for the wounding of the young man, if nothing more; for I am still unsatisfied as to her guilt on other matters.'

'And what form would her punishment take, if we were to relinquish her to Eyran law?'

'For the wounding, a blood-price to be paid by her family to the injured man's family.'

Rui Finco smiled. 'I fear that is not sufficient at all, my lord king.'

'What more do you want?'

'Let me ask my fellow lords.' He conferred briefly with Prionan and the Dystras, then turned back to group on the dais. In the Old Tongue he declared: 'There is no doubt that foul deeds have been done tonight. However, what is not in doubt is that this woman has admitted setting foot on land sacred to the Empire; land ceded to the south in the treaty made at the end of the last war. And she did this – not once in ignorance; but for a second time, in full knowledge of her act of defiance. And for this, my lord king I would seek your acquiescence to a burning.'

'A burning?' Ravn looked shocked. 'That is not the Eyran way.'

The Lord of Forent turned a placid face to him. 'Her violence has been against Istria, not Eyra. It is a cleansing fire we seek, to burn away the memory of this terrible night. I think if you check the Allfair statutes you will find this decision well within its parameters.'

Aran Aranson grabbed the Earl of Shepsey by the arm. 'Egg,

tell me what is happening? Someone here says they intend to burn my daughter.'

'They may intend it,' Egg Forstson returned, 'but they shall not do it.'

Southeye's face was flushed a dark and dangerous red. In Eyran he cried loudly, 'The Empire lords say they will burn her!'

A roar of challenge went up from the Eyrans in the throng. Istrians started to band into tight groups of their own. 'Bastard Istrians!' someone shouted. 'Murdering barbarians!' cried an Istrian voice. Scuffles began to break out all over the Gathering.

Ravn looked out across the angry crowd. Wine-flushed faces. Belt-knives glinting in the candlelight. An angry mob, ready to divide and tear at one another. Was this how his kingship should start, at his first Allfair, at his Gathering? A sudden wish for this to be over; so that he could be quiet and naked in his own pavilion with his new bride overwhelmed him. After all: it was just one girl they wanted, rather that than a war. 'Hold, Eyrans!' he cried. His own people quieted; but the Istrians did not.

'Burn her!' they cried – in both the Empire Tongue and the Old.

Aran Aranson stormed the dais. Without a thought for royal protocol, he gripped his king by the arms. 'Sire, this is madness! They are saying they will burn my daughter for climbing a *rock*—'

King Ravn Asharson stared down at the figure kneeling before him. There were tears in the man's eyes. At once he felt disgusted, repelled. No good Eyran man should shed a tear. A sudden recognition struck him then as he placed together the name and the face of the man before him and as it did so, a huge dislike welled up in him. 'Take your hands off me, man!'

'Save my daughter, lord, I implore you—'

'Aran Aranson, master of Rockfall, you once came to me seeking a ship.'

'I did, sire.'

'I asked you for some advice, I believe.'

Aran frowned. 'I— I do not recall, sire.'

Ravn Asharson laughed. 'Let me remind you, then. I asked you whom I should take to wife, and you said for all you cared I could take a troll.' He turned to the Istrian lords. 'Take the girl and burn her,' he said harshly in the Old Tongue.

In Eyran he said softly: 'I have my troll-wife to attend to.'

Sixteen

Holy Fire

The fighting started immediately, and with such explosive violence it was as if everyone had just been awaiting the opportunity, murderous thoughts seething away beneath a thin mask of gentility. At first it was just isolated pockets in the crowd and the damage was done with fists and feet; but then some Istrians started to smash apart the trestles and soon there were clubs and staves in the fray. After that, it was belt-knives and cutlery. A man with a paring knife rammed into his eye stumbled past a group of Istrian women, who screamed and fled for the exit. Suddenly there were five hundred desperate folk surging to leave the tent. Empire women, hampered by their voluminous gowns, tripped and fell and were trampled by the next wave of guests. The canvas belled and flapped where the strain on the fabric had caused the wind-ropes to pull free. Mast-pillars swayed and threatened to fall. Sconces were knocked over. In moments, the canvas had caught fire and suffocating thick black smoke started to wind its way through the Gathering. People coughed and choked and clawed their way blindly towards the edges of the tent. The lucky ones managed to make it into the night air by worming under the loose canvas.

A band of Eyrans led by Halli Aranson fought through the adverse tide of humanity to within a few feet of where Katla still stood on the dais, ringed around with Allfair officials, all with their swords drawn. Seeing the Eyrans coming at them, the guard captain set four of his men to holding them back with the only proper weaponry in the tent, while with his sword of good Forent steel he slashed a new exit in the side of the pavilion through which the troop retreated swiftly with their prisoner.

Screaming like a demon, Tor Leeson vaulted onto the dais, pushing aside a cowering group of Istrian nobles, and hurled himself through the torn canvas in pursuit. With a huge stave he laid into the unfortunate last guard in line. The man fell down screaming, but the sound stopped abruptly with a dull squelch, and Tor re-emerged into the pavilion wielding an Istrian sword, a mad battle-light in his eye. 'After me, lads!' he yelled, and the Eyrans cheered.

Aran grabbed Halli by the arm. 'I'm going back for as many weapons as I can carry,' he shouted above the din. 'Stay with Tor – and keep an eye out for Fent.' Of his younger son there was no sign: for as soon as the fighting had begun, Fent had been off into the midst of the fray like a mongrel into a dogfight.

Halli raised his fist in assent, swarmed through the hole in the tent after his cousin and was swallowed by the night.

In the midst of the chaos, Fent Aranson looked up from the man he had just knocked unconscious with a lump of wood, and saw three Istrian women in black sabatkas casting aside their all-encompassing robes to reveal themselves as tough-looking men in full wargear. Intrigued, he put his head down and shouldered his way through the mêlée towards them. Thirty feet away he realised that he recognised the one with the beard as Joz Bearhand, a mercenary from a steading outside Whaleness who'd been selling his services to the highest bidder ever since the end of the last war. Folk said he'd got a taste for action that farming on North Island just could not match, and had gone as a sellsword ever since. But why a group of sellswords should be disguising themselves as Istrian women at the Gathering he could not quite imagine. However, his fevered mind prompted him, not caring why this bizarre sight should have presented itself, they were Eyrans by birth and they had swords and just now that was all that mattered. Indeed, he thought, squinting through the smoke, the sword Joz had just drawn looked remarkably familiar. He ran closer until he could see it. Candlelight illuminated the Snowland Wolf wrapped in the coils of the Dragon of Wen . . . it was one of Katla's swords; one of her best.

'Joz!' he cried. 'Joz Bearhand!'

The grizzled man turned and scanned the crowd, but the chaos was too extreme to pick out a single detail. Urging on his companions, he charged towards the dais. A moment later, climbing across crawling backs and wounded bodies, Fent followed them.

Sitting on the top rail of the animal stockade, Saro Vingo watched the coils of thick black smoke rising from the other end of the fairground. He'd been wandering aimlessly for the past hour and more, at first in a fury, which had since cooled to confusion and doubt. It would, he had considered, be hard to go back, given what he'd done, what he'd said. In the heat of the moment – hating his brother for everything, hating his uncle for the vision he'd given him of his mother, hating his father for his unquestioning preference for Tanto – he'd truly meant to walk away from his family, from their greed and lack of principle, once and for all. But now he was unsure. For a start, where would he go? His first thought was of Katla Aransen: that hawklike face and strong hands, the way her touch had shivered on his skin. But Eyra was too foreign to him: he spoke none of the northerners' harsh language, had no skills by which he could survive amongst such a tough, warlike people. To wander with the Footloose, watching the world go by from the back of a wagon, traversing mountain passes and broad river plains, pine forests and high plateaux was a temptation indeed. But what nomad would welcome him – an Istrian nobleman's son; member of a race which had persecuted the Wandering Folk down the ages; brother to the man who had cold-bloodedly cut down Guaya's grandfather – into their caravan? Even Guaya had not wanted to speak with him.

He was still embroiled in this stew of indecision when he saw the smoke rising in the east.

He started to walk back through the fairground, at first curious, then touched by a strange compulsion. Deciding it would be quicker to go along the strand than to weave between the tents, Saro ran directly downhill and out into the open, and then turned towards the Istrian quarter and the grand pavilion. Illuminated by the bright moon above, a long northern rowing boat was cresting the surf about thirty yards out from the shore. A tall man was pushing it through the shallows, the pale light turning his hair and beard to silver; while in the bow sat a woman in a deep red dress. Saro stared at them intently, a horrible suspicion forming.

Katla Aransen had been wearing a dress very like that when last he saw her. And the man was surely the one who had come to her stall, the one at whom she smiled so warmly . . .

Saro felt his heart plummet as if he had just stepped over a long, sheer drop. The moment at which he had first seen her, up on the Rock in the pale dawn light, curved through to this moment of departure and loss in a smooth and perfect arc.

She was gone; and with the same tall northerner he had met at her stall. *Even then*, he thought bitterly, *even then I knew.* The smoke forgotten, he turned on his heel, putting his back to the scene that had given him such sudden, unexpected pain. Feet crunching on the black pumice, he trudged back towards the Istrian quarter, and prepared himself to face his family's collective wrath.

★   ★   ★

Mam slipped her dagger out of the folds of her preposterous green gown, slit the vile thing from neck to waist, and shrugged out of it like a mantis shedding its husk. Beneath it was her more natural carapace of mail and leather; her favourite sword strapped to one thigh, her throwing knives to the other. She grinned. A good fire always contributed nicely to the confusion. She'd tried to set it to create maximum smoke and minimum harm, but the canvas was parchment-dry after four days in the baking sun, and it had gone up rather more vigorously than she'd anticipated. As it was she took a robust view of such matters. Most of the folk here were at the Gathering for their own advancement – fat merchants finalising fat deals; fat nobles trying to sell off their fat daughters, everyone grasping after one thing or another. She had little sympathy with such people. From the age of eleven she'd lived off her wits, orphaned by war and raids. Her Uncle Garstan had taken her in for a while; but she soon found out why and it had not taken much soul-searching to decide that a life lived sleeping cold and hungry in hedge or ditch was preferable to one under a warm roof with a lecherous old hog.

Excellent vipers that they were, Joz and Knobber and Doc moulted their Istrian skins, and looked to their leader. She gave Dogbreath the signal. Dogo was immediately off and running, scrambling up onto the dais. Stormway and Southeye were busily bundling the King and his pale woman through a gash in the canvas, while Egg Forstson corralled another group of Eyran men and women, including the burly shipmaker and his pale-haired daughter.

As the others came storming through the milling throng, Mam made a quick gesture in the hand language they'd developed for use in the din of battle, and Knobber peeled off to the left to join Dogo, who was even now leaping enthusiastically through the hole in the tent like a trickster's terrier through a flaming hoop. Mam smiled. Her troop was the best, just as the bastard Istrian lord had said. She waited for Joz and Doc to win through to her, then leapt onto the dais and followed the King's group into the darkness. Ahead of her she could see the luminous glow of the nomad woman's robe, a beacon in the gloom. Very considerate, Mam thought. They caught up with them in seconds.

'Let us assist you, sire,' she called.

The King turned slowly. 'Who's there?'

'We should get you and your woman away from here,' Mam said smoothly, ignoring his question.

Southeye inserted himself between Mam and his king. 'Mercenaries, sire,' he said. 'You and your lady keep going. Bran and I will see to them—'

In the fey moonlight, Ravn Asharson saw his trusted old adviser slump to his knees, eyes bulging in shock. Blood began to cascade from his mouth. Then he fell to the ground. With the sound of metal grating on bone and gristle, Mam wrenched her blade clear of the old man's ribs. She gave the King a formal bow. 'Allow me, sire.'

Moving to Ravn's right side, she stepped over the body of Southeye and took the King by the arm. Doc wiped his sword on his leg. 'Nice night for it, eh sire?'

Joz grabbed up the Rose of the World, slinging her over his shoulder like a sack of grain.

'We shall now escort you to a place of greater safety, my lord.' Mam grinned with lupine ferocity. Twelve years ago it had taken her weeks to file her teeth to the points she owned now, but she'd never regretted it. Being a pretty child had resulted only in misery; but having the teeth of a wolf had extricated her from any number of difficult situations. She'd often thought about revisiting Uncle Garstan, but just knowing she could do so at any time was all she needed to keep her cheerful.

Blinking and confused, still in thrall to the bewitchment of the Rosa Eldi, King Ravn Asharson, Stallion of the North, followed her like a lamb.

Rui Finco looked up in surprise as Mam came shouldering through the door of his pavilion, pushing the northern King before her. He leapt up from his couch so fast that the slave who had been in the process of removing his boots catapulted backwards into Mam's knees. 'Outside!' he hissed to the boy. 'Fetch Lord Varyx.'

Mam noted with a certain pleasure that the suave lord's garb was in less than perfect condition. A sleeve of expensive Galian lace was charred and frayed; streaks of black marred the pale blue doublet. 'We've brought your delivery,' she grinned.

'You weren't supposed to bring him *here*!'

'How else to ensure we get the rest of our money in all this chaos?'

King Ravn Asharson stared around him like a man woken from a sleepwalk. 'Why have you brought me here?' he demanded. 'Where's Southeye?'

'I fear the Earl had inescapable business elsewhere,' Mam said cheerfully. 'So we've brought you to this fine gentleman instead.'

The Lord of Forent gestured for the northern king to take a seat. As Joz appeared in the doorway with the Rosa Eldi slung over his shoulder he said sharply, 'Stay outside, you, with the Footloose whore. I need the King's mind focused.'

Mam nodded. Joz winked. 'She's a rare one, this, Ravn. I can't say I blame you.' And he ducked his seven-foot frame out of the pavilion.

As soon as he felt he had the King's undivided attention, the Lord of Forent reached into a small drawer in the table, extracted something from it, and placed a small marquetry box on the table between himself and Ravn Asharson. 'Open it,' he said.

With a frown, Ravn picked it up. He examined it for some moments before finding the secret mechanism. Part of the box sprang open and he stared inside. The Istrian lord pushed a candlestick across the table. 'In case you need a little more light,' he said helpfully.

Ravn closed the box. His face looked drawn. 'Where did you get this?'

Rui Finco smiled. 'Shall we say, a family connection?' He held Ravn's gaze intently.

From the other side of the pavilion, Mam watched the interplay between the nobles with growing interest. Seen in profile, she noticed for the first time, they shared a certain resemblance, though the Lord of Forent had several years on the northern king. Similar reputations, too. Rui Finco had no wife, but it was said he'd spawned a hundred children, that in a short time he'd have bred his own private army. She narrowed her eyes and watched Ravn Asharson consider possibilities and consequences, alarm gathering about him like a stormcloud.

'Who else knows of this?'

The Lord of Forent dropped his voice. 'I'm so glad I haven't had to spell out the whole sorry tale,' he said. 'Unpleasant times . . . Let me see: your father of course, Falla rest his soul; my father, too: though being a proud man he took the secret to his grave. Not before he'd roasted a few hundred nomad magic-makers, however . . .'

'Anyone else?'

'A small and trusted consortium of my peers . . .'

'You bastard.'

Rui Finco laughed. 'An interesting choice of phrase!' He paused. 'And of course your lady mother. I'm sure if you ask her about it when you return she'll be delighted to tell you all. Such a burden to carry for what — twenty-three years? Hard on her to be barren as the Bone Quarter and have to accept another's child as her own. Discretion is a

marvellous thing in a woman,' he added, raising his voice for
the mercenary leader's benefit. 'And I shall pay you for yours,
madam, shortly. But first King Ravn has a certain document
to sign.' He unrolled a parchment and held it out for scrutiny.
'I think the rights to half the goods you bring back through
the Ravenway a fair trade for my continued silence, do you
not, my lord *king*? Though I would be curious to watch the
repercussions in your kingdom were your true parentage to
be revealed.' He stroked his chin thoughtfully. 'I have heard
the bloodlines of Eyra are much vaunted: how fascinating
it would be to match the shock and bloodshed that would
surely ensue were it to be revealed that Queen Auda is not,
in actual fact, your mother.'

Ravn paled. 'My father told me this before he died: but
who else would believe you?' He threw the parchment down.
'You know I will never sign this.' The light had come back
into his eye.

The Lord of Forent's smile widened. 'If you do not, I shall
merely have this good lady run you through where you sit
and dump your cadaver in some conveniently compromising
location—'

There was a rumpus outside the tent, followed by a shriek
of female outrage. A moment later, a woman with long
tousled hair came stumbling in at such speed it suggested a
hand had helped her on her way.

The candlelight illumined a round, ruddy face and golden
hair with the faintest tinge of green to it.

'Ah yes, the lovely Lady Jenna,' Rui Finco said carelessly.
He rose to his feet and swept her a bow. 'Welcome, my dear.'
He regarded Ravn's confusion with amusement. 'Jenna is
going to make a prolonged visit to Forent as my guest,' he said
smilingly. 'To ensure her good father's cooperation, though
Falla knows I've already paid him a more than decent
sum.'

'I am not!' Jenna cried hotly.

'Shut her up,' Rui Finco said to Mam.

Mam made a gap-toothed grimace at Jenna. 'You choose, my dear. Shut your hole or I'll be forced to make you shut it.'

Jenna quailed.

'Good girl.'

The Lord of Forent turned back to the northern king. 'Now then, my lord, the document.' He took a quill and inkpot from the table's drawer.

'And if we fail to negotiate the passage to the Far West?'

Lord Rui Finco shrugged. 'We shall have to come to some other arrangement.'

A slave appeared at the door. 'My lord Varyx, sir,' he announced, and the thin Istrian noble stepped through the entrance, ran his eye over the occupants of the room and laughed. 'Excellent, Rui. We shall be as rich as Rahai!' He nodded to the northern king. 'King Ravn, my honour entirely. Delighted to see you have so sensibly acceded to our scheme. Shall I act as witness?' He leaned over the table to peer at the parchment.

Ravn Asharson looked the southern lord up and down, his features as still as stone. Then he smiled. He nodded to Lord Varyx in turn. And then he pushed the document aside. Just as Varyx had started to frown, there came a sudden flurry of motion. The table went over, the inkpot flew through the air, and a moment later a gleaming swordpoint had appeared under Rui Finco's chin. Ravn's hand was on the hilt. Lord Varyx stared down at his empty scabbard like a simpleton. 'Falla's tits!' he exclaimed.

Without taking his eyes off the Lord of Forent, Ravn retrieved the marquetry box with his free hand and slipped it into his robe.

'Do something, woman!' Rui Finco screeched at the mercenary leader, all sang-froid gone. 'I'll pay you a bonus!'

'I'll double whatever he owes you,' Ravn grinned at Mam.

She laughed. 'Three times!' she cried.

Ravn's eyes shone. 'One of Finn Larson's finest ships,' he countered, 'and enough to buy yourself a crew: a king's word on it.'

Mam leered. 'Done!'

'When we're done here, take the girl back to her old man,' Ravn ordered. To Jenna he said kindly, 'You will tell your father I know about his treacherous arrangement with the old enemy, but that there will now be a new one.'

Jenna, flustered and tongue-tied in the presence of her idol, merely nodded and blushed a deep scarlet.

To the Istrian lords, Ravn inclined his head. 'Well, gentle-men,' he said, pressing the sword a little harder against Rui Finco's windpipe. A thin line of red flowered along the blade. 'Good Forent steel,' he mused. 'It would be most ironic were you to meet your end thus. But I'll not be called kin-slayer.' He withdrew the blade, tossed it lightly to the mercenary leader, then leapt over the fallen table and thence to the exit, noting with some satisfaction as he did so how the spilled ink had entirely spoiled Lord Varyx's fine silk cloak. 'Watch them for ten minutes,' he said to Mam, 'enough time for me to get my bride safely to the ships.'

Mam switched the Forent blade to her left hand, drew her own sword with her right and regarded the Istrian lords gleefully.

'Right,' she said. 'Which one of you's first?'

Out in the chill night, Fent Aranson ran swiftly and silently between the booths. By following the mercenaries to the southern lord's pavilion he overheard a conversation not meant for any Eyran's ears. His mind was in turmoil. Finn Larson a traitor to his country: it made his blood boil. It was not just that the shipmaker had been selling his finest vessels to the Istrian Empire: in doing so, he was selling every advantage the north had ever had over the old enemy – their mastery of the oceans, and the means with which to explore them. *The Ravenway*, he thought furiously, *that was their goal, the greedy bastards*. The Ravenway, that wonderful, mysterious ocean-passage to the fabled Far West: the Ravenway, that haunted the dreams of every red-blooded, sea-going Eyran. How could Finn Larson betray us all so? He had Katla's finest blade in his hand. He had used the pommel; now he meant to use the blade.

By the time Ravn exited the Lord of Forent's pavilion, he found Doc clutching his head and wandering about as if in a daze. Joz Bearhand lay on the ground with blood seeping from a wound on his temple. But the Rosa Eldi had vanished.

The fire had run amok and was threatening to consume everything in its path.

'We must leave this place!' the pale man said. He clutched at Lord Tycho's sleeve urgently. The Gathering had gone from celebration to what seemed instant riot in a way he simply could not comprehend. Such violence, such chaos. His head reeled. He remembered the outbreak that had engulfed the nomad stalls, resulting in old Hiron's death, but that had been a mere brawl in comparison to this savage tumult. And the smoke! His eyes were watering so hard he could barely make out the Istrian lord's expression as he made his plea. 'If we get out of here,' he advised desperately, 'I can fetch her back for you.'

At that, Tycho Issian gripped the map-seller by the arm and tugged him through the crowd. 'You will,' he said grimly. 'By the Goddess you will or I will spit you myself.' There was too much activity up on the dais in front of them: pulling Virelai along with him, Tycho made for a different exit. 'This way!' He looked back to make sure the map-seller had heard him, and saw that a great crest of flame had run up the central mast-pillar and was even now dancing amid the ropes that held the whole thing together. 'Hurry!'

Tycho shoved aside a weeping girl crying out for her father, trod firmly upon a man who had dropped in front of him, coughing weakly, and headed inexorably onward. The map-seller stopped to wait for the fallen to regain their feet, then was dragged off his own by Tycho's insistent hauling. Stumbling over the bodies, his mouth open in a silent wail, he found he had no choice but to follow. As they neared the exit, the pile of bodies and those struggling to surmount them grew higher. Ruthless to the bone, the Lord of Cantara removed the ceremonial knife from his belt and plunged it into the kidneys of a woman in front of him who was scrabbling ineffectually at the obstacle. 'Get . . . out . . . of . . . the . . . way!' Each pause punctuated by a stab. Though the knife might have been designed purely for ornamental purposes, the blade small and less than razor-sharp, in Tycho Issian's desperate hands it was as deadly as any combat dagger. The woman, without even a moan, slithered away underfoot. A man caught the blade in his throat as he turned to protest. The hot gush of blood spattered Virelai's face. He tried to scream, but found his lungs so full of smoke he could not.

'Climb, damn you!' the southern lord was shrieking at him. 'Get up there!' He trod on the dead woman and hauled the map-seller up by an arm, then set his shoulder under the pale man and launched him up the pile.

Virelai found himself falling; first up, then, at some speed, down. Cool air rushed past his skin, then there was the impact of hard ground under his back, and suddenly he was outside in the night, and the sounds and smells of horror from the place he had been seemed to have receded so far as to belong to another world. When he realised he was still alive and relatively undamaged, he opened his eyes and looked up to find the distant stars twinkling down upon him. The voices, loud at first on his contact with the ground, receded at last, as if appeased by his slowing heartbeat. He lay there for some time with his mouth opening and closing like a beached fish, and then there came a sharp pain under his ribs.

'Get up, damn you!'

The southern lord drew his foot back, and Virelai watched it coming towards him as if time had slowed, not understanding the purpose of it till it struck him again, at which point he yelped and scrambled to his feet. By the time he had come upright, Tycho Issian was flourishing the little knife at him. Blood glinted on its tip.

'I have saved your life, you miserable turd, and I'm not even sure why I've done so, considering that you have tried to dupe me into buying something it was clearly not within your power to sell; and I am less than convinced by your vaunted ability to get the woman back.' He took a step towards the map-seller, the blade trembling with his rage.

'My lord—' Virelai knew real fear now. He began to regret ever leaving Sanctuary: for all his faults, the Master had never treated him as ill as this. He willed himself to coherence. 'I can do magic!' he reminded his captor. 'I was apprenticed to a great mage, from whom I learned many mysteries.' This was overstating the matter, admittedly, but as long as he had the cat, it would be almost true . . . 'I can trace the Rosa Eldi and by spell draw her back to me.'

Tycho scoffed. 'Like you did just now?'

'My lord, it was all so confusing: I could not focus. Just bring me to my wagon, somewhere quiet—'

'And what about my daughter?'

Virelai frowned. The daughter. What was the daughter to do with him?

'Can you bring her back, too?'

She had been taken by others, he recalled as through a mist . . . 'I . . . can try, my lord.'

'If you can return them both to me, *sir magician*,' the Istrian said with venomous sarcasm, 'then I will spare your life.'

Virelai gulped air. He tried to concentrate on the problem. The scrying bowl; some water; he might at least espy the girl's whereabouts. As for the Rosa Eldi—

'You must permit me to fetch . . . certain items from my wagon,' he said. 'Then I will do what I can.'

Armed bands roamed the fairground like packs of hunting dogs. Tycho Issian and Virelai passed a pitched battle between a group of Eyrans and some southern youths, but in the darkness it was hard to tell which side was winning.

Further on into the northern quarter, all was havoc. People were running and shouting: there was smoke and fire everywhere.

'She's not in here!' came an Istrian voice. 'Nor here,' came another. 'Burn the ones you've checked!'

A tall dark boy in orange came skidding around a corner, torch in hand and was soon joined by another. Tycho thought he recognised them. Then some Eyran women came running out, armed with cooking implements. One of them belted the second lad with an iron cauldron on a chain that she whirled over her head like a mace; the next wielded a huge ladle. One of the Istrians went down with a split head; the other threw down his torch and took to his heels. Further along, they were forced to dive aside as a string of horses thundered past, whinnying in terror. No one seemed to be driving them. Past the end of the Eyran quarter they came into that part of the fairground designated for the nomads' use. Here it was quieter far, and darker, too. Virelai stared around. More than half the wagons were gone, and in the distance he could just make out the tail end of a line of vehicles and animals snaking away into the foothills of the Skarn Mountains. Wares had been cast aside in the rush to leave: pottery lay abandoned, fabrics trampled under yeka hooves; a puppet-theatre and its painted backdrop depicting the famed caves of gold lay forlorn and smashed beside an overturned cart. Virelai regarded it, head on one side, and a strange little smile touched his lips.

'Don't delay, you fool,' Tycho growled, shoving the map-seller in the back.

The wagon he had shared for these past months with the Rosa Eldi and the Master's familiar stood isolated, where before it had been hemmed in, and his yekas were gone. Something died quietly inside him. It was not that he had formulated any specific plan for escaping the southern lord; but without his animals even that option was closed to him now. But at least no one appeared to have tampered with the wagon, for the door was still latched as he had left it. 'I would ask you to remain here, sir,' he said to Tycho. 'While I pack my requisites.'

The Lord of Cantara nodded impatiently. Virelai opened the door a crack and slipped inside, shutting it quickly behind him. Inside, it was dark, and he felt the cat's eyes upon him seconds before he saw the beast. A movement on the divan betrayed its position. He watched as its outline stirred, then saw the wary green light of its gaze. 'Now, Bëte,' he said softly, but with despair already rising, 'nice Bëte, come with Virelai, who will do you no harm.' He picked up the woven-reed box he had made for the creature all those months ago when they had at last struck land, and placed it gingerly on the couch. Then he opened the flap. 'Bëte, my little dove, my pigeon, my sweetling . . .'

The cat purred, and he realised with some surprise that he had used the Master's voice.

Bëte rose from her resting place, stretched first her back legs, then her front legs, and then with the perversity that is the essence of the feline, strolled over to the box and sat down in it. She looked up at Virelai expectantly, then started to wash her face.

Virelai stared at her as if he could not believe his good fortune, then remembering what he was about he reached out quickly and snapped the catch shut. Moving methodically about the wagon, he gathered his most necessary belongings – his herbs, including the container of brome – though he had no confidence he would ever see the Rose of the World again; the little grimoires he had made for himself, the few spells he had rescued from the Master's efforts to destroy them; a sharp knife he suspected he might need. The gold and the maps he ignored for the worthless rubbish they were; but he managed to retrieve his scrying bowl and a few items of clothing . . . He paused. Draped over the back of the wagon's single chair lay a slip of silk. He picked it up, held it to his face. He ran it across his skin with his eyes closed and inhaled deeply. He could smell her. *He could smell her . . .*

There came a rap at the door. 'Hurry up map-seller—'

With the cat-box in one hand and his bundled possessions under his arm he shouldered his way through the narrow door and emerged into the night.

'My lord,' he said to Tycho, self-belief returning by the minute. 'I am ready.'

Feet dragging, Saro climbed the slope towards the Rock and was just about to turn west towards the Vingo residence when something moving fast across the strand snagged in his peripheral vision. He turned and stared back towards the Gathering. Moving away from all the smoke and flame of whatever celebratory bonfire had got out of hand there was a huge, many-legged beast. He could hear shouts – but whether of anger or high spirits he could not tell at such a distance. He watched the thing move quickly eastward until he could make out individual figures within the mass, a group of giants, it seemed, surrounding a smaller figure, and trailed by a great tail of ordinary mortals. He squinted. As they came closer, the giants resolved themselves into Allfair officials in their strange horsehair-crested helms, and in their midst a thin, dark lad bound with ropes.

Saro turned away. Clearly the wine had been flowing freely and someone had misbehaved. *Shame it isn't Tanto,* he thought savagely, and carried on up the hill.

At the family pavilion, he was surprised to find the lights on and slaves running about as if in a panic. Saro straightened his back, firmed his jaw and strode into the tent. Inside, his Uncle Fabel was sitting on the floor cushions with his head in his hands. He looked up, and his face cleared.

'Saro – thank heaven—'

'I had not thought I would be welcome,' Saro began, but his uncle jumped to his feet and ran to the adjacent chamber.

'Favio! Favio – Saro has returned hale and safe.'

There was a brief exchange of voices and Favio Vingo ducked out into the main room. His face was haggard, his eyes dull. He walked quickly across the floor and gathered his younger son into his arms. There were wet streaks on his face. Saro pushed back from him in alarm. 'What's happened?'

'It's your brother . . .' Favio could barely speak, emotion gripped him so hard. 'They think he will die—'

'Die? *Tanto?*' Saro was bewildered. The last time he had seen his brother the only death present had been the promise of his own. 'Die of what?' But his father was sobbing openly now.

A moment later a portly man in a dark-red robe emerged from the chamber whence his father had just come, rubbing his hands nervously. 'I have done all I can for him, sir. The flow of blood is quite stopped and the, er, wound is sealed, for the time being. If he wakes, you would do well to strap him down, in case the cautery does not hold. But I do greatly fear that even if he survives, your son will sire no children—'

Favio's shoulders quaked. Saro stared at the chirugeon in disbelief. *Sire no children? Cautery?* It was like walking into someone else's mad dream. Fabel, meanwhile, followed the man out of the pavilion, pressing a pouch of coins into his hand.

'I will be back first thing in the morning,' the chirugeon declared brightly, hugging the money to him. 'So many other calls to make in all this tumult, I bid you the Goddess's grace.' And with that he was away, his relief in escaping the place before the patient expired obvious in the speed of his retreat.

'What happened?' Saro asked again.

'My brave boy . . .' Favio started. 'My brave, brave boy—'

'It seems that Selen Issian was attacked by Eyran ruffians intent on rape,' Fabel said quickly. 'Tanto heard the rumpus and went in to stop them in their evil endeavour. By then they'd already killed her little slavegirl and were attacking the lady herself. He fought them off as well he could, but took a terrible wound.' He dropped his voice. 'They found her shift ripped clean in two, and the lady Selen gone . . .'

Something in this description sounded improbable to Saro, but he could not quite think what had made him so uncharitable in these dire circumstances. 'Have they caught these people?' he asked instead.

'Ah,' said Fabel. 'They took the girl who was with them.'

'The girl?' The idea of a band of rapists accompanied by a woman reinforced his sense of unease.

'A rough-looking young woman from the northern isles. Climbed the Goddess's Rock she had, too, the harlot.'

Saro's heart turned to ice. 'And they have her still?' he said, thinking of the figure in the boat.

'Going to burn her now,' Fabel said with a grimace of distaste. 'Feel I ought to go along to show my face – a Vingo presence, you know, given the state of poor old Tanto, but I could never stomach a burning. Nasty way to go, Falla's flames or no.'

A vision of the scarecrow figure in the midst of the guards offered itself to Saro then. It was Katla Aransen they had, he knew it now. And the woman in the boat? No time for such conundrums. Grim-faced, he strode across the chamber and into his own room, and returned a moment later with his sword in his hand. Then, without a word to his bewildered uncle or sobbing father, he disappeared through the door-flap and began to run as if he could feel the scalding breath of Falla's great cat on his neck . . .

'Mother, Mother!'

Alisha Skylark hammered on the stars-and-moon door of the old charm-seller's wagon. Frustratingly, there was no response. 'Mother, we must go now, before the riots reach us. There's no time: we must make haste!' Nothing. She applied her eye to the crack at the hinges and was rewarded by dim flares of light from the interior of the wagon. 'Mother!' she cried, 'I know you're in there!'

A moment later the door opened minutely and moonlight flicked off a dark and beady eye. Then a clawed hand shot out, collared Alisha and pulled her inside. The door slammed shut behind her.

'Shush,' said Fezack Starsinger, laying a finger on her daughter's mouth. 'You'll disrupt the crystal.'

In the gloom of the wagon, the great rock glowed and sparked. Alisha had never seen it as much as glint without the impetus of human contact before, but no one was touching it now.

'The magic is back,' the old woman whispered, hugging herself as if to contain this marvellous secret. 'It's truly, truly back, at last . . .'

'Mother, when we looked into the crystal yesterday, all we saw was death and hatred, and the fires, the burning fires—'

'Something has changed. Something has interrupted the pattern.'

'Let me see.'

Alisha arranged herself on the floor and, with a deep breath, laid her hands on either side of the great rock. Patterns of coloured light chased themselves across her face, flooded out across the wagon, to pick out a polished tin mirror here, a blue pitcher there; bundles of hanging feathers and shells, serried rows of little pots. Distended shadows danced out across the floor, travelled up the old woman's patched robe, the shiny bald forehead, the piercings and topknot. Within the crystal tiny figures ran about wildly, brandishing swords and torches, mouths open in silent shouts. Pockets of fighting went on between the tents: Eyrans against Istrians, Istrians against Eyrans, in threes and fours and fives, and in larger, more amorphous groups where space allowed. She saw a tall fair-haired man battling a pair of blue-cloaked guards, a black-bearded man at his shoulder grimly wielding a small but deadly axe. She saw a thin-looking lad in stained leather being tied to a hastily-erected stake; she saw Istrian slaves running to and fro with armfuls of smashed wood as fuel for the pyre. Further down the strand, a group of them were hacking at a northern faering. Another boat lay broken apart on the shore, its ribs white in the moonlight like the carcass of a great sea-creature. She saw a young, dark man with desperation in his eyes running for his life, sword aloft, into the middle of the fray; and another, keeping to the edges of the fighting, staring over heads and between burning pavilions as if he searched for something lost.

In the opposite direction, she scanned the unrelieved darkness, until she found Virelai the map-seller watched over by a cruel-eyed man with a curved and bloodied knife, scrying into a bowl of water which he held steady with one hand. With his other, he held a black cat tightly by the neck. She stared in disbelief. Familiar-magic had been forbidden for centuries now; but here was Virelai, the man she had lain with only hours before, who had held her gently and let her rock herself to a climax on his fingers, and had not complained once about his own lack of satisfaction, practising that ancient, abandoned art. Their eyes met. With a gasp, she took her hands off the crystal. At once the images dulled.

'Did you see it?' Fezack asked. 'Did you see the thing that has disrupted the pattern?'

Alisha shook her head, pushing away the unwanted intrusion. After a moment she gathered herself enough to answer her mother. 'I have seen just what I saw yesterday, no more, no less.'

The old woman clicked her teeth angrily. 'I have not taught you as well as I thought,' she said, pushing her daughter aside. 'Let me show you—'

She squatted down and grabbed the rock roughly. The same scenes of carnage and cruelty tumbled through the crystal facets, until, by the very power of her will, it seemed, Fezack found what she was looking for. 'There!' she hissed. 'See, there!' She nodded frantically. Alisha craned forward and placed her hands crosswise to her mother's. At the centre of the scene, something odd was happening. She squinted at it, twisted her head back and forth in case what she saw was caused by the angling of the facets. But no: something was moving through the crowd; something with no shape and no aura; something that cast no moonshadow, though folk moved out of its way as if by instinct. The crystal marked its progress with patterns of dancing energy, shattered waves of light that broke like a wave where it passed.

'What is it, Mother?' she asked, awed at last.

'I do not know,' the old woman said slowly. 'But if it can shield itself from the eye of the crystal, it has more power than any natural thing should possess.'

'Aiee!'

The map-seller shot back from the scrying bowl as if it had scalded him, and the cat yelped piteously as his hand tightened on its throat.

'What?' demanded Tycho Issian. 'What did you see?'

Virelai rubbed his eyes. They were red and sore-looking. 'Your daughter is alive, in a boat with a northern man—'

Tycho swore foully. 'And the Rosa Eldi?'

Virelai bowed his head. 'I thought I saw her, in the crowds at the burning, but I . . . could not be sure.' How could he tell this murderous man that where he had sensed her, she had pushed his eyes away, that she had clothed herself in shadow and deliberately disappeared from the scrying? That as he searched for her again he had met the eyes of another, also searching?

Tycho grabbed the map-seller up. The scrying bowl upset itself all over the cat, which yowled in disgust. It tried to wrench free from the pale man's grasp, but Virelai stuffed it swiftly back into its box. Furious at this undignified treatment, it hissed and lashed out, catching him smartly across the knuckles with its razored claws.

'Ow,' he wailed, 'the cat—'

'Falla take the blasted creature,' Tycho growled. 'Take me to the Rosa Eldi.'

At Finn Larson's booth, Fent found two mercenaries sitting outside, their swords across their knees – a big fellow with a lumpy face and a dwarf, it seemed, as round as an apple. They looked bored. When they saw him coming, they got to their feet and looked a little more engaged.

'Is the shipmaker within?' Fent asked carefully. His hands itched.

The two mercenaries exchanged glances. 'Who wants to know?'

'Tell him Fent Aranson is here, brother to his intended bride.'

The little man snorted and made an obscene gesture. The big man shoved him into the tent. 'None of that, Dogo. Watch your mouth.'

A moment later Finn Larson emerged. He looked white

about the eyes, a man embroiled in matters that had got out of hand. When he saw Fent standing there, he smiled in relief. 'Is the fighting over yet, lad?'

'No,' said Fent through gritted teeth. The sight of the shipmaker grinning away like a madman was too much to bear. 'How could you do it?' he wailed. Tears pricked his eyes. He blinked them away furiously.

Finn looked alarmed. 'Do what, lad? Your father offered her to me, fair and square, you know—'

'You know that is not what I mean. How could you give the Istrians the key to the Ravenway?'

Sharp panic infused the shipmaker's eyes. 'Not give, lad,' he managed at last.

'No,' said Fent, and his eyes were hard again. 'You sold it.'

Finn Larson, shocked, looked considerably more so when the Dragon of Wen slid home. Fent withdrew the blade and danced backwards, ready to fend off the mercenaries. The shipmaker stared down at his slit belly. 'It seems I have eaten well these past years,' he said puzzledly. Then his knees folded beneath him and he fell face forward.

'Mam won't be too happy about that, eh, Knobber?' said the little man, rolling the body over with his foot. 'Said to keep him safe, she did.'

'I did, didn't I?'

There came a howl and a figure lunged past Fent and cast itself on its knees before the body. 'Father!' Jenna Larsen wailed.

Fent began to feel uncomfortable, and not just for the blade he felt prod him hard between the kidneys. He released the Dragon of Wen on to the ground.

The pressure stopped. The woman he had seen disrobe at the Gathering appeared in front of him.

'What in the seven hells did you do that for?'

'He was betraying Eyra,' Fent said stiffly.

Mam rolled her eyes. 'Oh, do grow up,' she said. 'Now you've lost the King his shipmaker and me a ship.'

Something here was not right: he couldn't work out whose side these people were on. 'But he was making ships for Istria . . .' he started.

'We all sell our services for the price that suits us, whether it's money or some ridiculous notion of loyalty to king and country,' Mam sighed. 'Me, I prefer money, and that ship was my means of getting more than you can dream of.'

'My father gave Finn Larson all the money we had,' Fent said. 'But if you help me save my sister from the burning, you can have it and welcome.'

Mam laughed. 'With the old man dead, we can just take it anyway.'

Joz Bearhand, a lump the size of a duck's egg on his temple, appeared then beside his chief. He marked where the Dragon of Wen lay on the ground at the lad's feet, bent and picked it up and weighed it in his hands.

'I'd have been sorry to lose this blade,' he said slowly. 'It's fine workmanship.' He slid it into his empty scabbard, then looked up. 'Be a shame to see the girlie burn, Mam. A right shame, and for no good reason.'

'Sentimental old fool.' Mam reached up to cuff him across the ear. Then she placed a hand on Jenna's shoulder. 'Bring out your father's coffer and give it to Dogo. Dogo, you make sure she and the money get safely to the boat, right?'

The little man winked at the weeping Jenna. 'Right enough, boss.'

'Give the lad your sword.'

'But—'

'Give him your sword. You know you're at your best at close quarters with that wicked little knife.'

Reluctantly, Dogo relinquished his blade into Fent's hands. Fent looked enquiringly at the mercenary leader, but in response all she did was glare at him. 'You've caused me enough trouble, this night,' she said. 'See you don't cause me any more. Now let's go get your sister.'

Katla stumbled along in the midst of the guards. She had not realised how difficult it would be to walk quickly with her hands tied so and someone shoving her in the back with a spear-shaft. None of the guards spoke to her; now that they were away from the Gathering, they had reverted to their native Istrian tongue. At one point she caught herself remembering something her father had said after the two officials had visited their tent on that nerve-wracking occasion: how odd it was that the Allfair guard this year consisted solely of Istrian men. She had found her thoughts straying to the inconsequential and irrelevant since the moment they had declared the burning. Was this what people did when they were in fear of their lives, she wondered? Did it take the edge off their panic, to fill their heads with a jumble of nonsense before death came to steal them? As it was, her mortality was not something she'd ever given much thought to. She'd been close to death a few times climbing on the seacliffs near Rockfall: a name that should have given her pause, had she but thought of it. On one memorable occasion, a hold on which she was hauling had without warning come free in a shower of earth and scree and gone whistling past her ear, grazing her forehead as it went. Then, she'd not had time to think of anything at all but holding on with her other hand, jammed securely into a crack, while her feet flailed for purchase a hundred feet above the sea and the jagged rocks below; and as soon as she'd got them back on the rock, she'd scuttled to the top like a frightened rabbit, her mind a white haze of adrenalin. Or fishing with Halli in a storm a mile or more offshore, when the boat they were in had suddenly capsized, sweeping them into the freezing waters. She remembered the grey waves closing over her head, the burning sensation of the salt in her throat, her nose, her eyes; and how lucky they had been that old Fosti Goatbeard and his son had been fishing not a hundred yards away. Old Fosti . . . She found her eyes misting over. Had she not insisted on coming to the Allfair and taking his place in the *Fulmar's Gift*, she'd not be in this predicament now. It was her own pig-headedness that had got her into this situation, and there seemed to be nothing she could do to get herself out of it.

Up ahead in the distance, she could make out people scurrying about a dark structure – a blocky mass with a mast or something sticking out of it. She puzzled over this for some moments, with boats in her mind. But no vessel had ever looked so cumbersome. It was with some shock that she recognised it at last for what it was: a pyre, ready for the burning. The mast was some pole that had been stuck into the ground to form a stake, the blocky mass a great hummock of firewood stacked at its base. She felt her heart go cold in her. She'd heard tales of the southern burnings – how the Istrians had sent to the fires hundreds of nomad folk they accused of witchcraft and heresy, burning them alive so their souls would flee to the southern Goddess – but she had never expected to see such an atrocity, let alone be the victim whose skin would crisp and char—

'Katla!'

The familiar voice broke through her morbid thoughts. Her head whipped around. The rearguard of the troop seemed to be experiencing some problems. 'Keep walking, prisoner!' the man behind her shouted roughly, prodding her hard in the back.

'Damn this,' Katla thought. She made as if to trip, then cast herself urgently sideways, knocking one of the two soldiers guarding her right flank into his companion. The two of them stumbled, and the one on the outside suddenly found himself wrongfooted on the awkward shelving strand. With a cry, he went down. From her vantage point on the ground, Katla saw a familiar blond head bob into view. A sword caught the moonlight and disappeared from her sight; a man groaned. Then Tor Leeson appeared over the top of the dune. Blood had covered the front of his tunic, splashed up his arms, spattered into his hair and beard; but he was beaming from ear to ear. The second guard went at him with alacrity, but Tor merely laughed and, ducking inside the sweep of the Forent blade, hacked brutally upwards with his broad northern sword. The powerful, shearing blow took the front of the man's head off, so that his breath bubbled as he fell.

'Tor—'

The Rockfall man gave her his most feral grin, then danced around to meet the next challenge. The guard roared something unintelligible in Istrian. 'Your mother must have lain with goats!' Tor returned in the Old Tongue, smiling politely. The man frowned, trying to make sense of the accented words, then his face darkened with rage and he charged at the big northerner. Tor feinted and dodged, bringing his sword around in a whistling, vicious arc. There was a soft thud of impact, and the guard's leg came off at the knee, blood fountaining everywhere. The man looked down, brows knit, then lost his balance. 'It's a good sword, Katla!' Tor yelled. 'I said it would take a man's leg off nicely.'

She met his eyes for just a moment, just long enough to see something more in them than bloodlust and mayhem, before two guards hauled her upright and others closed the gap left by the wounded. Three of them rounded on Tor; then her brother Halli appeared beside him, teeth gleaming white amid his dense black beard. He was wielding an axe. Katla recognised it as the little adze they brought for chopping firewood, but by the look of it it had seen its share of bloodshed this night. The two men exchanged what must have been a jest, for Katla saw Halli's mouth open in what looked like a roar of laughter; then she realised her mistake. Tor suddenly pitched forward, blood gouting from his mouth. From the centre of his back, an Istrian spear protruded, the head sunk in the blond Eyran's body up to the barbs. She saw an armoured woman with shells in her hair dispatch the spear-caster, and then a big mercenary ran at her brother, but though she spun to try to watch Halli's progress the guards were pressing her so hard now that she was almost running, and she saw no more of him.

That was when Katla knew true despair.

Saro Vingo came running down to the strand just in time to see the guard captain tying Katla Aransen securely to the stake. At least, he noted, they had allowed her the dignity of the coloured silk shawl around her head, but it did not seem to have been a gesture of compassion, but rather one of mockery for the man tightened the knots with sadistic glee. Katla stared at him reproachfully, but she refused to cry out. Saro felt his heart swell till he thought it would burst. He scanned the scene. A great welter of fighting went on around the foot of the pyre – except for a small gap to the eastern side, where gleamed a pale, silvery light.

Saro stared at this light, and as he did so, the stone in the pouch about his neck began to throb against his chest like a second heart. He put his hand up to it wonderingly, distracted amidst all the noise and horror, felt its pulse beneath his fingers. When he removed it from the leather sac, it had gone a fiery red, but at its core, a scintilla of purest gold winked at him like a tiny beacon. He closed his hand over the moodstone and marvelled at how it glowed so hard that he could see the outline of his fingerbones through the flesh. Energy from the stone coursed up through his arm. It suffused his chest, his head; so he felt that light must be streaming from his eyes like lanterns, but as he moved forward, no one seemed to pay him any attention. Keeping his gaze trained on Katla, he made his way towards the gap, and was surprised to see a tall, pale woman standing there in

the midst of all the conflict, which went on all around her
unabated, though a circle of clear space maybe three feet
wide surrounded her at all times. The woman's gaze was
directed not at the girl tied to the stake, he noticed, but
at the torch the guard captain was even now applying to
the sere wood beneath her. Red flame blossomed and leapt.
He saw Katla Aransen's eyes widen, then shut tightly. With
his sword in one hand and the moodstone clutched tightly
in the other like a talisman, he walked steadily towards the
pyre. An Istrian he didn't know careered into him, pursued
by a black-bearded northman wielding a small-headed axe.
Terror, pure and desperate, consumed him for a second, so
that he felt his own feet urging him to follow the Istrian's;
then the moment passed and he was standing in the nexus
of space around the pale woman. When she turned to regard
him, he thought his heart would stop. Something in those
green eyes transfixed him, then searched through him like
red-hot wires. She smiled. Saro found himself taking a step
towards her. As soon as she was able to reach him, she took
his left hand in hers. At once the moodstone filled with such
heat that it burned his palm and he cried out, but her grip
on him only tightened. The energy he had felt in the stone
now increased a thousandfold. Burning up through his palm,
it travelled his arteries like a screaming horde sweeping down
from the mountains to scour its enemy from the plains; it
flooded through his muscles till each one, separately, swelled
in agony; it fled up the marrow inside every bone; but still she
did not let him go. Images exploded inside his mind: women
whose skin melted and sloughed from their bodies; men
staring at hands gone to charred black bone; death's-heads
and incandescent skeletons danced before his eyes.

And at last she released her hold on him.

Like a puppet on rods, Saro found himself walking past
the pale woman and into the flames. A blue-cloaked man in
a tall crested helm shouted at him, but Saro merely reached

out with his left hand and touched the moodstone to the guard captain's forehead. The man's eyes flared briefly to silver-white, then to fathomless black, and he dropped dead at Saro's feet. An Eyran and a southern man, joined in combat, pushed in front of him. One of them brushed Saro's left hand, and a moment later both had fallen lifeless to the ground. Saro stared at them uncomprehendingly. Slipping the moodstone back inside his tunic, he stepped over the two bodies like a man in a dream, his eyes fixed on Katla.

The fire was at head-height now and crackling so hard that it consumed the sounds of battle. Through the billowing smoke, Saro saw the northern girl's hands clenching convulsively behind her back. He saw her leather leggings steaming and bubbling in the heat; he saw the toes of her boots burst into flame.

'Katla Aransen!' he cried, and her eyes came open then, the flinty grey gone almost to purple in the conflagration's glow. When she saw Saro coming at her, sword upraised, they widened in disbelief.

When she saw Saro coming at her, sword upraised, they widened in disbelief. 'Go on, then!' she cried, her voice hoarse and cracked. 'Run me through where I stand, tethered like a sacrifice-beast. Kill me for your Goddess! At least it's a quicker way than the fire . . .'

Saro leapt onto the pyre, flaming wood skittering away under his feet where he landed, to roll out into the circle of combatants. At these close quarters the smoke was chokingly thick: he could hardly make out the difference between rope and skin, but he knew time was precious. Holding his breath, he swiped down with the Istrian blade. Miraculously, the ropes sheared away cleanly, leaving bands of clean, pale flesh against the char. Holding her by the arm to keep her upright, he bent and cut at the shackles that bound her calves and ankles, then stepped away, unsure what to do next. As soon as her support was gone, Katla stumbled and fell headlong into the fire. The shawl unfurled upward from her like a butterfly's wings.

From the opposite side of the pyre, Aran Aranson watched the Istrian wade into the fire, blade held aloft like some avenging hero, and every fibre of his will urged his good Eyran sword to transform itself into a crossbow. The boy was about to skewer his daughter before his very eyes and there seemed hardly anything he could do to prevent it. Words battered his skull like trapped pigeons: 'a flicker of hope may be fanned to a beacon,' old Gramma Rolfsen would say. 'Never say die.'

'Never!' howled Aran Aranson.

Not caring whom he struck to win through to his daughter, he launched himself through the press of bodies. He saw his daughter fall and marked her position by the bright flare of colour provided by the billowing shawl. With a howl of rage, he charged through the midst of the flames, heedless of the sudden stench of burning hair that engulfed him. Hurling his sword away, he buried his hands in Katla's jerkin and with a strength born of necessity, hauled her upright and over his shoulder. The silk blew around them and settled like a caul. He tore it aside and cast it down. Turning, found Saro Vingo in his path. 'Get out of my way, Istrian bastard!' he yelled, though the intake of breath seared his throat. 'If I ever see you again I will tear your lungs through the back of your ribs and send you to your bitch-goddess on bloody wings!'

Then he leapt back into the throng, and ran as hard as he could for clear ground. Behind him, someone shouted and pointed. The man next to him dropped his sword and stared.

Aran turned around. Down on the strand, the fire had become a shimmering white conflagration, each flame silver licked with gold; and the smoke had turned an eerie green. The flames that a moment before had been leaping at head-height and higher now flickered and diminished. As the smoke cleared, folk started to murmur. Weapons were dropped. Enemies stepped away from one another. All eyes now directed to the site of the burning, Istrians gestured nervously to ward off evil magic; while Eyrans stared and frowned.

To the side of the pyre stood the woman in the pale robe, her silvery hair touched by the golds and greens of the last of the bonfire.

'There she is – the Rosa Eldi!' Lord Tycho Issian pointed frantically across the remains of the pyre. 'Thank the Goddess, she's unharmed.' What he truly meant was that the northern king had not yet managed to make off with her as he had feared, so she was still here for the taking. 'Now! Work your magic now.'

Virelai bent to the cat-box. 'Now, Bëte,' he said cajolingly, 'you remember the Drawing Spell, do you not?'

The cat regarded him, green-eyed and unforgiving. Then it began to yowl.

'Extraordinary,' breathed Fezack Starsinger, her face radiant with the light from the crystal.

Her daughter frowned. 'It's certainly magic of some variety,' she said slowly. 'But quite what sort of magic it is, I don't know.'

They bent over the great rock again. 'Where's the girl?' Alisha asked softly. 'I can't see her.'

'Her father has her safe,' Fezack replied. She angled the crystal so that Alisha had a better view. 'See: he carries her down to the sea.'

Peering closer, Alisha could see how a small group of northerners had gathered around the faerings. She watched the big man, hair burned back to a dark fuzz, lay his daughter at the tide mark; saw how he cupped seawater and washed her face with it; how she did not stir. He called to a thin, red-haired man and together they lifted her into the thwarts of a large rowing boat.

'Why haven't they seen her escape?' she said, puzzled, indicating the crowd. 'Surely they can see she's gone from their damned pyre.'

They could. The two nomad women watched as a man waded in amongst the smouldering wood and drew a length of unsullied cloth from the foot of the stake. He held it aloft to the crowd and shouted something. At once, they could see faces contorting in rage and fear, mouths opening like caves through which night winds blow.

'They think it's witchery,' Fezack said. 'Tricks with cloth and lights. The fools.'

'And it's not?'

Fezack took her hands from the crystal and regarded her daughter solemnly. 'Oh, no,' she said. 'It's a great deal more serious than that. You might even term it a miracle; though it's not a good omen for our kind right now. We must flee at once. Get Falo. I'll harness the yeka. Quickly, Alisha, our lives depend on it.'

'Sorcery!'

The cry rose up into the air and was taken up by others.

The man with the shawl brandished it wildly. 'She flew up into the air: I saw her. She used this for her wings, till she needed it no more!'

'Witchery!'

'She did not climb Falla's Rock – she flew up it like a carrion bird—'

'Eyran sorceress!'

'Their men steal and defile our women—'

'They spit upon our Goddess—'

'Sacrilege, heresy and witchcraft: the way of the north!'

'How should we stand for such atrocity?'

'War, I say!'

'War!'

*   *   *

'At last, I have found you. I have walked the entire fairground in search of you, my love.'

King Ravn Asharson's arms closed around the Rosa Eldi's waist and she turned to face him with a smile that made his breath catch in his throat.

'We must away,' she said. 'He is trying to draw me to him: I can feel the tug of the old words . . .'

Ravn frowned.

'Quickly, now, before they use the Binding.' She took his hand and began to pull him towards the sea.

'There are serious matters afoot here,' the King said slowly, feeling his will drain away. 'There's talk of war . . . I will have my men take you to safety, but I must bide here—'

The Rose of the World laid a cool hand on his mouth and Ravn felt the blood rush so hard to his head that he swayed where he stood. 'Take me to your ship,' she whispered. 'Lay me down in your bed.'

Volitionless, he let her lead him down the strand, while behind him the cries for war swelled and burst like thunder-heads.

PART FOUR

Seventeen

North and South

The little boat rocked disconsolately on the dark sea. It was perhaps three hundred lengths out from the shore and far to the east of the fairground, sheltering in the lee of one of the barbaric northern ships with a prow carved into the shape of a bear's head roaring soundlessly into the night. Selen, shivering in the bow of the faering, stared up at it fearfully. In the course of a few short hours, she had come so far from the life she had known that she hardly knew who she was any more. She had killed a man and lost her future, and now here she was, dressed in nothing more than a rich robe made for an Eyran woman which left her face and the top of her breast exposed, alone in the world except for another man whose name she did not know, a man who did not speak her language and had uttered not a word since they had left the shore. He sat opposite her in the small boat, as great and as still as a rock, the moonlight shining in the whites of his eyes as he stared past her shoulder, scanning the silent stretch of water between them and the Moonfell Plain. He had shipped the oars and sat motionless like this for well over an hour now – as unblinking as a hawk watching for prey – but nothing had disturbed the oily blackness of the sea, neither seabird, seal nor the cropped red head of the barbarian woman who had left them on the strand.

Selen shivered. With shaking hands she wrapped the hem of the dress closer around her feet but the fabric had never been designed to keep out chill midnight airs on the sea. She had been shivering thus ever since they had left the Fair, when she had been warm from running across the dunes, away from any pursuit, so she knew it was not just the cold that was causing the great, seismic shudders to run through her body. For his part, the northerner kept staring past her into the night and if he remarked her discomfort he made no acknowledgment of it at all. The moon emerged from behind a cloud. When its light fell full upon his face and made a silver waterfall of his hair and beard, a silver mask of his face, she thought she had never seen a man in such despair. A few moments later darkness returned, and as it did so Selen heard him groan as if in pain.

Then: 'She's not coming,' he said.

He stated it with such flatness that she knew it was not merely his unfamiliarity with the Old Tongue that took the meaning from his voice; his tone was the sound of the loss of all hope. She opened her mouth to deny it, but the cold gripped her and wracked her body so powerfully that it was like a second invasion. The shivering went on and on. 'Oh,' she gasped at last, 'so cold . . .'

'By Sur – I had not thought!' The boat rocked violently as Erno came out of his seat and suddenly she was assailed by the smell of him, sharp and salty, terrifyingly male, and his arms were around her, and he was rubbing vigorously up and down her back. A moment later his hands came off her abruptly. 'My lady, I'm sorry—' he stammered and stopped, appalled. She had gone as rigid as a tree at his touch; he could even hear her jaw grind its protest.

In the midst of her fugue she was vaguely aware that he had pulled away from her, that the smell and the heat of him had receded, and that the boat was lurching again. But even while she was out here on the sea, with a chill in her bones and her feet bloody and bare in the bilges of an Eyran faering, somewhere in her mind she was back in the warmth of her pavilion, trapped beneath the oppressive weight of the man who was attacking her, her mind a shrieking storm of panic. In one world, Tanto was smothering her cries of outrage with his hand and reciting, shockingly and incongruously, Kalento's *Lay of Alesto,* punctuated by obscene movements in a region she could not even bear to contemplate; while in another someone was pressing a fold of soft fabric into her stiff fingers and talking to her in the sort of gentling voice you might use to calm a nervous horse. She blinked, brought back to herself of a sudden by the physical touch of the material on her skin, and looked down. In her lap there lay a cloak of felted wool. It had been crudely woven and even in the pale light it looked stained, but the fabric was as soft as the finest and priciest *pashkin.* Glancing up, she found the northerner was gazing at her, the moonlight delineating the angles of his face. His expression of concern was abundantly clear, but his eyes were too penetrating for comfort. She clutched at the cloak gratefully and, relieved to have the distraction of something practical to do, drew it tightly around her shoulders and tucked her hands under her armpits. For several minutes she sat like this until the shivering had subsided enough for her to speak.

'You're right,' she said suddenly, grasping at the tendril of conversation they had begun. 'She's not coming.'

Erno bowed his head, a gesture of defeat and resignation. 'I know,' he said at last. 'I know.'

She watched him retrieve the oars with a grimace. He slotted them into the rowlocks with exaggerated care as if eking out every possible last second; then with a last miserable look back towards the shores of the Moonfell Plain he began to row purposefully out from behind the moored ships into the ocean. For a long time there was nothing to hear but the slap of water against the sides of the little faering and the splash the blades made as they dipped and rose, and Erno's breath soughing rhythmically into the night air. Selen closed her eyes. *Sleep*, she thought. *Yes, sleep would be good* . . . She let the small noises of their passage wash over her and began to drift away from herself, out into the night.

Perhaps it was the sound of the man's laboured breathing, perhaps the salt smell of the ocean, or the rocking of the boat that tricked her, but what seemed only moments after she had slipped into a doze, panic rose in her like nausea. Images of her attacker assailed her again and again. She opened her eyes wide and stared out at the sea, but his lust-swollen face reasserted itself over the black waves, and the pattern of moonlight on the crests reconfigured into the splash of blood flowering on Belina's white shift . . . The horrible invasion enacted itself again and again, each time with the addition of a new and vivid detail; the grasping of his hands, the bulge of his eyes, the feel of the haft of the knife in her palm; how she had curled her fingers around it and improved her grip as reflexively as she might have picked up a hairbrush or a spoon; the way his body had stiffened and his mouth gone slack as the knife went into him the first time; the gush of his blood on her hands . . . The shock of the hot liquid on her skin, the easy parting of his flesh, had terrified her so much that her mind had fled away, leaving her in the grip of a revulsion so powerful that all she could do was to withdraw the blade and strike at him over and again until he, too, fell away.

No, she thought fiercely. *I will not think this. If I let myself dwell on this, I will go mad.* She willed her mind to blankness and stared determinedly past Erno's shoulder, out to sea. All she could see beyond the northerner was a featureless stretch of dark water, merging at some imperceptible point with the featureless dark sky. *My future*, she thought with sudden fear: *my future, as empty and mysterious as the night.*

As they rounded the first headland to the east of the Plain, Selen turned in the little wooden seat and watched until the lights of the torches and glowing fires of the Allfair faded to no more than pinpricks and were then eclipsed by tall cliffs stacked with silent seabirds, their ledges gleaming white in the light of the moon.

Erno rowed through all the hours of darkness. At some point Selen fell into an exhausted sleep that was blessedly unvisited by dreams. She awoke to the feeling of warmth upon her face, and when she opened her eyes, it was to see the red rim of the sun creeping above the horizon. It was the banners of light streaming out across the sea that had touched the skin of her cheeks and forehead and brought her to consciousness. Right in front of her, too close for comfort, was a figure in the stern of the boat, its outline limned with the weird dawn light, its face no more than a shadow to her against the fiery glow of its hair. Startled, she fell backwards off her thwart. 'Karon!' she cried out, and shielded her face with her hands. In her terror she did not know what to do, where to go. Wildly she looked around. There *was* nowhere to go. It was Karon, come to fetch her, for she was dying; or dead, and now the Goddess would take her heart and weigh it against a spent coal . . .

The figure leaned forward into the light and was transformed to the big northman who had rescued her on the Moonfell Strand. It was the first time she had seen him by daylight, and she couldn't help but stare. He was striking, she thought with a shock, in a bizarre sort of way; his hair and beard as blond as silver, and braided up in that barbaric fashion the northerners had, with bits of bone and shell, faded rags of cloth; the planes of his face as hard and chiselled as carved oak; and his eyes—

'Your pardon, my lady?'

Selen came back to herself with a gasp. In the shock of seeing the face of her rescuer she had forgotten the lack of the customary veil between the two of them. Flustered, she dropped her eyes from his intent gaze, focusing instead on the strange and intricate knotwork in his beard. 'I woke from a dream,' she lied, for she could not imagine having to explain her error to a foreign man. 'I did not know where I was.'

Erno smiled: another revelation, for it transformed his whole demeanour. Where before, by darkness, he had seemed dour and forbidding, his face set in grim and watchful planes, the smile brought a warm light into his blue eyes and loosened the tense muscles in his jaw.

'You called me "Karon",' he smiled. 'I have good ears. Is he not the boatman who brings unfaithful souls through the fiery river for Falla to judge and chastise?'

Selen stared at him, dumbfounded.

Erno's smile widened. 'We are not all such barbarians in the north, you know. Some of us own parchments. Why, one or two of us can even read. I have made my way through the whole of *The Song of the Flame*, translated into the Old Tongue, and even parts of *Strictures for a Life of Devotion to the One* in the original. I cannot say I understood much of either, but I liked some of the poetry a lot.' He paused. '"*And Karon lifted her body into the black craft, and with the black sail furled as tight as a crow's wing, he sculled silently into the black smoke that issued forth from the Kingdom of Fire*". I can't manage it in your own language, though, I fear: too many strange sounds for a poor Eyran to master.'

'I thought you northerners scorned such fancies,' Selen said, taken aback and therefore with a sharper tone than she'd intended.

'You thought all we do is to sail and fight and rape our captives? Well, I hate to disappoint—'

Selen's eyes went wide then, much to her horror, filled with tears.

'I'm sorry,' Erno said quickly, furious at himself. 'By Sur's raven, you are right,' he added bitterly. 'All I'm good for is swords and oars; I should leave pretty speeches to others. Lord knows, it's never done me any good in life.'

The Istrian woman wiped the back of her hand across her

eyes, blinking rapidly. 'Please don't say another word,' she said and watched his face fall still and hurt.

Silence hung between them, and into it fell the mournful call of a gull, far away over the land. Selen turned to watch it sweep across a green-edged bay and out across hills that rose and fell in gentle undulations punctuated by crescents of cliffs and wave-washed platforms of rock. When she looked back the way they had come, she could see the serrated tops of the Skarn Mountains, their snowy caps gleaming gold in the rarefied new light.

Three hours after the sun had climbed to its highest point they rounded a headland and found themselves confronted by the distant vista of a harbour in which a myriad of vessels bobbed close to shore and a hundred or more houses climbed the sides of the forested hills. A stone keep with a tall watchtower crowned one of the hills. The little town looked as small and peaceful as an answered prayer. Selen licked bone-dry lips and felt the gnaw of her empty stomach. Curious, that the body should make such simple but urgent demands even in the most dramatic circumstances.

Her companion pulled the oars in, shaded his sun-reddened eyes and gazed at it wordlessly. After a while he dropped his hand. 'I'm sorry to break our vow of silence,' he said reluctantly, 'but do you have any idea where this place might be?' He frowned against the bright light.

Selen looked at him in disbelief. 'Why should I know?' she asked. 'The Moonfell Plain is the only place I've ever travelled to in all my life. I come from Cantara.'

As if that explained everything.

'I thought you might be familiar with a map of your own country,' Erno persisted.

'Geography is not something they teach the women of Istria,' Selen said tartly. 'It is not thought to be useful to those of us who never have the freedom to travel any further than between house and garden, or to make the one trip required to sell us to a husband. In such a life, can you imagine the temptations the sight of a map might offer? We might realise the world is a much larger place than we had thought and feel even more confined than we already do; we might be seduced by exotic names and the call of faraway places. We might consider crossing the will of our fathers, who know so much better than we do the best course our lives should run. We might even run away to sea.'

Erno noted the glint in her eye and her acrid tone and was surprised to realise that this quiet, dark, southern woman could remind him of Katla in one of her more contrary moods. He nodded, not knowing quite what to say in response. He himself had seen a dozen maps of Istria, and now he wished he had paid rather more attention to them. Still, he considered, what difference did the name of the town make to them? It was a foreign port, as all ports here were foreign. He dug the oars into the water with even greater alacrity and pulled swiftly past the harbour.

'What are you doing?' Selen demanded with alarm.

Erno regarded her solemnly. 'What does it look like?'

'You've just rowed past the town.'

'Exactly.'

'But we need food, and water, and rest—'

'You may take some rest, and welcome,' he replied shortly.

She turned back to watch the town dwindle behind them. 'I don't understand. Why aren't you putting in there? Do you have any idea where it is?'

'In the end it is an Istrian sea port, and here am I, an Eyran sailor, alone at sea with a stolen Istrian noblewoman wearing nothing more than another's dress; a woman, moreover, who has blood on her face, and bruises on her arms.'

Selen's hands flew to her face. 'Blood?' Tanto's or her own? The thought of the Vingo boy's blood on her face was too horrible to contemplate. Convulsively, she leaned over the side of the faering and stared into the opaque green waves, but the chop of the water was too strong to give back a smooth reflection. Instead, she scooped a handful of it up and washed her skin vigorously, gasping at the chill, then mopped it dry with a corner of the red robe.

'Gone?' she asked at last, presenting her face to Erno as imperiously as a spoiled child might to its mother. Her skin, refreshed by the cold saltwater, glowed with vitality and her eyes were as dark and liquid as a seal's. For just a moment he glimpsed the beautiful and untroubled girl she must have been only a day ago; then, almost as if she drew back into herself under his scrutiny, the tense wariness had returned, and so had the dark shadows that lay in crescents beneath her eyes, and the lines that drew down the corners of her mouth.

It was as if he had been allowed to see too much. Suddenly he felt uncomfortable in her presence. 'Gone,' he affirmed quietly, and applied himself to his oars. He could feel her watching his face as he rowed and sensed the way she turned his words over in her mind, but for a long time she said nothing and he almost forgot she was there as he lost himself in the movement of the waves and the oars, the oars and the waves.

At last the open coastline gave way to more broken terrain: little firths and coves where the trees came right down to the water. Reefs broke the surface to the entrance of the first two bays they passed; but the third offered what appeared to be a clear passage to shore. Skewing the boat around with a single oar, Erno made for the land. He rowed in to what gradually revealed itself as a wide shingle beach fringed with birchwoods. The hull grated on the pebbles and Erno leapt over the side. He dragged the boat clear of the waves, lifted the Istrian woman out, and then hauled the faering up onto dry land.

Selen stumbled away from him up the beach, her legs

feeling weak and cramped. Swaying slightly where she stood, with the shingle pressing painfully into the soles of her feet, she stared around at these unfamiliar new surroundings. Behind her, she could dimly hear the rise and fall of the Eyran's voice; but already her demons were calling her, and so she pushed his voice away with them and applied her attention to careful scrutiny of the shoreline. Birch trees; ferns; brambles. *(Tanto's hands, his mouth . . .)* Rocky outcrops through the leaves; dark shadows beyond. *(The blood . . .)* To either side of her pale shingle stretched to cliffs at one end of the beach, and beyond a low headland at the other. *(Knife blade grating against gristle and bone . . .)* Amongst the tidewrack, driftwood; swathes of hard black seaweed; a dead fish, buzzing flies. Her heart sank. There was no shelter here, no sign of habitation at all, and the sun had begun its slow fall into the west. What was the northman thinking of? She turned back, only to find him gone. She spun around, feeling the panic in her rising again, but there was no sign of him – not on the beach, nor in the sea, nor, as far as she could tell, amongst the trees. The faering lay where he had pulled it up, canted onto its side, the bilgewater glistening away into the shingle. His pack had gone from beneath the thwart. She opened her mouth to call out for him, and then realised she had not even asked his name.

She ventured a little distance beyond the edge of the woods in search of him; but she had never been anywhere beyond a tended garden in her life, and then always in the company of the family slaves. Here, there were bramble-thorns that snagged greedily at the voluminous red dress, and loops of ivy to catch an unwary foot, and everywhere a silence that made the skin crawl along her shoulders and spine. A little further onward the silence was broken by the rustling of some creature in the undergrowth, which proved entirely too much for her unsteady nerves, and so she had made her way with haste back to the beach, wrapped herself into the woollen cloak and waited for him to return. *And if he doesn't, I shall no doubt starve or freeze to death*, she thought grimly, *and then he will have to bear the unwished-for burden of me no longer.*

Within minutes, the cold of the beach-stones began to seep its way up through the fabric.

It was many hours and full dark before the northman returned. Selen heard footsteps crunching on the shingle behind her and scrambled to her feet. 'Where did you go?' she cried angrily. 'You left me without a word. I thought you had gone for good and left me to my fate.'

Erno threw a bundle to the ground, where it landed with a rattle, a clank and thud, as if the cloth that swaddled it hid items made from many different elements. 'Almost I wish I had!' His voice was grim, his usual courtesy gone.

Shocked by the vehemence of his tone, Selen waited.

A few moments later he added: 'Besides, I told you quite clearly that I was going to determine the lie of the land. And I also said that when the water had drained from the faering, you would be best for warmth and comfort to take shelter inside it and wait for me there.'

Now Selen remembered the vague murmur of his words and how she had ignored them, and felt her face flush in the darkness, partly out of an embarrassment that did not come naturally to her; partly in angry reaction. 'How could you think I could stand to be in that filthy little tub a moment longer!' she stormed. 'Perhaps it would be better if I had stayed at the Allfair and trusted my fate to the judgement of civilised folk rather than perish due to the neglect of a barbarian.'

There was a moment of silence in which she could feel his eyes upon her face. Then the northman laughed, but it was not a pleasant sound. 'Civilised folk! If I did not mistake your words when Katla and I came upon you, you feared that your so-called civilised folk would burn you for your crime.'

'My crime?' Selen's voice rose to shrill indignation.

'You killed a man, or so I believed you to say.'

'He was a pig, a vile creature. He killed my slave. He . . . he . . . attacked me. I was defending myself.'

'I choose to believe you,' Erno said stiffly. 'Others – more barbaric than I – might not.' He started to undo the knot in the huge bundle on the ground.

'How dare you treat me so, as if you do me a favour by taking my word?' Rage overcame both cold and shock. 'I am the Lady Selen Issian, only daughter of the Lord of Cantara!'

Erno took a deep breath. Something in him had changed and hardened in the course of the last few hours; something that had made his jaw tight and his temper short. 'Yesterday, Selen Issian, you may have been the daughter of a noble Istrian house with slaves to bully and money to burn; but today you are outcast and alone in the world, unprotected by the law or by your family. I do not see that there is much between us in that respect, save that at least I own the clothes on my back.'

Her mouth fell open in incredulity. And then she flew at him. Her fists, small and hard with her fury, pummelled at his chest, his arms, his neck. One blow caught him painfully on the underside of the chin, so that his jaw snapped shut, jarring his teeth. He stepped back, appalled at the violence in her, appalled that he was responsible for unleashing it. She came after him, shrieking in the southern tongue, which sounded entirely unmellifluous in these circumstances, but all he caught was the Istrian word *hama* for 'man', over and over again. She scratched his neck and bit his arm. She tried to kick him between the legs, but he saw the red robe flap in the moonlight and dodged away. It was as well, he considered, that she had no knife this time. At last he managed to pinion

both her wrists in one hand, then with the other he pulled
her toward him and held her clasped against his chest so that
she could do no further damage. They stayed locked together
in this manner for some minutes until he felt the fight go out
of her. And still he held her, thinking as he did so that he had
never held a woman for so long before, other than his mother
as she was dying, and she had been as thin and as fragile as a
little bird as she reached the end, quite unlike this dervish of
an Istrian woman. And then he thought of Katla, and how
he had kissed her outside the Gathering, how her lips had felt
beneath his own; how her hands had grasped his shoulders,
how she had angled her jaw so that their noses would not
clash, and how he had wondered that she knew just what to
do to inflame his desire. And then he remembered the smell
of the charm as it ignited – the acrid, nostril-scorching stink
of the burning hair and suddenly he had to push the Istrian
woman away from him. He did so with more force than
he had meant, for she fell heavily to the ground, but in his
desperation he did not even notice. He ran down the shingle
to the edge of the water and there, with his eyes stinging and
a white heat in his head, he vomited noisily into the surf
again and again and again, retching and heaving until there
was nothing left inside him to expel.

Brought back to herself by the fall, Selen lay there listening
to the awful sounds the Eyran made and experienced a
moment of genuine terror. Had he eaten something poi-
sonous during his hours away from her? What if he died?
She would be left here alone, without provisions or shelter,
and with no one in the world to turn to for help . . . Could
she row the wooden boat on her own, to some little coastal
town where they had not heard of the Lord of Cantara and
his missing daughter? It seemed unlikely.

The retching noises had turned to something else, she
realised, while she had been thinking these selfish thoughts.
She frowned. Was the northerner dying? He seemed to have

gone very quiet, except for a series of soft gasps that might just have been the lapping of the sea. She held her breath and listened more carefully. He was *sobbing*.

She had never heard a man weep before and it made her even more afraid. She sat up, the shingle rolling and crunching beneath her, and the Eyran fell abruptly silent. Staring into the gloom, she saw a dark shape silhouette itself against the shining sea. Then the shape came upright and started to move up the beach away from her. She heard rather than saw the moment when the northerner left the beach, heard the sound of pebbles give way to sand beneath his boots, and then to the rustle of vegetation. For several minutes she stayed as still as stone, her arms clasped around her knees, listening to the small sounds he made in the woods, fearing to move again as if, hearing her, he might feel prompted to abandon her forever. *And who could blame him if he did?* she thought, suddenly ashamed of her outburst.

Then his footsteps sounded on the shingle again. There followed little noises she could not interpret, and then colour bloomed in the night and suddenly she was able to see the Eyran bending over a small cone of sticks sunk into a circle of stones, blowing until the small flame took hold of the kindling and burst into life.

'Here,' he said shortly, and cast something at her feet.

Whatever it was fell with a soft noise in the pebbles. Puzzled, she leaned forward, reached out and then drew back her hand with a sharp exclamation.

'A dead animal!' she cried in horror. 'Why have you brought me a dead thing?'

'You should eat.'

She stared down at the dark shape on the ground. It was small and furred. She prodded it gingerly with her foot and it fell sideways, the firelight revealing a white scut and long ears. A coney, its belly all bloody where the guts had been removed.

'How can I eat this?' she asked in disgust.

'Skin it and spit it over the fire,' Erno replied grimly. He turned away.

'I don't know how!'

'Then eat it raw and furry for all I care.'

Her brow furrowed in dismay. For a moment she thought she would weep again; then she grabbed the creature up and took it into the light. 'Give me a knife,' she said angrily.

Erno regarded her warily, then tossed her his belt-knife. 'Slip the blade between the fur and the meat,' he said, more kindly. 'Then pull the coat away. It's not difficult.' He watched for a moment while she wrestled awkwardly with the small corpse, then moved off into the shadows.

Tears of self-pity pricked Selen's eyes and she blinked them away furiously. *Damn him to the Goddess's fiery hell*, she thought: she would cook and eat the whole thing if he did not return, fur and all.

Some time later, she had managed to wrench most of the skin off the beast, though the touch of its slick, cool flesh made the bile rise in her throat, and cook it sufficiently to revive her appetite. When the northman did not return from wherever it was he had disappeared to, she gave in to her hunger and devoured as much as she could of the small thing, remembering only at the last that it was only propriety that she should save some part of the creature for him.

She sat and waited with the cooling remnant in her hands, waited until the fire burned low and the moon rose to its zenith. At last he returned and without a word sat down opposite her and gazed into the dying flames. He remained like this, inturned and uncommunicative, for several minutes until at last he foraged in his bag and took out a piece of coloured twine. This, he began to tie into intricate knots, chanting over them in the guttural Eyran language as he did so. He tied into one knot a feather, glossy and black; into another a shell with a hole in it. Finally, he reached inside his tunic and withdrew a small leather pouch. From it he took a length of gleaming red hair, charred at one end, and wove this into the last knot of all. He started a new chant for this most complex of knots, but after a little while his voice cracked and he stopped. Light from the embers gleamed in his downcast eyes as he turned the strange artefact over and over in his hands. She ached to ask him what it was and why he had made it, but she could not find the words. Erno, however, felt her eyes upon him.

'I am sorry for what I said earlier,' he said, looking up. 'Or rather, for the way in which I said it.'

She had the sense that this was in some way an evasion, but she could hardly ignore the offering he had given her by making it. 'Why did you not eat with me?' she asked, but all he did was shrug her question away summarily. Then: 'What is your name, northerner?' she persevered.

This, it seemed, was more easily dealt with.

'Erno Hamson, of the Rockfall Clan, who hail from the Westman Isles of Eyra,' he said.

'Then, Erno Hamson, the apology should be mine,' she said softly. 'In rescuing me from the wrath of my father, and the family of the man I killed, you risk your life. I had not thought there to be such nobility amongst the men they call our enemies, but I see that I have much to learn.' She paused, seeking for the right expression. 'The first thing I have learned is that an enemy is not always what he seems; nor a friend, either. And that the Goddess is less to be trusted than a tall, quiet northerner whose heart is broken.'

Erno's head went back as if she had lashed out at him again. 'How can you know that?' he demanded. 'Are you a seeress, able to peer inside a man's soul and pick out his most private thoughts?'

'I saw the way you kissed her, on the beach.'

He rubbed his hand across his face.

'And how you watched for her, all that time, till you knew

she would not come. And then I saw the light go out of your eyes.'

'It was dark.'

She smiled sadly. 'It was darker after that moment.' A heavy pause hung awkwardly between them, until at last Selen's curiosity got the better of her. 'And that last thing you tied into your length of knots is a lock of her hair, isn't it? I noticed the colour, where the dye had not taken, and I sense a story there, too. Tell me, are you a magician? Do you seek to draw her back to you by making this charm?'

Erno's hands clenched convulsively over the weaving he had made for Katla. She saw his knuckles whiten.

'When I left you I made my way across the hills to the town we passed on the coast four or five miles back, but it seems news travelled more quickly than we did. Already guards had come from the Fair, seeking a band of marauding northerners and a stolen Istrian lady. And they brought news, too. Katla Aransen – they were most specific about the name – is dead. She was captured when she drew them away from us. She had upon her the dagger you dropped and they did not believe her story. The man you say you killed rose up miraculously from the dead, it seems, and accused her himself. Then they burned her, your civilised people. Burned her like meat. Burned her till there was nothing left in the fires but a finely woven shawl, a shawl imbued with magical properties; a shawl, they say, which was far too expensive and far too fine for a barbarian daughter of Rockfall to have owned. They say she must have stolen it from you during the attack.'

His blue eyes had gone as hard and black as flint. Selen's gaze dropped to the remaining haunch of the coney in her hands, then with a shudder threw the thing away from her. It lay between them on the cold shore like an accusation.

'I bought her that shawl,' he said flatly, 'and now she is dead, and here are you and I, alive and free. We are murderers, you and I. I have killed the woman I loved more than life; and you, who thought you had killed one, have, it seems killed another—'

His voice cracked. He pushed himself heavily to his feet, turned the weaving over in his hands once more, his thumb caressing the thin lock of bright hair; then he tossed it into the embers, and walked away up the beach. He cast himself down on the shingle in the lee of the boat, but though she watched him for an hour or more, he did not once stir.

Eighteen

The Queen of the Northern Isles

Ravn Asharson, King of the North, lit a candle and looked down on the sleeping form of the woman he had taken as his wife. In truth, their union had not yet been formalised by all the rituals required by law – their departure from the Allfair had been accomplished so swiftly that there had been no time for such trivialities – but they had taken meat and salt together (the one for the earth, the other for the sea) and he had bedded her two dozen times and more, and that in a period of just a few days, and with only the shelter of a leather tent between themselves and the rest of the curious crew. In another day, with the wind set fair, they would see the hazy outline of the cliffs of the Tin Isles; and from there it was less than half a day's sail to his stronghold at Halbo. Then the law-speakers could indulge in as many of their dull and pointless ceremonies as they wished.

He brought the taper closer so that its circle of light illumined the curve of the woman's cheek, the long, straight line of her nose against the pillow, the way a lock of her hair had tangled itself during their exertions and now lay criss-crossed about her throat and one exposed white shoulder: she looked like a mermaid caught in a golden net. And such a magical catch, too.

He found he was holding his breath for fear of waking her, and he smiled to himself: the wide, lazy smile of the cat that has been locked in the fish-store. He was, he thought, the luckiest man alive.

Before he could help himself, he had taken hold of the snow-bear fur and moved it down a hand's breadth to lay bare the aureole and nipple of her left breast, as pale and demure and flower-like as the sea-pinks on the mainland's western cliffs, and remembered how in the throes of lust it had flared to a deep and carnal red. Even now, spent and weary as he was, he felt a spasm of hot desire lance his groin and felt faintly ashamed of himself for it, stricken by the contrast between the vulnerable, sleeping creature before him, who looked barely more than a child, curled in on herself like this, and the wild temptress who had ridden him to oblivion in the late hours of the night, her hair snaking around her head and the sweat running down her belly.

He had known a lot of women in his life, but none like this one. The women of Eyra were often beautiful, whether dark or fair, or with the distinctive red hair of the Westman Islands; long-limbed and slender, or with bodies as sleek and sturdy as their highly-prized mountain ponies: he had loved them all. He had never needed to seek out sexual pleasure – somehow it had always found its way to him. It was good to be the King, for certain; but well before his crowning and in times when the succession seemed chancy there had still been all sorts of girls and women offering themselves with such a free and cheerful grace that he could not bear to show them such discourtesy as to send them away unsatisfied.

Ravn loved women, and women loved Ravn. For his part, in his early years he found each of them fascinating, an undiscovered country to be mapped and explored. They all smelled different; they all felt different; they had different ways about them. And when they talked, late at night or early in the morning, shut away in his bedchamber, reclining amidst bearskins and otterskins, fox-furs and rabbit-pelts, he had listened to them and learned more than he had ever expected to learn from the talk of women; more, often, than in the company of other men, for the women gleaned snippets of knowledge here, there and everywhere, like little pied-crows gathering shiny objects for their nests, and then fitted them together into intriguing shapes, making stories out of the most unlikely collection of incidents and observations.

It had been surprising to Ravn just how often these stories had proved to be true, in part or in whole, when the sources from which they had been patched together had been so diverse. A missing button found in an unusual location (a passing comment from Janka, who bathed him); a sly look between two unconnected courtiers – noticed by Therinda Rolfsen – and a plain wife sent away across the mainland on a wild-goose errand, as reported by Kiya Fennsen, suddenly added up to the rumour of a lustful affair between one of the highest ladies of the northern court and one of the King's handsome but poor land-managers; while away, the man's wife dies from a fall from her pony, crossing the treacherous Wildfell Moors; and some weeks later the previously impecunious land-manager finds himself elevated to the position of steward at the Earl of Jorn's hall. Within less than a year, when her husband, Earl Jorn, has been lost at sea, Lady Garsen and the steward become man and wife. From a small carved button of whalebone to two unwitnessed deaths: from such details Ravn had learned to take notice, when he could be bothered, of the smaller things of the world; and so he wondered, gazing down at the Rosa Eldi, how it was that a nomad woman who travelled for months on end across mountains and plains and the wide southern deserts at the mercy of the sun and the wind, could possibly possess a skin of such surpassingly pure whiteness. It was as if the world could make no mark on her; or as if she were not of the world at all.

He had not asked her much about herself for they had spent little time talking, in truth. But the few questions he had asked her, when they lay together in the night, with the wind cracking in the sail overhead, the roar of the sea all around them and the muffled voices of the night-watch at steerboard and bow, had not been altogether informative. Sometimes she had gazed at him as if she could see right through him, through the hull of the ship and into the deep, dark waters below; sometimes she merely gave the smallest of smiles and reached out to touch him on the face or the arm, and then every word he had been preparing to speak to her flew right out of his head, like starlings out of a tree.

As if she felt his eyes on her now, the woman stirred. Other women, Ravn had noticed over the years, came awake in stages, with a flutter of eyelids, a roll, a stretch, a yawn; momentary disorientation. The Rosa Eldi, in contrast, seemed to sleep as lightly as a cat, going from drowsy stillness to full alertness in the space of a moment.

'Where am I?'

She sat bolt upright, blinking against the candlelight, and the furs fell away from her in a drift of white.

For a moment he was rendered speechless by the sight of her naked body revealed in all its sudden perfection, then he lowered the taper and knelt beside her. 'Where you were yesterday, and the day before that, my love: safe aboard my ship, crossing the ocean to my kingdom.'

Each time she awoke it was if sleep had washed her memory clean: each time her first words were to question him in this way. Now, she followed the first question with a strange second:

'Who am I?'

The first time she had done this, he had thought that she toyed with him, that it was a game in which she liked to indulge as if seeking extravagant compliments, and so he had replied, then and since: *My heart's desire;* and *My wife and my queen;* or: *The loveliest woman alive, the most perfect creature in all the known world,* but each time she had persisted, her eyes mysterious in the first light of dawn that stole through the doorflap: *My name: tell me my name.*

And so he had crooned to her: *You are the Queen of the Northern Isles, now; the Lady of Eyra*; but she would shake her head in wild frustration until he told her: *The Rosa Eldi: you are the Rosa Eldi, Rose of the World . . .*

'You are known to me only as the Rosa Eldi,' he said again. 'You are the Rose of the World. It is all I know of you, since you will tell me no more.'

'The Rosa Eldi. Rose of the World.'

She repeated it over and over, like a prayer; or as if she were committing it to memory. On this, the fifth day he had spent with her, she repeated the information only four times. On the first day she had told her name to herself a dozen times or more; so at least there seemed to be some improvement in the situation. He had wondered whether being cast alone into a strange ship with people whose language she did not know had made her understandably nervous and unsure of herself; or whether, and this was harder to accept (especially after her fearless and uninhibited demeanour in the night) she was afraid of him. But now, like a revelation, there came to him a recollection of a man at the Halbo keep, one of his father's counsellors who had inadvertently been struck by an ox-bone hurled across the hall by a member of the King's Guard in the midst of a rowdy brawl at the winter feast. It had been a large bone, he recalled; a thigh-bone, or perhaps the jaw, and it had caught the man squarely on the side of his head and knocked him instantly unconscious. The next day he had been up and about, with a swelling on his temple the size of a gull's egg; but he had no recollection of what had happened to him; or even his own name. The guards had thought this a fine game, and had managed to persuade the counsellor – a mild-mannered, courteous man who would hardly dare to look a chicken in the eye – that he had brought the damage upon himself by goading one of the serving girls too far with lewd suggestions of what she might like to do with him later, and she had given him a good whack with her ladle. The counsellor, horrified at himself, had even gone so far as to seek out the girl in question and apologise abjectly to her for his behaviour, which had merely added to the guards' mirth. The counsellor had regained his memory eventually, as Ravn recalled, though he never did remember the events of the night on which he'd lost it.

Leaning forward now, he cupped his hand around his wife's head, feeling as ever the jolt of excitement run up through his hand and into the bones of his arm as he touched her. He spread his fingers wide, pressing her skull with the pads, but the bone felt smooth and even beneath his touch, and a moment later she jerked her head away.

'What are you doing?' she asked without expression.

'Did you ever hurt yourself?' he asked softly. 'On the head?'

There was a pause, as if she was considering the meaning of this enquiry. Then: 'No.'

This was said with such flatness that it brooked no further discussion, and as if to emphasise the end of the conversation, she pulled away from him and stood up out of the bed so that the top of her head brushed the roof of the tent and the taper on the deck illuminated only the smooth skin of her legs and the perfect ovals of her knees while the rest of her was cast into darkness.

'I wish to go outside,' she said, moving past him towards the door-flap, as naked as the day she was born.

In the past few days, Ravn had learned to be swift to his feet in these circumstances; he reached her before she could duck through the tent-flap, enveloping her in his cloak.

'It's cold out there,' he said. 'The wind off the sea in early morning can be remarkably . . . bracing.' He had found himself unable to explain to her the unseemly interest the crew would take in the sight of her bare flesh, and, somewhere in an obscure corner of his mind he had no wish to acknowledge, he suspected that their scrutiny would in some perverse way please her.

Together they emerged out onto the open deck. It was true: the wind was sharp and chilly, invading fabric and flesh alike on its path to the bone, but the Rosa Eldi seemed to take no notice of it at all. Ravn's own skin, tanned and weathered by years of exposure to the elements, was fast puckering to gooseflesh, but his wife's naked feet and shins remained as smooth as Circesian silk. To the east, the edge of the sun had just crept above the horizon, so that a long low back of purple clouds was edged with deep gold, and streaks of deep red were smeared across the lower sky, like the mottled parts of a bad egg.

'Storm later,' the helmsman stated sourly, his eyes fixed not on his king but at the woman standing at the gunwale with her pale hair flying and her face thrust into the battering air.

Ravn grinned. 'Faster winds to drive us home, Odd.'

The man laughed, throwing his head back to show an array of yellow teeth as curved and as sharp as a rat's. The sound caught the attention of Egg Forstson who crossed the pitching deck warily to Ravn's side, his face bearing the slightest tinge of green. In the past few years, his stomach had started to rebel against the oppressive rhythms of the ocean, urging him with a genuine gut-feeling to return to his steading and enjoy the peace of a life on land.

'You should not encourage . . . your lady-wife to show herself,' Egg said quietly to the King, unable to bring himself to use the strange name the woman had adopted. 'It disturbs the men.'

It was not the first time on this voyage the Earl of Shepsey had made this warning, and indeed all around them signs of work had ceased and a curious hush had descended over the crew. A knot of them, who had been playing knucklebones amidships, had on the last cast lost interest in the game and were now all staring in the same direction as if they possessed only one set of eyes between them. Elsewhere on *Sur's Raven* men had stopped polishing knife-blades, preparing the meal-porridge or gutting the morning's catch; and two men who were adjusting the rigging off the yard allowed the tacklines to fall from slack hands so that they snaked out into the wind, catching a man who was engaged in patching his leather sleep-bag a wet crack across the face. His howl of outrage broke the Rosa Eldi's spell and gave Ravn the chance to cross the deck to her, place an arm around her shoulders and draw her towards him.

At first, she resisted his hands, pulling instead towards the sea, but then something went out of her and she relaxed into his grip.

'What is it that fascinates you so, my love?' Ravn whispered into her fragrant hair. 'Have you never seen the sea before this voyage?'

She seemed to digest this question, as if translating it slowly from the Old Tongue into some more complex language. At last she said, 'It frightens me. The greatness of it.'

Ravn nodded slowly. He remembered his own first voyage, when he had been exhilarated to be on board one of the fine dragon-ships in his father's presence, entrusted with duties and treated like any other member of the crew: a man at last. But when they had rowed beyond the natural harbour at Halbo, with its curving seawalls and protective cliffs, set up their sail and ploughed through the sheltered coastal waters off the mainland and out into the wilds of the Northern Ocean, he had felt the first buffet of the sea-winds, strong and inexorable, whipping the tops of the waves into angry white crests, making the timbers of the ship creak in protest. He had watched the land behind them diminish to a mere line of grey; ahead, nothing but rank after rank of high waves as far as the eye could see, and he had thought then, as he had tried not to do since, that there they sat in their tiny ship, like the cup of an acorn borne volitionlessly along in the spate of a flood, with nothing between them and the cold, sucking water below that stretched down and down and down until it reached the Great Howe on the ocean floor, where lay many of his ancestors amongst the bones of the drowned, except for a thin skin of clinkered wood, that might buckle and burst in the hand of the sea as easily as he might break a hazel twig.

So he held the woman closer and said, 'We are all at Sur's mercy, out here, that is true. But I have a stout ship and a fine crew and home is no more than a day's sail away now; and then we will be in my capital, and you will be welcome into my keep, where my mother will cherish you and her maids will cosset you, and you will never have to journey out over the heart of the sea again.'

At this, the Rosa Eldi merely frowned. A tiny line appeared between her gossamer brows, where no line had been before.

'Sirio?' she said.

Ravn quirked an eyebrow at her. 'Sirio? Forgive me, lady: I do not know what you are saying. Our languages are very different, I believe.'

'Ah,' she said. Then: 'Sur,' she repeated; and: 'Sirio.'

'You have another name for our god?' Ravn asked, amazed.

The frown deepened. 'God?' she echoed. 'What is a god?'

'Don't you know?'

In reply she merely shook her head.

Ravn rubbed a hand across his face. If pressed, he would have to admit that he found these conversations a little trying. It was like interpreting the world for a child, and a foreign child at that; and children were fine for games of rough-and-tumble and for surprising with gifts or sweetmeats – but being forced into explaining religion to them was not something he felt comfortable with. But, he reasoned, this lady was his wife now and knew nothing of their northern ways, and he had chosen her above all others, so he must do his best. He cleared his throat.

'A god is one we pray to for his favour and his aid: for fair winds when we make a voyage, or a farmer may pray for good weather when he brings in his crops . . .'

'What is "pray"?'

He stared at her in disbelief. 'You must pray to your own deity, surely? Everyone has a god, even the damned Istrians have their bitch-goddess, their fire-demon, Falla.'

She shrugged. 'My life has been very . . . enclosed.'

'Egg?' Ravn beckoned his first lord closer, sensing that the conversation was beginning to teeter too dangerously close to a discussion of metaphysics for his liking. 'You're better at explaining these things than me. Make her comfortable out of the way of the crew and tell her about Sur and how we make our worship in the north, there's a good man. Can't have her shocking my devout lady-mother with her odd nomad ways, can we? By the time we dock at Halbo, I'll expect her to be able to recite the Mariner's Prayer backwards. Meanwhile, I must check our bearings with the navigator!'

He clapped the Earl of Shepsey on the shoulder and with a grin bounded away towards the bow, stepping lightly over braces and thwarts, between bales of cargo and casks and outstretched legs until he reached the fabulously-carved prow and the stern-faced man stationed there. Egg watched him go with a sinking heart before turning back to the pale woman.

'My lady,' he said, bowing politely. 'Please come with me and I will answer your questions as best I can.'

When she smiled at him and placed her hand on his arm he felt an unaccustomed warmth in the pit of his belly and a few moments later caught himself grinning back inanely like a green lad of eighteen. He patted her hand, then carefully removed it from his arm, feeling at once the sensation in his loins recede and clarity returning to his mind. Almost, he thought, he could see why Ravn had selected this creature as his bride; almost, but not quite. A king had to be able to think with more than his cock, especially when making a strategic decision that affected not only the matter of which woman would warm his bed, but how, as a result of his choice, the rival factions surrounding him would line up their swords: before him and in clear sight, on bended knee or in antagonism; or behind him, with poisoned edges and whispered plans. To have chosen this unknown nomad woman was quite the worst choice Ravn could have made, and typical, Egg thought, of this wild, untutored lad. Sur knows, they had tried with him, he and Stormway and Southeye—

He shook his head to dispel the image, but he knew it would come back to him again in the night as these things did, no matter how many wars he fought or deaths he witnessed, along with the sight of severed limbs and the burning woman; and this strange young wife wandering untouched amidst the violent crowd as if she belonged in entirely another world.

'Have you hurt your head?' the woman asked, reaching up and spreading the pads of her fingers over his skull exactly as Ravn had touched her earlier.

Startled by the intimacy of this gesture, Egg jerked away from her hand. He felt hazed, confused, curiously violated.

'Many times,' he whispered. 'Both inside and out.'

'Inside?' She closed her eyes for a moment, rocking slightly on the balls of her feet, in perfect rhythm with the pitching of the boat. Quite the natural sailor, he thought disjointedly, for all her closeting. When she opened them again, the extraordinary green of her irises seemed to swirl and clear, like clouds moving across a sunlit sea. And then she laughed.

He found himself laughing, too, feeling a little stronger now that the connection between them was broken. But was it? Out of nowhere, it seemed, rose a clear vision of his own wife, just as she had been all those years ago when he had sailed away to war, a beautiful fair-haired girl of twenty-five with flushed cheeks and merry eyes, their two small children hiding behind her skirts, unsure what to make of their father in all his mail and leather, with his great helm under his arm and his father's sword slung across his back; and how Brina's belly was well swollen with their third, the child he had never seen . . .

'She is alive,' the nomad woman said, and the smile she gave him was dazzling. 'She is older than she is in your head, but it is her all the same. Her hair is red now, and short, beneath the veil.'

'Brina, alive?'

'Her name is Brina? I have not heard that name before. This is the woman, yes?'

Her fingertips brushed him lightly on the forehead. At first he saw only the outline of a woman wearing an Istrian sabatka in a shade of blue that was almost black, and then it was as if the veil she wore became transparent to him and he could *see* her, his wife of so long ago, his Brina, stolen by the raiders. Her face was lined and her mouth dragged down by age and hard experience, but her eyes were still the bright blue he remembered – the startling blue of a periwinkle – and her hair, as the woman had said, was no longer plaited into long golden braids, but had been dyed a dark red and cropped close to her scalp . . .

'How . . .' he started.

He backed away from the pale woman, his hands instinctively making the sign of Sur's anchor to root him safely to the earth in the face of this wild magic, his mouth working silently, as if the words that boiled up inside him – *fakery – witchcraft – the worst kind of sorcery, to steal and twist a man's memories so –* could find no sound to carry them beyond his lips and out into the cold air whence he could never take them back.

Then he turned on his heel and ran from her, stumbling over the obstacles his King had avoided so agilely but a few moments before, and reaching the gunwale on the steerboard side, vomited noisily and urgently into the churning waters below.

This brought a chorus of raucous cheers and catcalls from

the crew. Ravn, turning from his conversation with the navigator, stared at his first lord in disbelief. For near on fifty years the Earl of Shepsey had been sailing, and in far stormier conditions than this. If he could not handle a clear dawn sea with barely more than a chop to it, how would he manage in the storm the helmsman was predicting? It was time the old man retired to his steading, Ravn thought, not for the first time; before he became a laughing-stock and worse; before he made a laughing-stock of his king. Meanwhile, he could see that in abandoning his post Egg had left the Rosa Eldi alone at the rail, where she stood now, her chin jutting into the wind like the fiercest of figureheads, her hands resting lightly on the top plank. With her feet apart and her knees slightly bent, she rode the pitch and roll of the waves like a seasoned shipman; except, that is for the royal cloak billowing away from her white, white skin . . .

Without a word to the navigator, he was away down the deck like a stag, taking the cauldrons and kettles, the paraphernalia of the morning meal; the mast-fish and bodies and casks in his stride, until he was at her side, clutching the soft folds of wool close about her.

'Come with me back to the shelter of our bedchamber, my love,' he said, 'and I will bring you a bowl of porridge and a fine, fresh mackerel to break your fast.'

'Do you not wish to take me again?' she asked, her face as innocent as a child's, but her hand, less chaste, reached down to cup his genitals.

Ravn shivered. 'Not now, my lady, no: for I have other duties to attend to.'

'Later, then, my lord.' The hand, unerringly, closed upon the hardening stalk of his cock.

Despite the rapture that rose in him, he reached down and prised it loose.

'Later, indeed.'

Nineteen

Nightmares

Quarter-sun came and went and still Tanto did not regain consciousness. Healers came and went, too, sucking their teeth and shaking their heads – crowlike men with bald heads and flapping black robes; wizened physics with beady eyes, who departed with more gold than they'd arrived with, and left the patient in no better shape, despite their tinctures and leeches, their herb-soaked swaddlings and heated cups. And then at last a chirugeon had been found, and what he had had to do in order to save the patient's life had been shockingly brutal.

Through it all, Tanto sweated and groaned. His eyelids fluttered, so that Favio Vingo's heart fluttered with them, but then rolled up to reveal only the pained white corneas beneath. In the third week after the chirugeon had cut away what was left of Tanto's manhood, his hair began to fall out as his father combed it; and then the hair from his chest and legs, his armpits and groin followed suit, leaving him at last as pale and smooth as a girl, except where the wound he had taken from the dagger, and then from the surgeon's knife, was swollen and inflamed. Foul-smelling pus and other noxious fluids leaked incessantly into bandages that had to be changed three times a day. The cost of fresh linen and medicines was becoming astronomical. As the barge forged its way slowly down the Golden River, Favio Vingo sold his best cloak, his jewellery, and two of his stud-horses to finance Tanto's treatments. By the time they had passed beneath the city of Talsea, its great stone buildings rising on their ancient ochre columns into the mercilessly blue sky, and into the trading-post of Pex, he found that not only had he little left to trade, but also that he had lost all faith in traditional medicine. At Pex, then, the nondescript riverside town in which it was common to break one's journey on the Allfair run between the Moonfell Plain and the southern provinces, Favio ordered the barge be moored downstream of the five-arched bridge and jumped ship.

An hour before sunset, when Fabel Vingo and the crew were beginning to get restive, he returned, dragging behind him a screeching woman with feathers in her hair, three or four long braids of shells clattering down her back and a huge black bag bumping against her thigh.

'What in Falla's name do you think you're doing?' Fabel demanded, staring past his brother's shoulder at the bizarre nomad woman. 'You can't bring her aboard.'

It was one thing to wonder at the Footloose from afar: to marvel at the yeka caravans wending their odd and colourful way to the Allfair, to buy trinkets and gifts for the womenfolk from them; even, in direst need, to worship the Goddess with one of their dexterous whores – so long as it was done only during the two-week bustle of the Fair; but to allow any woman to set foot on a ship was well known to bring bad luck, and to bring a nomad woman and her heathen magic on board was madness. Especially given the penalties against magic-peddlers and those who frequented them that had been announced by the Council following the events that brought this latest Allfair to a close.

'She can save him: I know it!'

Favio bundled the woman up onto the gangplank and pushed her along in front of him, while she whistled and shrieked her protest. At the end of the plank she stopped dead and stared at Fabel, who stood blocking her way. Then, with a single, long-nailed finger she reached out and touched him on the forehead, and gabbled something high-pitched and unintelligible at him.

Fabel stood his ground, glaring at her. 'Are you mad? She's a Wanderer, Favio; a witch.'

'So let her use her magic on Tanto.'

'It's heresy, brother!'

Favio thrust his jaw out. 'I don't care.' He pushed the nomad woman in the back until she had nowhere to go but to cannon into Fabel, who stepped backwards quickly, making the superstitious sign of Falla's fire to ward off her touch.

'Would you damn his soul as well as your own, man?'

'He's not going to die. I won't let him die.'

Stepping past the nomad woman, who was staring around the barge in bewilderment, Fabel put a restraining hand on his brother's arm. 'Favio, hear me: in the condition he's in, it might be a blessing—'

Favio's face blackened with fury. 'He's not one of your precious horses, to have his throat cut when he's past performing.' He shot Fabel a venomous look. 'If it were Saro lying there, you'd not say such a thing.'

It was the nearest either of them had come to acknowledging the truth of Saro's parentage. Fabel paled. Then, without another word, he pushed past the nomad healer and headed off down the barge, his back hard and straight, his legs carrying him across the deck in angry strides towards the pens where the horses were tethered. He was halfway there before realising that the subject of this last part of their conversation was standing quietly at the stockade, watching him with hollow eyes.

It was too late to turn back, Fabel thought, and now Favio would think he had deliberately set this course, as if aligning himself with the son he had sired. Well, there was nothing for it. He quickened his pace, feeling his brother's eyes drilling into his back like awls.

'The horses are quiet, lad,' he said with forced cheerfulness.

Saro managed a wan smile. He'd had little sleep on this voyage, and the past few weeks had been amongst the worst of his life. He had tended his brother night and day as well as he was able, gritting his teeth against the agony and the seething hatred he could feel bubbling away like magma beneath the surface of Tanto's consciousness every time he had to touch him — to turn him over to stave off bedsores, to change his foul bandages, to feed him; to clear his waste away. For some perverse reason, Favio had deemed it 'good' for Saro to undertake these tasks. *After all*, he had said, regarding with flinty eyes the lad whom he presented to the world as his second son, *you owe it to your brother, for if it hadn't been for your overweening pride and selfishness none of this would have happened*.

Saro had never succeeded in drawing a fuller explanation from his father as to *his* guilt in Tanto receiving a knife-wound and the time when it might have been possible to discuss it in a civilised fashion had been and gone in the single look that had passed between him and Favio as they stood over Tanto's sickbed that first night, before Favio, with a disgusted sigh, had broken the contact and left the room with his head in his hands. It was the clearest indication he could ever have had that his father wished it were Saro lying there instead of Tanto, the Vingo family's pride and joy; Saro, who failed at everything his older brother excelled in; Saro who had the look of a young Fabel about him, who reminded him at every turn of his wife's unfaithfulness, and of his own weakness in not revealing the adultery. And so he had endured the dual hurts of his father's resentment and the horrible empathy that linked him more closely than they had ever been linked before with his dying brother, and every day felt less like living himself. And the dreams . . . He forced his mind away from that worst hurt of all.

'Good day, Uncle Fabel,' he said now. 'They're happy that the barge has stopped moving; but Night's Harbinger is off his feed.'

Fabel looked alarmed. They'd been forced to leave the Moonfell Plain before he could conclude the deal he'd been negotiating for the sale of the stallion. It had been a good deal, too, and luckily with a horse-breeder less than a day's ride away from Altea town, so he was still hoping to close the bargain when he returned. After their disastrous Fair, it was the only bright prospect on the horizon.

He climbed laboriously over the stockade and made his way to the separate pen where the stallion was tethered. The horse rolled a weary eye at him, threw his head up and backed away.

'Ho there, lad—' Fabel reached out and touched the stallion's arched neck. It felt warm and hard beneath his hand, but not unusually so. He made a face. The boy had an over-active imagination: the horse seemed fine. 'Well, likely he'll eat when he's hungry,' he called back over his shoulder.

Saro shrugged. 'I don't think he's well,' he persisted. 'And one of the mares is wheezing, too.'

He pointed out a handsome chestnut to his uncle.

'She's drinking a lot of water.'

Fabel shook his head. 'The horses get nervous on the barge, you know that, Saro.'

'I saw Father bring the nomad healer aboard,' Saro started tentatively. He had gone from animal to animal that day, touching them as he groomed them and listening to their silent thoughts, even though it distressed him to do so. They were hot and listless, which might just have been due to the change of climate as they moved further into the south of Istria; but he also picked up on a certain level of anxiety from the horses, separately and as a group, that spoke of sickness and fear, even though few obvious symptoms had yet expressed themselves. What concerned him most was that it might be the sickness that had swept through the livestock a couple of years past, immediately following an Allfair. It had seemed a mystery, a plague from the Goddess at the time he had thought, smelling the awful stench of burning horseflesh when their neighbour Fero Lasgo had been forced to slaughter all his livestock and incinerate them on towering great pyres whose greasy black smoke had drifted low across the fields on a stifling, windless day. As he recalled, that sickness had started as innocuously as what he intuited here today. Nomads were known for their clever ways with animals, and if it could be detected early, and treated . . .

'I thought, perhaps, when she's tended to my brother, she might take a look at—'

Fabel shook his head impatiently. 'Your brother's life is in Falla's hands now, and it won't do to anger her with heathen magic. If the Lady thinks we have no faith in her, she'll take Tanto to her for sure, but your father won't see reason. We must stop him, lad, but he won't listen to me. You might try, though.' He looked at Saro hopefully.

But Saro shook his head. 'He won't listen to me, either. But even so, I must speak to her.' Superstition or no, he couldn't see the horses sicken and die if such could be prevented.

Fabel looked dubious. 'Oh, I don't think so, lad: all she seems to be able to do is shriek and whistle. I doubt she understands a word of Istrian. But you might be able to remove her bodily from the chamber before she has a chance to do her mischief on him—'

But Saro was gone.

His brother's chamber was as stuffy as a bread-oven; which was no wonder, with three people crammed into a room that barely contained the bed that had been set up there. At one end, Favio Vingo peered desperately over the bedstead as the nomad woman laid her hands on his son's fever-ridden body and slowly shook her head.

'Bad wound,' she was saying in heavily accented Istrian. 'The knife that . . . made this . . . hole . . . *kalom*.'

'Speak Istrian, woman; or at least the Old Tongue, you illiterate old hag!' Favio threw his hands up in the air and began pacing the three steps back and forth that the chamber's dimensions allowed. 'Can . . . you . . . mend . . . my . . . son's . . . wound?' he shouted, emphasising every word as if for the benefit of a deaf child. 'Can . . . you . . . make . . . him . . . well?'

'No, no . . .' The nomad woman shook her head faster, her hands scything the air in her frustration. '*Kalom ealadanna . . .* strong magic . . . the oldest. *Ealadanna kalom; rajenna festri*.'

Favio frowned. 'I don't understand.'

Saro, drawn by an urge he did not fully comprehend, took a step through the doorway. Finding himself inside the room, and at a loss as what to do next, he placed the palms of his hands together and bowed to the healer in the polite nomad way he had learned from Guaya and later observed, but this time without the error he had first committed. '*Rajeesh, mina konani*.'

The healer's eyebrows shot upward like lark's wings. She smiled delightedly and then rattled out a great stream of nomadic gibberish: '*Felira inni strimani eesh-anni, Istrianni mina. Qaash-an firana periani thina; thina brethriani kallanish isti – sar an dolani fer anna festri. Rajenna festri: er isti festriani, ser-thi?*'

Saro waved his arms frantically. 'No, no,' he said quickly in the Old Tongue. 'I don't understand what you're saying—'

But the old woman was not to be stopped in mid-flow. '*Ser-thi, manniani mina? Brethriani thina ferin festri mivhti, morthri purini, en sianna sar hina festrianna. Rajenna festri en aldri bestin an placanea donani. Konnuthu-thi qestri jashni ferin sarinni?*'

Without thinking, Saro put his hand on the healer's arm to stop her words and all at once was overwhelmed by her horror at the wound that would not heal, could never heal. For the blade that had made the wound had been forged with

the old magic – *ealadanna kalom; rajenna festri* – the earth magic
had returned; ill to those who do ill – and the blade *knew*: his
brother had done an evil deed, he had murdered innocence,
and so the wound the blade had dealt would fester and boil
and never be brought to health until the evil his brother had
done was atoned for and forgiveness given by the one who
had made the wound.

Konnuthu-thi qestri jashni ferin sarinni?

Did he know the knife that had made the wound?

How could he? But somehow he had his suspicions: the
dagger that . . . *she*, the beautiful swordmaker . . . had given
him had disappeared on the night of the Gathering, and he
had not seen it since. But he remembered the way it had
shivered in his hand, the magical sense of it he had imputed
to his feelings for its maker, rather than to its true nature. Saro
believed in magic now: oh, yes he did: was he not haunted by
it day and night?

Wide-eyed, he turned to his father. 'I think she is saying that
my brother's wound has festered because the knife that made it
judged him evil.' It sounded mad even as he said it, and Favio
Vingo looked as if he might explode at the very idea, but still
Saro persisted. 'I believe the blade that made the wound was
the one the Eyran girl—' he could not bring himself to say
her name '—forged. She made a gift of it to me at her stall
when Tanto and I were looking at her weapons, but Tanto
must have taken it . . .' He faltered, for something here was
wrong: he had not thought through the implications.

Favio looked triumphant. 'I knew it! I *knew* it! She tried to
kill him with her witchery, the Eyran whore. She poisoned
the blade against him: no wonder my poor boy will not
heal!' Perversely delighted to have a solid reason for Tanto's
persistent fever, he grinned wildly. 'That little Eyran witch:
it was she who did this to my lad; not Selen as she lied. I
knew we were right to feed her to the flames. She poisoned
him with her foul magic and then tried to poison him further

with her words. Damn it, boy—' he reached over and shook
Tanto by the shoulder as if to share this wondrous knowledge
with him '—she went to the fires, and thank Falla for it! Now
all we need is for this Footloose witch to give you a spell that
will counter the Eyran's vile sorcery—'

Saro looked back at the healer in desperation. He could he
make his father understand the truth of it? But the nomad
woman was backing away now, her face distorted with terror.
For a moment, Saro thought Favio's lunatic happiness at the
death of the knife-maker had upset her; but then he realised
with a cold jolt that her eyes were fixed on him, eyes that were
so wide with shock that he could see the yellow of her corneas
all around her great black pupils. It was *him* she was terrified of,
not his father, nor his wicked, unhealable brother: no, it was
the touch of him that had brought about this change in her.

But why?

'Don't fear!' he cried out in anguish. 'Please: I mean you
no harm.'

She would have to pass him to leave the room: they could
both see that. It was why she was staring wildly around for
another exit as a frightened cat, confronted with a snarling
dog, might desperately seek an escape route that would take
it even through flood or fire out of the path of its enemy.

He took a step towards her and was horrified to see her
cower away from him. Crossing the floor between them in
two swift strides he caught her by the shoulders, thinking to
reassure her, but as soon as contact was made it was he who was
swept away by the sensation. No reassurance here: nothing
but sheer, mindless terror: for in front of her, *touching* her,
was one who carried a fabled death-stone around his neck as
thoughtlessly as one might wear a silver trinket. Yet all he had
to do to carry her soul away into the howling wastes between
the stars was to take the death-stone from its leather pouch
and hold it in his hand; just the merest touch would rend
body from soul, as had happened to the others. She could

feel their deaths on him. Men, all of them, and fighters, to be sure; but what was to say he would not scruple to take a defenceless woman's soul, too, in his dangerously unaware state? He had already taken three − or was it four? − lives without understanding what he did. It was hard to tell, for the ghosts of their tortured souls seethed and blurred in the dark aura that surrounded him; an aura that smelled sharply of fire and smoke, of burning clothes and hair. By the Twins, the burning times were back again, as they had heard, and surely they would all perish . . .

'Aieeeee!'

With a shriek, the nomad woman wrenched herself away from Saro's hold. In the stunned moment that lay between them, as Saro fought against the deluge of images that had tumbled out of her mind and into his, she took advantage of his bewilderment and ducked past him and out of the door, careful despite her desperation not even to brush his clothing as she did so.

The sound of her bare feet slapped on the wood of the stairs and the deck above them, then echoed away into the distance.

'Well, go after her, then!' Favio roared.

But his idiot son had collapsed onto the floor, holding his head and sobbing like a child.

For the rest of that day, and through the night and the next morning, Saro took to his bed and would not be roused, despite his father's threats, or lately − and in some panic (for to lose one son to a wound; then another to madness was more than Favio could bear) − his entreaties. He drank the wine and the water the slaves brought and ate the bread, the spicy meats and dates they left at his side as if in a kind of daze. All the while, the images reaped from the nomad-woman spun through his head like the bright shards of a broken mirror: fractional memories that would not fit into any shape that he could make sense of, no matter how he tried to reorder them. He saw the faces of three men he did not recognise: an Allfair guard with fierce dark eyes and a tall, crested helmet; a blond northerner with plaits in his hair and a long, forked beard, his nose as hooked as a bird of prey, his pale eyes spitting cold fire; an Istrian man with a jowly face, sword raised and mouth open in a cry of fury which turned suddenly, and for no cause Saro could name, to fear.

He saw his own hand reaching out, touching the first man lightly on the forehead, saw how the guard's eyes flared briefly to silver, then to empty black space. He saw the other two, who seemed to be fighting each other, drop dead, for no apparent reason, at his feet.

He saw himself staring down at the stone which he held in his palm; saw how it went from the red of a glowing ember to a white heat that made the bones glow through his skin as he closed his fingers over it.

Try as he might to connect these disparate images, nothing – except the thing that made his mind skitter sideways every time he approached it – could knit them together into any coherent shape.

And finally, again and again and again, from many different angles, as if he were in more than one place at once – somehow approaching from the right, then the left, and once, disconcertingly from *above* – he saw the Eyran girl (*Katla, Katla, Katla,* his broken heart echoed piteously) bound to a stake. He saw the smoke from the pyre billowing in great black clouds into the air. Then he was back in himself, graced with a single viewpoint that was recognisably his own, so that he was able to see with a terrible and unwanted clarity how the toes of her leather boots crisped and bubbled; how the bonds cut deep into her bare skin; how her eyes filled with hatred as she saw him coming towards her through the lung-scorching fumes; how her mouth opened and closed on a stream of words he could blessedly no longer hear.

After that he had seen nothing else; and even now, despite the nomad healer's touch, he could still recall nothing more beyond these events until he had woken up the day after Katla's burning in his own bed in the Vingo family pavilion with a sense of awful doom, a foreboding of cataclysm. When his uncle had entered the chamber at noon (he had known it was, for he heard the priests calling the observances, their cries falling loud and haunting into what seemed even then to be unnaturally still air) to check on his well-being, he had clutched Fabel by the arm and demanded to know what was happening; why he sensed imminent disaster. Why it was so quiet out there.

And Fabel had thrown back his head and laughed.

'You're a hero, lad!' he'd cried. 'All Istria will hear how you waded fearlessly into Falla's fires to make sure with good Forent steel that the Eyran witch's soul reached the Goddess's judgement before her sorcery could save her.'

'I killed her?' Saro was aghast. His heart had thudded painfully against his ribs. His mind raced. He could never raise a weapon against Katla Aransen, surely there was some appalling error, a joke made in the worst of taste? 'I took my sword to the Eyran girl?'

'We all saw you, my lad,' Fabel had said proudly. 'It was a noble attempt, a hero's act. They're already making songs of it, I swear, even though it was in vain.'

'What do you mean?' Saro's heart had stopped its beating; he had felt it flickering in place like a hummingbird poised in the most delicate of motions. 'In vain?'

'The witch used her sorcery to escape the fires, or so they say.'

'But how?'

Fabel shrugged. 'Who knows the ways of witches, Saro? Disappeared into the air, she did, leaving nothing behind but that outlandish shawl she had wrapped about her head.'

The shawl. Somewhere in Saro's smoke-hazed mind he

recalled the shawl, a thing of many colours, glowing with a light of its own amidst the flames.

'And how – how did I get here?'

Fabel smiled fondly and his chest swelled with pride. 'Ah, well, that was me, you see, lad. The smoke and fumes had done for you, it seemed: you'd fallen down on the edge of the pyre, would have been burned yourself had Haro Fortran and I not seen you there. We came in after you, dragged you out and I carried you back here. Amazing the strength you find in yourself under dire circumstances,' he pronounced smugly. 'Haro already has half a song written for you. "In battle's heat, midst flame and fight / He drew his sword in blackest night / To give the witch to Falla's might / Such was the act of a true knight." Rather good, I thought. He'll be delighted to hear you've come round, I know he'll want to perform the rest of it for you.'

'But I'm not a knight,' was all Saro could say.

It was inexplicable, bizarre; profoundly disturbing. He had turned his face to the pillow and wept, though for what, exactly, he could not have said. Fabel, embarrassed by such an unmanly display, had left silently.

And that was all that Saro had managed to discover, from Fabel, or anyone else, to this day. He had been visited by fragments of nightmare, a dull, vague sense of failure and misery; and worst of all, he had been haunted again and again by the vision of Katla's eyes, the searing hatred she had turned on him as he came toward her through the flames. For all the evidence, though, he would never accept that he had meant to kill her, or the men whose faces the nomad woman had shown him, for surely it was not in his nature. But no matter how strongly he urged himself to believe this, still more strongly the suspicion grew that although he had not intended their deaths, he was still, in some terrible, incomprehensible way, fully responsible for them.

Twenty

Homecoming

But Katla Aransen had not died, though she lay as one dead.

She had done so for day upon day as the *Fulmar's Gift* cut its way home to Rockfall through the churning waters of the Northern Ocean and was aware of no more of the voyage than the fiery sting of salt on her face and the dreamlike sensation of falling endlessly through the peaks and troughs of that hostile sea. Drifting in and out of consciousness, she heard the voices of the crew as from a great distance, and to her they sounded like the cries of carrion birds over a battlefield, a battlefield from which she fled over and over in her dreams: on foot, on her hands and knees; lashed to a dark horse that galloped tirelessly through the night.

No one, it seemed, could do anything to ease her from her fugue. They had put to sea in such haste that Aran had had no time to locate a healer, deciding rightly that to escape the killing grounds of the Moonfell Plain must be their foremost concern. Once out of sight of the fires, and beyond pursuit of the inferior Istrian vessels, he had bathed her burns himself – treating them with seawater and covering them gently with strips of his best linen tunic, which he had torn to pieces with shaking, furious hands, cursing his own failings all the while – but for the hurts he could not see, which were the deepest of all, he could do nothing.

In the two weeks it took for the passage – weeks in which

the winds blew steadily and the currents ran true – Katla's hair began to grow back, a fiery red that graded through to the coarse and patchy black; an uncompromising colour that looked violent and ugly against the dark burns and scabs left by the fire. But the fact that it had appeared again even on the side where the fire had caught her – as if Erno's shawl had truly acted as a magical shield between her body and the pyre's worst destruction – offered hope. Every day Aran Aranson came and touched this new growth, the feel of it as soft as down against the callused pads of his fingers, as if it gave some sign if the inward health of his daughter, and prayed (for the first time in his life to the women's deity, Feya) for a miracle.

The miracle came on the day before they made landfall.

Fent was sitting beside his twin, as he did between watches and chores, knotting twine and making nonsense verses and riddles. Today, he had made a new one for her:

> *'I own no great hall*
> *But I do have a bed;*
> *I travel to and fro*
> *But I never leave home.*
>
> *I whisper and roar*
> *Yet I have no mouth*
> *My bounty is endless*
> *And so is my wrath.*
>
> *Silver streams through me*
> *And azure above*
> *I let you rest on my skin*
> *But death lies within.*
>
> *Who am I?'*

There was the smallest of movements from the huddled

figure beside him and then, with the utmost clarity, a voice said: 'The sea.'

Surprised, Fent stared around. Halli was the closest to him of the crew, but his back was turned and he was in conversation with Kotil Gorson, the navigator, and there was no one else in hearing range. Frowning, he went back to his knots.

A moment later the voice came again. 'Didn't you hear me? I said, "the sea". Too easy – far too easy: the seabed and tides, the silver fish and the sky and all. Pity your rhyme scheme is so lacking. Old Ma Hallasen's goat makes a better poet!'

Looking down in astonishment, Fent found his sister's eyes – as deep and indigo as the ocean itself – were wide open and fixed upon his face, glinting with amusement.

He grinned from ear to ear, then let out an ear-splitting whoop: 'Da! Da! She's awake! Katla's awake!'

Such a fuss, Katla thought, *over one who'd just been asleep.* She tried to lever herself up into a sitting position and was utterly defeated by the effort it entailed. *Sur's nuts, such pain! And how odd, for Fent not to react to her gibe . . .*

Suddenly afraid, she reached up and tried to catch Fent by the sleeve, but her hand felt heavy and weak: she couldn't feel her fingers. 'How long have I slept?'

Exhausted by even this slight exertion, she sank back down, her eyes closing involuntarily. Confused images of a frantic pursuit overtook her at once: a chase between tents, along a dark, moonlit strand in the shadow of a great rock; in and out of a crowd of people from which familiar faces loomed and then vanished in turn: Jenna; her father, Finn Larson, his red lips all wet with greed; Halli with the wood-adze raised above his head; Erno entwined with a strange dark woman; a blond-bearded Eyran man, his mouth open on a scream, the head of a spear protruding from the centre of his chest; and an Istrian coming at her, his sword raised, a strange, pale, silvery light burning in his eyes . . .

With a sudden convulsion, she brought her right hand up in front of her face and stared at it. It was a bundle of cloth: a great, swaddled club of a thing.

'What happened to me?'

The thought came, swift and sure, that the man with the sword had cut off her hand, that this clumsy, bandaged stump was all that was left. She would never climb again; never beat the iron, never wrestle, never even feed or clothe herself easily . . . Made desperate by this certainty she started to tear at the cloth with her teeth.

'Katla!'

Distracted from her efforts, she looked up to find her father gazing down at her. Rather than his eyes – brilliant dark with unlikely tears – it was his stubbly beard, missing eyebrows and short, frizzled hair she noticed first.

'What happened to you, Da – got too close to the cook-fire?'

'You could say that.'

Aran Aranson gave his daughter a lop-sided grin. It was, she thought with curiosity, the first time she had ever really looked at his mouth. In her just-awake state everything seemed preternaturally vivid, every detail a crucial piece of the world's design. It was a good mouth for a man, she decided: the teeth sharp and white and as gappy as a dog's, the lips clearly delineated and well-shaped, though the line of the upper lip was marred by a pale white scar which ran up towards his nose. She had never noticed it before.

Aran watched Katla's eyes scan his face. Unconsciously, his hand went up to the scar, his fingers tracing its unfamiliar line through the new stubble.

'Where did you get that, Da?'

His face fell solemn and rueful. 'I wish I could say it was an honour-wound, won against the south; but I fear it was at my first Gathering, outside of Halbo. Some of the other Rockfall lads and I overdid it on the ale, got caught stealing another jar: I tripped and fell – and was too drunk to save myself from the rocky ground! Used to trim my beard as close as Fent does, but after that—' He leaned forward and winked at her conspiratorially. 'Told your mother I got it in a duel.' He put his fingers to his lips. 'No telling, now.'

Katla felt tears come to her own eyes. 'Did I lose my hand, Da? Tell me quickly—'

Aran knelt beside her and began to peel the bandages away with a delicacy that was surprising in so large and powerful a man. As the strips came away, Katla could see the shape of a hand underneath; and then she could feel her fingers, stiff and sore, to be sure, but fingers nevertheless. But when the last piece of linen fell to the deck, what was revealed was an abomination: a hand and wrist swollen to twice their normal size, the skin ruched and shiny-pink, where it was not black and scabbed; and where before her fingers had been long and thin and brown and hard, now they were fused together into one great red rut of burned flesh. Katla gasped. She stared at the monster on the end of her arm. This thing could surely not belong to her, could it? Was this her own hand, or were her eyes playing tricks on her? She blinked and stared; blinked and stared again.

'What happened to me?'

'They tried to burn you, my love. Even now, I'm not sure why – whether it was for the Rock, or the other nonsense.' The end of the Gathering had become a blur of outraged fury to Aran: all he could recall was his daughter in jeopardy; the insupportable arrogance of the Istrians; their glee at the prospect of a burning.

Katla frowned. 'I remember climbing the Rock.' At the very thought of it, her right hand started to itch and buzz. She pushed away the image, determined not to dwell on the horror of the injury. She had seen worse, she told herself, remembering young Bard's dreadful scalding in the smithy the previous summer. His skin had fused too, but it had healed. Somewhat.

'I cut your hair off for it,' Aran said, running his palm over her scalp.

'I climbed it again, Da: just before they caught me.'

It was coming back to her now, the sequence of events: running from the Gathering after Erno had kissed her (*no*, she corrected herself sternly, *after you kissed Erno* – charm or no charm, that was how it had been); climbing Sur's Castle and feeling the power of the rock roaring its way up through her hands and arms; seeing the southern woman – shockingly naked – stumbling down the strand between the pavilions; and the dagger – *her* dagger, one of her best – the fine, pattern-welding of the blade as sure a trademark as if she'd etched her name on it – all stippled and smeared with blood.

She looked around – saw Halli and Fent behind their father, both smiling with relief; beyond them, Gar and Mord, Kotil Gorson, Ham the tillerman. Turning toward the bow, she could make out a knot of a dozen oarsmen playing knucklebones, and while there were several blond heads among the dozen bent over the sheep's knuckles, none were quite as blond as Erno—

'Where's Erno, Da? And the girl?'

'What girl?' Aran asked sharply.

'Erno was helping me run away rather than be betrothed to Finn Larson,' she said simply, and watched as her father's face clouded. 'Down on the strand we came upon an Istrian woman, terrified for her life; someone had attacked her, she said, and she thought she had killed him. I made Erno rescue her, told him to get her safely away in a boat, for she feared they would burn her for it.' Her brow knitted; then she grinned, wolfish and wild, a flash of the old Katla. 'But instead they tried to burn me, didn't they? I remember bits of it now; getting caught by the guards, the Istrian man appearing at the

Gathering, blood all over, and such a liar; and the fire and such – but what happened to Erno, and Tor?'

'Erno I know nothing about. Tor—' Aran hung his head. He would have the hard task of telling Ella Stensen how her beloved, if wayward, son had perished.

Halli cut in, his jaw grim, his eyes hooded. He looked, Katla thought, as if he had aged ten years since they had left home. 'Tor died in the battle, trying to save you from the Istrians. Took a spear in the back.'

The image of the blond man with the head of a spear bursting obscenely through his chest flickered for a moment through her head. She closed her eyes. *Tor Leeson, dying to save her from the burning. Such a brute – whoever would have thought it?* And at once felt ashamed for her dismissive judgement. *Brutes make good heroes, under the right circumstances*, she thought. *It was a brave death, and I was the cause of it. I'll make an offering to Sur when we're back home in Rockfall, pray that his soul is safely in the Great Howe.* But dying a land-death, would he be accepted into Sur's ocean hall to join the heroes' feast? Or would his soul be carried through the rock veins of the world, into the heart of the holy mountain, wherever that might be? The intricacies of these matters had not previously given her much pause for thought: death-in-battle had never touched her so closely before now. Everyone knew that when they died, they became one with the earth and sea; clay for Sur to remould into whatever form he most required; but those who died at sea or in battle he reserved for himself, surrounding himself with the soldiers and the sailors he would need for the great conflict at the end of the world, when he and his fellow deities – the Snowland Wolf and the She-Bear – would do battle with the monsters of the world – the Dragon of Wen, the Fire Cat and the Serpent – to decide the final outcome. All such had seemed merely entertaining stories, dressed with telling details and embroidered with fine jokes and aphorisms: tales for children to memorise and invent variations for; songs for travelling bards to entertain them all at High Feast. Now, she realised, they gave you a framework for your life, and your death: like the wooden frames that the women used for keeping the cloth taut when making their tapestries, keeping the picture in one place, stopping it all from sliding into a chaos of tangled wool . . .

'I'm sorry he died,' she said softly. 'And I hope Erno got the poor woman away.'

Aran shook his head. 'I hope he's made it onto one of the other ships,' he said grimly. 'I don't give much for his chances if he's caught in a stolen boat with a naked Istrian woman.'

'Oh, she wasn't naked!' Despite everything, Katla's laugh rang out. Shaking off her father's helping hand, she pushed herself up into a half-sitting position until her head and shoulders were wedged up against the lower plank of the gunwale. 'I gave her my handfasting dress.'

Fent snorted. 'Probably suits her a lot better than it did you, troll-sister.'

Katla's good hand snaked out and caught him a sharp jab in the kidneys that doubled him up, more out of surprise than pain.

'Ow!'

'Never anger a sleeping troll, or one that's just woken up.'

During the next few hours Katla discovered the full extent of her injuries. Where the shawl had not reached, her boots had protected her feet and legs from the worst of the flames, but even so, she found charred and reddened patches all over her legs where the leather had blistered away, some as small as pennywort, others the size of her palm. Beyond the club of her hand, her right arm had lost the top layer of skin from shoulder to elbow, but Katla had always healed quickly, and new skin was already beginning to grow back, tight and glistening, around the scabs. Even so, the whole limb was stiff and excruciatingly painful, as if the damage went far deeper than was apparent, so that even the touch of fresh linen upon it could make her shout – except for an area of her upper arm, where a band of skin on the outside of her biceps remained glowing and unsullied, an area which did not hurt even when prodded. Katla knew this because she had poked and pinched at it unmercifully ever since discovering this odd fact. If anything, it looked healthier and smoother than it ever had before. *One small mercy, at least*, she thought. *I'll have skin as rough and scaly as a dragon's all up and down my left side, except for the softest, most beautiful skin in Eyra on my upper arm.* 'I shall start a new fashion,' she announced to Fent, when he remarked on it. 'By cutting a large hole in all my tunic-sleeves and showing only this patch of bare skin. Like the Istrian women and their mouths.'

'Ah, indeed,' Fent grinned appreciatively. 'Incredibly seductive, being able to see nothing of them but those painted lips. Tor said—' He stopped suddenly. 'Damn.'

Katla looked away. 'He asked father for my hand, you know—'

'I was there,' Fent reminded her flatly.

'—to try to save me from Finn Larson.' She paused. 'Will Da go through with it, after all this, do you think?'

Fent looked puzzled. 'With what?'

'The marriage – to Finn.'

Some indecipherable expression crossed her twin's face. 'I doubt it,' he said. He looked uncomfortable.

Katla, who could usually read her brother's thoughts as if they were her own, frowned. 'What? Why? There's something you're not telling me. Out with it, fox-boy.'

'He's . . . dead. Finn Larson.'

'Dead?' Her mind worked swiftly. There had been an extraordinary mêlée as the guards had dragged her to the burning, and fighting had broken out all around the edges of the pyre as they bound her there and lit it, but she could not remember seeing the portly shipbuilder amongst the combatants, try as hard as she might. Apart from which, she could not ever imagine him fighting the Istrians for her—

'I killed him.'

Katla stared at him, dumbfounded. Her brother, her little brother, as she liked to think of him, had killed a man. And not just any man – not even an enemy – but the man with whom their father had struck a marriage-deal, Eyra's finest shipmaker; Jenna's father.

'But how – *why?* Not for me, surely?'

Fent, unable to help himself, barked out a laugh. 'The entire world does not revolve around you, you know.' And then he told her what he had overheard of the conversation in the Istrian lord's tent, and how he had taken the big mercenary by surprise and borrowed his sword. 'It seemed right at the time,' he said. 'To take the Dragon of Wen, you know, since you made it, it seemed almost mine . . . and it fit my hand so well: it felt almost that it was singing to me as I plunged it into him: the traitor.'

Katla watched with astonishment a mad blue light enter her twin brother's eyes. *He feels no remorse for it*, she thought. *None at all.*

'But we aren't at war with Istria,' she said carefully, 'and our King might even have taken one of theirs to wife; where's the harm in Finn selling the southerners a few ships? I'm sure he fleeced them well—'

Two deep red spots appeared in the centre of Fent's cheekbones. 'Do you understand nothing of the history between our races?' he said, and his tone was as cold and cutting as one of her blades. 'They have stolen our land and murdered our folk for hundreds of years, driving us ever northward, until all we have left are a few poxy, inhospitable lumps of rock in the middle of a treacherous ocean and the skill to make ships and sail them. And now war looms and you would just sit back and let them take that as well? You would have done well as a traitor's wife.' And with that he shot to his feet and stalked the length of the ship to sit at the helm, face pressed fiercely into the wind like one of the avenging Fates.

She watched him till it was clear he would not turn and give her the satisfaction of meeting her gaze. Then, exhausted, she fell asleep again.

Early the next morning, Katla felt the old familiar draw of the blood in her veins, pulsing and buzzing beneath her skin. *Land. I can feel the land, calling me.* It was stronger this time than it had ever been before. She could even feel the reefs below the keel as they passed through the deep, dark waters of the Westman Sea; a counterpoint to the more tenacious song of the islands. On unsteady feet, she made her way forward to the helm, where Kotil Gorson stood with her father, staring away to the long grey horizon, as yet unbroken by any hint of Eyra.

Rain spattered down out of an overcast sky. *Fitting weather,* Katla thought, *for our not-so-glorious homecoming.* At that moment, the *Fulmar's Gift* caught a big roller of a wave – another sign that land was close now – and all three of them had to grab the gunwale to save their balance.

'Whoa!' The roller passed. Removing her hands from the gunwale, she turned to Kotil and her father. 'Did you feel that?'

They regarded her blankly.

'Big wave,' Kotil remarked in his usual taciturn fashion.

'No,' Katla said quickly. 'Not that—' She stopped, then gingerly replaced one hand on the top plank.

Beneath her palm, the oak of the ship thrummed with energy, a powerful ripple of reaction that spoke of more than the simple aftershock of the impact between sea and planks. '*That,*' she said forcefully. She took one of Aran's hands and pressed it down flat onto the same surface. 'Can you feel it? It's almost as if it's humming, as if it has a pulse—'

Aran gave her an odd look. His fingers closed over the wood, then unclenched. 'I can feel the pull of the sea, the knock of the waves . . .' he started. He frowned. 'Should you be up, Katla? You look pale. Why don't you go lie down until we make land? It won't be long now, hours at most.'

'I know,' Katla said distractedly. 'I can . . . feel it . . .'

Shakily, she turned from them and struggled back amidships, unaware of their puzzled eyes on her back, unaware of anything now that she had made the connection except the trembling of the wood beneath her feet, and the answering call it seemed to receive from the land from whence that wood had come, a call that was conveyed and amplified by the cold grey water through which they travelled. It was as if more life had somehow – in the time she had slept on this voyage – been invested in every part of the living world, and that life was speaking to her, Katla: making itself known to her, and only her.

They came into view of the Westman Islands at midafternoon: Long Man first of all, its north-south axis presenting to them a strangely curtailed sight as they skinned its western coast. Once into the channel between Long Man and Rockfall, Katla could see smoke rising from the settlements surrounding the Great Hall even from five miles or more out: drifting peacefully eastwards with the prevailing wind, and the sudden sharp nostalgia she felt for her home took her by surprise. Minutes later, Aran was striding about the deck issuing orders with the clear, deep voice she identified as that of a man happy and sure in his task, for ships were what Aran knew best: sailing the ocean on a following wind, reading the weather and the run of the sea, making delicate manoeuvres into port. The big square sail was lowered and furled and the long yard was dismantled and stowed away lengthways down the deck. With six of the crew manning the stays, down came the great, thick mast – a tricky procedure even with an experienced team – out of the mast-fish and onto the deck with barely a thud. Katla, impressed, watched it all closely. *One day,* she thought, *one day I will have a ship of my own to sail where I will.* It came out of nowhere, this notion, so that it felt almost like someone else's thought, foreign and improbable; but somewhere at the root of her soul, the idea had taken seed.

Soon the men had taken their rowing places and unshipped the sculls, and within minutes the ship – riding high and light in the water without the burden of cargo – was into the calmer sea of the Rockfall Sound and the blurred mass of grey and green began to resolve itself into the myriad details of the island she called home. Out to the west, stark against the pale-blue sky, the sea-stack known as Sur's Needle rose like a great white tower, crowned by circling gulls and guillemots. Inland from the Needle, the little bays of the southern coastline dipped in and out of the surf, some guarded by foaming reefs, others open to the winds and the tides, their pale sands visible as crescents of gold before giving way to the tangles of gorse and bramble that marked their landward boundaries. From here, the cliffs began to rise steeply towards the awesome overhangs of the far eastern coast, the furthest visible point topped by the impressive Hound's Tooth. *They'll have a watchman up there*, Katla thought. *He'll have spent a good hour climbing to the apex to watch for sails.* And the palms of her hands began to itch and burn, almost as if she could feel the rough-grained granite, its sharp mica crystals pressing painfully into her skin. They always kept a look-out at Rockfall: Aran had insisted on this discipline since returning from the war. Often, Katla had volunteered for the duty, for the climb she favoured as her route to the top was a delight: not difficult if you took the southern corridor, where two columns of the rock folded into one another to make a wide corner you

could bridge comfortably and in perfect balance; and Katla
also preferred this route for the added thrill of the open sea
at her back and the glorious exposure of three hundred feet
of sun-warmed granite beneath her feet. She would sit up
there in the summer with her feet dangling over the edge,
entirely unfazed by the dizzying descent below her, looking
down on the backs of the dark-winged gulls as they slipped
by below her, and the bright orange patches of lichen that
bloomed like marigolds on the shelves and ledges.

Sure enough, as they ghosted in towards the shore, she
could make out the silhouette of a tiny figure atop the Tooth
– one of the lads they had left behind when they sailed: Vigli,
most like, or his cousin Jarn; for both were nimble climbers
– and her heart leapt. *I'll climb to the top first thing tomorrow
morning*, she promised herself, *before the sun comes up so that
I can watch the shadows of the fish shoals moving round the coast
before the boats go out.* And then, with a dull thud in the
pit of her stomach, she realised that climbing the Hound's
Tooth would be the last thing she did the next morning –
or for many mornings to come – and the disappointment of
it all made her eyes sting and her throat swell as if she had
swallowed half a turnip. *I won't weep*, she told herself fiercely.
*I won't have any of them see me weep. It was my own choice; my
own fault, and I must bear it bravely.* She brushed the club of
her bandaged arm across her face and stared furiously into the
wind, lids narrowed to prevent the escape of her tears.

The *Fulmar's Gift* rounded the headland and was at once
engulfed by the cold shadow first of the Hound's Tooth,
then by the looming Raven's Ness as it sailed beneath that
chill curtain of rock. At last, the natural harbour at Rockfall
opened itself to them like an embrace and suddenly they could
see the pastures and crags, the enclosures and barleyfields; and
then the longhouse and outbuildings, the turf roofs of the
cottagers' dwellings, the sandy lanes leading up through the

furze and bracken to the quarries; and people everywhere, running like insects. Too far away to make out identity, still it was possible to trace their paths as they ran down towards the harbour – all the natural dyes of the islands on display at once in their garments: blues and heathers, greens and browns, ochres and dusky pinks. A great knot of them had gathered on the seawall built by Aran's grandfather when he had settled Rockfall a hundred and more years ago; more were arriving on the strand behind it.

As the ship sailed around the breakwater, Katla began to make out individual faces in the crowd: on the seawall as they passed – waving and shouting – were Uncle Margan and Kar Treefoot; Bran Mattson and his daughters Ferra and Suna; Fellin Grey Ship and his wife Otter, Forna Stensen and Gunnil Larson. A sheepdog – a great grey hairy beast with a tongue half as long as its head – ran neurotically up and down in front of the assembled group, its tail lashing the air in a paroxysm of delight. Small children were hoisted onto shoulders. *For many of them*, Katla thought, *it will be the first time they've seen a big ship like ours come in from the Allfair; pray Sur it won't be the last.* Fent's talk of war had unnerved her, truth to tell.

In the lee of the seawall, a few small fishing craft bobbed at anchor. Most would still be at sea completing their day's catch; and those that remained were likely owned by crewmembers of the *Fulmar's Gift*, or the other ships that trailed them.

On the strand, faces now became distinct. The Erlingsons – all four in their fifties now, all identically clad, with the same iron-grey beards and vast noses – stood a little aside from the main assembly, amongst which Katla could make out Stein Garson and old Rolf Finnson, Ma Hallasen and her friend Tian; Fotur Kerilson and the old women of the Seal Rock clan – *they must have picked up their skirts and run like rabbits to have got here ahead of the others*, Katla thought, her lips quirking at the image thus conjured. Fat Breta, Kit Farsen and Thin Hildi were fighting over a basket. Pies for the lads, no doubt; it had become something of a tradition, trying to bribe one of the returning seafarers to your bed with some home-cooked food in the hopes of a piece of nice jewellery or a pretty shawl. No one thought the worse of them for it, and one or two girls had even married their sailors in the end and no harm done.

At the end of the front row she could make out Ella Stensen, Tor's mother, anxiously searching the ship for a sight of her ne'er-do-well son, and her heart contracted. Tearing her eyes from that ravaged face (for Ma Stensen had lost husband, brother and another son in the last year – to the sea; a drunken fight and a throw from a horse respectively), she scanned the eager faces for a sight of her mother and grandmother, but to no avail. Incongruously, she was suddenly gripped by dread. *But what could happen to them here in Rockfall?* she reasoned. The worst that had touched these shores had been odd, isolated acts of nature, freaks of wind and tide, like the great storms that had ripped up off the sea a dozen years ago, stripping the turf off the roofs of the steadings, demolishing the stockade and the plantation that Halli had planted as a zealous thirteen-year-old, determined to grow his own trees and build his own ships. Katla remembered how he had so proudly brought the saplings back from the mainland and dug them in with loving care, against all advice, on the hill behind the longhouse. He'd told the family in great detail about the beautiful ship he would build from the oaks – until Gramma Rolfsen had taken him by the hand and led him down into the valley where the oldest trees on the island grew, the ones that had been preserved as a sacred grove to Feya, and showed him a mark on one particularly fine specimen that his grandfather had carved on the day they had been betrothed. 'Fifty years ago, that was,' she'd cackled, pointing to the twining love-knot a few feet above her head. 'Fifty years, my lad, and you might just have enough tree for a rowing-boat; but you'll have to live as long as the Snowland Wolf before you'll grow a longship from these twigs!' But when the great wind came and flattened them like grass beneath a giant's hand, Halli had wept like a child and Katla, at barely seven years of age, had thought the end of the world – that apocalyptic event she had heard about in stories from her earliest childhood – must surely have come at last. Then, a few days after the storm had blown itself out, the bodies of five men had been washed up at Seal Point. No one recognised them: they were not Westman Islanders; indeed, from their odd clothing and dark and strangely marked skin, they appeared not to be Eyrans at all. Many said they must be Istrians from the far south of their country whose ship had been caught in the storm and blown northwards way off their course, but no wreckage from the stricken vessel had ever been found. They had dug a firepit for the bodies on the beach where the sea had brought them ashore and had sent them to their Goddess in fire, rather than returning them to the ocean in the northern way. Within a week, two of the women and four of the men who had arranged the disposal of the bodies fell ill with rashes across their skin; rashes that were then followed by high fevers and a sudden wasting. Three of the six died; and within a month half of Rockfall had been afflicted by the mysterious sickness and everyone was terrified. Katla remembered being swaddled in cloths soaked in tinctures of pungent herbs by her grandmother; but despite all such precautions the whole family had caught the disease and been covered in fiery rashes from head to toe. Their fevers broke early, and the wasting never set in: they were lucky, but others were not. Thirty-five people – hale men, strong women, lively children – died in that mysterious blast; then, as quickly as it had struck, the plague passed, leaving weakness and exhaustion in its wake; but no further deaths.

Has the sickness come again? Katla wondered. Or had some other misfortune kept her mother and grandmother away from the homecoming crowds? But even as the thought crystallised the crowd parted and she caught a sudden glimpse of her mother's bright red hair, and the redoubtable Gramma Rolfsen, belabouring those in her way with her trusty knobkerry, and Katla let out a huge sigh of relief.

With a great splash a dozen or more of the crew leapt out into the chest-deep water of the harbour, exclaiming at the cold, and hauled ashore the great ropes they would use for drawing the *Fulmar's Gift* up onto the strand, where it could be recaulked and refitted for its next voyage. Faerings were let down over the side and people began to clamber down into them eagerly. Katla glanced down at her bandaged arm; felt the pain and stiffness in her legs. It wouldn't be easy lowering herself into a boat, but she was damned if she was going to return home after her first Allfair as a useless invalid. When her father and brothers approached, their faces set in identical expressions of concern, she waved them away like bothersome gnats.

'Leave me be! I'll see to myself.'

Used to the ways of his headstrong daughter, Aran shrugged and turned away.

'Been missing the chilly kiss of the Northern Sea, have you, sister?' Fent teased.

Katla stiffened, more determined than ever to prove her point. Hobbling like a lame goose, she made her way across to the gunwale above the nearest boat.

Halli followed her. 'You could wait, you know,' he said, pitching his voice so low that no one else could hear. 'They'll fetch the rollers and haul the ship ashore soon enough and you can just step out onto dry land. No one will think any the less of you.'

'No!' Katla was adamant: her eyes flashed dangerously.

Without another word, she bent and held the gunwale tight with her good hand, then swung her right leg grimly over the side, wincing despite herself at the burst of fire that shot up through her spine. It was a long way down to the faering, with the *Fulmar's Gift* sitting unaccustomedly high in the water, and so she set her jaw, shut her eyes and dropped.

Willing hands broke her fall. The little boat rocked precariously, but she was safely aboard. A pair of the crew unshipped the oars and pulled vigorously for the shore.

'Are ye all right, girlie?' a gruff voice said, and she whirled about to find Kotil Gorson behind her, his blue eyes shining unnaturally bright in the web of dark and weatherbeaten creases of his face.

'I'll do,' she grinned back, though her entire body hurt like hell.

He nodded. 'Good effort, lass. Glad they didn't burn yer. 'Twould have been a sore loss after Tor and Erno, too.'

Katla bit her lip. Her eyes returned to Ma Stensen: a tall, slight woman whose long blonde hair had faded in the course of the last year to an unhealthy-looking white streaked with yellow, like the mane of a pony Katla had once owned. She would have come here all the way from Falls Ness in the north of the island, hoping, no doubt, for her share of the money Tor would have earned from the sardonyx. Life was tougher the further north you went: the farms yielding less and less; the fishing wild and treacherous, and with only Tor's little brother, Matt, to aid her, times would be hard indeed. *I will make the finest sword I have ever fashioned, as soon as I am able,* Katla promised herself, *and I will sell it and give Ella Stensen the proceeds.* It was hardly enough to compensate for the loss of her son, but the gift would be worth more than soft words.

Some minutes later the faering crunched its way onto the pebbly strand and more willing hands were assisting her out onto the shore. The ground felt strangely unsteady under her feet, as if it were the sea that had been motionless all these days of the voyage, and the earth beneath that had moved and was moving still. Katla tried to pitch and roll with the absent swell, and fell flat on her face, to the great

amusement of the crowd who had not yet remarked the
bandaged arm or her other, less obvious, injuries. She lay
there, stunned, and the voices and laughter washed above
her head like another sea; then a counter-rhythm began to
pulse through the cheek that touched the ground; through
her hip, her ribs, through her chest and arms and legs. Heat
followed – not fiery, but a warm, engulfing flow – so that she
felt almost that she was floating in a hot spring. Blood buzzed
and sang in her head. Someone pulled at her shoulders and
began to lever her up, and she went unwillingly, feeling ever
more light-headed and disorientated as she came away from
the ground. Upright once more, she was vaguely aware of
people talking to her, of one embrace and then another, and
the familiar scent of the lavender water her mother used; then
she was moving through bodies, propelled by others' hands,
away from the water.

An unknowable time later, she came back to herself
with a start, and found that she was standing before the
Great Hall at their Rockfall steading. How she had got
there, she barely knew. People milled about in front of the
outbuildings, and animals roamed the pastures beyond. The
grass seemed greener than it ever had before she went away;
the sky lucent with hidden light, the birds sang as loudly
as they did at the onset of spring. Behind the steading,
the waterfall known as the Old Woman plunged off the
crags and into the upland tarn in a neverending stream of
white water and surf; and beyond the crags, the mountain
rose preternaturally distinct against the pale sky. She took a
deep breath and felt her body respond to the rush of air in
her lungs. Then Ferg, their hound, came bounding out of
the gate, barking fit to wake the dead, and launched himself
at her at full speed, slobbering with adoration. Instinctively,
she turned slightly away from him, and he hit her full on the
injured arm. With a yelp that had more to do with surprise
than pain, Katla stepped backwards and fended him off with

her other hand, till Aran called him and he ran obediently to his master's heel.

Katla's arm throbbed dully from shoulder to fingertip; but the nausea-inducing wave of agony that should have ensued from such an onslaught never materialised.

Brows knit in confusion, she allowed herself to be led away into the longhouse, feeling like a fraud as everyone fussed around her.

Twenty-one

Silver and Stone

In his castle in Cantara, far in the rocky south of Istria, Tycho Issian seethed and raged. To have come so close to owning the Rosa Eldi and to have had her snatched from his very grasp was desperate enough; but to have lost her to the licentious embrace of the barbarian king was far, far worse. The fact of her loss plagued him whether he were awake or asleep, for night after night she visited his dreams with her green eyes, her hot mouth and willing hands. Some mornings he had felt her presence so powerfully that he could even smell her perfume – a light, earthy scent with just a hint of musk to it – and had turned in the bed to draw her to him yet again, only to find the left side of the mattress cool and smooth and entirely unoccupied.

By contrast, the loss of his daughter Selen seemed a minor privation, except when he remembered the words of the map-seller (whom he had now grudgingly come to regard as 'the sorcerer', though the man's sorceries were as yet grossly deficient): 'in a boat with a northern man' – a statement which, under intense questioning, had rendered a little further detail; 'a tall, young man with a beard so blond it was almost silver; a man with plaits and shells bound into his hair'. It was this last particular that stayed with Tycho. The bizarre braidings and knottings that the Eyrans made – in their hair, their beards, their tally-ropes and those dreadful pieces of string that seemed to stand in for decent parchment and quill – were yet more proof to the Istrian lord, if proof were needed beyond the heretical worship of their ocean-god, of their primitive and boorish nature. What fate did Selen face in the hands of an enemy; an enemy, moreover, who could neither read nor write, a man who tied strange, uncrafted objects into his own hair?

He had had Virelai scry again and again for the whereabouts of both women, though he knew even at the outset it was a useless exercise: for where else would either be bound but to the vile and frozen north? Nevertheless, he had forced the sorcerer into the practice of these searches, as much to stamp his will on the man as for any valuable information. The crystal, time after time, gave back nothing but bland images of fog and cloud, rocks and sea, and eventually Tycho grew bored with the whole procedure and switched his attention to the matter of persuading the sorcerer to find ways of turning brass and alloy into pure silver. Virelai, however, smarting from the Lord of Cantara's unrelenting contempt, practised the scrying in private in his room; and one night, perhaps aided by Bëte being uncharacteristically curled up in his lap, his persistence had been rewarded by a single tantalising glimpse. On a headland that looked too green and forested to belong to the bleak northern isles, a tall man with his head swathed in a turban, and a small dark woman in a red gown climbed a steep path through a rocky brake. He watched as the dress was caught by a bramble runner, forcing the woman to spend some seconds trying to disentangle herself; but the tall man did not even turn, let alone stop to help her; and a few moments later, she ripped the fabric free, leaving a small rag of red on the bush, and ran after him in what seemed some panic. Virelai had seen no more of Tycho's daughter than that one brief sighting in the crystal amidst all the chaos at the Allfair; but her dark, frightened eyes had struck a deep, empathic chord in him: he knew he would recognise them anywhere.

After some deliberation, however, he decided to keep this tiny nugget of information to himself. It might not, he reasoned, in an attempt to justify his decision, be a true vision – which would only result in further vilification and probably even another of the lord's unusually painful punishments, and Virelai was in no hurry to incur a repeat of this experience. All that he had suffered at the hands of the Master had paled into mild discomfort by comparison, and it was with increasing frequency that he regretted the way he had poisoned the old man and left him wrapped in a sleep that might – he realised rather belatedly – eventually kill him by starvation or dehydration before any of the eager northern expeditioners reached the island. And if the Master died thus by Virelai's hand, albeit so belatedly, then the geas that the mage had explained to him so grimly and in such grisly and elaborate detail would surely be invoked. He had thought his little ruse with the maps and the promise of gold beyond measure so foolproof, so clever, for surely to have the old man fall to another's hand could not count against him? The thought evaporated into panic, and a moment later he found himself wondering desperately how he might find a way to escape Tycho Issian and return to Sanctuary in time to save the old man. *Perhaps*, he thought, *if I pretend it was all a terrible accident* . . .

Miraculously, the horses recovered, due to Saro's care and a fresh source of clean water; but Tanto failed to show any significant improvement, and it was with a sinking heart that Saro viewed the prospect of his home. He had always loved the town and environs of Altea but as the Golden River debouched into the great fertile plain at the foot of the southern mountains and he had gazed out across the winding terraces of orange groves and vineyards, punctuated by stands of tall poplar and pillar-firs, the fields of spice and balsam, and the mauve haze of the lavender plantations, instead of feeling uplifted by the beauty of the scene he had found himself in the grip of a cold dread. There was no denying that he was now a completely different person to the naive and hopeful young man who had set out from his home only a few weeks before; and that a very different future from the one he had always envisaged for himself awaited him there. Consigned to tending to his festering brother (the smell alone some days was enough to make him retch) while grieving relatives came and went, shaking their heads and (no doubt) privately opining that it was a shame the two sons' fates were not reversed, he would surely go quite mad.

Then there was the small matter of his mother, now that he had been made aware of the secret of his parentage. He dreaded her looking into his eyes for fear she would divine the knowledge he had acquired: her shame would be unquenchable, and how could he bear to bring her that pain?

Time and again he stared off into the distance, where the Dragon's Backbone rose like a low bank of grey cloud on the farthest horizon, and wondered whether he had the courage to just disappear; maybe even to take Night's Harbinger and gallop off into the distance. *And do what?* he thought bitterly. He would last but a few days in the southern wilderness; be murdered, most likely, by the fierce tribes that infested the foothills of those mountains as he wandered, clueless and waterless, through that hostile landscape. And if he were to travel alone anywhere else in civilised Istria his furious father would have spies out looking for him and he would be spirited home again before any further dishonour could attach itself to the Vingo name.

And so, here he was, about to set foot on the family land once more. With each step he felt himself a step closer to a prison he might never leave.

'Ach! No one's going to mistake *that* for silver, you fool!'

Tycho's toothmarks were clearly visible against the grey shimmer of the coin as dull brown marks where the original copper shone through.

'Can't you bribe the damned cat, squeeze it harder, or something?'

Virelai stared dully at the pile of metal. All day he had worked, with poor Bëte chained to the table-leg, mewling angrily: all day to the effect of transferring the *appearance* of silver to the stuff; but as Tycho said, the result would barely fool a blind man for long.

'I'm doing my best, my lord,' he said wearily. 'But it's not perfect yet, I admit.' He had started a week and more ago by melting down some of the plain coins and attempting to work a spell of transformation upon them, but all that had earned him was a single foul lump of slag worth less than the sum of the coins; that and a beating. The Lord of Cantara was very fond of beatings. After persisting to no greater effect for some days with attempts to make the metal what it was not, he had suddenly struck upon the idea of working with illusion instead, which had earned him a moment of Tycho's most extravagant praise – until he realised that what the sorcerer had offered him was not a nugget of solid silver and the answer to all his pecuniary problems, but a shoddy trick. It was not until a day after the savage beating the southern lord had so promptly administered that Virelai had been able to speak well enough to explain his stratagem, for which he had won himself a grudging nod.

The demands from the Council for the repayment of Tycho's debt were becoming ever more pressing. This very morning he had received a messenger from Cera advising him that his fellow peers in their bounty had decided to extend his period of credit for a further thirty days; but no more. The parchment the messenger so hesitantly brought (his manner suggesting to Tycho that the man had done the unthinkable and actually unwrapped the scroll and *read* the contents) also went on to point out in the most polite terms that the funds were urgently needed by the state, and that if the Lord of Cantara failed to comply with this request, the Council would have no choice than to declare him apostate, requisition his castle and all his chattels and place them in the hands of Balto Miron. That grotesque fool! The thought of Balto's fat arse squeezing itself into his exquisite oak chairs, hand-carved by the finest craftsmen in the Blue Woods, let alone swiving his comeliest slavegirls in his own bed, gave Tycho physical pain; at once he began to formulate a plan that would satisfy all his needs at one fell swoop.

Saro watched his mother kneel beside Tanto's litter and realised with bitter relief that he hadn't needed to worry about her reaction to him at all: he might as well not exist. She knelt there, running her hands across Tanto's pale face and the bald pink dome of his head, and her shoulders began to shake. It must be a shock for her to see her beautiful boy so reduced. Gone was that glossy mane of black hair; gone was his dark golden tan, the hard, flat planes of his cheeks, the strikingly sharp line of his jaw, to be replaced by this pale and sunken mask. Tanto's brows and lashes stood out in stark contrast to his now-sallow complexion; but while these remained intact, no stubble broke through the skin on his jaw and slack jowls, and the changes did not stop there, Saro thought grimly, recalling the appalling vista currently hidden by the blankets, though the general stench must give Illustria some indication of Tanto's state, for he smelled as if he were rotting from the inside out.

When at last Illustria raised her head, he could see that the front of her sabatka was so wet that it was almost as if he could see the glitter of her eyes through the sodden veil, though she had made no sound at all. *Was the fabric so fragile; or were the tears a mother cried for the loss of her favourite son unusually potent?*

It was an uncharacteristically uncharitable thought and he felt ashamed at once. Without thinking, he took three steps across the room and laid a hand gently on her shoulder; and at once was assailed by her grief. It was so powerful that for a few moments he forgot to break the contact, as wave after wave of despair rose and broke upon the shore of his consciousness; and when at last he removed his hand the room swayed and canted and his knees gave way.

'Saro!'

His mother's dark shape loomed over him, her mouth, painted in Falla's colours, all red and gold – *to welcome her husband home, he wondered incongruously; or his brother, Fabel?*

'Don't touch me,' he said sharply, as her hand hovered towards him. 'I'm all right, truly.' He levered himself upright.

'You look . . . terrible.' Her voice dropped almost to a whisper.

'It's been a long journey, Mother. I'm very tired, that's all.' He pushed himself quickly to his feet, wincing as his body registered the impact of his fall. The moodstone, safe in its leather pouch, thumped coldly against his breastbone; and he raised his hand unthinkingly to still it. As he did so, an acrid smell filled the room. It was an aroma he had become all too familiar with by now.

'I must wash him again,' he said dully, turning to his mother. 'Perhaps you could ask one of the girls to help me?'

'Nonsense,' Illustria was brisk, all trace of tears gone from her voice. 'I looked after him for years when he could do nothing for himself, and I shall do it again now. He is only ill: I shall nurse him back to health myself.'

Such assurance in the face of overwhelming evidence to the contrary, Saro thought; and how quickly she had gone from hysteria to this controlled calm. It was no wonder she had managed to mask her infidelity so effectively. 'Father said I must care for him.'

'And I say that my women and I will do it, and that no one else shall enter this chamber without my express permission.'

'He will be angry.'

'Let him be angry: I am not going to lose both of my sons. You look dead on your feet, Saro: go and rest. I will talk to your father.'

And so for the next fortnight, Saro had found himself with time on his hands, as Illustria held to her word and in this one matter forced her will upon his father. Saro had heard their raised voices permeating even the thickest walls of the villa, rising from Tanto's chamber (they had laid him in one of the guest rooms on the ground floor, where water could be fetched and carried more easily); then from the corridor outside, and finally from the entrance to the women's room, and had marvelled how so demure a woman as his mother could become so fearsomely strident when her protective instincts were thus engaged. There had come the sound of a heavy oak door slamming shut with such force that the walls reverberated; and then silence, and Saro reckoned his mother had won her argument, for thereafter during the daylight hours he found the way to his brother's chamber barred by the presence of Fina, a large woman whose grim and silent demeanour had as much to do with her bad temper as the loss of her tongue to a cruel slavemaster at the Gibeon market whence they had purchased her.

He had occupied himself mainly in walking the hills, ostensibly to exercise the hounds, but more to escape the smell of his brother's rotting body and the oppressive quiet of the villa. He would sit amid the sage brush and wild mallow watching the larks soaring into the deep-blue sky and eating the bread and cheese he had taken from the breakfast table, while the dogs rootled cheerfully among the rabbit holes and limestone terraces and brought him sticks and stones and even once a small brown snake with one head at either end of its twisting body which, miraculously unharmed by those sharp canine incisors, had observed him cautiously out of its four unnervingly unblinking copper eyes before slithering quickly under away into the shadows. And sometimes he caught himself thinking about a wild northern girl with hair which had blazed like a beacon on the top of Falla's Rock; and then he would catch the thought and stow it carefully away before her dark fate came back to torment him.

Some time later a merchant train came through Altea town and Favio, in a sudden and uncharacteristic burst of hospitality, invited the visitors to the house. They too, it transpired, had been at the Allfair and had left early like the Vingos, making their slow path south on a roundabout route that meandered from town to town selling the wares they had come by there. As well as silver, they had gleaned a wealth of rumour on their passage.

'There are a lot of angry people in Cera and Forent,' said the leader of the caravan, one Gesto Ardum. He was a stout man in his middle fifties and liked to make it plain he had seen a lot of the world and knew well its workings. Every other sentence was peppered with famous names, as if he thought his perorations would somehow carry greater weight because of his passing acquaintance with these nobles and artists. Saro had taken a hearty dislike to the man. Even now he was citing another of them, punctuating his words by waving a half-chewed chicken leg in the air. 'My friend, Lord Palto – who has a large castle, you know, on the outskirts of Cera – says Rui Finco was quite furious after the Fair; that he was storming around swearing the northerners had become far too confident, and that their new king is a dangerous man and needs taking down a peg or two. And of course the Dystras are quite distraught that he spurned the Swan in favour of a Footloose whore, though the poet Fano Cirio, who often passes his summers at the court at Jetra, told me in confidence that the lady herself is relieved not to be taking the trip north, for she was quite alarmed at the barbarous appearance of the Eyran men.'

'And the Lord of Cantara has rather been inflaming the situation,' one of the other merchants added, intent on parading his own subtle understanding of Istrian politics.

Fabel laughed. 'Bloody madman.'

'Bloody *rich* madman,' Gesto corrected. 'We've done some fine business with Lord Tycho in the past month; I won't have him maligned.'

'His is not a name that is spoken lightly in this house,' Favio Vingo said, tight-lipped.

Gesto's hand flew to his mouth. 'My apologies, sir: I had forgotten the unpleasant matter between yourself and the Lord of Cantara at the Fair. Something about a marriage settlement, I believe?'

Favio glared at him. 'You should not listen to the gossip of fools,' he said shortly. 'The man is quite insane, and where you get the idea that he is rich, I do not know: he was clearly so desperate for funds at the Allfair that he insulted me and my family beyond point of forgiveness.'

'With the greatest respect, I must beg to differ with you on this subject, for the Lord of Cantara paid for his purchases from us – some superb Jetran jewellery (very collectible) and an assortment of the finest gems – with ingots of pure silver. He didn't once dicker over the price I quoted – a very fine gentleman I thought him – and he had great piles of the stuff in his revenue chests: I saw it with my own eyes.'

Favio frowned and fell silent. After a moment he said: 'I thought you had not travelled as far as Cantara yet.'

Gesto Ardum laughed. 'Ah, no: and with the lord away we probably shan't venture that far south. No, it was in Cera that we met with him; and he was cutting quite a figure there. He travels with a nomad servant – a tall, strange, pale man with a black cat that he keeps on a lead: I never saw the like. Very striking.'

Someone else cut in enthusiastically: 'A very pious man, he is, Lord Tycho Issian. Pious and patriotic.'

'Aye,' said another of the merchants bitterly. 'Pious and patriotic, some might say; me, I'd say he was a bigoted zealot.'

Gesto laughed politely and leaned across the table. ' Lindo took a northern woman to wife, would you believe?' he said softly, with an unpleasant grin. 'He likes them a bit wild. Anyway, the Lord of Cantara arrived at court in a great whirlwind of fervour, paid off his Council debt with a flourish and has been whipping up all sorts of fury against the Eyrans ever since: says we should send ships north to "liberate" their women from the cruel yoke of their heretical religion and convert them to Falla.'

'Liberate them into our brothels, most like!'

An ironic round of applause and table-thumping greeted this statement.

'And is anyone listening to this nonsense?' Fabel asked.

'It's been twenty years and more since we last fought them; those that remember bear grudges, and those that weren't old enough to fight last time around fancy a bit of sport, I dare say. The ones who favour war are in a minority now; but more are listening to Tycho Issian every day.'

Favio laid aside his knife grimly. He had barely touched his food this night, or any other since the night they left the Allfair. His cheeks were haggard, the skin around his eyes dull and crinkled with new lines. 'It pains me to agree with that upstart lord, but my son lies dying at the hands of Eyran brigands . . .'

Gesto Ardum exchanged a glance with another of the merchants, a tall, dark man with closely set eyes and a thin mouth. This man, who had never, Saro thought, given his name, looked away now, applying himself instead to the delicious platter of saffron rice and fragrant baked lamb and apricots that was the local speciality.

'Ah, well it's only *talk* just now of course,' Gesto went on. He leant forward conspiratorially. 'It would be a most expensive undertaking, to storm the north. Lord Palto says we simply do not have the ships for it, nor the expertise either; and to engage the services of the necessary number of renegades to forge the passage to Halbo would be costly; and not just in terms of the money—'

'How do you mean?' Fabel drained his goblet and sat back in his chair, his hands folded over his neat little potbelly in a parody of satisfaction. 'Surely we have had several good years from the mines and the fields? Certainly, we've paid enough taxes recently for their damn coffers to be overflowing in Cera! I wonder where the hell it all goes sometimes: for it's certainly not coming back here: the damn bridge at Costia's been down for near on five years now!'

Gesto looked over his shoulder and around the room in the most melodramatic fashion. Then he leaned even closer to his hosts. 'They say,' and his eyes gleamed, 'that there's a significant sum missing from the treasury; that or the Lord Steward has failed to keep his records true, and *he*, of course, is adamant the shortfall is nothing to do with *him*. Threatened to resign when the books were questioned and then started ranting about some fire at the Duke of Gila's palace last year, at which point a number of the lords all rushed around trying to mollify him. Something odd, there, Lord Palto reckons, though why anyone should bother to fire that old miser's castle is beyond me. One way or another, though, the Supreme Council has been forced to call in debts all over the country well short of the agreed grace periods, and that's certainly not pleased some people I could mention.' He shook his head sadly. 'It's been bad for business, that it has, and that's without all the bizarre accidents.'

'Accidents?' Favio frowned.

'One of the Duke of Galia's barges was overturned in a flat sea off Pig Island. One minute the oarsmen were making good speed; next thing, some devil wind whipped up out of nowhere and capsized her. Damn nuisance for the Duke – lost over a hundred new slaves.'

'Couldn't they swim?' Saro asked naively.

There was a bellow of laughter from around the table. Gesto choked on the lamb shank he had just inserted whole into his mouth.

'Swim! Ha, ha! Excellent, laddie!' He coughed and banged the table with the flat of his hand, spluttering bits of lamb everywhere. 'Swim!'

Saro stared around bemusedly.

Fabel leant across to him and said gently: 'It's the leg-irons they wear, Saro: no chance of escape, see – and if the ship turns turtle . . .'

A sudden, horrible picture presented itself to him then: dozens upon dozens of terrified men and women trying to drag their limbs free of their shackles as the murky Southern Ocean claimed them amid an avalanche of broken timber and crashing water, their eyes bulging, their mouths open on silent screams, the sea rushing in to fill up every available void, whether living or inanimate . . .

By the time he had rid himself of this nightmarish vision, one of the other merchants was deep into the tale of how a caravan bearing a consignment of carpets from Circesia had been trampled by a huge herd of wild horses that seemed to be running for their lives out of the Bone Quarter.

'Finest rugs in the world – reduced to tattered scraps!' was his indignant closing comment; but Saro shivered: horses, running out of the deathly Bone Quarter? That was bizarre indeed.

'I heard how a huge serpent rose up out of the Southern Emptiness and swallowed a yeka entire—'

'Serpent!' laughed another. 'Ridiculous nonsense!'

'I heard the same tale,' piped up another of the merchants. 'And worse.' He regaled them with the unlikely details of how an eagle had carried off a child on the Tilsen Plain, bearing it off on vast wings to its eyrie deep in the Golden Mountains. 'Snatched it right out of the arms of its poor mother!' he cried. 'Had wings as wide as this room!'

'I saw no giant eagles when I was in the mountains; but I do know there are gouts of steam coming up out of the Red Peak,' the unnamed dark man interrupted softly, and across the table all other conversation fell away as everyone strained to listen to him, even though a mountain emitting vapour seemed a lesser wonder than colossal serpents or immense raptors. 'I saw such a sight myself but five days ago.'

The Red Peak was deep down in the great southern mountains. Saro wondered what the man had been doing in that strange, remote region; and how he had come to join a merchant train that had travelled from the north of the country.

'But the Red Peak hasn't erupted for over two hundred years!' Fabel exclaimed.

The dark man cast a sardonic eye at him. 'Maybe not – but I felt the ground move beneath my feet and I didn't stay around to find out more. Rode my horse till its knees broke and had to buy a new nag from hillmen in the Farem Heights.'

Favio Vingo raised an eyebrow. 'I'm surprised they'd do business with you: there's little kindness between our people and the hill tribes.'

The dark man smiled. He reached under his cloak and drew out a pouch, which he then upended onto the table. A shower of bright stones tumbled out, the candlelight sparking off the rough crystal facets of gems as large as eyeballs.

Saro shivered. Moodstones. Even uncut and unpolished, he would recognise them anywhere.

'Pick one up,' the man said to Favio.

Favio reached out and selected the largest, a lump the size of a hen's egg. Upon contact with his skin, the stone flared a deep, unnatural blue shot through with darker veins of purple. The stone in the pouch Saro wore around his neck, concealed beneath his tunic, began to throb as if in sympathy; or was it just that his heart had begun to beat loudly?

Favio dropped the stone as if it had burned him. 'What in Falla's fiery halls is it?'

The dark man laughed and retrieved the stone. In his palm it became a warm, rich orange that glowed like an ember. 'The nomads call them moodstones,' he said. 'They cut them till they're pretty and make them into trinkets that you can buy for your lady and judge her mood – very popular at court, I've heard: a powerful aid to seduction! But the hillmen around the Farem Heights call them "the Goddess's Tears" – some tale about her weeping over a lost brother or lover or such – and say they channel her power. He went on at interminable length about their miraculous properties, the chap I got the horse from, but he gave me his finest nag for a pair of these things, so I'm not complaining.'

'May I?' Fabel extended his hand and the man dropped the stone into it, whereupon it lost its fire and took on a duller, ochre hue. Fabel made a face. 'Doesn't seem to like me much.'

The man laughed. 'A worry on your mind, I'd say.'

Fabel gave him a sharp look and tossed the stone back to him. In the dark man's hand it flared to life again. Then, feeling Saro's intent gaze upon him, the man turned. 'Here: you take it, son: see what pretty colours you can coax from it.'

Saro pushed away from the table. 'I fear I must excuse myself!' he said quickly, and ran from the room, clutching his mouth as if he might vomit. Behind him, he heard catcalls: 'Make some space, lad: plenty more wine to get through yet!' one man laughed; 'Better get the lad in training!' and: 'Do you raise girls here in Altea, then, Favio?'

Out in the corridor, Saro pressed his forehead against the cool plaster on the wall and waited for his racing pulse to slow. He remembered the old nomad healer's terror of the moodstone he carried, how she had called it a 'death-stone' and how he had seen it in her mind's eye as a white, glowing thing, quite unlike the innocuous object the dark man had them toying with at the feast-table. *I'm being a fool*, he thought. *I should have just touched the stone, watched it change colour; passed it back again and let them have their joke.*

He took this thought with him out to the privies where he relieved himself, then washed his hands and face at the ewer. Across the enclosure, an owl hooted, the sound carrying on the night air with extraordinary clarity. A moment later, the call was met by another sound – a wild, distant ululation that made the hairs rise on the back of his neck. He listened, but the noise was not repeated, and he wondered whether he might have imagined it. There had been no wolves in the hills around Altea for generations for they had been hunted into extinction in his great-grandfather's time, and the nearest he had ever come to one was peering at the stuffed head adorning the wall of his father's chamber, a trophy now so moth-eaten and dusty that it bore little relation to the proud living creature it had once been.

He stood out there for a few minutes, feeling jittery and out of sorts, listening to the horses whicker and shuffle in the stables, to the breeze in the poplars, and the crickets in the bushes. A short while later he heard voices and turned to see two of the merchants stumbling out of the door. Unable to make it as far as the privies, they pissed into the flowerbeds, clutching one another and laughing raucously. *Mother's poor marigolds*, Saro thought, and felt a desperate urge to yell with laughter. He watched them stagger back inside, completely unaware of his presence, and then turned and followed them back into the house.

Inside, the noise from the hall was loud and boisterous and

suddenly Saro found he did not have the stomach to return
to the drinking games and lewd jokes which had undoubtedly
started up in his absence. Such activities had never been his
forte, and since Tanto loved to show off in the company of
men as much as he did with women, it usually proved possible
for Saro to slip into the background, his hands cupped around
the goblet of wine he had nursed for the past hour, smiling and
nodding and pretending to share the coarse humour, while
he longed for the solitude of his room. Even without Tanto
present, he doubted he'd be much missed. He could always
say he'd passed out in the enclosure, and provide them with
another laugh in the morning.

He walked quickly past the door to the feast-hall and along
the cool corridor beyond, passing the solar where his mother
entertained any women accompanying their guests; but it was
already quiet and dark. The candles had been extinguished;
though not so long ago, for he could smell the hot wax from
them as he walked by. Beyond lay the guest quarters, and
his brother's chamber. He was about to set foot on the stairs
when he was distracted by a sound. Someone was in Tanto's
room: he could hear the murmur of a voice rising and falling.
He frowned. His mother had forbidden any but herself and
her women access to her unconscious son; but the sound he
could hear was a low drone – a man.

Saro crept to the doorway and hovered outside. Here, the
words became more distinct.

'Oh, Tanto, Tanto, to see you lying like this, dead to the
world . . . I do not even know if you can hear me. I look
for signs of life in your eyes, but they are as black and empty
as the Poisoned Pools of Beria.'

A sob. It was his father, Saro realised, which caused him
no great surprise.

'When I remember you as a boy, so swift both with feet
and tongue, so handsome, everyone charmed by your beauty
and your energy, and now . . .'

There came a brief rustling noise, then Favio went on: 'I must know if you are still alive in this rotting shell, my boy; I must know if you are aware of me, or even if you dream, for I do not think I can bear to watch you dying before my eyes much longer. Forgive me for disturbing this long rest, Tanto, if disturb it I do. They say the soul carries on living for long after the body has failed; but they say nothing about this living death, and I must *know* . . .'

Saro twitched the curtain that draped the door and saw how Favio Vingo was bending over his brother's still form. Something in his hand throbbed out light the colour of a deep bruise.

'Let the stone tell me what goes on beneath this cold, white brow—'

'No, Father!'

Without a second's thought, Saro took two strides forward to stop him, just as Favio Vingo pressed the moodstone to his son's forehead. For a moment as it made contact with Tanto's sweating skin, the stone pulsed a pale and sickly greyish blue; then as Saro caught his father by the shoulder, it flared to a white so brilliant it hurt the eyes; then to a powerful, coruscating gold. A bolt of pure energy coursed through Saro's right hand, making him tighten his grasp on Favio's shoulder until it felt as if their bones might melt together. It raged up his arm and into his head, so that he shrieked with the pain of it – a deep, scouring pain that burned as mercilessly as any pyre – and his father's howl rose in counterpoint, agonised and terrified. It ignited the stone in the pouch around his neck so that Saro felt both moodstones like two vast, external hearts and himself a tiny seed trapped between them, filled with so much life he might just burst apart and spill it all out into the night in an incandescent rain; and a moment later their shared cry took on a third, higher note that rang and echoed off the chamber walls like a trapped animal.

With a savage vigour, Saro wrenched himself free of the

contact. At once the light went out of both moodstones, throwing the chamber into such complete darkness it was as if someone had blown out the sun. He heard his father collapse onto the floor, heard his stertorous breath and a mumbled prayer: 'Oh, Falla, oh, Falla, oh, Falla . . .'

And then another voice, pitched high with panic:

'I'm blind! By the bitch, I'm blind!'

Twenty-two

The *Seither*

Time passed and Katla continued to improve. By the end of the summer she could run, and ride a pony one-handed; but everything else – climbing and metal-working, swimming and fishing; even clothing herself and visiting the outhouse on her own – had become a desperate frustration.

The burns on her legs and shoulder mended to pale scars; but her right hand remained stubbornly gnarled and fistlike, the fingers fused together in an ugly mass of red-and-white scar tissue which, though she had never thought of herself as a vain person, she preferred to conceal. Small children took one look at the wound and ran away: it was upsetting, especially since others at Rockfall had taken worse injury and not attracted such attention. Kar Treefoot – so called for the wooden peg he had attached to the stump of the leg he had lost (he claimed) to a sea monster – was certainly a local curiosity; but his wound was not on view to the world, and no longer caused comment; and Grima Kallsen had been born with a dark-red stain running across her face, but her smile was still the first thing you noticed about her. Older men had scars, from the war, from horse-fights and drunken brawls and fishing accidents, it was true: but women in Rockfall rarely carried wounds, and Katla's story had anyway carried far and wide. Taking pity on her granddaughter, Gramma Rolfsen had adapted a number of her tunics so that a long sleeve could be gathered with a leather thong to hide the nub.

Healers had come and gone, applying poultices and admin-
istering potions to the damaged arm; but none had had any
effect other than to make her retch and run for the outhouse.
All the while, Gramma Rolfsen had sucked her teeth and
tutted over their efforts, and then one day she had caught
her daughter by the elbow and whispered something to her.

'Festrin One-Eye!' Bera had exclaimed. 'You can't be
serious.'

'Nothing else has worked: how can it hurt?'

'But Festrin One-Eye is a *seither*!' Bera hissed, glancing
quickly to make sure Katla had not overheard.

Katla had. 'A *seither*? Really?'

Bera whirled around, blue eyes snapping with irritation.

'Ears like a bat!' Gramma cackled.

Katla had never come across a living *seither* before, though
when she was twelve she had crept into the Old Howe with
several other children to see the bones of the one who lay
there, as a dare. Nothing had happened, though Fent had
sworn he'd seen them *move* when a cloud passed across the
moon; and two days later the wart Tian had had on the end
of her nose had mysteriously vanished, which was surely proof
of some sort of magic in the place. The bones were long,
Katla remembered; attenuated and yellowed and thin and very
brittle, and people said the *seither* whose skeleton it was had
been an old, old man for as long as they could remember, a
result of the ancient earth-magic he wielded.

'Besides,' Bera addressed her mother, ignoring her daughter's
outburst and with one shoulder turned resolutely to Katla as if
to physically block her from the discussion, 'how would you
know how to contact Festrin One-Eye?'

Gramma tapped the side of her nose and shot her daughter a
crafty look. 'The old have their ways,' she replied cryptically.
'I hear we'll be able to greet the *seither* shortly.'

'What? Here?' Bera drew herself up to her full five foot. Her
pale skin was flushed, and two red marks had appeared on her

cheeks. *Just like Fent, when he was angry*, Katla thought. And just like her twin, her mother could be remarkably pig-headed and difficult. 'No one has informed me of this.'

Gramma Rolfsen, who was used to her daughter's flare-ups, merely shrugged. 'I hear Festrin is travelling with the mummers.'

High Feast was just a few days away, and even though crops in the wild and rocky Westman Isles were not usually abundant, this year the weather in the crucial last few weeks had been perfect – a period of soft rains had been followed by unseasonably warm sunshine resulting in a late surge of growth: unusually, the wheat was shoulder-high; the barley a lush pale-green swathe; and they had to prop the branches of the appletrees in the orchards at Rolf's Dell to save them from the weight of the fruit. The seas around the islands had not been immune to this bounty, either; lately the fishermen had brought ashore line after line of pollock and bass; shoal after shoal of mackerel and herring. The drying-racks were full, the store of salt almost depleted, and the smoking-house sent billows of fragrant fumes into the air both day and night. And the fine weather had held through harvest, too, so that the barns were stuffed to overflowing. It would be a fine feast this year, which was as well, for the mummers numbered twenty or more including the musicians; and it was Rockfall's turn to accommodate them.

Bera frowned. 'Why didn't Aran tell me?'

'Tell you what?'

Bera spun round to confront her husband, who had come in silently behind Katla. Many women would be intimidated by a man so large that his shoulders filled the doorway with barely an inch to spare on either side, but Bera planted her hands squarely on her narrow hips and glared up at him like a little fighting cat.

'That the mummers think to bring a *seither* with them this year.'

Aran's eyes darted guiltily to his mother-by-law and Katla watched her grandmother's gap-toothed grin widen challengingly and immediately read the situation.

'I . . . ah,' Aran struggled. 'I didn't know,' he lied unconvincingly, and Gramma Rolfsen bellowed with laughter.

'Poor lad,' she said. 'Don't blame him, Bera dear. It was my fault. You remember when he sent the messenger off to Halbo to ask Morten Danson if he'd take on a commission for the ship—?'

Bera bit her lip. 'That ridiculous ice-breaker,' she said grimly.

'The very same. Well . . .' She looked sly; but then, Katla reasoned, Gramma Rolfsen had got 'sly' down to a fine art. 'I slipped a message of my own off with the lad. To Tam Fox.'

Tam Fox was the leader of the mummers: a well-built man in his middle years, with strikingly green eyes and a wealth of braided russet hair. Katla had thought him fine-looking, if, at thirty, a bit old. She'd only been fifteen the last time his troupe had visited Rockfall, fifteen and skinny as a spear-shaft; but that hadn't stopped him plying her with ale while her mother wasn't looking and trying to sweet-talk her outside into one of the barns. Her ears pricked up. This could be very interesting.

'And?' Bera gave her mother a hard stare, a look that had been known to make grown men quail and stammer; but Gramma Rolfsen was indomitable.

'I suggested he might win himself some favour here if he were to bring my old friend Festrin with him.'

'Your old *what*?' Bera's voice rose sharply.

Gramma Rolfsen chuckled. 'I've lived near twice the length of your life, my dear, and not all of it as transparent to the eye as one of your beloved rockpools.'

Poking about in rockpools was one of Katla's favourite childhood pastimes. She looked at her mother with renewed interest: perhaps there was something they had in common, other than the bones and hair . . .

Bera snorted. 'More like a foul and muddy pond by the sound of it. Consorting with necromancers and ne'er-do-wells behind my back – inviting them into *my* house . . . to treat with *my* daughter . . . calling them *friend*. I won't have a filthy *seither* in this hall. If the mummers bring this creature with them I will not offer them hospitality. They shall not take bread and salt at my table; no, nor fish and ale, neither!'

'Bera!'

'By Feya, I swear it. No *seither* shall not set foot over this threshold. They are abominations, and not to be tolerated by the god-fearing.'

Aran regarded his wife with horror. 'Wife, you cannot mean this: it is the worst of insults – you will bring shame down on all of us.'

In response, Bera merely took two steps forward, placed one splayed hand on her husband's shoulder, pushed him firmly backwards out of the door and marched past him into the yard outside without another word.

It was three days before she spoke to any of them again.

It seemed that during this time Bera's dangerous pronouncement must have been withdrawn, for before long everyone was making preparation for High Feast. Katla took to hanging around the harbour with Ferg – after all, there was little help she could offer in the kitchen with but a single hand. *And absolutely no culinary skills, thank Sur*, she grinned to herself. The club-hand had its uses when it came to avoiding such dextrous, and tedious, chores as peeling and baking, skinning and sousing and roasting; but it didn't prevent her from swiping a chicken pie on her way out of the door on this, the fourth day she had made it her business to watch for the incoming ships. She ate it sitting on the seawall with her back against an upturned rowing boat and her legs dangling over the side. Ferg turned his nose up at the pastry – *Too much soft living, my lad!* she chided him – but wolfed down the pieces of savoury chicken so fast it was impossible he could have tasted them; and then he licked her good hand all over to mark his gratitude and curled up next to her on the warm stones, his eyes reduced to satisfied, gleaming slits. Together, they listened to the gulls crying overhead and watched the sun make its scintillant patterns on the water. A little while later, the hound began his sonorous snore; and a short time after that Katla, too, fell into a doze.

Katla!

She heard her name clearly; but the voice was unfamiliar. In her dream she was running, and something was pursuing her. She did not dare to turn around to check its progress for fear she would miss her footing and tumble headlong, but she could hear its roar – wintry and elemental – it was coming for her, and had (she knew, in some cold and certain corner of her heart) already consumed her family. Overhead, the skies had turned dark red, and malignant black clouds limned with crimson had swallowed the sun. She felt the first drops of rain on her cheeks. She lifted her right hand to wipe them away and found it was whole and perfect, the fingers long and thin and separate as they had always been before the fire. Mesmerised, she stared at it, and then she realised she could see her bones through the skin like dark shadows shrouded by her thin, translucent flesh, as if the sun had the power to glow right through them. And then the glow passed away and she saw that there was blood on her fingers, and when she lifted her gaze to the sky, more of it spattered down onto her face. A terrible dread gripped her then. But there was a bright light in the distance, and someone was calling her from it, and if she could only just outrun the thing that was behind her—

'Katla!'

She came back to herself with a start and found herself standing in her brother Halli's shadow. Behind him, the sun made a red halo of his dark hair.

'I . . . ah . . .' She suddenly felt terribly guilty. *Was it the pie?* a small voice in her mind asked; *or something worse?* The dream had left her with gooseflesh all down her bare arms; her spine prickled in some atavistic reaction. The hound, touched by her mood, or perhaps, in some ineffable way by the dream itself, began to whine.

Halli put his hand out to Ferg, who sniffed it warily, then settled again. He grinned at Katla, then pointed out to sea. 'Look – the mummers' ships!'

And there they were on the line of the horizon: two big rectangular sails dark against the blue sky, coming closer all the while.

Katla shook the remnant of the dream away from her and, craning her neck to look up at him, forced a smile. 'Did you come to tell me that, brother, or are you here to reprimand me for my missed errands?' Halli got older and more responsible as each day passed, it seemed; as if he were somehow stepping into their father's boots, since Aran could talk of nothing but his mad scheme for an expedition to find Sanctuary, much to their mother's fury. There had been angry words exchanged between them (the first Katla could remember in all her nineteen years) for several nights after he had first announced his plan – to commission the finest ice-breaking ship that could be made (which, since the coin earned by the sale of the sardonyx at the Fair had subsequently found its way into the hands of a group of mercenaries, would cost all the money the family had saved and more) and take every able-bodied man in Rockfall to search for the fabled land marked on his precious map. 'You are not the man I married!' Bera had stormed. 'I chose a father for my children and a husband for myself, a man I could trust, who would provide for his family: not some madman obsessed with a legend, who carries about a scrap of paper some trickster fobbed him off with at the Allfair like Jack and his bean-seeds!'

On three separate mornings Katla had found him lying flat out on the hay in the barn when she'd been to saddle up her pony for a dawn ride.

'No.' Halli looked hurt. 'I just thought—' A pained expression crossed his face; then he sat down beside Ferg on the seawall. The old hound looked up at him reproachfully, then shifted over and laid his head firmly on Katla's lap, where he began to drool. 'I'm sorry, Katla. I really am.'

She frowned. 'Sorry for what?'

He cleared his throat and looked down at his hands and his dark eyebrows became a single unbroken line, just like Aran's when he was angry or perplexed. 'That we didn't save you from the fires. That . . . your arm got burned. That you can't climb any more.'

Katla felt her throat contract and her eyes prick. 'It was my own fault,' she said huskily. She reached out with her good left hand and gripped him by the forearm, feeling the warm cord of muscle and the curling black hair under the pads of her fingers. 'You did everything you could. You and . . . Tor. I saw you. You killed a man with the wood-axe.'

'I killed three.' He looked ill. 'I never killed anyone before. I keep thinking about it.' A pause fell which Katla did not know how to fill, then Halli said: 'Fent reckons war will come soon, you know. Then I'll have to kill again. We all will. I wanted to catch Tam Fox and his men before they get to the hall, find out what the news is from court, whether the King is calling a muster.' He glanced up and his face was harrowed. 'Perhaps father's expedition is not such a stupid idea, after all.'

Katla laughed. 'Oh, it is. But what fun, eh? Do you think he'll let me come, Halli?'

He snorted, taken by surprise. 'I doubt it – you cannot even row, let alone man a line – what use would you be?' Katla's face went stiff and still and a few seconds later Halli grimaced. 'I'm sorry. I didn't mean—'

'You did and it's true,' Katla said gloomily. 'I'll never get out of here again. I'll go mad and end up like Old Ma Hallasen, living alone with my goat and my cat, talking to myself in some language no one else can understand.'

'You're already halfway there!'

Ferg's head came up sharply, the ghost of a snarl in his throat; but it was only Fent, grinning widely.

'Do you think Ravn will have called a muster?' His eyes were bright and avid. 'I'll take ship back with the mummers if he has. And, Katla, that sword, the one you made last summer on a commission that was never claimed? Can I have it?'

'The one with the carnelian set into the pommel?'

'That one, yes. A beauty – though not as fine as the Dragon. Now that was a weapon. Slid home like a dream.'

Halli looked at his brother suspiciously; then he turned to Katla. 'I thought Joz Bearhand bought that sword from you.'

Katla glared at Fent. Somehow it seemed very important that Halli did not know his own brother had murdered Jenna's father. 'He did. And, no, you can't have it. The Red Sword is mine and I'm going to learn to use it left-handed. Ah – look – it's the *Snowland Wolf*—'

The lead ship was now close enough that you could make out the great wolf that adorned its sail, the coil of a huge serpent in its jaws. The head of the serpent loomed up over the wolf, jaws open to strike, while its tail looped in extravagant twists and flourishes in and out of the wolf's legs to form a decorative border around the canvas. A line of colourful ornamental shields had been strapped along the outside of the gunwale and the sun glinted off the bronze bosses and studs. The *Snowland Wolf* was a fine sight, enough to lift the spirits of any who saw it. Tam had always had a flamboyant streak.

The second ship, meanwhile, displayed a rayed sun on its sail and had the head of a great bear carved into its prow. Squatter and shorter than the *Snowland Wolf*, it was nevertheless a seaworthy little vessel and Katla watched it breast the rollers appreciatively. 'I wonder which ship Festrin One-Eye's on,' she mused.

Fent shot her a suspicious look. 'What would you know of any *seither*?'

'Gramma sent a message to him,' Katla said smugly, cheerful to have acquired knowledge that Fent had failed to ferret out. 'To ask him to look at my hand.'

Fent made the sign of Sur's anchor. 'That's witchery, sister. I'd have thought you'd had enough of such at the Moonfell Plain.'

Katla glared at him. She waved the club of her hand in his face. 'See this, fox-boy? Its only use at the moment is for thumping idiots like you: but I'm damned if I'll live with it forever.'

'You'll be damned forever if you let a *seither* touch you.' Fent strode off down the seawall and waited for the ships to come in, fists planted firmly on his hips.

Halli put a hand on his sister's shoulder. 'Whatever you need, Katla,' he said. 'You must do whatever you need for your poor arm. Fent's a hot-headed fool and you should take no notice of him. I've come across no evil caused by this Festrin; nor indeed of any other of these magic-makers; but if Gramma thinks the *seither* may be able to do something for you, that's all right with me. I'll keep an eye on Fent, I give you my word.' His fingers tightened on her shoulder and then he levered himself upright and went to join his brother.

Katla watched them standing there with their backs to her: one so tall and broad and dark that he could almost have been their father, were it not for the diffidence with which he held himself; the other red-haired, smaller of frame and wiry, all that pent-up energy fair sparking off him in the afternoon air. She often felt closer to Halli than to her twin; as she did to her father rather than her mother, despite all their difficulties and differences. How was it, she mused, that good qualities in one became so exaggerated and dangerous in another? Sometimes she hardly felt she knew Fent at all any more.

With a sigh she extricated herself from the hound, gathered her feet under her and got up. Ferg, comfortable on the warm stones, stared at her sorrowfully. 'Come on, boy,' she said.

'Let's go see what monsters these mummers have brought with them, eh?'

Festrin One-Eye was not as easy to spot as she had expected. Of the two dozen and more folk on the ships, all seemed to be hale and in possession of both eyes. There was no old, bowed man amongst them, as far as she could tell; not even one with white hair. There were several women: two in their middle-years, who filled out their low-necked tunics to admirable effect, some younger girls, all blonde-haired and willowy and one very tall, all dressed in striped trousers and jerkins like the men, moving with swift efficiency around the deck, clearing lines and stowing the sail, and Katla, overtaken by a rare moment of insecurity, felt a sudden stab of jealousy for the sure way they went about their allotted tasks. Of the men, Tam Fox was immediately visible, standing up on the prow of the *Snowland Wolf* in a fine crimson-and-gold tunic, his wild red hair flaring behind him like a fire. She recognised a number of the others too – men as lithely muscled and exotic-looking as the big cats she had seen in the pens at the Allfair. *The tumblers*, she thought. She remembered how they had sprung and cartwheeled their way around the hall on their last visit, and how she had given herself a bruise the size of a hen all down her right hip and thigh while attempting to copy their extravagant capers on the beach after they had gone.

She watched Halli and Fent go to make the ritual greeting from the men of the house to the visitors, and waited until the last of the mummers had disembarked. But there was still no one-eyed man, nor any likely-looking *seither*. Perplexed, she tailed the troupe up to the longhouse with Ferg lagging at her heels. Clearly the sorcerer had not come, despite her grandmother's request. She would have to try to catch a quiet word with Gramma Rolfsen to find out what had gone amiss.

But when she arrived at the hall, there was already a

commotion taking place. Her mother was standing in the doorway with her arms crossed, dwarfed by the carved posts and by the knot of shouting men in front of her. At the head of the knot was her husband.

Bera waited for the noise to subside. Then: 'Until you tell me which is the *seither*,' she said grimly, 'none shall enter my house.'

'Wife, this is no way to greet people who have sailed hundreds of miles to bring us all entertainment! They are hungry and thirsty—'

'Aye!' came a chorus from the mummers. 'Thirsty, that we are!'

'—and we are bound by the kingdom's law to offer them bread and salt—'

'And ale as well!' chimed a lone voice, and others joined the chant.

'—for if word reaches the King of such lack of hospitality, he'll make outcasts of us all.'

Bera's face flushed. 'Our so-called king did nothing to save my daughter from the Istrian fires, and this is what I think of him and his laws!' She spat on the ground at Aran's feet, and a hush fell over the assembled crowd.

Then a tall woman carrying a bulging knapsack pushed through the crowd, stepped neatly around Aran Aranson and knelt before Bera, her hair a flag of gold that swept the ground. 'Mistress of Rockfall, I beg your pardon: I had not meant to cause you offence by coming here. Indeed, having come by invitation, I had thought to find a better welcome.'

Bera looked down at the woman suspiciously. 'I find no offence in *your* presence,' she said stiffly. 'I shall turn no travelling woman away from my home.'

The woman rose and shook back her long hair, and Bera's hands flew to her face. Katla saw with a start that in the midst of the visitor's sharply-boned, handsome, sun-weathered face, she bore only one eye, and that set squarely in the middle of her forehead.

Gramma Rolfsen hustled past her daughter and embraced the one-eyed woman. 'Festrin, Festrin – you have aged not a day since last we met.'

'Oh, I have aged, Hesta, that I have. It just does not show in the ways that your people look for.' The *seither* regarded Gramma Rolfsen solemnly, then graced her with a smile of surpassing sweetness. Then she reached out a hand to Bera, who looked at it as if she had been offered a nine-day herring and declined to shake it. Festrin shrugged. 'So be it. I shall go and visit my grandfather's burial mound, and I will return later. If you still do not wish me to set foot over your threshold, I will honour your decision, but the Fates may regard your decision with less equanimity.'

Hoisting her knapsack over her shoulder, she turned and made her way back through the mummers, who parted for her, eyes averted and heads bowed.

'She threatened me!' Bera turned to her husband. 'Did you hear that? She threatened to turn the Fates against me.'

'Hush, wife,' Aran said, though even he looked white about the eyes. 'It was no threat she made, and you are behaving badly. Let us welcome the company into our home and make them comfortable. I pray the *seither* will return quietly of her own accord, and that you will say no more against her.'

And clearly, Katla thought, watching Bera nod quietly and step back inside the hall, the *seither*'s magic was working, for she had never seen her mother back down in an argument. The mummers, meanwhile, piled up their baggage in the outhouses and followed the Master of Rockfall into the longhouse, ready to enjoy their meat and ale. But Katla's appetite had been subsumed by her curiosity. And so, when no one was watching, she slipped away, with Ferg silent at her heels, and headed for the Old Howe.

★   ★   ★

The *seither* was waiting there for her – or so it seemed to Katla. She was sitting on her knapsack outside the entrance to the ancient burial mound with her feet crossed neatly at the ankles, paring the skin from an apple with her belt-knife. When Katla appeared over the knoll, Festrin held out half of the apple to her and Katla walked over, trying hard not to stare at the single blue eye, took it without a word, and sat down beside her.

They sat together like this for a short while, eating the apple, while Ferg slunk around them, belly to the ground, ears flat against his head; but even he made no sound. At last, the *seither* said, 'Show me your hand, Katla Aransen.'

'You know who I am,' Katla said wonderingly.

Festrin threw her head back and laughed, a great harsh bark of a sound that had Ferg bounding away in fright. It was not the response Katla had expected. 'I came at your grandmother's request: she told me in her message just how her talented and beautiful granddaughter had been afflicted and—' She gestured at Katla's wrapped club of a hand. 'It's hard to miss, even for one without the eye.'

Katla smiled, feeling foolish. Then she began to unbind the bandages until the awful pink-and-red thing on the end of her arm was exposed in all its ugliness. Festrin did not flinch at the sight. Instead, she put her belt-knife carefully away, then reached out and took the hand between her own two. At once, waves of tingling heat ran up each of Katla's arms, crossing at her chest and running back down the opposite arm. It was the most bizarre sensation.

Now Festrin smiled. 'I was right,' she said. 'I thought so as soon as I saw you.'

'About what?'

'You have been touched. Not directly, maybe, but in some other way.'

Katla frowned. 'I don't know what you mean. Touched by what?'

'It must have been latent in you before then, though,' the

seither mused, ignoring Katla's question. 'I have rarely come across the gift so strongly.'

'What gift?'

While this tableau was being played out, Aran Aranson had appeared quietly behind them, and Ferg, obviously relieved to know his place again, took up his rightful position at his master's heel.

The *seither* regarded the tall West Islander thoughtfully. 'You are not entirely immune from its power yourself,' she said cryptically, 'but in you the mystery has taken another course, and not one for the good, I fear.'

Aran frowned. 'Where I come from folk say what they mean straight out, rather than hide the sense in such glib and abstract notions.'

Festrin stood up, and Katla was surprised to realise that she was very tall, topping the big man as she did by half a hand. This was puzzling, until it dawned on her that, arriving at the Great Hall, the *seither* had carried herself stooped and with her head bowed. With a shiver, Katla remembered the long, yellow bones in the howe behind them.

'Most folk do not usually like to hear straight out what I have to say,' Festrin said. 'It discomfits them to hear it plain and simple.'

'I am not "most folk",' Aran said sternly. 'And in matters concerning me and my family, I like to know exactly where I stand.'

The *seither* reached a hand out and touched him on the cheek. Aran felt a pulse of heat, then nothing. 'Ah,' she said. She withdrew her hand, looked at her fingertips for a moment, then rubbed them together as if dusting flour from them. Then: 'Now is not the time,' she said. 'I am hungry and I am weary. May I sit at your table, or is your wife still adamant that I should suffer the elements? Because if she is, then I will stay here with my kin—' she gestured at the burial mound '—and make my own repast.'

'And I will stay with you!' Katla said hotly.

Aran rolled his eyes. Then he bowed to the *seither* and said of course his wife had not meant to bar her from their table and that he had come out here expressly to fetch her to the feast.

They walked in silence back to the hall, where their arrival was marked only by a brief pause in the conversation and supping. It was amazing, Katla thought, that their longhouse could accommodate so many people. Trestles had been set up along both long walls and laden with every sort of delicacy and staple food – wheat-bread and apple-bread; goats'-cheese and ewe-cheese, pressed meats, soused fish, great haunches of lamb and beef, roasted chickens and seal-steaks and shark-steaks; hen pies and mackerel pies, whole roasted seabass and trout stuffed with fruits; and great barrels of ale and casks of the islands' best stallion's blood wine – and folk were ranged along either side of the trestles, with their backs to the wall or to the firepit that burned merrily down the centre of the hall. If you were particularly susceptible to the intoxicating power of stallion's blood, it was as well to sit on the outside of the tables, Katla recalled.

Aran took his place at the high seat and beckoned the *seither* to sit beside him. Bera's eyes flickered malevolently at the woman, then she pointedly turned away to talk loudly and flirtatiously with Tam Fox. Katla viewed her possible placements – on Tam Fox's left hand or beside Festrin One-Eye, and slipped quickly in beside the *seither*.

'So tell me, Tam,' Aran said loudly, breaking into his wife's conversation. 'What news of the King's new shipmaker – will he take my commission?'

Tam looked shifty. He coughed. 'Ah, no, Aran. Morten says he cannot leave his yard: he's inherited a lot of Finn Larson's unfinished business, and that work alone will take him through next spring. He recommends one Fly Raglan, though, who was his apprentice and has now set up on his own.'

'I don't want his damned apprentice! I want the man who built the *Snowland Wolf*, if I can't have Finn Larson—'

'Aye – it'll be only the Lord Sur who can avail himself of Finn's skills from now on!' laughed one of Tam's men.

Tam dropped his voice. 'Morten says he won't meet with you because he heard a rumour it was your son who slew Finn Larson.'

Aran looked aghast. 'What, Halli kill his future father-by-law? That's sheer madness.'

Tam put a finger to his lips. 'Fent,' he mouthed.

Aran's eyes went wide.

'What?' Bera thrust her head between them. 'What did he say?'

'Nothing,' Aran said irritably. He shook his head as if to dislodge this unpleasant piece of information, then leaned around his wife. 'So he won't take the commission? What if I were to offer a better price?'

Tam Fox shook his head. He applied himself to half a chicken. '"Wouldn't touch it with a barge-pole," was what he said,' Tam reported indistinctly, hot juices running down his chin and into his beard. '"Load of mad dogs, the Rockfallers" were his exact words. Besides, I gather he's already undertaken a commission for a vessel from Fenil Sorenson.'

'Has he, now?' Aran's face went thoughtful. 'Big one?'

'Sixty-oar, I heard.'

Aran nodded. 'Interesting.' He'd seen Fenil briefly at the Allfair: he and Hopli Garson, never usually that friendly, had had their heads together in a conspiratorial fashion; but he'd not have had either of them down as adventurers – they were solid landsmen, both with sardonyx mines on the mainland within fifty miles of one another; as far as he knew, the only time they took to the ocean was on the annual trip to the Fair.

After that, Aran was remarkably quiet. Gossip and rumours and news alike washed about him and occasionally he nodded in an abstracted manner, though it was clear he had not really taken in what had been said to him. Someone told how freak tides had washed a monster ashore on the beach at Whale's Ness – a giant narwhal with human eyes, some said; others reported the dead thing as being a humanlike being with flippers and a great whiskery chin. Someone else chimed in with a tale of a sea-creature swallowing a fishing boat whole in the Blue Channel west of the Sharking Straits, a beast longer than three ships, with teeth like swords; but others said it was just a whale that had strayed from its usual path which had risen up and capsized the vessel; or maybe it was just a big wave. But for all her love of such tales of monsters, Katla was most intrigued by talk of the King and his new wife: it was, after all, indirectly because of the pale nomad woman that she had been burned; for King Ravn would surely never have allowed such to happen to one of his subjects were he not under some spell; and now it seemed she had worked her magic on others, for one of the troupe reported she had quite stolen the hearts of all at the northern court; all, that is but Queen Auda, Ravn's mother.

'Took one look at the Rosa Eldi, she did,' said the mummer, a dark and wiry man called Mord, 'and turned her back on her, went to her chamber, and hasn't come out since.'

There was a murmur of surprised chatter at this from the Rockfallers: far from court, such tales of royal affairs were always fascinating to them. Bera quite forgot how angry she was with her husband, and pressed Tam closely for as much detail as he could provide her about the strange foreign woman. Even the *seither* appeared to be interested in this subject, for she leaned forward and turned her powerful blue gaze unwaveringly upon Tam Fox.

'She's a rare one,' he said appreciatively. 'Got the King completely bewitched: not a mention of war in all the time we were at court, not from Ravn, anyway. Spent most of his time holed up with his new queen, and looked a bit shaky when he did make an appearance, if you know what I mean. Amazing, really: I never saw a woman so pale and fragile-looking; but those eyes – they transfix you. She could kill you with a single glance.' He clutched his chest and tumbled backwards off the bench, to the amused roar of those around him.

This was the signal, it seemed, for the entertainment to begin. The mummers leapt up from their places, some rather the worse for wear, and the musicians vanished outside then reappeared with their arms full of odd-looking instruments and costumes, and assembled at one end of the hall. Tam conferred briefly with them, and they struck up a lively tune.

Tam Fox retrieved a fur-lined cloak from the pile left by the door, and a large wooden sword, a black wig that looked suspiciously as though it might have been made from horse-hair and a vastly overstated crown. Meanwhile, one of the other men had donned an abundant white dress and a long mane of golden straw and was prancing around in a ludicrously provocative fashion, lifting his skirts to flash first a bit of leg, and then his bare and hairy arse.

Katla touched her father's arm. 'Why dress a man as a woman when they have women in their company?' she asked, bemused.

Aran, startled from his reverie, smiled. 'Would you laugh if a pretty girl played the part of the Queen and not some lumbering oik?'

Katla thought about this. Then, ever-logical, she said: 'So why not have a woman play the role of the King?'

Aran looked shocked. 'That would be surely be trea-sonous.'

Katla frowned and turned her attention to the loud non-sense that was taking place at the other end of the hall. There, Tam Fox lay swooning in his beloved's arms, while one of the minstrels sang:

'The King he did a-wooing go
To find himself a bride
The girls paraded to and fro
But he wasn't satisfied.

He saw fat and thin and in-between
Dark and fair and red
Even one girlie whose hair was green!
"They're not for me," he said.

Oh, there were gals with long—'

And here, with a gesture, Tam encouraged the audience to join in:

'Noses!' shouted one of the women.

'Legs!' cried Kotil Gorson, raising his flagon.

'Tongues!' called another, and various voices were raised in enthusiastic accord.

'Hair!' corrected Tam loudly.

The 'Rosa Eldi' twirled her appalling straw wig around, coyly covering her face with it; and one of the players fell dying at her feet; another reached up for a single touch of her hair, and then of course the wig fell off and she had to retrieve it after a tussle with her admirer, put it on back to front, stumbled about blindly, then managed to get it the right way around again.

'And some with big—'

'Teeth!'

'Tits!' yelled Fent, drunkenly.

'Arses!' cried Gramma Rolfsen, grinning insanely.

'Eyes,' supplied Tam demurely, and the 'Rosa Eldi' pranced around some more and clutched his enormous false chest.

'Eyes!' repeated Tam with a bellow, and there was a great gale of laughter.

'All the ladies were fair, so fair
But not one of them could compare
With the Rosa Eldi, the nomad Queen
The prettiest girl he'd ever seen.'

And now Tam had his hands on the Rose of the World's huge fake breasts as well, which earned him a hefty swat from the other player, who made an obscene and unmistakable gesture to the crowd, then proceeded to pick the King up, hoist him over her shoulder, arse in the air, and march from the room to a great crescendo of horns and catcalls.

Even her mother was laughing, Katla noticed; but Aran sat there with a faraway look in his eyes, as if the minstrels had performed some ballad telling an affecting tale of tragic heroism. A little while later he took a small piece of folded parchment from inside his tunic and gazed at it lovingly for a moment; then he got up and went over to his sons and the three of them left the hall. Curious, Katla shifted on her seat and also made to rise, but Festrin put her hand on her arm.

'Stay and talk to me, Katla Aransen,' she said softly.

Katla, surprised, settled back again.

'What do you believe in?' the *seither* asked.

It was a hard question to answer, because Katla did not know what level of response she was expected to give, so after a while she laughed and said simply, 'Myself.'

It was supposed to be a joke of sorts, but Festrin put her head on one side and her big single eye regarded Katla solemnly. Then her lips quirked. 'I sense that that belief has got you into quite a bit of trouble so far in your life. I also sense there's a lot about yourself you do not yet know. What are the things you do best?'

Mesmerised by the eye, Katla blurted without thinking: 'Oh, climbing cliffs and rockfaces, and making my knives and swords—' And then stopped dead as she realised what she'd said.

Again Festrin smiled. 'So what belief is left when, with only one hand, you can do none of those things?'

Katla felt unaccustomed tears well up. 'I . . . I don't know.'

The *seither* leaned in closer. 'What of Elda, Katla? What of your connection with the world – don't you feel it? I think you do, but that you don't understand it yet.'

Katla stared at the one-eyed woman. She remembered how the palms of her hands tingled when she worked metal in a particularly pleasing fashion; how a jolt of energy would sometimes run up her arms when she climbed; the way that the rock of Sur's Castle had spoken to her, in some language that only her blood and body comprehended; how the timbers of the ship had thrummed with life beneath her hands as they neared the islands. How even lightly running a hand across the warm granite above the hall that very morning had made a jelly of her bones and how for just a moment she had sensed words in her head, as if the world itself were communicating with her.

'Something has happened to you recently, Katla Aransen, something not unconnected to your injury, to bring you to the earth-magic. I can feel it in you, and all around – I can feel it everywhere lately, but in you, Katla, it is strong. What happened to you? All your grandmother told me was that you had been burned. Was it in the smithy?'

'The Istrians tried to burn me at the Allfair.'

Festrin's eye flashed. 'They are superstitious, dangerous fools. They have destroyed thousands of poor souls who carry the magic without even knowing it and have never done anything more harmful than to offer a few weak potions or charms.'

'It was not for witchery,' Katla said, and went on to tell her tale. When she came to the burning itself, she frowned. 'I remember seeing my brother Halli and our cousin Tor in the crowd; I remember being tied to the post, and the lighting of the fire; and I remember an Istrian that I thought was my friend coming at me with his sword – then I can remember nothing until I woke up on our ship, bound for home.'

'And this—' Festrin touched the unbandaged hand '—happened in the burning?'

Katla nodded.

'Would you like your hand back, Katla? As it once was, strong and fine, with four fingers and one thumb, as perfect as before the fire?'

No need to think about that. 'Of course.'

'Then you must find a way to believe in yourself as you have never done before, and if you can do that, I can help you to heal yourself.'

Katla felt obscurely disappointed. Somehow she had expected either arrant fakery, or an instant and magical cure. Helping her to heal herself suggested a lengthy and tedious process and no miracle to look forward to at the end of it. She hung her head. 'Oh,' she said.

Festrin laughed, the harsh note of it making several around the tables look in their direction. 'Take me and show me the knives you make,' she said.

Outside, it was full dark and the stars were scattered across the sky. Katla, holding a brand she had taken from the pile beside the firepit, led the *seither* across the enclosure towards the smithy. They passed the outhouse, where someone was being noisily sick, and the stables, where the ponies whickered softly as they passed. As they neared the barn, Katla realised that someone was inside, for a lantern cast long shadows out of the open door. Puzzled, she motioned for Festrin to follow quietly and together they crept closer. Even before they reached the door, Katla could hear her father's voice carrying quiet clearly in the crisp night air.

'We need Danson. The *Fulmar's Gift* isn't up to the job – it would never withstand the floes to the far north.'

'We could modify it ourselves.' Halli's tones now, deep and rich, sounding remarkably like Aran's.

'It's just not suited to having an ice-breaker fitted: the

Fulmar's Gift is built for speed. With the extra weight, it'd capsize in a high sea,' Aran replied impatiently.

Now Fent joined in, his voice, like his mien, lighter and sharper than his brother's. 'I say we kill Tam Fox and take the *Snowland Wolf*, modify that.'

'Fent! You don't mean it.' Halli seemed shocked; but Katla knew her twin only too well.

'Of course he doesn't. Besides, we'd still need Morten Danson to do the work – and if I'm going into uncharted waters I want a ship that's been custom-built, not some other vessel that's been hastily cobbled together out of old scraps.' Aran sounded annoyed now. 'Damn the man for turning down my money. I've already lost a fortune to Finn Larson.' He paused, suddenly thoughtful. Then: 'You didn't happen to retrieve my money when you butchered him did you?' he asked Fent bitterly.

There was a moment of appalled silence. The *seither* gripped Katla by the arm. 'We should away,' she whispered. 'I mislike the turn of this.'

But so bound up was she in her family drama that Katla barely even felt the woman's touch. There came a scuffling noise and an inarticulate cry, and then Halli's voice rang out. 'You! You killed Jenna's father? Tell me it isn't true, Fent! Surely not even you—'

'—would kill a fat old traitor?'

'Enough!' Aran roared. 'This family stands together. I'll pay Tam Fox to take the pair of you with him when he returns to Halbo to provide the entertainment for Ravn's marriage ceremony: no one there will notice another pair of numbskulls amongst the company. He'll not be able to resist an invitation to such an event, Tam reckons; then you can take Danson aside and make our case to him and see how . . . persuasive you can be.'

'You mean, knock him over the head and bring him whether he will or not?' laughed Fent.

'Whatever it takes. You'll need to borrow two of his big knarrs, and load the necessary timber onto them. And don't bludgeon him senseless till you've made him tell you which men and which tools he'll need for the job—'

'We can't just abduct people!' Halli's voice was thick with emotion. 'You're mad and he's a murderer, and I want no part of this!'

'If you don't, then you're no son of mine,' Aran said harshly.

Festrin leaned in close to Katla. 'This is an ill-fated night. I want to hear no more.'

Katla nodded reluctantly. To her, it all sounded rather exciting. *If Halli won't go*, she thought, *then I will*. She glanced down and the torchlight made a gleaming orange cudgel of her hand. Her heart sank. Silently, she led the *seither* to the smithy.

Once inside, she lit two lanterns, hung them up and discarded the torch. The warm light offered up a well-ordered workshop in which tools were hung neatly along the walls, or lay oiled and gleaming on shelves. The great leather bellows smelled of wax and showed but a thin dusting of soot; but the fire was out and not an ember glowed, which endowed the place with the faintest air of neglect. Katla's face told the story: suddenly drawn and tense, it looked to Festrin for a few seconds that she might break down.

'Your father is in the grip of a dangerous obsession,' she said, to capture the girl's attention. 'A ship is made from the living stuff of Elda – borrowed from the world and eventually returned to it; but a ship built with ill-will may not serve its master well. Your father is tempting the fates: they may measure his cloth and cut it short if he persists in his plan.'

Katla said nothing.

'And you, Katla Aransen. What of you? I felt the earth-magic in you; but has it touched your heart, or is that part of you as dark and riddled as your kin's?'

'My father and brothers are brave, good men,' she said angrily. 'Don't talk about them so.'

The *seither* pressed her lips firmly together as if imprisoning her next words. Then: 'Very well,' she said. 'Show me your work. Maybe I can tell the colour of your heart from your working of the metal.'

This seemed thoroughly unlikely to Katla, but she walked over to the great wooden chest at the back of the smithy and opened it up. Inside, wrapped carefully in soft wool and oiled cloth, were some of her finest pieces – the carnelian sword which Fent had so coveted, some of her best knives (the less well-balanced ones she had flintily melted down and worked anew), and some of the Allfair weaponry that Aran had grabbed up from their booth. From this collection she selected the Red Sword, an ornamental knife with a beautifully decorated pommel, and one of her more recent creations: a simple but elegant pattern-welded dagger. These three she brought and laid out on the table before the *seither*.

Festrin leaned over them. She ran a finger along the Red Sword. 'Fine work,' she said appreciatively. She hefted the blade and tested its balance. 'I've not had much use for weapons in my long life. At least, not simple makings of metal and stone.'

Katla felt vaguely annoyed. So Festrin thought her work simple, did she? She reached out and took the carnelian sword from her. At once, a pale-red light played down the length of the blade to culminate in a bright glow around Katla's grip. Surprised, she laid it quickly back on the table. When she looked up, there was an expression of intense and amusement in the woman's eyes.

'So,' she said. 'So.' She smiled at Katla then, passing over the ornamental knife, picked up the pattern-welded dagger. In her long hand, it looked little bigger than her paring knife. She angled it into the light and made appraising noises deep in her throat. The noises became more distinct until they sounded almost like a language Katla could not quite grasp, though her skull itched and buzzed with the effort. Then the word *beautiful* crept into her mind; then *rare*. She kept staring at the *seither*, but the woman's lips did not move.

'Did you say something?' Katla asked puzzledly.

Extraordinary.

The *seither*'s lips curved upwards into her sweet smile. 'Oh yes,' she said. 'But in a way only you might hear.'

Katla frowned. 'I don't understand.'

The woman pressed the dagger into Katla's hand and again the light shone, brighter this time, as if the metal were lit by an inner fire. Katla gasped. She watched lines of flame lick up and down the patterns in the blade, illuminating each gorgeous detail. When the woman withdrew her hand the light faltered for a moment and gained a bluish tinge; then it flared out again, brighter than ever.

Festrin laughed delightedly. 'Your heart knows more than your head, my dear. And it was with your heart that you worked this blade. Just think what you might achieve now, with the magic awakened. I wonder if it is just metal with which you have this affinity,' she mused. 'I'd be curious to see how you worked with stone or wood.'

Katla, shaking, placed the dagger back on the board. Her knees felt weak. Little tremors of aftershock ran up and down her arms. 'It's hard to work anything one-handed,' she said dully.

'Then let us try to remedy that situation,' the *seither* declared. She took Katla's right hand in both of hers. *Pick up the dagger, Katla.*

Katla's left hand went to the hilt before the thought had completed itself. Light flamed out, red and white; and then, without knowing what she did or why, Katla found she had poised the point over her injured hand and was cutting down. The *seither* placed a guiding hand on top of Katla's. 'Don't falter,' the woman said aloud. 'Trust yourself. Trust me. Trust the magic.'

The scar tissue began to part, but there was little blood. Katla stared disbelievingly. Again the dagger descended into the club-hand and she watched it with awe, as if it moved of its own accord, or as if it were an entertainment performed for her benefit by others. A piece of dead flesh fell to the floor, followed by another and Katla watched with a kind of fascinated repulsion. *Much more of this*, some part of her mind thought, *and I'll have nothing left there but a bloody stump.*

The glow from the dagger was so bright now that it hurt her eyes, leaving a jagged white after-image even when she looked away, and the whole of her left arm was abuzz, hot vibrations chasing one another through the bones and up into her shoulder joint; then spiralling around her ribs, down her pelvis and into her legs. The soles of her feet tingled and burned; the energy flowing out into the flagstones. She could feel them absorbing it all; she could *feel* how it was sucked away into the veins of the ground below, only to gather itself and rebound to her anew.

The *seither*'s face was awash with the light: her single eye gleamed like a moon.

Another cut and Katla 'saw' the image of her forefinger and thumb, limned by a red glow, but separate and true. *I could pick up a spoon now*, she thought incongruously. *I could hold a pair of tongs . . .* Another release of pressure, followed by the urgent wish to flex her hand, but the resistance was still there. She bore down again with the knife, feeling the incursion of the blade more deeply than ever, and had to bite her lip to prevent herself from screaming out her fear and horror. Remarkably, there was still no pain – just a sense of applied weight and coercion. She became aware of another finger being freed from the club.

The buzzing got stronger, the light blinding.

Suddenly she was conscious of another voice amongst the

vibrations: deep and low and a long way off – more of a rumble in the earth than a voice, in truth; more like the deep heart of the ocean, beating and retreating. The sound was hard to distinguish, but it was not the *seither,* not this time. She closed her eyes so that the light could not distract her and reached after it, down and down, through the flagstones, down into the rock beneath. Then: *Hear me!* the voice rumbled. *I feel you: even in my prison of stone I hear you: hear me! Sirio calls you, through the veins of Elda, I call you to free me. I have been incarcerated here for three hundred years and none have heard me. Come to me—*

'Katla!'

Her eyes sprang open. In her shock at this new invasion, her hands fell away, leaving Festrin in sole control of the blood-stained dagger.

'My god! What are you doing to her?'

Wild-eyed in the blazing light, his hair a blood-red corona, Fent snatched up the carnelian sword and rushed at the *seither.* 'Leave her alone, you witch!' he howled, and with a single vicious lunge spitted the one-eyed woman on the perfect blade.

Festrin stared down at where the hilt had come to a violent halt against her ribs. Her eye blinked furiously. Then one long hand floated up and wrapped itself about Fent's throat, the fingers tightening convulsively so that his eyes bulged and his hands came off the Red Sword.

'An . . . evil deed . . . to interrupt . . . a healing . . .' She coughed and dark blood bubbled out of her mouth and ran down her chin. 'May all . . . your ventures . . . meet with . . . disaster . . .' She smiled sweetly, grotesquely; then crumpled to the floor, where she lay canted at an odd angle, half-propped up by the sturdy hilt.

Katla, jarred out of her inertia, pushed Fent aside and dropped to her knees beside the *seither.* 'Festrin, hear me!' Her voice felt odd to her, deeper and more sonorous. She turned the woman over with surprising ease, and laying both hands on the hilt, withdrew the carnelian sword. A gout of blood shot into the air, striking Katla in the face, but she barely registered the fact beyond noting the unaccustomed warmth on her skin. The weapon blazed like lightning in her hands, and she became dimly aware that Fent had staggered back, shouting something incomprehensible. Behind him, another figure appeared as a blur, but Katla's attention was on the dying woman. She laid aside the Red Sword, but the light continued to pulse up and down her arms. Without a thought, she plunged her new-made hand into the hole in the woman's chest, and the light went out like a doused fire. Heat surged and ebbed inside her; and ebbed again and again. She felt the tide of power draining away and something inside her mourned it. *Let go!* came a voice in her skull. *Let go!* It reverberated back and forth, a miserable, tiny thing like a bat in a cave, echoing until her head ached. It was all too much. *I am dying*, she thought desperately, feeling the last of the fire go out of her. *Here and now, I am dying*.

With a gasp, she fell backwards, and felt the cold night claim her.

Twenty-three

The Use of Magic

Exhausted after a long day's work for his new master, his hands stinking of tin and other cheap alloys, Virelai stood at the window of his room in the High Tower and stared out at the city of Cera. No matter how long he spent here, he thought, he would never get used to the idea of there being so many people in the world. It had become his favourite pastime whenever he was able: watching them scurrying to and fro along the narrow streets with their baskets and carts, their pack-animals and their slaves, all so busy, so preoccupied, each with their own lives, anxieties and dramas. *Why did the Master never tell me about all this?* he wondered, as he had wondered every day since Lord Tycho Issian had brought him here. But he knew the answer; just as he had known it as soon as he had spied the Rosa Eldi in the Master's chamber: Rahe kept the world secret from him because he knew Virelai would be tempted by it, that he would be unable to withstand the lure of its secrets. And now he had exchanged one master who sought to keep him cloistered for another. For the view from this elevated window − like the view from an eyrie on an inaccessible peak − was the closest that Virelai had come to the world's temptations: Tycho had seen to that as soon as he had managed to work the shaping spell on the base metals he had been brought, creating for the Lord of Cantara a fortune in what appeared as perfect silver to all eyes except those of a trained mage. And to begin with, Virelai had hardly cared for the world, so thrilled had he been at the success of his magic. Twenty-nine years he had been apprenticed to a mage; yet in all that time Rahe had taught him only the most rudimentary spellcraft, keeping him ever distant from the magic that changed nature or even the appearance of nature. In truth, his apprenticeship had amounted to little more than slave-work: fetching and carrying, cooking and skivvying. He ground the powders for the Master's alchemical experiments, heated the crucible and polished the retorts; he cut the hearts from the little birds that Rahe conjured for his darker magic, and burned them with blood from his own finger. He had felt nothing for the tiny fluttering things: for they were spellborn and shortlived, given life only at the Master's whim; but he was beginning to experience odd pangs of remorse, especially now as he watched the small blue-and-black swallows swooping beneath the eaves of the villas on the hill below the castle. Suddenly he found himself wondering if he had been in some way cruel to deny the tiny magic-made birds the same freedom to find mates and make nests and raise young.

'Every creature has the right to its own life,' he said now, aloud, 'no matter how they come into this world.' Even as he said it, he knew it to be a deep truth. Behind him on the bed, Bëte the cat stirred and yawned and a moment later he felt a voice tickle the inside of his skull.

At last, it said. *At last he wakes.*

Two days later, Rui Finco strode down the Amber Parade in Istria's capital city, hardly noticing how elegant the avenue of poplars looked this year, nor how the fountains played at the intersection with the Great West Road; nor even how the sunlight made a golden curtain of the wall of the Duke's palace at the top of the hill. A trader carrying a pitcher of wine on his shoulder jostled him as he entered Market Way, but rather than roundly chastise the man as he would usually do, the Lord of Forent hurried on grimly, his handsome face set in a scowl. Ever since the fiasco at the Allfair – when he had lost the northern king, his most useful piece of blackmail evidence, the services of the best shipmaker in the known world (let alone all the funds tied up in their many and various projects) and the trust of the other lords in his cabal, all in the space of a single evening – Rui's plans had been going further and further awry. He owed money to Lords Prionan and Varyx, and Prionan had been less than understanding about the loss of his investment. Varyx, of course, had been witness to the proceedings; more, it had been through his stupidity that Ravn Asharson had armed himself and escaped; even so, that did not seem to have prevented him treating Rui with unwonted familiarity, where before he had been all suitable deference and submission. Losing face amongst his peers had been the worst of it, he admitted to himself. It would require a bold move to win them back to him; and win them back he must, if he were ever to proceed with his overarching strategy. And so he walked the capital, desperate to escape the stifling confinement of the palace, with its whisperings and snide laughter, the little knots of men who fell silent or broke apart as he entered a room; the sense that he had fallen irrevocably into that social quagmire from which it was impossible to crawl alive.

Forcing his busy mind to quietude, he made his way through the early afternoon traders and customers, stooping beneath awnings and stepping around crates of oranges and limes, in and out of great skeins of herbs, ropes of garlic and hot peppers, bundles of wind-dried chickens and Jetra ducks, between stalls selling confectionery in the most lurid hues, jars of spice, silver jewellery, gemstones and tapestries; rolls of silk and lace from Galia; rugs and carpets and huge bronze vases; ornamental braziers, censers and garlands of safflower; flasks of wine and araque and the bitter, resinous spirits of the deep south; he passed them all with barely a look, beyond registering a slight surprise that it seemed easier to make his way through the market than it usually did at this hour of Fifthday.

Emerging from the agora into the backstreets beyond, he found the city even more deserted. Two bony, striped cats lying in a pool of sunlight between the fish shop and the grain store darted away so swiftly at his approach that all he saw was a movement in his peripheral vision; and a moment later he was out into the wide avenue bordering the gardens below Speaker's Mount.

Here – where there was usually only sporadic traffic and the occasional recitation of self-penned verses – the place was heaving with humanity and a great hubbub of noise. Hundreds upon hundreds of folk seemed to have gravitated towards the Mount and were surrounding it for fifty yards in all directions. Rui Finco stopped still on the outside of the crowd in amazement. It was not like the citizens of Cera to gather for any reason other than to celebrate feast-times and fire festivals; but this, this sounded like some religious ranter holding forth at the top of his voice, and religious fervour was a rare thing indeed in the decadent Istrian capital, where everyone made dutiful but unenthusiastic obeisance to the Goddess and went on with their usual business of fleecing their neighbours and visiting the bordellos without a qualm; or turned the very worship into a public ostentation, to score social points and win political favour.

He craned his neck to view the man who had generated such interest, and was horrified to find that he knew the speaker.

It was Tycho Issian, the Lord of Cantara.

Behind him, standing slightly to one side, and taller by a head, stood the pale man Rui had seen accompanying the Lord of Cantara to the Gathering; and curled in his arms there appeared to be a small black cat all tricked out in a fancy red harness and muzzle. Rui frowned. What bizarre

entertainment was this? He pushed his way into the crowd
until he could better hear the proceedings; which proved
easier than he had expected, for the assembled crowd was
as rapt and silent as if held under a powerful spell, hanging –
against all likelihood, for, even if he had suddenly come into
some huge and extravagant fortune which he was spending
left, right and centre, was the man not a low-born upstart?
– on every word that Tycho Issian uttered.

'They are *not like us!*' he was crying now, his hands striking
the air as if it were a solid mass. 'They are an abomination!
They treat their women like the cheapest Footloose whores,
exposing their most intimate features to the lascivious gaze of
every man who has the shame to look upon them, unveiled
as they are. Any man who has visited the Allfair can vouch
for the truth of this – you can see every detail of their faces,
and sometimes their bare arms and breasts—'

The crowd sighed as one.

'You could brush a woman's cheek or touch her hair; you
could even stare into the very pupils of their eyes, these
women have been raised to be so brazen, and to have so
little knowledge of the true way of the Goddess.'

'Shame!' someone cried, and others echoed the sentiment.

'And rather than cherish them in the safety of fine houses,
keeping them away from temptation and trouble as we do
with Falla's own, they have no care for their charges at all
– they let them walk where they will; they allow them to
work in the fields, on ships or even – and I find this the most
shocking evidence of their barbarism of all – to go as warriors
and fight alongside men in conflicts all over the world.'

Rui was granted a sudden vision of Mam – that most
delicate of Eyran ladies – in her boiled leather and scars,
spitting into her fist and grabbing his hand, and missed the
next pronouncement; which was unfortunate, since it had
raised a great cry of outrage.

'Yes, the Swan of Jetra!' Tycho roared, leaving the Lord

of Forent in no doubt as to the current subject of discussion. 'When she had offered herself as the ultimate sacrifice of our people, the very symbol of the hand of friendship we had extended across the Northern Ocean; the Swan of Jetra was left weeping in the care of her family, while the filthy barbarian king chose himself a Footloose woman as his bride!

'Shall we stand idle and watch heresy and sacrilege committed before our eyes? Shall we shrug and walk away as the flower of Istrian womanhood is spurned in favour of a foreign whore? Shall we merely pray that Falla will bring them gently to their senses in time? Rather I say we should offer ourselves as her messengers, the bearers of her fire! I say that we should carry a holy war against these worshippers of false gods – these monsters who treat civilised peoples with such contempt that they will even abduct noble women at a peaceful assembly and carry them away for their vile pleasure—'

A murmur of consternation rose in the gathered men.

'My daughter!' Tycho shrieked. 'My beautiful, devout daughter Selen, stolen by northern brigands and rapists from my own tent at the Allfair, and never seen again. She may even now be stripped naked amid a baying pack of northern wolves, her face and body bared to their greedy eyes, her tongue ripped away so she may not even speak Falla's name, her back bloody with welts—'

Rui felt himself swaying like one intoxicated, felt his mouth open to echo the horrified shout of the crowd, and wondered, with the small piece of his mind that remained unaffected by the man's strange tirade, what on Elda was happening here.

'She may be thrown to the ground and pawed over by these beasts, with their feathers and shells and their braided beards. She may be set upon by a dozen of them at once; she may be impregnated! Forced to bear the child of monsters! Imagine: a noble Istrian woman treated so; as they treat all their women; as they would have treated the Swan!

'Shall we allow this foul behaviour to go unpunished? Shall we not rather take Falla's fire to them, and cleanse them of their sins? Shall we not rescue their women and put their men to the sword? Shall we not expunge their kind from Elda?'

'We shall!' shrieked the crowd.

'Falla's fire!'

'Put them to the sword!'

'Save the women!'

'Cleanse the world!'

Rui felt the words buzz in his head and began to shake it rapidly from side to side as if to dislodge a wasp that had become trapped there. He took a step backwards, then another and another, and with each step the buzzing receded, until he found himself once more beyond the crowd, in the cool eaves of the chestnut trees, an area that seemed to be untouched by whatever spell the man's words had cast. From the safety of the shadows there he watched for another ten minutes with interest as Tycho Issian whipped a crowd of upstanding Istrian citizens into a crazed rabble, baying for the blood of the old enemy. He listened carefully, and as he did so the suspicion that had first come to him at the Gathering hardened into a belief, and he felt a plan of his own beginning to form.

'My Lord of Forent.'

'Lord Issian, a pleasure,' Rui Finco returned, lying through his grin-bared teeth. 'I am delighted that you acceded to my invitation.'

The southern lord entered the Lord of Forent's luxurious chambers (Rui liked to live well whenever he was in the capital, and although he did not much himself care for ostentation, it impressed others no end) as wary as a cat entering another's territory. Rui watched with satisfaction as Tycho took in the carved and gem-encrusted settles; the silver-framed mirrors and lush Circesian carpets, the expensive Santorinvan candles, the beautifully decorated shrine to the Goddess, all wound around with gold-and-red silk to look like sacred flames; and the priceless wall-hanging depicting the Battle of Sestria Bay (chosen most carefully from his small private collection this very afternoon for a most specific purpose). *At least*, Rui found himself thinking, *he has not brought the pale servant with him*, and felt a considerable relief.

Tycho crossed the room and arranged himself with fastidious care on the finest settle beneath the ornate candelabrum, spreading his robe around him to show it in its best light and to ensure that the Lord of Forent was made well aware of its fantastic cost. That it was a most expensive garment was in truth hard to ignore, for despite the conservative cut and sober midnight blue of the cloth, the candlelight picked out every silver thread in its facing, every bit of hem and cuff and collar, and played off the tiny, intricately-worked silver buttons adorning the breast of the tunic in numbers too great for pure functionality. It was a robe that had surely set the southern lord back by several hundred cantari, Rui thought, and it was designed to speak its message: *the Lord of Cantara is a man of both excessive wealth and fine taste; in the right cause, he will spend his money generously, and be trusted to keep a secret close*. It did not encourage the Lord of Forent to trust him any the more; but trust was hardly the issue here.

'In Falla's faith I serve your lordship,' he now said: the traditional greeting between peers of similar rank, and thus a blatant flattery, since little was known of the southern lord's heritage, where Rui's noble lineage was impeccable.

Tycho smiled, a small, tight smile that barely twitched the polished muscles of his face and made no attempt to reach his eyes. 'You should ask rather how I may serve *you*, my lord.'

This was neither a traditional nor a polite response. Rui bit back the retort that sprang too easily to his tongue, and returned the cold smile. 'You must think me remarkably inhospitable,' he said with chilly grace, and clapped his hands.

An instant later a pair of willowy serving girls in identical sabatkas of such a sheer, pale pink gauze that it made a mockery of the very concept of the veiling nature of such garments, wafted into the chamber bearing a flask of araque spiced with attar and ginger, another of springwater, beakers of expensive frosted glass and a dish of sweetsmoke. With some satisfaction, Rui watched his guest's avid eyes scour the women as they set each item down on the low table, bending almost double before the Lord of Cantara's face. He could smell the rosewater and musk they had bathed in from nigh on twenty paces away. It was the closest concoction he had been able find to the perfume with which the Rosa Eldi had filled his pavilion at the Allfair on that fateful night before he had – by immense effort of will – sent her away with the mercenary, and it was clearly having the desired effect on the southern lord, for Tycho's eyes – usually so black and fierce – had gone wide and dreamy, and his mouth had fallen open like a tomcat's tasting a scent. It was all the Lord of Forent needed to prove his theory.

The women bowed low, white hands fluttering in gestures of extreme politesse, and made their exit. The second girl, unseen by the visitor, made a pout of her mouth as she passed her lord, the very tip of her tongue protruding for an instant to leave a small bubble of saliva on her full lower lip; then she too was gone. With effort, Rui kept the smile he felt from his face. Marla: she was a provocative imp. He would look forward to enjoying that mouth later.

While the Lord of Cantara was still flustered, Rui poured out a tall beaker of araque, barely drizzled a few drops of diluting water into it and handed the beaker to him. Tycho took it from him mutely and drained off a good half of the pure spirit before coming fully to his senses. With a start he stared at the glass in his hand and in that second Rui knew his thoughts.

'I would never stoop to poison, my Lord Tycho; besides, as you say, we may be of assistance to one another. And what man does not need an ally in these turbulent times?'

Tycho replaced the glass carefully on the table and wiped his mouth. He was not used to araque; he could already feel it going to his head. Taking up another of the beakers, he poured a long measure of water into it and drank it down quickly.

'Allies, yes.' He glanced quickly at the door, which was closed; and then back at the Lord of Forent where he had sat down opposite him, thinking even as he did so in this strangely heightened state how very like the northern king this smooth-faced eastern lord suddenly appeared, despite the discrepancy in their ages and races. He found himself staring for a moment, taking in the high planes of the cheeks, the bone that shelved so close to the eye and hollowed itself out so elegantly beneath, the long, straight nose and powerful, dented chin, which in the northerner was obscured by the close dark beard; the lupine jaw and sharp teeth . . . It was a disconcerting comparison, since whenever he thought of the barbarian who had carried off his love a red tide of hatred swept through his heart. 'You would welcome war in the north, then, my lord?'

Rui raised an eyebrow. He did not usually encourage such a direct approach. However, the man was from the deep south of the continent and little was known of his heritage; he had much to learn of the ways of court intrigue. 'There are . . . certain advantages to be gained,' he said carefully. 'But of course to wage such a war is an expensive affair, what with ships to be built and mercenaries to be paid, let alone the cost of arming ourselves against our enemy, and the disruption to trade . . .'

Tycho smiled. It was a smile of great contentment and con-fidence; it made gimlets of his eyes. He leaned forward. 'Ah,' he said. 'I do not think that money will be the problem.'

'And what does your lordship think may provide an obstacle?'

'Men's hearts and minds. It will take much persuasion to raise the Council to war: not everyone will see the right of it.'

Now it was Rui Finco's turn to smile. 'Ah yes,' he said. 'Men's hearts. And loins.' His smile became unpleasantly personal. He leaned across the table and touched the Lord of Cantara on the arm so that the man recoiled. 'Do not be alarmed, my lord: I harbour no desires for my own sex. A willing woman – or even an unwilling one – eh, my lord? – is all I ever crave. Women hold a great mystery, do they not, my friend? Veiled or unveiled, we are blind to their true natures; but how they draw us in, with their subtle signs and their perfect hands, their mellow voices and their soft lips; their seductive scents and the promise of that slippery, hot flesh beneath.'

Tycho looked appalled.

'You see, my lord of Cantara, I know your inner mind; I have seen into your heart: I know your true desire and motivation.' Rui stood up, set his palms flat on the low table and bent across to place his mouth an inch from Lord Issian's right ear. 'The Rosa Eldi,' he whispered, and withdrew.

Tycho's face became a mask of stone, his turbulent emotions betrayed only by the draining of the colour from his skin, leaving it an unhealthy, sallow colour in which the veins stood out like marbling.

Rui Finco settled back upon his bench with his back against the wall and stared pointedly at the tapestry over the Lord of Cantara's head showing scenes from the Battle of Sestria Bay, a campaign fought during the Third War which had saved the north coast of Istria from the Eyran invaders. Above his head, ancient galleys cut through the azure water of the Istrian Sea, their serried rows of oars delineated in precise lines, their sails furled for close-range fighting and to prevent damage from the northerners' fire-arrows. *Using the enemy's own weapon against him,* Rui thought with a vicious inward smile. Unbeknownst to the Eyrans, the commander of the southern fleet – his own grandfather, Luis Finco, Lord of Forent – had armed his ships with great iron battering rods, fitted to the keel beneath the waterline, and thus invisible to the eye. He had invited the northern fleet to engage them at close quarters, and then, with the rowers suddenly ordered to full speed, the Istrians had rammed and holed the great Eyran vessels, and a vast slaughter had taken place. It was one of Istria's most famous victories: the only Eyrans to survive had been gelded and sold as slaves. Men whose grandfathers had fought in the Third War still heralded the Battle of Sestria Bay as Istria's finest hour, citing it as proof that Istrian vessels were as fine as those made in the north; but Rui knew the truth: they had won that engagement only because of his grandfather's wiliness, and because it had taken place in Istrian waters, close to home. There was no skill in the south at making the sort of ships at which the northerners excelled – the sort of ships that would breast stormwaves and hurricane winds, that would skim the ocean like great birds – and no great skill at sailing them, either. Carrying war to the north would require the services of another Eyran shipmaker turned traitor, and enough mercenary northerners to navigate them there. And if the Lord of Cantara had the money and the will – for whatever reason – to help to fuel that war, he was just what Rui had been looking for. Especially, he thought, since Tycho would owe him the very great favour of keeping his correct deductions to himself, and Rui liked to have others owe him favours.

'How did you know?' the other man breathed.

There was desperation in his eyes, Rui noted with some satisfaction. To harbour such lust for a nomad whore that you would invoke the Goddess in your call for a holy war just to lay your hands on her was hardly the honourable behaviour of a devout and patriotic Istrian nobleman. Nevertheless, he leaned forward again and patted the Lord of Cantara on the arm. 'I have eyes, my lord. Love burns powerfully inside you, I can see. And what better motive for a conflict than to rescue the frail sex from the barbarians in the name of love?'

Tycho breathed out a great sigh. 'It is a relief to me to be able to speak of this at all,' he said softly. 'I have never felt such fire for any woman. I do not think . . .' He paused, considering. 'I do not think she is entirely human, the Rosa Eldi; for she is like no woman I have ever seen, or hope to see again. I believe she is touched by the divine, and so I must have her, you see. I must save her soul.'

Absurd, Rui thought. *The man is clearly so obsessed with the creature that he raises her on the highest of pedestals and like an alchemist turns basest emotion to pure silver.* 'Assuredly an extraordinary creature,' he returned blandly.

'And what, pray, my lord, do *you* hope to gain from carrying a war to the Eyrans?' Tycho asked, his tone suddenly sharp.

Ah, now we come to the nub of it. 'I want the Ravenway,' Rui said smoothly and looked the southern lord hard in the eye. It was only half of the truth, but he could see by the calculating look that crossed the Lord of Cantara's face that it was sufficient explanation.

Tycho nodded slowly. 'The Ravenway,' he repeated. 'Seaway to all the ancient lands. Do you even know it exists?'

'The northerners believe it does, and that's enough for me. Ravn's been assembling a fleet to attempt the crossing for the last two years and more; just think of all those fine Eyran vessels, ready for the taking—'

'But in a war, those vessels will be sailing against us.'

'Indeed, my lord. But imagine if we were to make a pre-emptive strike on Halbo before war is formally declared, storm their capital, steal their ships – and their Rose—'

Tycho became very still. 'Finding the right men for that job will take time, and a lot of money . . .'

Rui shrugged. 'The genius is all in the planning; but with my strategies and your silver . . .' There: it was said. He watched the Lord of Cantara digest the idea and wondered which way he would jump. They would have to kill him, of course, if he made the wrong decision; but there were many misfortunes that might befall a naive southern visitor to the decadent city of Cera.

The ensuing silence was long and uncomfortable. Rui began to count the ways the man might most safely be disposed of. At last Tycho smiled. 'My silver is at your command, my lord of Forent.'

At first Virelai had wondered if the voice he had heard had merely existed in his imagination. He knew he had been preoccupied of late by the Master's fate, and his own, by extension; so for a time the refrain 'he's awake' had given him considerable pause for thought. But then, if it was the mage that had woken, who was informing Virelai of the fact? He had left the Master alone on Sanctuary: of that he was sure. And if Rahe were awake, Virelai had no doubt that he would know about it from the mage himself, and in none too gentle a fashion.

So then his suspicions had fallen upon the cat – for who knew what the magical beast was capable of? – but no matter how he cajoled or threatened it, Bëte offered him no more than a contemptuous expression and an annoyed flick of the tail.

Ever since he had first heard it Virelai had been as jumpy as a mouse hearing the cry of a predator, snapping out of deep sleep in the dead hours of the night at the slightest sound, jumping at odd noises during the day, and listening, always listening, for the return of the voice.

Then one night his new master had come to him in a highly agitated state, his eyes gleaming as if someone had lit a fire in his head. Unable to stand still for a minute, Tycho had paced the room, talking at such high speed that Virelai could make out barely one word in three, his hands opening and closing like ravenous mouths. Unnerved, Bëte had fled away under the bed where she bubbled and hissed like an overheated kettle.

More silver, seemed to be the import of his babblings; a lot more silver was needed, as fast as possible. Was there not, he had asked Virelai, another way of producing it? He was having trouble laying hands on sufficient tin and brass for the sorcerer to work on; besides, he had bought up so much of the stuff recently that the price of the lesser metals had soared. Soon the transformative process would be barely profitable, given the time and effort he had to put into trading on the goods he had to buy quickly with the fake silver. Could not Virelai work his magic on bricks, maybe; or even bread? But when Virelai had once more tried patiently to explain the difference between the magic required in changing the appearance of like for like, metal for metal, and that required in changing the essential nature of things, Tycho had merely ignored him and carried on in like vein for several minutes about ships and something called the Crow's Path or the like. Several times in this tirade, Virelai had caught the name of the Rosa Eldi and, with some venom, Ravn Asharson, King of Eyra; that barbarian, scoundrel and pirate. And then the Lord of Cantara had clapped his sorcerer on the back and left in as great a hurry as he had arrived, leaving Virelai to ponder on his instructions.

And so Virelai had redoubled his efforts; until Cera ran out of tin ingots. Then they had had to bribe a local blacksmith out of his premises and Virelai had worked by night as well as by day, for now he had to smelt his own raw materials from the pewter dishes and tin mugs, brass ornaments and candlesticks that Tycho sent his slaves out across the city's markets to purchase or steal. And ever Virelai kept the cat by his side, trussed up in its ridiculous red harness and the muzzle to stop it from mewing incessantly, drawing on its strength and on its well of spellcraft. There would come a time for reckoning between them, he could tell: for the cat's eyes reflecting the smithy fires gave back a stare as inimical as death.

And then one night the Lord of Cantara sent a slave down to the smithy to fetch him back to his chambers – *for a drink*, the boy said, *just a drink*. Virelai stared at the lad. 'What, now?' The alloy was bubbling in its great cauldron; the ingot moulds lay waiting, and he was behind schedule again. 'He wants me to come back to the castle for a *drink*?'

The child – Felo, Virelai thought, though he and Tam looked so similar it was hard for him to tell – nodded urgently and grabbed him by the hand. 'Now, now, or he will beat me. And he said, "bring the cat".'

As if cognizant of this request, Bëte wound herself around the boy's legs till he laughed and scooped her up himself. Virelai watched this little charade through hooded eyes. *She would rake me bloody if I tried the same*, he thought bitterly, aware that all over his forearms and hands there were scars that told that very story.

The Lord of Cantara's rooms were on the floor below Virelai's own tiny chamber, rented from the Duke at no little expense; but where Virelai's were plain and unadorned, consisting only of a stone bed carved out of the wall, fitted with a straw pallet and covered with an insufficient and smelly woollen blanket (which privation suited him well, reminding him as it did of his room back in Sanctuary) Tycho Issian's rooms professed his master's love of fine living. The floors were covered with Circesian rugs woven with ancient and mystical symbols said to bring wealth to those who walked upon them; the furniture was all by craftsmen from the Blue Woods; and statues of the Goddess adorned every alcove and cranny. Tonight, the air was thick with safflower incense: it appeared that the lord had been engaged in prayer.

But Tycho did not seem like a man whose soul had been soothed by long meditation; rather he looked flushed and manic, and his breath smelled of undiluted araque.

Virelai looked around. On the settle outside the lord's own chamber there was an unfamiliar cloak, and on the floor below it a streak of some smeared substance, dark enough to have stained the wood. Virelai frowned. It was rare that the lord drank the red wines of the region, declaring them as he did detrimental to the health, since they heated the blood and blurred the mind. Felo let go of the cat, which ran at once to the stain and sniffed at it with great interest. A moment later, there came a muffled sound from behind the door, and when Virelai stared at his master in puzzlement, he was alarmed to see the white showing all around his dark pupils.

'Damnation, I thought he was dead!' With two strides, Tycho was at the door to his chamber and had flung it open. On the floor inside lay a dark shape which groaned and clutched at something that looked suspiciously like the Lord of Cantara's ornamental knife, the one with the curved, serrated blade that he used for cutting apart his morning grapefruit. Virelai stared down in dismay. The shape resolved itself as a man, a plump, dark man with greying hair, his face turned in agony into the floor, his body curled around his wound like a dying wasp.

'My lord—' Virelai started, and at the sound of his voice the man turned over. Virelai gazed at the face thus revealed. He had seen this man somewhere before . . .

It was Gesto Ardum, the merchant to whom the lord had paid what to others would seem a great fortune for a consignment of jewellery and gemstones which he had then traded on or given away to buy favour with the Council lords.

Tycho grasped his sorcerer's shoulder with a vicious hand. 'He came here complaining,' he hissed furiously. 'It seems that the silver we paid him is not as pure as it first appeared.'

Ah, thought Virelai, feeling his heart hammer. *I wondered how long the illusion would last.* It had been a month or more since they had done business with the merchant.

'You have to get rid of him! No one can find him here: it would ruin my reputation. Kill him and transform him into something . . . small; something you and Felo can carry out of here and dispose of without attracting attention to yourselves.'

Virelai stared at him, aghast. 'I cannot!' He took a step away, but the Lord of Cantara came with him.

'You will! You must!'

'I cannot kill, my lord: I beg you – there is a geas on me—'

'A curse? What care I for such?'

'If I kill, I will die myself, and you will be left with no sorcerer—'

That stopped Tycho. His faced twisted with fury, then he stepped back to the merchant, and, setting his foot on the man's capacious belly, dragged out the belt-knife. The man squirmed and shrieked. A hot jet of blood fountained up, followed by another as Tycho buried it in Gesto Ardum's fat throat. The squirming and shrieking came to an abrupt halt and a heavy silence descended over the chambers.

Tycho Issian turned to his sorcerer. His face was a dripping mask of red. The knife was red, and so were his hands. Virelai had seen demons in the Master's books which looked more human. His head began to buzz and itch, his own words ricocheting around and around his skull until he had to open his mouth and let them out: 'Every creature has the right to its own life,' he said now, aloud, 'no matter how they come into this world—'

'I have just saved *your* life with this act,' the lord said unfairly, 'and it will be many years before you earn it back. You can make a start by getting rid of this *thing*.'

And so Virelai had laboured long over the body of Gesto

Ardum; but flesh will transform only to flesh, and no matter what he tried all he could manage was a change in the merchant's appearance. At last, he managed to make the merchant such an aged crone that Tycho cried, 'Enough! At least no one could lay *her* at my feet and claim a link!' He had the sorcerer make rags of the merchant's rich clothes, and then ordered Virelai and Felo to hoist the corpse up onto the sill and lever it out into the night air. Virelai watched it tumble away, a pale, stiff thing that disappeared into the canopy of trees below. Pigeons came shooting up out of the boughs, startled from their sleep; but beyond that there was no sound of discovery.

Two hours later, after much aggressive scrubbing and polishing, Virelai was back in his own bed, lying as rigid as the corpse, staring at a ceiling silvered by moonlight. It was a colour he had come to hate.

He could not sleep. He *dared* not sleep; for whenever he closed his eyes all he could see was the blood on Tycho's face and the murder in his eyes. At last, he got out of bed and walked across the cold stone floor to the window. With his hands set squarely on the sill, he stared out into the darkness, his skull as empty as a drum. A moment later, the tower vibrated, a great thrumming that started under his fingers and overran his arms and shoulders, and then the bones of his throat and head. Through it, he felt how the stone of the tower met its deep foundations in the rocky veins of the earth; how those veins travelled out and away, far away—

Come to me! cried a voice; and Virelai knew it for *the* voice, the one he had been waiting to hear again. *Come south, far south, to the mountains!* From desperation, the voice took on a note of cunning. *Come south and free me, and I will reward you.*

How will you do that? Virelai made the question inside his own head.

I know who you are.

Is that you, Master? Is it Rahe who speaks? Only the Master knew his history. Virelai felt very afraid now.

There was a silence, then the world trembled.

I am Sirio, the voice boomed. *Come south to the great caves beyond the Dragon's Backbone. And bring my sister, and the cat . . .*

A great heat filled the room, and the vibration took on a noise all its own. In panic, Virelai pulled away from the sill, breaking the strange contact. But the sound was still loud, and something was breathing in the room behind him. In trepidation, he turned, and found that Bëte the cat was gone, and in its place was a monstrous creature: a vast black jaguar with eyes that glowed like coals and a purr that filled the world. It opened its huge red mouth so that Virelai was treated to the unwelcome sight of its knifelike teeth and great red flag of a tongue.

The Man, the Woman and the Beast, it said into his mind. *We shall be reunited.*

Interim

The hand of night reaches down to enfold the islands of the Northern Ocean. Already it has cast its inky net over Blackwater Moor and the Nag's Head, over Long Eye Lake and the Old Man of Westfall; over Halbo and Southeye and Rockfall in the Westman Isles. In the bay at Ness, the fishing boats bob on a sudden churn of current, the waves slapping against sturdy wooden hulls to send them dipping and rocking, before breaking in a crash of white water on the seawall. On the greenstone cliffs bordering the chill waters of the Sharking Straits, the last of the seabirds have found their roosts and laid their heads beneath their wings. Their cries have ceased, but they do not sleep: out of nowhere, a cold wind has just barrelled up the precipitous sides of the chasm, ruffling their feathers and waking their young. On the quayside of the village at Wolf's Sound, on the northernmost and ill-named Fair Isle, the only movement that might catch the attention of an observer is that of a pair of cats, out on the prowl for their dinner and some sport, as they cross the starlit space between the fishing nets and crab-pots. As a cloud passes across the silver eye of the moon, one of the pair startles, the fur on its back lifting and jagging as the muscles shiver and contract. The other cat drops uncomfortably to its haunches, ears flat. In the distance, a child wails, its sleep disturbed by a nightmare. At Stormway, all the dogs begin to howl at once; and in the upland saeters, where the sheep have spent the day cropping the sweet summer grass, the flock shifts about anxiously.

Something wild has stirred; something ancient and elemental. The animals feel it, though they do not know what it is; the birds sense it, though they know not whence it comes.

Two thousand miles away, herds of wild horses on the Tilsen Plain feel the ground move beneath their feet and flee in panic. Swans on Lake Jetra, disturbed from their refuge among the reedbanks, take to the water, honking and hissing. In Cantara, the women in the stronghold's kitchens steady pots and bottles that are rocking unsteadily on the shelves. In the Golden Mountains, five days' ride to the south, there is a rumble as deep as thunder and a slab of granite as long as a beach and as high as an oak detaches itself from a snow-capped peak and comes shattering down through the gullies. A great white eagle, its eyrie demolished, wheels angrily, crying its protest. Below, a mountain goat, its horns curled exotically around its narrow skull, is less lucky.

Minor tremors are not unusual here in the southern continent. The oldest inhabitants – the nomads, and the stunted pines bordering the high desert – can remember a time when such earth movements occurred daily; and witnessed the relentless passage of lava-rivers that swallowed everything in their path. But there has been no true earthquake, no great volcanic eruption for two hundred years and more; not since the old one was laid beneath the ground.

In the Golden Mountains, a nomad caravanserai comes to an abrupt halt, for the old woman, Fezack Starsinger – who had been scrying into the great crystal while seated on the back of her wagon – has just let out an ear-splitting shriek and tumbled from the step, beneath the plunging hooves of the startled yeka drawing the next cart. Her daughter, Alisha, is immediately at her side; but there is nothing she can do, for Fezack is dying: of that there is little doubt. Her eyes have lost all focus and blood is bubbling from her mouth, along with words that Alisha can barely make out amidst the hubbub around her.

'Save us! The Monster wakes!'

And then she expires, passing swiftly and irrevocably into the Beyond.

The crystal lies where it has fallen in the scree, miraculously undamaged, and utterly inscrutable.

Amid the jumble of bergs and floes at the top of the world, an old man passes a cold and weary hand over his face. Emerging from the world's longest dream, he opens his eyes. Without the magic to keep the place habitable, his fastness has become a freezing wasteland; the sconces are dark, the fire has gone out, icicles have formed around the doorframe.

Can this elderly being possibly embody the monster of whom the old woman spoke? Surely not: he is feeble as a mouse woken from long hibernation: his muscles wasted on his already-gaunt frame; his skin as stretched and sallow as old paper.

The Master sits up stiffly. How long has he slept? It feels like an age. His joints are creaky with disuse, his mouth as dry as cotton. His stomach, which aches dully, feels tight and empty. He frowns, recalling his dream. In it, a creature he had raised from dust and spit, loved and cared for more than it knew, had risen up and attacked him, robbing him of his powers, his mind and his most prized possession.

'Rose,' he calls querulously. 'Rosa, my dear, why have you let me sleep so long?'

He turns to investigate the great, carved wooden chest in which his love usually lies sleeping: only to find it gone, its absence marked by a thin felting of recently-fallen dust.

'Virelai?' he calls into the freezing air. And: 'Bëte—'

But they are gone, all gone, out into the world – he knows this without having to wait for the answering silence. Magic has slipped from his grip, and now he feels a true chill: not from the icy air, but deep within.

Fate has just laid its freezing hand around that ancient organ he once called his heart, and squeezed it tenderly: a gentle reminder that the natural — or unnatural — order of Elda is reasserting itself. While he has slept, the world has turned. Chaos beckons, chaos and death, and not just for himself. It will take a miracle to retrieve the situation; for out there, beyond his will, outside his control, sorcery is rising . . .